HOMER'S ILL ILIAD

&

ODD SEA ODYSSEY

HOMER'S ILL ILIAD
&
ODD SEA ODYSSEY

Jay Dubya

BOOKSTAND PUBLISHING

·PUBLISHING·

ESTD 2006

www.bookstandpublishing.com

Published by
Bookstand Publishing
Pasadena, CA 91101
4967_3

ISBN 978-1-956785-67-8

For Homer (but not Jethro)

Other Books by Jay Dubya

Adult Fiction

Black Leather and Blue Denim, A '50s Novel
The Great Teen Fruit War, A 1960' Novel
Frat' Brats, A '60s Novel
Ron Coyote, Man of La Mangia
Pieces of Eight
Pieces of Eight, Part II
Pieces of Eight, Part III
Pieces of Eight, Part IV
The Wholly Book of Genesis
The Wholly Book of Exodus
The Wholly Book of Doo-Doo-Rot-on-Me
Thirteen Sick Tasteless Classics
Thirteen Sick Tasteless Classics, Part II
Thirteen Sick Tasteless Classics, Part III
Thirteen Sick Tasteless Classics, Part IV
Thirteen Sick Tasteless Classics, Part V
So Ya' Wanna' Be A Teacher
RAM: Random Articles and Manuscripts
Mauled Maimed Mangled Mutilated Mythology
Fractured Frazzled Folk Fables and Fairy Farces
FFFF&FF, Part II
Nine New Novellas
Nine New Novellas, Part II
Nine New Novellas, Part III
Nine New Novellas, Part IV
One Baker's Dozen
Two Baker's Dozen
Shakespeare: Slammed, Smeared, Savaged & Slaughtered
Shakespeare: Slammed, Smeared, Savaged & Slaughtered, Part II
Suite 16
Time Travel Tales
Snake Eyes and Boxcars
Snake Eyes and Boxcars, Part II
UFO: Utterly Fantastic Occurrences
The Psychic Dimension

Young Adult Fantasy Novels

Content Chapters

Background

Homer did not invent the game of baseball. Instead, the popular sport had been organized by a fellow named Abner Doubleplay.

The poet/bard Homer, reputed to have been blind, is credited with orally describing the *Iliad* (the story of the end of the ten-year Trojan War), and the *Odyssey,* the epic tale of the Greek hero Odysseus, who had been punished by Poseidon (Neptune, the sea god) for ten-long-years after the Trojan War. Homer had lived during the time when alphabets and writing were being developed (around 1,000 BC), so his epic poems were later recorded by educated scribes, and both stories exist today in their present forms.

Around 1184 BC, King Agamemnon of Mycenae, and his brother, King Menelaus of Sparta, had led the great expedition of a thousand Greek ships and 50,000 warriors against the Asia Minor city of Troy. The kings of the Greek city states were notorious pirates and marauders, but to glamorize their siege upon Troy, a mythological story involving Helen of Sparta, wife of King Menelaus, claimed that she had been wooed by Prince Paris of Troy to elope to Asia Minor. Thus, Helen of Sparta soon became Helen of Troy, and her abduction became the principal cause of the Trojan War.

The Trojan War had taken almost ten-long-years to fight, and the lengthy conflict was finally won when Odysseus, a brilliant schemer and ball-breaker, had a magnificent Wooden Trojan Horse built, and then had the Greek warriors situate the structure outside the main gates of Troy. The city was strategically located at the Hellespont Channel between Greece and Persia (now Turkey). Greek heroes were hidden inside the stomach of the colossal horse, and during the night, the warriors stealthily climbed-down a rope, opened the gates to Troy, and allowed thousands of Greek warriors to enter, rampage, sack and plunder. The Trojan War was fought during the late Bronze Age, which according to historical records, was around 1184 BC.

Mythological Background

Zeus, king of the Mt. Olympus gods and ruler of Heaven and Earth, and his brother Poseidon, king of the sea, both loved and desired Thetis, a beautiful sea-nymph. Zeus was aware of a prophecy that a son would be born to Thetis who would be mightier than Zeus himself, and *that* son would be capable of overthrowing the king god, just like Zeus had rebelled against his Titan father Cronus. In order to prevent that possible insurrection from happening, mighty god Zeus arranged a marriage between Thetis and a common mortal, a fellow named Peleus.

"It is not right for either my brother Poseidon or myself to sire *that* foretold rebellious child," Zeus thundered to his wife Hera. "We'll invite all of the gods to the wedding of Thetis and Peleus." But one particular goddess, Eris (goddess of discord), was overlooked and not invited. Eris appeared at the reception and rolled a golden apple onto the marble floor.

"This apple will go to the fairest goddess of all," Eris coyly announced. "The leading candidates are Hera, Athena and Aphrodite. And Prince Paris of Troy is to be the judge whose selection will be final!"

"I'll offer you the most gorgeous woman on Earth!" Aphrodite promised Paris, without revealing to the knucklehead that Helen of Sparta had already been married to King Menelaus. "My prize will be more valuable to you than the power and fame that Hera and Athena have offered."

Cunning Aphrodite, goddess of love and beauty, assisted Prince Paris in journeying to Sparta and seducing Helen, bringing her to Troy. Sometime later, Menelaus, and his brother King Agamemnon of Mycenae, assembled an armada of one-thousand ships to depart to Asia Minor to retrieve Helen of Sparta, who then had auspiciously become Helen of Troy.

But the sea-nymph Thetis and Peleus did have a very famous son, whose immortal and legendary name was the Greek champion Achilles.

Greek Name	Roman Name
Zeus	Jupiter
Poseidon	Neptune
Hades	Pluto
Athena	Minerva
Hera	Juno
Aphrodite	Venus
Apollo	Apollo
Hermes	Mercury
Ares	Mars
Cronus	Saturn
Hephaestus	Vulcan
Artemis	Diana
Thetis	Thetis
Odysseus	Ulysses

Gods Supporting Greeks	Gods Supporting Trojans	Neutral
Athena	Aphrodite	Zeus
Hera	Apollo	
Poseidon	Ares	
Hermes	Artemis	

HOMER'S ILL ILIAD

Jay Dubya

Chapter 1

"ACHILLES AND AGAMEMNON ARGUE"

Brain-dead-but-awesome Ancient Muse, amuse and speak to me now of those intrepid heroes who had pillaged and looted the corrupt bordellos and brothels of Troy. You can begin your unique narrative with the verbal dispute occurring between King Agamemnon, leader of the Greek armies against Troy, and the mighty hero from antiquity, Achilles.

"Agamemnon, you' totally obnoxious bastard," Achilles brazenly insisted. "You've caused plenty of anger from Lord Apollo for insolently yelling-up to high heaven, 'A-pollo is a chicken! A-pollo is a chicken'!"

"Get real, Achilles," Agamemnon vehemently maintained. "True, I have been a trifle irreverent. All I did was create a minor crisis by mildly offending Chryses, Apollo's favored high priest, who is only four-foot-tall!"

"We have been plagued with various plagues ever since your mounting arrogance had insulted Phoebus Apollo," Achilles screamed, almost rupturing his tonsils and adenoids. "Lord Apollo had heard Chryses' pleas for retribution, and the dispassionate god shot thousands of arrows of death and disease down-upon our afflicted Achaean armies. You're to blame for all of the recent destruction and devastation to our apprehensive troops," alleged Achilles. "For nine whole days and nights, Apollo's silver arrows came-down like torrential rain, killing good warriors, and having us cremating the corpses upon makeshift funeral pyres. The bodies were easy to burn because your defiance of Apollo and his lethal arrows had already scared the shit out of thousands of our brave warriors, making our enemy, the Trojans, both jealous and envious of the sky chariot god's awesome shooting ability. No mortal in his right mind wants to have Apollo as an enema, or, I meant to say 'as an enemy'!"

On the tenth day of massive death, Achilles called all of the Greek captains to a general council and firmly stated that under Agamemnon's dangerous leadership, the Achaean military campaign against King Priam and his Trojan minions was doomed to utter failure. "The Trojans cannot defeat us, but Apollo's wrath very easily can slaughter our' frustrated soldiers. I suggest that we forget this unproductive siege upon Troy, unless one of you morons can reveal to this assembly exactly why the immortal gods have apparently sided against us!"

"I'll tell you precisely what you desire learning," Calchas calculated and volunteered a viable answer to Achilles' imperative request. "But first, you must guarantee me safety from the wrath of a bitter rival. I need inclusion in your secret government protection program."

"Look, Calchas!" Achilles yelled. "Even if your alluded-to foe happens to be King Agamemnon himself, I'll kick his royal ass good, along with easily crushing his tiny testicles bouncing-around inside his miniature scrotum sac!"

"Lord Achilles; Phoebus Apollo is especially angry on two counts," Calchas anxiously disclosed. "First, our leader against Troy called all-powerful A-pollo 'a chicken', rather repeatedly; and second, your adversary Agamemnon refused to surrender his handsome ransom Chryseis, high priest Chryses' beautiful daughter. Apollo will not stop shooting silver arrows into our vulnerable assholes and puncturing our' delicate scrotum sacs until Chryseis is safely returned to Chryses! It's that plainly simple! What a fully fucked-up situation this Chryses/Chryseis crisis is! After you return Chryseis to Chryses to avoid further crisis, I suggest that we alter our errant ways and make abundant sacrifices to Lord Apollo upon a newly constructed altar!"

But Agamemnon, king of Mycenae and the Achaean leader against Troy, became infuriated at Calchas' Chryses/Chryses commentary. "Look, Calchas, you feckless wimp," the king of Mycenae bellowed. "All of your prophecies are basically doom and gloom in nature. Chryseis is a tremendous piece of ass, and she's better in bed than my wife Clytemnestra is at daily humping and pumping. And as you know, my captains. My brother King Menelaus of Sparta had married that cold-hearted bitch Helen, and I have regrettably married Helen's frigid sister, Clytemnestra!"

"Do you value this religious-freak girl Chryseis over your entire army of fifty-thousand men?" Achilles audaciously challenged Agamemnon. "Surely, you should not jeopardize all of us simply over a well-endowed whore. But first, you must scream-up to the sky, 'A-pollo is *NOT* a chicken! A-pollo is *not* a chicken!"

"I shall surrender my pride and obey Apollo's greedy will," Agamemnon reluctantly agreed. "But then it would look like I am weak if I must surrender my prize at a belligerent underling's prompting. Now Achilles; I assert that I must be given another horny harlot in the place of me giving-up Chryseis."

"What woman do you wish to pump the poop out of?" Achilles demanded of Agamemnon. "You might just lose your confused head over a stupid piece of ass!"

"I might just consider possessing your prized concubine, Briseis, Achilles, or perhaps instead, I'll decide to confiscate Ajax's prized hussy. I can't emphasize how terrific it is for me being the chief chauvinist with absolute authority on this military expedition. There's plenty of time for my' heart to determine which sexy bitch I'll choose for my personal gratification! But first, I must avoid future crises by appeasing Apollo by giving that excellent piece of ass Chryseis back to that lunatic dumb-dick priest Chryses."

"You dare belittle super-strong Ajax, the great warrior who had cleaned-out several Trojan platoons like an ivory-skinned white tornado!" Achilles loudly challenged.

"As leader of the forces against Troy, I can do whatever I please," Agamemnon articulated, using the rank card. "Your might is no defense to my acclaimed and established wisdom!"

"You're a very greedy bastard," Achilles accused the Mycenae King. "Quite truthfully, I have no particular grievances or quarrel against the Trojans. I had led my troops here to Troy to help your brother Menelaus retrieve your sister-in-law Helen from the clutches of Prince Paris. In fact, I've contributed more to this battle than you have. Just look at all the cities I've sacked, and all of the promiscuous whores I've bagged! Yet, you; you stubborn asshole, get to keep all of the plunder to your own avaricious self! Frankly, I've had enough of your abusive bullshit!" livid Achilles screamed. "I'm inclined to gladly sail for home and return to Phthia in my native Thessaly, and leave you to fight Paris, Hector, Priam and the rest of the Trojans over the stolen wife of Menelaus, who is reputed from Greek gossip to be a third-class piece of ass!"

Agamemnon then accused Achilles of being an emboldened coward, and to demonstrate his supreme authority, deliberately belittled the greatest of Greek warriors. "Achilles; enough of your snarky innuendo; now hear me out! You cannot defy the will of the Lord King, namely myself, captaining this formidable armada! Since I shall give Chryseis back to the short high-priest Chryses, I demand that you make a reasonable concession before this military council and give me your prized female, Briseis, to compensate for Chryseis, in order to avoid more crises with Chryses, the dwarfish high-priest of Apollo."

When Achilles and Agamemnon were about to commence dueling with bronze swords, Hera, wife of Zeus, urgently dispatched Athena, daughter of Almighty Zeus, to whisper powerful words into enraged Achilles' ear.

"Hold your hand from your' sword, dear Achilles, and I urge you to forget about using your bronze weapon at this moment," Athena softly and discreetly recommended. "For your exhibition of self-control, I assure you, brave warrior, that soon you'll be fully rewarded with endless fame and glory, if you just wisely practice self-control and restraint against Agamemnon. Slice the garrulous asshole with your clever language, but not with your awesome sword!"

"As is our tradition, the meeting scepter has been passed along to me, and as you all know, I am the only one entitled to speak at this moment," the Phthian prince insisted. "Now Agamemnon; here is my general evaluation of our' impasse! I've concluded that I shall refuse to fight on your behalf," Achilles boldly addressed Agamemnon while standing erect before the other noble captains attending the assembly. "As Hector and Paris courageously lead their soldiers against *your* invading armies, I will not participate any further in *your* futile battle!"

Elderly Nestor was then handed the scepter by Achilles, and the old fart slowly addressed the aggregate of Greek commanders. "I am the oldest one here, and had once fought with the hero Theseus, slayer of the Minotaur on the island of Crete. But I must confess to you, King Agamemnon, that this is indeed a black day! I advise that you give-up Chryseis to Chryses and not take Briseis from Achilles. And I say to you, Lord Achilles; I further extend this fair compromise as a viable solution to this ongoing argument. Please help us to defeat the Trojans and not sail back to your homeland with your battle-proven Myrmidons!"

"Well said, Nestor," Agamemnon complimented the distinguished philosopher from Pylos. "But Achilles is obviously extremely envious of my prowess, and the covetous fool evilly wishes to pilfer my authority! I shall never relinquish my newly acquired prize Briseis to *his* jealous disposal, and if the son-of-a-bitch dares to double-cross me, *his* pathetic blood will soak my trusty sword!"

Fearing the infamous wrath of Achilles, double-talking Agamemnon quickly relented from his demand, and the King of Mycenae instructed Odysseus of Ithaca to transport Chryseis back to her father, the midget high priest Chryses, in order to avert continuing crisis involving Apollo's revenge. But soon thereafter, Agamemnon instructed two guards, Eurybates, brother of Eurabadass, and Talthybius, father of the pygmy-runt

Tallthebes, to escort Briseis from Achilles' tent and transferred into *his* personal custody.

"Lord King; can't I sail to Lesbos instead and eagerly watch some kinky lesbians in action?" Odysseus begged and asked Agamemnon. "I understand that there are some tri-sexuals living on that bizarre island, in addition to the notorious female homos!"

Meanwhile, aggrieved and thwarted Achilles, suffering from emotional distress, ventured to the distant seashore and beckoned his petulance to his mother, the sea nymph Thetis.

"Why do you sorrow so extensively, my dear son?" Thetis curiously inquired. "Did that antagonistic heel Apollo castrate your exposed testicles with one of his silver arrows? I've heard that the chariot sky rider's major beef is when a mere mortal like yourself yells-up to the clouds, 'A-pollo is a chicken'!"

"You already know the reason for my demeanor being quite disconsolate," Achilles replied to his immortal mother. "I've been horribly disgraced by Agamemnon, and have currently lost my slave girl Briseis to *his* imperial command. Now mother; I understand through hearsay that Almighty Zeus owes you a colossal favor. I'd like you to intervene for me and ask Lord Zeus to side with the home-team Trojans against the visiting Achaeans, and let all the Greek Captains finally realize the abundant crazed madness of Agamemnon! The Trojans must temporarily gain the upper-hand in the ongoing conflict! Then, the Greek Captains will finally comprehend exactly just how important I am, and just how unimportant Agamemnon really is!"

"My son, I see on the horizon a dim future for you as a mortal being. Confidentially, you have so little sand left falling inside your hourglass. Zeus and several other Mt. Olympus gods are presently attending a major feast in Ethiopia, but when they return from their merry festival, I'll plan to speak to him on your behalf."

Fulfilling his vital errand, Lord Odysseus reunited Chryseis with her father Chryses, and in the process, the current ever-escalating crisis with vindictive and arrow-gant Apollo had been successfully averted.

"In the future," the midget high priest/prophet commended, "I see you, Odysseus, going-down in history and standing next to fantastic contributors to world civilization such as the great Michelangelo, the magnificent Leonardo da Vinci, and a political genius with the weird appellation Thomas Jefferson," Chryses articulated and informed.

"Who the hell are those three anonymous assholes that you've just mentioned?" the King of Ithaca instinctively asked the tiny high-priest. "Those jerk-offs you've just indicated don't sound like ordinary Greeks or Trojans to me! Are the three others you've just mentioned distrustful Etruscans, or perhaps itinerant, fucked-up Chinese cavemen?"

Chryses ignored Odysseus's dumb-ass comments and solemnly proceeded with his preferred reverence to *his* adored god, Lord Apollo. The senile priest then offered monotonous prayers, dissonant songs, and cheap libations in the form of watered-down wine to satisfy the god's enormous ego.

"Odysseus, I bless you, valiant hero, in your gallant pursuit of evasive glory," Chryses advised. "The future of civilization depends on your genius in bringing the Trojan War of East versus West to a reputable end! Go now, oh illustrious champion; go in quest of your honorable destiny!"

And then Odysseus, with his essential mission of delivering Chryseis to Chryses being fully accomplished, sailed back to the shores of Troy with his crew upon his reliable Bireme.

On the twelfth day after the initial argument between Achilles and Agamemnon, Zeus had merrily returned to Mt. Olympus and granted an audience to Thetis, obsessively representing her tantrum-plagued son Achilles. But learning of the sea-nymph's visit, Hera, wife of Zeus, boldly confronted and challenged her husband's fidelity.

"I had witnessed you submissively bowing your head to that sea-whore Thetis, so what the Hades did you ever promise that conniving strumpet? I think, husband, that I already know the correct answer. You'll create a convoluted scenario where the Trojans will drive the Argives back to their anchored black ships upon the shoreline, just to satisfy the will of that over-ambitious heel, Achilles, son of Thetis."

"Leave me the fuck alone, wife!" Zeus boomed. "If you continue goading my sensitive ass, I'll turn you into a horny frog who is de-evolving-down into an insignificant tadpole. Depart from this chamber immediately, or else woman, you'll most certainly feel my tempestuous anger when I become excessively pissed-off!"

Upon Hera exiting the Mt. Olympus throne room, Zeus snapped his fingers and suddenly, his devout attendant Dream appeared to honor his master's imperative command, which happened several dozen times a day atop Mt. Olympus.

"Dream; I want you to take a brief trip to the distant shores of Troy and visit beleaguered King Agamemnon while the idiot's still sound asleep.

Instruct the dumb-fuck to wildly attack the city with his entire force. Whisper into his defective brain that the day of the Achaean victory will soon arrive. This activity, meaning the power of suggestion as enacted by you, will be phase one of my most recent war game scheme. Now Dream, I hereby insist that you get your shit together and complete your assignment in forty-winks!"

"Yes, Master Zeus. I see much merit in your most-recent canard. As always, your imaginative wish is my loyal instruction!" Dream obediently declared. "But honestly, my dear Lord Zeus. You could call me by my other popular name if you'd like: Mr. Sandman!"

Chapter 2

"RALLYING THE WARRIORS"

The following morning, Agamemnon summoned his commanders to an important assembly to reveal the detailed essence of the deceitful dream that unscrupulous Zeus had fabricated, and that Dream had deposited deep inside *his* thick skull.

"Generals," the King of Mycenae prefaced his remarks. "Last night Mighty Zeus had sent me a dream, but unfortunately, it wasn't a marvelous white one. The king god had informed my subconscious mind that *our* day of triumph has finally arrived, and that a phenomenal victory will soon be within our grasp. The walls of Troy will soon topple and disintegrate into dust, for Zeus now favors us Achaeans; the chief deity wants us to stop kissing butt and to start kicking ass!"

Agamemnon then held a brief private side-bar conference with Odysseus and Nestor, the two major officers that he most trusted. "The under-ranking men's loyalty must be tested. I'll feign honesty and announce that the troops should board their boats and be ready to sail back to their native lands. If the idiots desire to be reunited with their wives' smelly crotches and with their aberrant, wise-ass kids' undisciplined antics and semantics, then I command that you, Odysseus and Nestor, convince your loyal confederates to rally the lower-echelon morons if the ridiculous dolts appear to be succumbing to my brain-dead test."

"This is an idiotic notion that you're foolishly commanding us to implement," Odysseus complained to the expedition's leader. "Do you think that the fifty-thousand soldiers in our landing party will facetiously obey your silly intent and stay on the battlefield, risking their lives fighting against the rabid Trojans?"

"Odysseus is absolutely right!" Nestor chimed-in. "Your plan, Lord Agamemnon, is evidently more fucked-up than the fucked-up gods on Mt. Olympus are!"

"Do as I command, for although the dumb-ass plan sounds like a dumb-ass plan, the fucked-up scheme had originated from Zeus, who might be a dumb-ass, but whose electric lightning bolts are notorious for cauterizing mortals' assholes so that the afflicted victims die because they can no longer shit or fart!"

Agamemnon then climbed to the top of a recently reinforced rickety platform and non-persuasively spoke gibberish to his assembled minions. "Achaeans; for nine difficult years we've battled the enemy outside the walls of Troy, and have suffered misery, plagues and persistent heartache. I know that you dumb-shits miss your bratty delinquent kids along with your sex-starved wives' stinking vaginas. The riggings and hulls of our ships are slowly rotting away, and the Biremes all smell worse than your spouses' pungent pussy holes. Now, we happen to outnumber the Trojans ten-to-one, but please remember; we had to also fight surreptitious sneak attacks from their myriad allies arriving on the battlefield from neighboring cities."

"What the fuck are you saying? What the fuck are you saying?" the fifty-thousand soldiers all amazingly chanted in unison. "Stop speaking nonsense out of your asshole! Stop speaking nonsense out of your asshole!" the irate contingent of exhausted soldiers continued yelling and cursing their leader.

Agamemnon raised his hands to achieve silence, which was finally accomplished after a half-hour of incessant wild protesting. "Men," the King of Mycenae resumed his address. "I do not disparage you! I now ascertain that Zeus has lied to me in my dream, where the villainous immortal has deceitfully promised us victory. Let's euphorically board our awaiting ships, and depart from accursed Troy in defeat."

The Achaeans leaped up and down in joyful celebration, and jubilantly dashed across the arid plain to their respective ships, eagerly scrambling on board their separate Biremes. But Athena, who for sheer mental diversion favored her mortal champion Odysseus, placed courage into the Ithacan king's heart, enough strength to settle-down his rambunctious troops and to encourage the fatigued warriors to not obey Agamemnon's dumb-ass frivolous command.

"Attention, all you goons and loons. Our erudite leader has tested your fidelity to our Greek cause. Stupid-shit assholes; you have failed the challenge by complying with his preposterous orders!" Odysseus admonished his confused troops. "Get back in line, and stop behaving and acting out of line! Your deplorable deportment is both shameful and cowardly!"

And then, Odysseus screamed-up to Agamemnon, still standing atop his rickety platform that was swaying back and forth in the heavy, gusting wind. "Mighty King and Fearless Leader! Your men have forgotten their oath to you and to our absurd mission to not leave these foreign shores until they have plundered Troy, and have raped and screwed at least a dozen gorgeous women each. Men," Odysseus then shouted to the fifty-thousand soldiers. "Wouldn't you like humping and pumping fresh, young pussy rather than returning to your haggard wives with their crotches that smell like rotten tuna? I insist that you dunce-like dimwits remember the prophecy of Calchas, where a tremendous red snake had surfaced from behind the pedophile priest's altar. The slimy reptile slithered up a tall tree, and ravenously swallowed-down eight tiny birds, that weren't swallows, but actually sparrows, I believe. After digesting the eight defenseless chicks, the voracious snake then lurched-out and caught the alarmed mother sparrow, and upon lunging at the panicky wing-flapping bird, devoured the cawing mother, but as a result of the viper's appetite, the venomous red snake, according to Calchas, immediately turned to stone."

"What nincompoop puts credence in such totally bullshit mythology?" a cynical witness named Thersites yelled-out in opposition. "That dumb-fuck story lacks credibility! It's truly the mantra of a born loser! And old fart Agamemnon; you are completely wrong in your fucked-up quarrel with indispensable Achilles, the whole argument being over a dumb-cunt kinky slave girl!"

Odysseus was not deterred by the critical objector's negative comments. "Calchas had told me to interpret those nebulous signs, and I suddenly became inspired to perform some basic analysis. The nine devoured sparrows symbolically indicated our nine years fighting our bitter enemy here outside Troy. The serpent turning to stone indicates that soon, the stone walls of Troy will fall to our fierce onslaught, and despite the petty interference of the Greek gods on either side of the war, the Argives shall prevail and win this fucked-up hostility being fought over Helen, Menelaus's whoring wife!"

The troops, encouraged by Odysseus's plausible explanation of the snake and birds' parable, all yelled in accord: "Yaaa!" and "Hooray!" Their boisterous exclamations were hollered in loud appreciation of the prospect of each soldier screwing at least a dozen hairy slit holes.

"Ha, ha, ha!" Nestor congenially laughed to Ajax. "Odysseus had once told me that existing on his stranger-than-fiction island of Ithaca, there grows a fabulous Cunt Tree Shrine out in the country, that a man's nostrils could smell from miles away!"

"Ha, ha, ha!" the gargantuan Ajax jollily answered the famed philosopher, Nestor of Pylos. "That remarkable Ithacan Cunt Tree out in the country must stink worse than the world's largest rotten fish market. I suspect that the emanating malodor would be so bad that the filthy stench would both attract and 'deter gents' who would be alertly coming to the shrine from all directions! Ha, ha, ha!" Ajax replied.

Nestor suggested that the time was ripe to organize the various clans and tribes into attack groups, and to then prepare for the mighty battle awaiting them. Agamemnon, feeling relieved from not being assassinated by Achilles and his allies, praised Odysseus and Nestor for their wisdom and military strategy.

"Let's have an ox slaughtered, and then wrap its corpulent thighbones in greasy fat. We'll burn a wholly wonderful sacrifice to Almighty Zeus, who, according to tradition, is basically carnivorous, and definitely not an avowed vegetarian. Then, let's have the various, skilled brigade butchers' carve-up the thousand fattened steers that we had stolen in previous raids, and thereafter, we'll excitedly feast on the beasts. And gentleman," Agamemnon continued his exposition. "Make sure that the butchered meat has been pounded correctly, because our sex-deprived butchers have been seen pounding their own meat for lack of accessible pussy."

After feasting and anticipating their forthcoming victory following nine years of frustration, the heralds announced for the fifty-thousand or so remaining troops to muster upon the open plain situated between the narrow sea and Troy. In what later in history became known as a Homeric Catalogue, Agamemnon of Mycenae had brought a hundred ships from Mycenae; Menelaus had led sixty; Nestor of Pylos ninety vessels; Diomedes of Argos eighty Biremes; Idomenus of Crete had amassed eighty ships for the war effort, and Agapenor of Arcadia, where primitive versions of simplistic amusement games had been invented, led an armada of sixty Biremes. Some of the other captains who had navigated their vessels in lesser numbers were Odysseus, twelve ships; the giant Ajax, the detergent king, a dozen also; Tlepolemus of Rhodes, an academic scholar and the son of Hercules, had aggregated nine ships, and delirious Podalirius from Thessaly, who was green in complexion, and according to mythology, had been miraculously born inside a four-foot-long peapod, had assembled thirty vessels.

Of course, because of his ongoing personal dispute and conflict with King Agamemnon, Achilles, proud commander of fifty sea-worthy Biremes, and his famed Myrmidons, who incidentally looked a bit like prehistoric Trachodons, all refrained from participating in the battle preparations just to deliberately spite Agamemnon. The classic story of the acclaimed Achaean assault on the wealthy Asia Minor citadel was about to be finally fought and chronicled. "We shall destroy Troy!" became the

Greeks redundant battle-cry. "We each can't wait to get laid with a dozen hairy-holed Trojan whores!"

Back on Mt. Olympus, unscrupulous Zeus was now temporarily allied with the Trojans, since the king of the gods had promised the alluring sea-nymph Thetis that the Greek army would eventually realize how essential her son Achilles would have been in the ensuing battle, and that Agamemnon was not nearly as intrepid or audacious as the renowned Phthian hero was to winning the Argives' cause.

In the interim, Iris, the irascible Goddess of the Rainbow, and also a dependable disciple and pupil of devious Aphrodite, (who obviously had sided with Prince Paris), upon Aphrodite's insistence, disguised herself as King Priam, who then instructed the Trojan captains to be vigilant and to keep a lookout for the impending Greek siege upon the city.

'Paris must be favored, since the handsome prince had chosen me over Hera and Athena in the fairest of goddesses beauty contest at the wedding of Peleus and Thetis,' Aphrodite imagined and recalled. 'My will and the Trojan cause must ultimately prevail! I have had the upper-hand ever since Eris's golden apple got rolling upon that ancient dance floor! I respect and admire both Eris and Iris's allegiance to my imperial will!'

Chapter 3

"PARIS DUELS MENELAUS"

The impressive battle scene was now set for a spectacular confrontation. The dedicated Trojans and their allies flowed-out of the city's main gates, screaming war cries as the soldiers hustled forward through a dense cloud of dust, all troops dressed in full battle array. King Priam's warriors were loud and clamorous, while on the contrary, the Greek advance was deliberate and methodical, with the silent Argives moving shoulder-to-shoulder in strict military fashion.

Feeling responsible for the tremendous loss of life on both sides, Paris boldly stepped-out and challenged any of the reticent Achaeans to fight him in mano-to-mano combat. Seizing the opportunity, Menelaus, recognizing the abductor of his wife Helen, accepted the fortuitous invitation. But when Prince Paris realized that his forthcoming opponent would be the red-headed King of Sparta, the youth scampered like a frightened rabbit back into the Trojan ranks, where his older brother Hector began berating his cowardly sibling.

"I feel disgraced and ashamed in calling you my brother," Hector adamantly criticized. "Inspired by Aphrodite, you had sailed to Sparta on a prospective good will mission, and soon wound-up abducting King Menelaus's wife. Your grotesque greed has brought-down a perilous wasp nest upon all our heads, including the damned innocent Achaeans. Now Little Brother, you cravenly state that you'll duel with any of the Greeks, and when Menelaus agreed to honor your terms of engagement, you speedily retreat and are gone with the wind into the shadows, as if you were a frightened antelope."

"You're correct in verbally rebuking and hectoring me, Hector," Paris reluctantly admitted. "But Aphrodite had afforded me the enticing gift of love, but regrettably, not that of courage. Right now, Hector; I wish that I had remained a common shepherd boy tending my lambs and sheep out on the non-fruitive plains, and not be acting as the bragging warrior that I have pretended to be!"

"You're scared shitless of Menelaus, aren't you?" Hector asserted to Paris. "If you foolishly duel with the livid King of Sparta, I believe that you'll soon be wasting-away in Diarrheaville! Indeed, Little Brother Paris;

Menelaus will most certainly plaster you! You'll be pounded so brutally hard that you'll think that you're a slab of veal cutlet on a table inside a butcher shop!"

"Please Hector. Show respect for my sensitive ego that has been severely damaged. In all honesty, I feel like a disintegrating snowflake quickly melting-away in the hot sun. What constructive wisdom can you advise besides constantly belittling my vulnerable self-esteem? Why can't you be my substitute high school guidance counselor?"

"Look here, you disoriented juvenile asshole! Your eighty-pound, spastic sister Cassandra has always beaten your' ass in basic arm-wrestling; and numerous times, the nasty bitch has easily pinned your butt to the mat in two out of three falls. And also, everyone residing and gossiping inside Priam's palace secretly knows that Cassandra is a neurotic heroine on heroin!"

"Okay, you win this totally peculiar discussion," Paris conceded. "I'll duel with formidable Menelaus to the death, and in so doing, I hope to end this absurd ancient war and save Troy from utter destruction. Whoever triumphs in the ensuing death struggle, then that victor will get to keep Helen, along with all of her wealth and precious jewels. Then, the soldiers in both armies will put-down their spears and bows, with the Greeks merrily voyaging back to their homeland, and the Trojans re-entering the gates of their city, and hopefully, co-existing in harmonious friendship with the asshole Achaeans. But first, a fight to the death must commence in order to attain such an honorable solution. I want to be a 'victor', Hector, even though my name is Paris!"

Hector then yelled and commanded for his expert battalions to halt from advancing ahead, and in a matter of seconds, Agamemnon hollered similar instructions to the Argives, stating that the troops should cease mechanically marching forward. Hector proudly stood between the two armies and orated directions to both the Greek and Trojan warriors, whose keen ears listened attentively to his specified rules.

"Trojans and Argives!" Hector loudly enunciated. "Paris now officially challenges King Menelaus to wage single combat, even though only Menelaus is presently married. All warriors on both sides should put-down their spears, and other weapons and paraphernalia, while these two pugnacious pugilists desperately fight for Helen and her Spartan gold."

"I'm the afflicted party here, and I accept the adolescent punk's proposal to fight to the death!" red-bearded Menelaus confirmed. "Enough strife has already occurred between our armies over these past nine years! I submit that there will be no compromises during this lethal altercation. After my imminent vanquishing of my callow opponent, let the Greeks peacefully depart from this non-fruitive Troad Plain, accompanied by my purloined-back wife Helen. Now, before the confrontation happens, we should seal the deal by slaughtering a black and blue ewe and a white, rambunctious ram, both of which to sacrifice to all the gods, some of whom favor the Greeks, and others that staunchly support Troy. And I believe that King Priam should arrive and attend the upcoming bout, so that His Imperial Majesty can verify the oath of peace after my swift triumph is easily attained. For, in all sincerity, I am sagacious enough *not* to trust one iota the statements of Priam's two wild and crazy sons!"

The thousands of tanned warriors representing both sides knelt-down, placed their weapons and shields upon the hot sand, and quietly sat upon the dusty plain, hoping that death to either Menelaus or Paris would finally terminate the near decade-long conflict.

* * * * * * * * * * * *

Meanwhile, Queen Hecuba, King Priam's corpulent wife, called Helen over to the palace's high ramparts to witness a "marvelous spectacle". "Look-out onto yonder battlefield, my dear. The soldiers on both sides are getting sand fleas stuck inside their assholes by stupidly sitting upon the hot desert sand. Yes, the men have ceased fighting; have thrust their sharp spears into the dry earth, and the pathetic fools are so moronic that they're leaning on their shields instead of intelligently sitting upon them!"

"Come and join the Queen and me to witness mythology in the making," King Priam beckoned to Helen. "After all; you have caused all of this needless bullshit to occur! You cannot claim irresponsibility for all of the mayhem your lust for Paris has generated!"

"I love you as if you were my biological father, whom I had despised and never either listened-to or cared about!" wily Helen prevaricated. "I wish that my vindictive brother-in-law and my jealous husband had not come here to reclaim me for their own greed, which has been cunningly disguised as being 'glory for all of Greece'."

"My blurry eyes are not quite as sharp as my peepers once were," Priam revealed while squinting his dilated pupils. "I think that my cataracts are bigger than the fabled ones existing at the source of the Nile River over in Egypt, or is it Ethiopia? Anyway, my child, who most-definitely is not my biological child. Inform me; who is that awesome-looking figure on the *far left?* He doesn't look like a political conservative to me!"

"That idiotic antagonist is my husband's bastard brother, King Agamemnon of Mycenae. He is the son of Atreus, who was quite renowned for designing and building magnificent atriums in various Greek palaces. Vindictive Agamemnon is the elected leader of the Argive expedition to retrieve me and my face, that has launched a thousand ships to Troy, organized to conduct me back to Sparta. Oh, King Priam. I absolutely love living my dream in fabulous luxury here inside your opulent palace, and I totally despise my former nightmare Spartan existence!"

"Pardon my rather impulsive histrionics, Helen. King Agamemnon commands the greatest army ever assembled in history, er, I mean 'in mythology'," Priam declared and clarified. "I've noticed that the Argive captains are all standing erect and not crouched-down, squatting in the hot sand. And who is that portly, psychotic fellow standing next to Agamemnon. He looks as strong as a beastly ox, and as dumb as one, also."

"Don't allow first appearances to deceive you," Helen mildly reprimanded elderly Priam. "That hero you're referring-to is the inimitable Odysseus of Ithaca, son of Laertes. No one on either side can match his genius at practicing shrewd trickery and clever military strategy!"

"And who is that five-hundred-pound giant who towers over everyone else?" astonished Priam asked. "The very imposing ogre looks more powerful than a white tornado! He's probably here to do some ethnic cleansing!"

"That humongous individual is Ajax, who the roads scholars on Rhodes plan to model a colossal statue after, which after being financed by means of exorbitant taxes, will become one of the Seven Wonders of the Ancient World. And standing beside Ajax is famous Idiomeneus of Crete, who metaphorically speaks jabberwocky, mostly mumbled and stuttered in dumb-ass cliches. However, I do not see among the Greek captains my brother Castor, who had perfected manufacturing a certain type of oil, and his twin, Polydeuces, who liked to play poker with the number two cards being wild!" Helen elaborated. "According to recent palace scuttlebutt, I now sadly understand that both of my mentally deficient brothers, who in real life were actual called by others 'mothers', are now the exclusive properties of morbid King Hades and Queen Persephone, with both my brothers now dual disconsolate and miserable spirits mutually residing in dark and dismal Hades!"

The conversation between King Priam and Helen was suddenly interrupted when a gay messenger arrived and announced in a high-pitched voice that Prince Hector desired a black ewe and a white ram to be religiously sacrificed to appease the gods before a specially scheduled duel was to transpire. "Prince Paris and King Menelaus will soon wage hand-to-hand combat. The sought-after prize will be Helen along with her gold and jewels' fortune. And after the contest's victor is determined, the Greeks promise to leave in peace, regardless of the outcome," the staccato-voiced courier divulged.

Priam hobbled out of the palace and was soon escorted onto the Troad Plain battlefield in a well-designed miniature chariot. The Trojan King somberly presented the black ewe and the white ram to grim-faced Agamemnon, who swiftly used his dagger to cut tufts of fleece from the designated animals in order to distribute the sacred wool among his captains. Then, the Ruler of Mycenae orated a short speech to further inspire, perspiring and revenge-minded Menelaus.

"Father Goose, er, I meant to say, Zeus," Agamemnon reflexively corrected his faulty pronunciation. "And also, Lord Poseidon, Lord Hades, and all of you other mercurial-minded Mt. Olympus gods. I hereby request that you very bored deities stay out of this lengthy conflict, despite the fact that many of you have already taken sides. If Paris luckily kills Menelaus, allow the juvenile delinquent to retain possession of Helen, along with her incomparable wealth, and then we melancholy Greeks will dejectedly sail back to our native cities. But if Menelaus plasters Paris and sends the puny punk's skinny ass down to Hades, the Trojans will be obligated to surrender Helen and her fantastic gold as just compensation to my brother, the King of Sparta, and also to my avaricious self. And so, you two royal Trojan dumb-dicks, namely Priam and Hector, you'll both have to invent a new method of birth control in order to rebuild your city's largely-diminished fortune."

The throats of the sacrificial animals were then viciously slit, and the finest of wines was mixed with the ram and ewe blood, and quickly poured-out to pay homage to the generally apathetic Mt. Olympus gods. Every Greek warrior solemnly prayed for Menelaus's victory, to be followed by *their* safe voyage back home.

Priam, in a raspy tone of utterance, then spoke as loudly as the old fart could to aggrieved Agamemnon. "Eminent King; I must take my leave from this impending assassination of my wimpy son. Although I'm not a carnivorous ursa, I cannot bear to witness my dear scrawny and feckless son

Paris die from extensive body mutilation. I'm certain that the gods already know my doomed son's fate and ultimate destiny."

Hector and Odysseus stepped forward and began measuring-out the square perimeter of the proposed (and highly-anticipated) duel. "The inside area of the square must be around one fourth of a hectare," Hector confidently communicated to Odysseus. "And according to my general knowledge of mathematics, there are approximately two and a half acres in a hectare."

"Hector, cut the lousy bullshit!" Odysseus explicitly chided his Trojan adversary. "If Menelaus kicks Paris in his tiny testicles, your younger brother will already be sporting two acres! Ha, ha, ha!"

After the perimeter had been officially established, Odysseus placed two non-building lots inside his bronze helmet to determine which dueler would be the first to hurl his spear at his opponent. Paris's lot was chosen and removed, and the sorrowed Prince discernibly mumbled, "What a lot of fucked-up horse-crap this whole scenario is! I'm in a lot of trouble, and worst of all, being on this raunchy battlefield every day and night, I haven't even yet had the chance to pump the poop out of Helen! Thanks a lot! I can't even get marmalade, let alone get laid!"

The pair of combatants stood a mere fifty-feet apart, and soon, impulsive Paris awkwardly tossed his bronze spear at Menelaus's chest, and the sharp weapon merely deflected off the Greek king's shield, and after the weak carom, harmlessly fell upon the desert plain.

And to Prince Paris's great apprehension, Menelaus frightfully yelled-up to the cloud-laden sky, "Father Zeus! Grant me total revenge upon this skinny wimp who has egregiously wronged me. Let his death be interpreted as a strong message to all of today's witnesses that such a fate as being brutally killed is what awaits any warrior who maliciously betrays another!"

The King of Sparta quickly and accurately hurled his sharp spear at Prince Paris, with the razor-like projectile speeding toward his foe as if it had been a lethal javelin tossed by Hercules himself. The airborne weapon penetrated Paris's sturdy shield, and the abominable tip more-than-grazed the prince's abdomen. The force of the impact immediately knocked the Trojan heir to the sandy ground, and immediately, Menelaus grabbed the hanks of hair extending out from Paris's helmet, and the enraged Spartan proceeded to drag his disgraced victim around the half-hectare outlined perimeter that had been carefully drawn by Odysseus and Hector.

But feeling compelled to intercede on her hero's behalf, beautiful-but-invisible Aphrodite mystically appeared upon the scene and cut Paris's helmet strap, so that her favorite Trojan could continue breathing. And then, the coy Goddess of Beauty enshrouded and enveloped her favored royal Trojan in a dense mist, which hid the prince's form from everyone's scrutiny, while saying to her admired Beauty Contest judge, "Dear Paris; I give you inspiration to inhale so that your respiration will not expire! I shall now mysteriously conduct your lily-white ass to a neutral place of safety, where you, my beloved handsome champion, will adequately recover from your exceptionally bad battlefield encounter!"

"Where the fuck did my craven opponent go?" astounded Menelaus shrieked to the earless heavens. "This whole fucked-up ordeal involving gutless Paris is positively insane! His appearance in this abbreviated duel has resulted in an incredibly dumb-ass, abrupt, magical disappearance!"

Again, employing her supernatural ability, gorgeous Aphrodite miraculously transported Paris to his palace bedchamber and meticulously cleansed the sweat and grime from his entire body, focusing mostly upon his tiny testicles, and also the fatigued prince's limp pussy-plunger. After comforting and caressing her unconscious hero, the devious goddess, disguised as a common palace maid, gracefully flew like a majestic eagle out of the bedroom's open window, and glided over the palace ramparts to visit bewildered Helen.

"Come, Helen of Troy. Paris's privates require your immediate presence inside his private bedroom. His once-abused body is again fresh and fair, but the prince's erratic emotions need immediate solace and comfort. And who the hell knows? Perhaps some perverted pre-marital sex is about to occur?"

'How in the world did Paris ever zoom into the palace after being wounded on the plain by Menelaus?" Helen wanted to know. "I know that the prince sometimes flies off the handle, but he's never before mysteriously flown into his own palace bedroom!"

"Your esoteric wisdom marvelously transcends your splendid beauty!" Aphrodite facetiously complimented and commended Helen. "You are indeed a credit to all of Troy!"

"Holy divine deity shit!" Helen wildly exclaimed. "Ah! Now I understand. You are famed Goddess Aphrodite in wonderful disguise. Why don't you, er, I mean, why *do* you seduce me? Haven't you administered sufficient pain to Paris, to all of Troy, and also to myself? If you love Paris so much, I believe that you should experience inferior sex with him, instead of him having poor sex with me!"

"Do not refuse my generous assistance, ungrateful mortal bitch!" insulted Aphrodite promptly and effectively chastised Helen. "If you ungratefully refuse my liberal favors, then Paris, Hector, Priam, Hecuba and all the combined Trojans and Achaeans alike will be exposed to extreme, powerful hatred coming from all directions, and I emphatically predict Helen, that your dim future will also transform into a very grim one!"

Chapter 4
"THE BATTLEFIELD"

"Lord Zeus, thank you for calling this emergency meeting of the gods," Phoebus Apollo commended. "What particular issues and concerns are presently dominating your superior mind? Are you running out of your supply of thunder and lightning?"

"On the contrary, Apollo," Zeus smugly replied. "I have more lightning bolts at my disposal than you have silver arrows accumulated in your secret personal arsenal. But I do want to review some matters in regard to those pesky mortals meandering-around down on the Earth. As you know, archer god," Zeus stressed, "it is a dumb-ass law of Olympus that once humans acquire a certain knowledge or a particular skill, then the gods are supposed to allow the dimwits to keep their acquisition, without receiving or suffering any major consequences."

"True," Apollo readily confirmed. "But for instance, Almighty Zeus, if mortals ever accidentally discovered the nature and location of nectar and ambrosia, then they too could obtain immortality, and eventually, after developing moderate science and technology, the mischievous race could rival our current dominance over them!"

"Husband, I believe that you are too paranoid worrying about those weak humans down on Earth having a violent rebellion against you," Hera accused Zeus. "And I think that you're afraid that the mortals will someday overthrow you, just like you had an insolent insurrection against your Titan father, Lord Cronus. Do you concur with my assessment?"

'Yes, dear wife. And I've punished Cronus along with his Titan cronies by banishing the whole rebellious group to the dismal black pit of Tartarus, located in the most dark and gruesome center of Hades. My brother Hades and Queen Persephone have made sure that their Titan captives are permanently secured with enormous shackles and chains."

"And just look how you had penalized poor, good-hearted Prometheus," Hera accused and indicted her spouse. "Just because the compassionate Titan felt sorry for the humans living in caves during the winter and had taught the mortals how to make and keep fire, you felt it necessary to severely disciple empathetic Prometheus for all eternity."

"I had tolerated Prometheus after I conducted my usurping of my father Cronus and allowed the Titan to stay here living atop Mt. Olympus. But Prometheus had violated my supreme will by giving mortals vital knowledge that could be used to manufacture metal weapons," Zeus argued. "Now the do-gooder fool is chained to the top of Mt. Etna over in Sicily, where two squawking eagles persistently claw and peck away at his injured heart and tender testicles."

"And don't forget your ongoing quarrel with the Titan Atlas," Hera reminded her volatile-minded husband. "He had been penalized by your verdict to perpetually hold-up the sky from collapsing onto the Earth!"

"Atlas has to be diverted from entertaining a rebellion against me by performing his eternal labor, my wife, so that the temperamental Titan doesn't get any wild ideas about having the other Titans also revolt, with their plan being to again rule the sky along with the entire planet. But now, dear Hera, I would like to change the subject of discussion to what's going on among the Greeks on the nearby shores of Troy!"

"Please be more specific and hurry-up your speech," Apollo assertively butted-in. "Pretty soon I need to get my golden chariot and my four immortal white horses ready to pull the sun across the bright blue sky."

"Gods of Olympus, and I especially mean you, Athena," Zeus commenced, acknowledging the principal reason for convening his special council session. "I've recently been eavesdropping on strange conversations between Odysseus and his five illiterate lieutenants, and I want you other deities to listen-in on their current ass-backwards communications. Just watch my newly installed monitor screen placed by Hephaestus on the side marble wall, and fathom the hilarious full extent of these dumb assholes' oddball comedy dialogue."

"What the hell happened to Prince Paris?" Odysseus forcefully asked his five subordinate lieutenants. "I'm initially asking you, my first-in-line Eurshiddenme. Did the royal Trojan punk apply vanishing cream to his entire body? We all were witnessing and enjoying that King Menelaus was assiduously kicking the Trojan prince's butt really good when all of a sudden, the young loon amazingly disappeared into either thick or thin air!"

"Well, King Odysseus," Eurshiddenme replied. "I must state that I've often turned our ship's stern directly into the wind, but I never ever had the Bireme disappear inside the swirling gusts. It seems that Prince Paris had just mysteriously evaporated, like a mystifying vapor trace, integrating right into the atmosphere around him. Maybe the royal Trojan dimwit had been absorbed by a low-drifting cloud."

"What do you think about this conundrum now being discussed, Eurballsourout, my very intelligent second-in command. Do you have any revolutionary theories to explain this confounded disappearing mystery?"

"Well, Lord Odysseus," Eurballsourout uttered. "I truly believe that some sort of divine intervention had incidentally occurred during our' peculiar observation. Perhaps Lord Zeus was performing a demented magic act, but instead of a white rabbit, he needed a new available human, namely Prince Paris, to pull out of a high silk hat."

"You're shittin' me?" Odysseus bellowed.

"No, Commander Odysseus. I'm Eurballsourout; the guy standing and farting over to your right is Eurshiddenme!"

"Your balls are not out," the fourth mate Eurdicisin observed and commented to Eurballsourout. "Let's not get testicle, or, I meant to say 'technical'. Perhaps our fifth mate Eurcockisnum has a better answer to contribute to this discussion than I can," Eurdicisin suggested.

"Look, Lard-butt; Eurcockisnum thinks with his dick and not with his dysfunctional cerebrum," Odysseus aptly indicated to Eurdicisin. "Why should I make any inquiry to a dumb-dick like pecker-headed Eurcockisnum?"

"King Odysseus," Eurcockisnum ejaculated. "Don't be so hard-on me! How am I ever expected to rise to the occasion?"

"You five dumb-fucks need to become transsexuals and grow inflated tits and massive pink vaginas," Odysseus screamed and commented, "so that after this bizarre Trojan War terminates, my other crew members can enjoy some semi-normal sex instead of perpetual day-and-night, up-the-ass sodomy. When are you' uneducated Danaan jerk-offs ever going to learn that you can't defy the natural laws of biology. An asshole is an exit, and not a friggin entrancing 'entrance!"

"What's wrong with a little up-the-ass, pleasurable sodomy?" astute third lieutenant Eurassisgras challenged his four nutcase companions. "I mean, every once in a while, since we're so far from our native Ithaca, I say that we ought to have a little homo-sweet-homo!"

"The ship's doctor has told me that you need more fertilizer up your anus," Odysseus angrily interrupted, "because I think that a cluster of nasty weeds are growing where your ass-like hairs should be showing as artificial turf!" the incensed Ithacan King sarcastically scolded his third mate, Eurassisgras.

"Now fellow deities," Almighty Zeus imperatively stated as the god of thunder and lightning waved his left hand, and successfully canceled-out the

Achaean images off the screen of his visual monitor. "I believe that we immortal gods have nothing to fear or worry about in regard to these earthly nincompoops ever having any organized insurrection successfully waged against us! Lord Apollo. We Mt. Olympus residents have nothing to apologize for to these incompetent, imbecilic Greeks!"

"You're precisely right on target, Lord Zeus," arrow-shooter Apollo praised. "We don't have to worry one scintilla about the inferior human race, simply because the zany dolts are morally corrupt, but more importantly, those defective mortals are, beyond a doubt, mentally retarded."

"As you all well-know," Zeus replied, "I wish to remain neutral in the escalating conflict between the Argives and the city of Troy, as does my brother Hades, who also doesn't give a pregnant fart about who wins the monotonous war, just so that many warriors will die on both sides to populate Hades' underground Kingdom of the Dead. I'm also aware that my daughter Athena; my wife Hera; my brother Poseidon; the blacksmith Hephaestus, and my trusty messenger Hermes have all sided with the Agamemnon and the Greeks. And Aphrodite; Artemis; Ares, and you, Apollo, have sided with Prince Paris and the Trojans. Without objection, and with nothing further scheduled on my short agenda, I'd like to call this meeting to adjourn until there are new developments in the dull and boring Trojan War. Everyone is now free to leave, except Athena, with whom I would like to confidentially confer for a brief-but-constructive exchange of essential ideas."

Zeus privately revealed to Pallas Athene that the Ruler of Olympus was fully aware that Aphrodite had wholeheartedly committed her personal assistance to helping Paris and the Trojans to gain the advantage of soundly defeating the Argives, but then the chief god disclosed to his daughter that he wished to remain neutral, even though Zeus had an inclination to support Thetis's Achilles in his obstinate power-struggle quarrel with Agamemnon. "It's a good thing, Athena, that your Greeks don't have a lot of donkeys in their' camp, or else, your favored Argives might just get their asses kicked!"

"Father, this is no time for merriment or for amateur comedy hour," Athena rebuked. "If I am your favorite goddess who you revere even more than your spouse Hera, then I need your loving allegiance more than ever."

"Dear Athena; allow me to get serious for a moment. I feel that Helen should nostalgically return to Sparta and reunite with Menelaus, so that peace can once again prevail throughout both Troy and Greece. I could almost guarantee that King Priam and Agamemnon would each be satisfied with such a viable solution being implemented."

"Father, I've labored so hard in organizing the Danaans' armada of a thousand ships, and now you want to spoil my great enterprise by arranging a truce," Athene futilely argued. "As your omniscient mind already knows, I positively love the Greek cause, and my heart especially favors my splendid hero, Odysseus of Ithaca. If Troy is salvaged from destruction, and if the citadel in the future flourishes and prospers, then all of my industrious input in defense of the Argives will have been done in vain. Please don't spoil my great achievement!"

"The Trojans have always obediently and fearfully worshipped me," Zeus impatiently explained to his independent-minded daughter. "And their sincere sacrifices paying homage to me have been most respectful and satisfactory. At this juncture in time, I'm thinking about favoring Priam, Paris and Hector in their noble cause, and being objective, my mood is presently opposed to *your* spite for Paris pilfering Helen away from Sparta. However, precious daughter. I don't want to see a dangerous wedge materialize that would separate you from me. To reinforce our long-standing sentimental bond, I shall see that the in-progress war vacillates back and forth like mercury moving around a person's palm, as one manipulates his or her hand."

"Thank you, father," the fair goddess of wisdom professed. "Sparta, Argos and Mycenae are indeed my favorite cities, so if you decide to exercise your notorious wrath upon any of those places, I shall sadly endorse your wrongful decision. For I know that you'll stubbornly enact whatever whim enters your obstinate head, since you're the most potent and fickle-minded immortal up here on Mt. Olympus. In the end, I love and admire your omnipotent existence, and I maintain that you and I should not quarrel in a parallel manner that corresponds to what Greece and Troy are currently disputing and fighting. Do you agree with my general assessment?"

"Your devotion has encouraged me to endorse any stealthy trickery that your conniving loyalty to your hero Odysseus and the Danaans will engender. Go now Athena, and fly down to Earth and initiate any down to Earth policy that your sly mind can produce. For instance, if you desire for the Trojans to break the present truce, then my dear, you have my expressed permission to aggressively go for it!"

Pallas Athene gratefully thanked her dominant father for his vote of confidence, and in a matter of seconds, expeditiously zoomed-down from

Olympus, and soon zipped over to the plains of Troy in order to implement her new-found, devious strategy. The determined goddess's intended target was accessible Pandarus, a highly-skilled Trojan archer, who before the war, was an award-winning baker of delicious wheat and rye bread, and also, a producer of quality doughnuts, pies and bagels.

'Listen to me, Pandarus,' Athena's power of suggestion whispered into the famed archer's subconscious mind. 'This dream is of paramount importance to establish your high place in contemporary mythology. Now Pandarus, you can easily attain historic fame and fortune if you could deftly utilize your bow and arrow ability to instantly kill Menelaus of Sparta. Please recall that your trusty bow had been hewed from an ibex's four-foot-long horns, taken from the beast that you had hunted up in the Greek mountains. Now, audacious Pandarus; first off, you need to devoutly pray for imminent success to Phoebus Apollo, so that your' humble solicitation can obtain the courage for your name to go-down in the anals, er, I mean, the annals of history!'

'I could expertly shoot an arrow through a doughnut or a bagel with my incomparable bow and easily eliminate Menelaus without ever using-up any of my more lethal, poisonous arrows,' Pandarus's influenced brain creatively imagined.

After Pandarus made the recommended and appropriate sacrifice to Apollo, who incidentally favored the Trojan cause, in imitation of impish Cupid, the former baker-turned-archer drew back his bow and let the old arrow fly, straight toward the vulnerable navel of Menelaus. Using her natural guile inherited from Zeus himself, Athena surreptitiously guided and diverted the shot arrow into the targeted king's thick leather belt, with the sharp tip only slightly wounding Menelaus; the arrow's penetration merely gouging his abdominal flesh.

As Menelaus was lying upon the ground experiencing non-life-threatening-pain, vigilant King Agamemnon, witnessing the suspicious result of the surprise ambush, rushed to his brother's aid. "The tentative truce has been shattered, Menelaus. I'll bet you dollars-to-doughnuts that *that* villainous Pandarus has wounded you. Brother, I don't hardly understand how all of this happy horseshit has ever happened. Your intestines have been grazed and your damaged navel has sunken-inside your lower stomach. Now brother, here's the riddle that I can't completely comprehend," Agamemnon stated. "When shepherds graze their rams and lambs in a pasture, the sheep do not bleed from their grazing. How serious is your bleeding? I'll summon a herald to get our best surgeon, Machaon, to seal your wound."

"Don't worry a cunt hair, Agamemnon," Menelaus insisted. "A bagel or a sea gull shot from Pandarus's infamous bow would've created more bodily injury than that flimsy errant arrow had done! In the final analysis, I suppose that I have been most fortunate. No vital internal organs have been hit, not even my scrotum, my colon, or even my semi-colon!"

Feeling desperation and emotional panic, Agamemnon frenetically yelled to the Greek forces his patented *alarm:* "All to arms! All to arms!" the frustrated Greek leader reiterated. "Menelaus has almost been made into an invalid! But this invalid invalid lying superficially wounded upon the desert sand will quickly recover, rise to the occasion, and join us in battle! If we kill more than a thousand Trojans during this engagement, then King Menelaus will administer quality fellatio to each and every one of you!"

The two armies quickly assembled into their standard, customary ranks, and slowly advanced towards each other's straight (and gay) infantry lines. Soon, the roar of loud, hysterical shouting, along with delirious screaming, was discerned by human ears a full mile away, as heavy metal swords clanked, and bronze shields experienced terrible continuous impacts. Warriors on both sides met their ultimate fates, and their released spirits were swiftly conducted-down to shadowy Hades.

Various soldiers attempted to claim the bodies of fallen comrades, but during their valiant pursuits, those brave troops also became indiscriminate victims in the ongoing dual massacres. A horrendous, macabre and hideous-looking site had evolved. The entire battlefield was terribly strewn with blood-soaked Trojan and Greek corpses.

During the massive imbroglio, the incomparable giant Ajax slayed brothers Antiphus and Antifa, both fucked-up bastard sons of King Priam. And then, intrepid Odysseus of Ithaca, showing plenty of 'spear-it', hurled his sharp projectile at Democoonis, son of Racoonis, with the javelin immediately striking-down the pusillanimous-but-bellicose son-of-a-bitch. Symbolically, during the raucous and clamorous military encounter, the Trojans were buoyed by interference from Apollo and Ares, and conversely, the Greeks were provided adequate encouragement, inspiration, and required stamina from sympathetic Pallas Athene.

Chapter 5

"DIOMEDES BECOMES AGGRESSIVE"

"May the unpredictable gods acknowledge my urgent plea. When I get my sweet revenge on that son-of-a-harlot Pandarus," infuriated Agamemnon promised his aching and bleeding brother who was lying upon the hot desert sand, "the perverted bastard will be breathing out of his ears, will be pissing out of his nostrils, and will be shitting out of his new-found Z-shaped dingle. And Menelaus, I'll have my personal medic rub a healing sea-bass against your gory wound, because the injury appears to be only a super*fish*ial gash!"

The Achaeans were gaining the initiative and were pushing the Trojan forces back towards their towering citadel. Showing diversity in an ancient age of conformity, Athena soon chose Diomedes for attaining glory as her special hero of the day. Diomedes instantly embarked on a killing rampage, slaughtering high-ranking Trojan military personnel along with their contingent bodyguards. But then, the expert archer Pandarus spotted emboldened Diomedes riding in a chariot that was not on fire; the baker-turned-archer took aim with his ibex bow, and the marksman shot an arrow that hit his enemy target's thick leather shoulder pad.

"Sthenelus, er, I'm sorry," Diomedes corrected himself. "Stenny; please pull-out that toxic arrow from my shoulder guard. "Then I'll elicit Athena's help in paying back that furtive Pandarus for mildly scratching the surface of my right shoulder. I'm gonna' make sure that *that* former dough-rolling, bagel-baker will never again be able to munch on any delectable female muffin!"

Pallas Athene heard Diomedes's beckoning and promised her new-found champion to grant the selected Greek warrior deserved revenge on Pandarus. "You'll be able to distinguish me from the remainder of the interfering gods, particularly my foremost rival, Aphrodite. But I caution you, Diomedes; avoid wounding any of the immortals with the exception of my main family opponent, namely Aphrodite, who Prince Paris had frivolously chosen over me as the winning contestant in a past beauty contest."

The surging attacks, led by chariot-riding Diomedes were ferocious, as the archer's accurate arrows downed several dozen additional Trojan lieutenants, among the group Astynous, Hypeiron, Hyperbolla, Xanthus, Thoon, Typhoon, Eurydamas, Euradumass, Chromius, Echemmon, and the always-overzealous Trojan officer who had a bad case of psoriasis, Itchentogo.

Aeneas, a spoiled sissy rumored to be a favorite of Trojan-biased Aphrodite, appealed to Pandarus in a non-sexual way. "Quick famed archer; say a fast prayer to Zeus and then aim your arrow at that insane bastard Diomedes, who is massacring a slew of our baby-faced infantry officers. Don't aim to please, but instead, aim to kill!"

"Some god or goddess, probably Pallas Athene, is apparently inspiring that son-of-a-bitch Diomedes to go berserk. I've already hit him once," Pandarus bitched, "but my dart seemed to change course on a windless day, veering from the scumbag's chest over to his shoulder guard. I won't be able to send the troublesome jerk-off down to Hades until I get a worthy chariot to best engage my fanatical foe; my imaginary chariot should have two stellar white horses that perfectly match Diomedes' black stallions."

"Pandarus, forget about piercing Diomedes in the breadbasket," Aeneas weirdly yelled back. "Here, now; stop loafing around; hop aboard my chariot that is pulled by my marvelous white horses that had been bred by Tros. If I had a third equine to hitch to my chariot, we could have a friggin' Tros-fecta going-on here!"

But observant Agamemnon alertly noticed Pandarus boarding the fantastic Trojan chariot with Aeneas being the driver, and the vengeful King of Mycenae simultaneously briefed Diomedes of the most-recent battlefield development. "Great warrior. I know my mythology inside and out. Here comes Pandarus as a passenger upon Anus's, er, I mean Aeneas's chariot. A popular myth has it that *that* youthful driver happens to be the son of the goddess of beauty, unrivaled Aphrodite!"

Diomedes clambered-aboard Agamemnon's stationary chariot. "If I get lucky and kill both Pandarus and Aeneas," Diomedes hollered-over to the King of Mycenae, also standing on *his* chariot's platform, "then hop-off and collar the two white horses that were bred in Sicily. I'd like for us plundering Greeks to possess and own that exotic pair of magnificent Italian stallions!"

Pandarus, whose wife had given birth to a baker's dozen bratty kids with another one already in the oven, came-up with one of his half-baked ideas. The Trojan archer was the first to draw his bow and shoot, but his on-target arrow penetrated the shield of Diomedes, and only scratched the Greek hero's right forearm. But then the Danaan warrior, selectively favored by

Athena, tossed his bronze spear at Pandarus. The lethal projectile pierced through the Trojan's helmet's facial flap, and the tip severely impacted his nostrils, brutally separating the victim's sinus cavities, as an immense amount blood and snot squirted-out of Pandarus's already deviated septum.

Aeneas, seeing Pandarus's blood-soaked corpse prone and motionless upon the desert plain, leaped from his stationary chariot and dashed toward Diomedes, who immediately lifted a nearby jagged boulder and flung the huge rock, as if it were a pebble, at Aeneas's vulnerable stomach. The Trojan prince buckled-over in pain; Aeneas's hip socket had been violently shattered, and the valiant warrior fell to his knees, incessantly groaning and moaning in excruciating pain.

Aeneas was about to succumb to death and have his spirit become the custody of King Hades and Queen Persephone down in the dank Kingdom of the Dead, but Aphrodite appeared upon the scene, and first protected Aeneas with a shielding mist, and then prepared to transport the wounded combatant to a place of safety where his broken hip could be administered advanced medical aid.

Not seeing Aphrodite rendering supernatural assistance to her wounded son, Diomedes flung a second spear at Aeneas to make certain that the valiant Trojan had truly perished. But amazingly, the Greek's toss hit invisible Aphrodite in the lower thigh, just above the right knee, and Ichor, the perfumed blood of the immortals, came squirting-out as if the goddess's punctured right leg were a fractured fountain. Aphrodite hobbled-off, holding her wounded knee.

"And then, with Aphrodite being injured, Apollo, another ally of King Priam and Troy, appeared on the battlefield to rescue ailing Aeneas, but maniacal Diomedes lunged his spear at the chariot/sun god, whose voice boomed at the Argive aggressor, "Back-off, you dumb-ass, puny mortal! Are you insane enough to actually think that your meager bronze spear can best an Olympus god at the fine art of death-struggle survival?"

Without any hesitation, Phoebus Apollo carried Aeneas off to the lofty heights of Pergamus, and there, Artemis, the famed goddess of hunting, volunteered to heal and reconstruct the afflicted Trojan's disintegrated hip.

Ares, nasty-tempered Greek god of war, showed-up and quickly aligned with Apollo. The duo combined their talents and caused an ominous gloom to settle over the dusty battlefield, and their collaboration also inspired Hector to lead a savage charge in the direction of the Achaean front lines.

While the wild assault led by Hector was occurring, Sthenelus was confiscating the resplendent white horses that had pulled Aeneas's chariot.

"Well done, Stenny," Diomedes sincerely commended his dependable comrade. "Yes, Stenny; well done in*steed!*"

Meanwhile, oddball Odysseus, accompanied by his five lieutenants, Eurshiddenme, Eurballsourout, Eurassisgras, Eurdicisin, along with Eurcockisnum, heinously slaughtered thirteen Trojan officers who were brandishing and wielding bronze swords in their immediate vicinity. "It's a good thing your dick is in," Odysseus said to exhausted Eurdicisin. "Or else, your erect wiener would never be able to slide into a female bun, ever again! And also, Eurballsourout; you're lucky that your scrotum sac wasn't sacked, and that your tiny Greek meatballs weren't cruelly castrated! I mean, your annoying soprano voice right now is bad enough!"

Athena, appearing inside Zeus's marble temple situated atop Mt. Olympus, requested a favor from her sometimes more-than-tolerant father. "Great Lord of Thunder and Lightning; I'd like to enter the exciting fray on the Trojan plain and perform what I've always desired doing; kicking Ares' lard-ass black and blue."

"Be my guest and pursue your pleasure, Daughter Athena," Zeus smiled and then laughed. "Kick his obnoxious ass good, but not with both feet at the same time! That quarrelsome war-monger has caused me more than a century's worth of accumulated grief and misery!"

In the interim, Hera, who like Athena, favored the Greeks over the Trojans, entered the combat zone. The wife of Zeus said to Diomedes, "Greek warrior: are you a wimpy coward, or what? You have retreated from the battle as relentless Hector attacks your inexperienced, baby-faced infantry."

"My sage intuition recognizes you as Hera, goddess wife of Great Zeus," replied Diomedes. "I do not shirk my military duty. I should not attack either Ares or Apollo, because Athena had instructed me that I should only aim my arrows at her bitter rival, Aphrodite, promiscuous wife of Hephaestus, the ugly, lame blacksmith god, who manufactures all of the bronze equipment for the fickle Olympus deities to utilize."

"Then if you have any virile sperm left in your testicles," Hera asserted to Diomedes, "you'll join me in a dual duel with Hector and my major nemesis, Ares! Now get your craven ass upon Aeneas's chariot, and in pursuit of liberated woman's equality, I'll do the damned driving!"

While Hera was erratically and wildly bumping along, holding the reins of the Trojan chariot, her partner, Pallas Athene, cloaked herself from Ares' scrutiny, and the goddess found the god of war stripping-away the armor and breastplate from a deceased Trojan general. Without any warning,

Athena thrust her spear into the gut of Ares, and Ichor oozed from the hollowed-out gash.

Instinctively, tattle-tale Ares flew-up to Olympus to register a verbal grievance against Athena, whom Zeus so often favored.

"Ares, you fucked-up, trouble-making crybaby," the king god austerely admonished. "All the fuck you ever do is make mortals quarrel and wage combat against one another. In short, you demented ignoramus, I have no degree of sympathy for your present physical suffering, or for your current emotional anguish. Court surgeon, come hither. I command you to heal this imbecile's wound so that this feckless asshole can go-down to Earth and promote additional dissension among the just-as-stupid humans!"

"Why do you favor Athena over me?" Ares insisted on knowing. "Do you prefer females over males? Are you' prejudiced against me? Are you some kind of weirdo heterosexual?"

"Listen to basic truth, Ares," Zeus demanded. "Even though we gods of Olympus are immortal, don't underestimate these cantankerous human vermin. The inferior race must always fear our power, and should never be able to challenge our authority. As you have just learned on the battlefield, you are *not* invincible, and can be injured. Whether a mortal can actually kill a god, well, that possibility remains to be seen. Nectar and ambrosia just make us immortal, but those ingredients cannot protect either you or me from being either wounded or assassinated! Much of our supremacy over mortals is assumed by both us and them."

Feeling relieved that Ares had been at least temporarily sidelined, Athena and Hera, relishing their recent battlefield accomplishments, returned to the comforts and luxuries of Mt. Olympus, leaving the rest of the day's impending events to the maneuvers of the fatigued Greek and Trojan armies.

Chapter 6

"HECTOR AND ANDROMACHE"

With Ares sulking and sobbing inside Zeus's Mt. Olympus temple, Diomedes led a military phalanx that pushed the Trojans back towards the gates of Troy, with the stench of rotting corpses permeating the air around their' strategic maneuver. Hector was worried that the gods were turning against his army, so Priam's son told his commander Helenus to first rally the troops, and then sprint into the city to instruct his mother Hecuba to make rich sacrifices to appease Athena, which might consequently stifle the coordinated Greek onslaught led by inspired Diomedes, who in reality, was imitating and substituting for absent Achilles.

"Intrepid Trojans!" Helenus shouted. "Show your strong mettle along with your heavy metal! Defend your city as if it were your girlfriend's hairy pink pussy hole!"

Carrying his armor and a small hammer, Hector dashed into Troy, and immediately, the renowned hero was swarmed by concerned women requesting news about the fates of husbands, uncles, cousins, brothers, sons, kindergarten kids, and great-great-grandfathers. Fleeing from the raucous mob of information seekers, Hector sped past King Priam's white castle's closed window, which had a large overhead painted sign, featuring hot dogs and hamburger images, that explicitly read: "War Is No Picnic!"

The enormous palace contained a variety of fifty-seven bedrooms for Priam's impotent sons and their respective wives, and across the expansive courtyard, there had been built thirteen "honeymoon honey-well bedchambers" for Priam and Hecuba's dozen promiscuous daughters and their sex-driven cheating husbands.

"My precious son, what brings you to the palace?" Hecuba cried. "Is it true that the insane Achaeans have mastered weather control and are about to storm the city walls? This is no time for sour grapes or for tart tarts! Let my servants find you some sweet wine to specially offer as a libation and tribute to Zeus!"

"Bring me no wine, mother, because the liquid would only soften and weaken my knees like blueberry buckle. And just observe how dusty and dirty I am from continuous fighting out yonder on the Troad Plain. Zeus and his family will be offended if I were to offer impure sacrifices with my skin and body being so unclean that not even the Greek white tornado giant Ajax cold cleanse my hide."

"When then, Hector. What assistance could I do to help you?" Queen Hecuba wondered and asked. "I'm too friggin' old, wrinkled and fat to perform a striptease inside the palace temple, or do a private-audience naked lap-dance to entertain Zeus, Ares, or Apollo!"

"Here's what you should do," problem-solving Hector stated. "First pray to Pallas Athene inside the palace temple. Then, have your most reliable servants sacrifice twelve hefty virgin heifers; that is, female cows, and not corpulent lard-ass teenagers, on the temple's recently-altered altar. Hopefully, your sincere act will give the Trojan army a respite from ruthless Diomedes and his barbarian minions."

Hecuba gathered her two finest scented robes and carried the garments to the palace temple, where she met the Old Ladies Civic Club of Troy members, and led the former hot prostitutes in prayers to Athena, which was followed by cremating the dozen hefty heifers to Athena in the temple's brick pizza oven. But unfortunately, for Hecuba, the goddess's heart was in harmony with the enemy Achaeans, and the well-intended sacrifices were completely ignored by the contemporary Mt. Olympus powers-that-be.

In the meantime, Hector made it his mission to visit his younger brother Paris's room, where the Trojan commander's initial impulse was to reprimand his cowardly sibling for embarrassing Troy in his recent, overmatched duel with incensed Menelaus.

"Paris; you hide and sob inside your room, grieving about your obvious incompetence, while your loyal peers are on the plain doing combat against the dastardly Danaans," Hector vehemently scolded. "You have humiliated your city, and your family, you craven, pusillanimous pussy! If you had a clitoris above your ass slit instead of your tiny dingle, I'll wager that Helen's clit would be much larger than yours! Even larger than both your diminutive testicles and your miniature pecker put together!"

Helen, curiously eavesdropping on the verbal harangue, entered the bedchamber and pleaded to Hector to cease browbeating Paris. "Stay inside the palace with Paris and me," the estranged wife of Menelaus begged. "You must be exhausted and weary. I don't blame you for despising and resenting me being here in Troy. If you want to learn the truth, I regret ever being born, and I wish that I could be thrown off the highest mountain peak, or be drowned in the deepest sea. But most of all, Hector, I wish that I could have both love and power, but with your brother Paris being a feckless wimp, I might as well shave my golden beaver and throw all of my precious gold coins, along with all of my soft blonde pubes, into the palace temple's flaming brick pizza oven!"

"War is hell, Helen," Hector heckled and hectored. "So, I must abandon my craven brother, and also you, his problematic hussy, and now my desire prefers reuniting with my faithful wife, Andromache."

Soon thereafter, Andromache affectionately greeted her militant husband, and showered the Trojan General with abundant hugs, kisses and crotch-grabs. "Oh, my wild and savage husband. Our son now sleeps inside his cradle, but before long, I dread that he will be fatherless, and that I will be spouseless! Oh, Hector! When you are gone forever, both I and your helpless infant son will have no one around to protect us!"

"My only hope is that baby Scamandrius will not turn-out to be a scam artist just like all of the other males on your side of the family," Hector angrily remarked. "It figures that you'd like me to stand on top of the city wall, above the large fig tree, where the Greeks have attacked three times, attempting to climb said fig tree, which is not a fake figment of my fig tree imagination. But please clarify certain relevant facts, Andromache. You and your name are of Greek origin, I believe, growing-up in Thebe, just below Troy."

"Yes, my strong, muscular husband. The town was founded by Hercules, and was named after the place where the Greek hero had been raised, the original Achaean city of Thebes. Because of my upbringing, I know quite a lot about Greek culture and history."

"You're shittin' me, aren't you Andromache?"

"No, Hector. I'm not shittin' you. As you should know, Eurshiddenme is a lieutenant under the command of the Greek champion, Odysseus of Ithaca! Oh, what the heck, Hector. I'll tell you everything you want to learn!"

"Well, wife; we are aware that the Greeks are here after Helen's gold, and that Menelaus is here after his wife's golden beaver, but kindly describe for me the hereafter in Greek religious belief."

"If you insist, Hector; here is what academic knowledge I can share. The ancient Greeks loved music as much as they loved adventure, lesbians, vacationing on the Isle of Lesbos, and wild unlimited sex orgies. When the famed Achaean musician Orpheus sang, trees would extend their boughs downward and shade the handsome lad from the sun, because the wandering minstrel was a damned albino with milk-white skin. The poison ivy' vines often reached-out their tendrils in response to Orpheus's majestic music, and everybody in the vicinity that already had venereal diseases didn't like the notion of doing additional skin scratching, so the worried area residents very discreetly stayed out of the forests, ponds, streams, marshes, marketplaces and swamps."

"So far, your revelations sound a lot like a shit-load of ethnocentric bull-crap!" Hector cynically criticized. "I hope that your rendition improves as your fragile explanation progresses."

"May I continue enlightening you?" Andromache politely rebutted. "When Orpheus sang and played his sensational tunes upon the lyre, rocks would rumble and tumble-down mountainsides, causing widespread devastation to nearby villages and outhouses. Wild beasts skulked-around low to the ground, because the dumb-ass creatures simply felt like continually pissing and shitting, and woodland gods would stop masturbating and screwing each other up the yazoo, just to benignly listen to the boy wonder's glorious, enchanting music."

"Those woodland creatures sound a lot similar to the fucked-up Greeks we're now fighting," Hector interrupted. "I trust that your lackluster story will get better as it evolves."

"Well, Hector. Orpheus *madly* loved a gorgeous girl named Eurydice, who had inspired the minstrel to go beyond 'madly', straight-on to 'insane', and then on to totally 'crazy' rap lyrics. The musician's creative powers to organize imaginative love songs had originated from *his* passionate longing to lose his disgusting virginity and pump the excessive poop out of Eurydice's eager beaver. All nature celebrated with the 'mythology period bard' on his wedding day, but unfortunately, Eurydice didn't want to get laid or have her swollen box munched, because the moody bitch was starting her own lousy bloody *period* cycle during the aforementioned 'mythology period'. What a lousy bummer!"

"The minstrel's girlfriend was having her menstrual cycle," Hector laughed. "Now your mediocre tale is most definitely getting somewhere!"

"Just listen to this next part," Andromache urged. "On the morning of the wedding ceremony, no pedophile priest arrived to officiate, because religion had not yet been invented in ancient Greece. Disappointed by no priest showing-up, and pissed-off because she was having her monthly period, Eurydice ambled-down to the riverside to have lesbian sex with her equally pissed-off bridal attendants. The despondent girls' gathered bunches of flowers to shove-down the throat of the first Greek priest to ever show-up, and then the bridesmaids were prepared to choke the sanctimonious son-of-a-bitch if and when the reputed pedophile should ever come around to their village after the eventual establishment of religion."

"So, what happened next?" Hector hypothesized and curiously asked. "Don't keep my fascination in suspense!"

"Unfortunately, Eurydice was suddenly bitten in the foot by a huge, poisonous snake, and her totally shocked maidens instantly became frightfully snake-bitten themselves, and then quickly serpentined their' exit the hell away from the river before the foul, venomous viper reloaded its fangs for a second more-lethal attack."

"Sounds like the bitches didn't enjoy playing with reptiles!" Hector stupidly joked. "The dumb-ass lesbian broads probably would also run-away from an erect fadorkenbender, too!"

"Allow me to tell you more," Andromache diplomatically objected. "Orpheus became quite despondent when the minstrel heard the bad news about Eurydice, and the horny adolescent was so extremely pissed-off that he couldn't get a hard-on with which to jerk-off, no matter how hard he tried. His somber songs were now very sad, and reflected *his* totally disconsolate disposition, and all of the wild male forest beasts got pissed-off too, because suddenly, they could no longer lick each other's long dicks, and also, the aroused creatures couldn't get laid either after vainly attempting to achieve even weak erections. 'Go to Hades you dumb stupid bastard!' the pissed-off animals all repeatedly yelled at Orpheus, no matter where he roamed."

"I'm getting pissed-off just listening to your fucked-up story," Hector butted-in. "But I've always believed that it's much better to be pissed-off than to be pissed-on! Ha, ha, ha!"

"Will you please let me resume my tale?" Andromache somewhat-courteously retorted. "Now then; the rather-depressed Greek minstrel picked-up his lyre and made his way to the wide cave that led-down to eerie Hades; yes, the Greek underworld, where as you already might know, ancient gangsters and mobsters hung-out after the ill-tempered scoundrels had died. Orpheus believed that Eurydice's soul had already journeyed-down to bleak Hades, and the young lover theorized that *that* was where her *spirit* could ultimately be found. 'Who the hell wants to have sex with a damned thin, two-dimensional ghost?' Orpheus objectively conjectured. 'Eurydice no longer has a body, and her massive tits are probably now just hollow air bubbles; her ass is probably two noxious farts glued together, and her former hot-wet pussy is probably like a primitive air pump. Who needs this kind of fuckin' illogical shit in their already-troubled life?' Andromache asked."

"And I thought that my unenviable existence here in Troy was miserable," Hector commented to Andromache. "How could this character Orpheus ever screw a two-dimensional ghost, even if the lovestruck asshole ever was lucky enough to find her down there in dark Hades?"

"Anyway, Hector, the melancholy minstrel descended a vast vertical tunnel inside the diagonal cave, and successfully clambered-down a twelve-mile-long rocky subterranean cliff to finally reach the dreadful *River Styx,* which historically separated the land of the living from the morbid kingdom of the dead. Charon, the macabre, hooded, skeleton ferryman monotonously rowed his barge to shore to pick-up his next passenger for transportation across the stranger-than-fiction underground river to bleak and mysterious Hades."

"Did any conversation occur between Charon and Orpheus?" a now-fascinated Hector inquired. "Your tome is actually becoming quite intriguing! Please continue."

"Yes," Andromache tersely answered. 'Hey jerk! Ya' gotta' be dead in order to get to the *other side,'* Charon chastised his still-living. mournful guest. 'Ya' just can't look dead, asshole! Ya' gotta' *be* fuckin' dead! Go back to Earth and get assassinated, murdered or eaten by a famished shark or lion. Have you ever fuckin' considered chugging-down either hemlock or arsenic?' Charon suggested."

"But my spirit is dead already, but not my body!" bitterly grieved and argued Orpheus. "So, what's an empty, pitiful mind and body to do?"

"Seeing her husband with his mouth agape, Andromache continued with her extraordinary myth. 'Just hand me a coin to pay for your toll of passage, and then simply commit suicide,' the ghastly, ghostly specter firmly recommended. 'Then you'll officially leave the *sticks,* and I'll take ya' across the *Styx* to some other part of the even more incomprehensible post mortem' *sticks,* ha, ha, ha,'!"

"What did the minstrel say in response?" Hector wanted to know. "Did he develop a case of instant laryngitis?"

Andromache proceeded with uttering her descriptive narrative. "Permanent death?" Orpheus exclaimed. "I'm not ready for that type of esoteric bullshit yet! I just gotta' find-out if I can get my rocks-off with my girlfriend's ghost, and that's all I wish to especially accomplish on this particular expedition."

"That's terrible," Hector concluded and mentioned. "The poor kid hasn't even gotten laid with Eurydice, and now the unlucky dumb-ass doesn't have a ghost of a chance of screwing her flitting two-dimensional specter!"

Smiling at her husband's fairly humorous response, Andromache proceeded with her most-excellent rhetoric. "The *dispirited* musician had to devise a fast solution to effectively remedy his present dilemma. So, the disenchanted minstrel went into his mystic, creative mode and sang a haunting love song that completely mesmerized the heartless barge-rower, Charon. The ferryman felt wonderful ecstasy for the first time in his eternally dismal life, so the skeletal figure voluntarily led Orpheus onto his barge, which would allow the saddened passenger to *barge-in* on the pathetic silent underworld. If the minstrel could enchant the fearful god Hades with his powerful, stirring lyrics, then the singer might be able to retrieve Eurydice's ghost and transport it back up to Earth where the dismal, itinerant spirit could be reunited with its no-longer-active 38-24-36 hourglass figure."

"It sounds as if Eurydice has run out of vital sand inside her temporal hourglass," jested Hector. "I need to hear this pathetic story simply to get my troubled mind away from the fucked-up Achaeans and that dangerous bastard Diomedes."

"Now then, Hector. Cerberus, the three-headed dog that growled ferociously and snapped its jaws and bared its fangs, was steadfastly guarding the narrow portal leading into Hades' interior. The fierce monster was so hypnotized by Orpheus's song that the awesome beast cowered-down like a puppy, and then the fierce mutt was so thrilled by his newly-discovered blithe nature that Cerberus began wildly using all three heads to lick its erect dick, and then did the same to Charon's *boner*, giving the ferryman a pleasurable 'triple *head*er'."

"But what about the inconsolable minstrel," Hector wondered and asked. "Did the soprano punk suddenly become impotent with erectile dysfunction? Did Orpheus acquire a choir down there in Hades?"

"As Orpheus entered the dismal, dank, gloomy world of Hades, pale, spooky ghosts crowded and flitted-around the apprehensive hero, with all of the attracted shades being wholly captivated by his beautiful song. The visitor's extraordinary voice resounded throughout the myriad caverns and stagnant marshes, artificially giving the appearance of life to the formerly silent and ominous fucked-up place."

"Managing all of those deceased souls must've been a huge undertaking for Lord Hades and Queen Persephone to supervise," Hector contributed.

"Your compelling story makes me glad to be alive and fighting the crazy Argives."

"The determined musician cautiously stepped into the well-manicured, flowered fields of Elysium. And all of the daffodils, the petunias, the dainty dahlias, and the 'creeping' myrtle that ordinarily gave everyone the creeps leaned towards the sound of the lad's marvelous voice," Andromache orally related. "The suddenly-happy dead danced and frolicked through the colorful floral meadows and shadowy dells, finally experiencing delight and pleasure as part of their' promised eternal reward. The jubilant ghosts held hands, and jumped and pranced around, inadvertently crushing all the beautiful flowers, and giggling incessantly, while acting like a billion ludicrous faggots and gay-spirited lesbians."

"Your depiction makes the spirits in Hades seem like the kin of the myriad whores and pimps that frequent the bordellos and brothels in downtown Troy," Hector realized and articulated.

"Then, my dear husband; Orpheus advanced through a shadowy cave and entered the spooky area of atonement where the pathetic, grieving ghosts of dead individuals were posthumously punished for violating the capricious Mt. Olympus gods' supreme laws. Even Sisyphus, who labors for all eternity pushing an enormous rock up a hill, only to have the boulder roll down the incline so that the process would have to be repeated over and over again; the punished fellow's sad spirit stopped his monotonous enterprise to appreciate and enjoy Orpheus's unique song. Sisyphus was so inspired by the marvelous melody that the ghost immediately organized his own underground rhythm band called 'The Rolling Stones and Pebbles', and instantly began mimicking Orpheus's fine example. Even the crackling flames that blazed and flourished in leaping fences of fire in that atonement section of Hades danced around, and soon magically heated-up the whole damned area."

"Your fascinating tale, Andromache, is pretty interesting bullshit heaped on top of pretty interesting bullshit," Hector candidly commended. "I hope I don't ejaculate an explosive orgasm during its exciting climax!"

"Next, my dear husband. Orpheus and his music encroached upon thirsty and hungry Tantalus, who had been eternally punished by having to stand chained inside a pool that was filled chest-high with delicious, cold, fresh water. An abundance of fruits on tree limbs dangled above the hungry and thirsty man's head. When Tantalus was 'tantalized' to drink, the manacled figure would bend-over, and the cool water would rapidly drain out of the tank. When the penalized apparition would reach for a ripe peach, or for a savory apple, the fruit would either disappear or be blown away by a sudden wind gust. The unfortunate ghost was so enraptured and entranced by Orpheus's song that the brain-dead specter ceased performing his eternal sentence, and Tantalus's rejuvenated spirit fondly recalled what it was once like being alive."

"Holy Hades!" Hector exclaimed. "Tantalus, acting in a complete vegetable state, had to experience a totally fruitless posthumous existence!"

"Finally, husband. Orpheus arrived at the stone-cold, black-granite, pillared *Halls of Hades*. The ashen faces of past Greek heroes were sadly sitting at Hades' dark, ebony table. Even King Hades and his pallid-faced Queen Persephone showed rare animation, and began smiling in the direction of the young troubadour, dually acknowledging his wonderful music. The gods' cold hearts knew all misery, and cared not one iota about any of it, but amazingly, Hades and his pale, morbid wife were touched and moved by the magical rhapsody that their dull ears were then wondrously hearing."

"It's too bad that Orpheus wasn't accompanied by a full band of musicians; the minstrel could've orchestrated a wild rebellion down there in subterranean Hades!"

"You haven't lost your deranged sense of humor," admitted Andromache. "At length, Orpheus became fatigued from his difficult descent down into the underworld, and also, the musician had become exhausted from his extensive singing and meandering. The shades of the assembled, swirling ghosts mingled-in with the gentle winds, and at least temporarily, all nature in eerie Hades was one and the same. Then, morbid King Hades frightfully addressed his latest visitor, and the awesome god's deep bass voice reverberated throughout *his* usually silent, cavernous, dark world."

"What did Hades say?" Hector wanted to know. "Did the scary god offer Orpheus an entertainment contract?"

"Hades emphatically said, 'Orpheus. Go back to the sunshine while my monsters are still under the spell of your hypnotic songs. Climb-up the steep vertical tunnel to the warmth of broad daylight, and I promise you, the spirit of Eurydice will follow your' ascent. But there is one caveat to this special arrangement,' Hades austerely warned. 'Whatever you do, don't turn around for verification of my words, and therefore, by doing so, doubting my promise. If you dare to turn around, Eurydice will return down here to the underworld, and your fond hopes will immediately vaporize into utter despair. If you learn to trust and believe my imperial decree, you can have living and breathing Eurydice back as your three-dimensional fiancee'!"

"Did Queen Persephone agree with King Hades' decree?" intrigued Hector asked Andromache. "The pair of deadbeats both sound like royal pain in the asses!"

"Yes, go back Orpheus," Queen Persephone implored from her dark ebony throne. "My crotch is getting wet for the first time in three centuries, and I actually feel like getting laid. Get the hell outa' here and give us some damned privacy! I'm as horny as Hades is right now, and I absolutely need to be pumped and humped like there's no tomorrow, right away!"

"Andromache, was Hades sexually aroused, too?"

"Yes, go back quickly," Hades anxiously concurred. "I'm getting a massive erection, and I think I know exactly what the fuck to do with it! Show me some pink, Persephone! I'm headin' right toward the center of your hot juicy love tunnel!"

"Holy shit!" Hector exclaimed to his wife. "Hades and Persephone were ready to have some high-spirited sex!"

"Well, dear husband. Orpheus turned and retreated from the great *Hall of Hades,* and the teeming ghosts separated into two divisions, and made sufficient room for the wanderer to exit. The young minstrel desperately searched on both sides, and in front, for any sign of his lost Eurydice's spirit, but his eyes dared not look behind him in honor of Hades' stern edict. No sounds were discernible anywhere around him, as the talented musician advanced through the major dark rock mineral corridors, moving past Tantalus and Sisyphus, and then through the now-wilting flowers in the Elysian Fields. Soon, the sorrowed lover passed Cerberus's narrow portal, and then stepped assertively onto Charon's barge, which quickly sank-down two feet in reaction to *his* weight being onboard."

"I hope that Orpheus did not go overboard by violating Hades' specific instruction!" Hector gleefully concluded and shared. "I definitely prefer Greek comedies to Greek tragedies!"

"Is Eurydice behind me?" Orpheus asked macabre Charon. "I dare not look and violate Hades' weird prophecy."

"If Orpheus turned around," Hector remarked to his spouse, "then I think I'm going to lose my erection!"

Andromache disregarded her husband's semi-humorous comment and resumed her graphic exposition. "Behind every man, there is a woman!" Charon diplomatically and arcanely answered. "If you are *that* curious, you asinine asshole, why not turn your damned neck around and fuckin' see for yourself if Hades had been bullshitting you?"

"Oh, my Zeus!" Hector yelled. "This dumb-ass story is amazing! I promise not to interrupt you, dear wife. Please tell the remainder of your incredulous tale in its entirety!"

"No thanks!" Orpheus answered in response to a very magnetic temptation that he felt. "You must have virgin ears, Charon, because what woman in her right mind would want to suck on a piece of lousy cartilage dick for the remainder of eternity, or have sex with someone that looks exactly like the fuckin' Grim Reaper's twin brother?"

"Did you feel any additional weight shift the boat's equilibrium after you entered?" Charon replied with a question, enjoying his self-appointed role as an accomplished and sophisticated eternal ball-breaker."

"No, but I must value Hades' promise in spite of your biased sarcasm; your pessimism, and your fucked-up cynicism," Orpheus proudly volleyed.

"Finally, the surreal ferry left Hades' bank, and slowly made it across the dreary *River Styx* to the shadowy opposite shore. The ascension to the upper-world of mortals was an arduous climb that was filled with strange shapes and alien forms floating around inside the tight, chimney-like cavity's tomb-like silence. Orpheus ceased his scaling to listen for any remote sign of his beloved Eurydice, but there was not a trace of a noise, or a hint of an echo of her soft voice. 'Maybe Charon was right and Hades was just bustin' my balls about Eurydice following my ass back up to Earth?' Orpheus suspiciously reckoned. 'I wonder if that miserable bastard is still getting it on with Queen Persephone? Both of those imperial, pallid-faced assholes looked like they needed ten blood transfusions each'."

"Orpheus feared that the God of the Dead had deceived him, and that *he* was alone and isolated between two worlds, but his soul had been belonging to neither one. 'What if I climb-up to the bright sunlight, turn around, and Eurydice is not there?' the adventurous minstrel skeptically considered. 'I had fascinated Charon, Cerberus, Sisyphus, Tantalus, Persephone and Hades once with my spellbinding music, but could I repeat those remarkable results with a second daring expedition into the underworld? Maybe I've lost Eurydice with my naïve eagerness to believe any and all bullshit from men and from gods?' the mirthless singer lamented. 'Gee; I wonder if Hades has enough blood to sustain an erection for a full century? I wonder if the diabolical prick has any blood at all'?"

"With every step upward, my dear husband, the befuddled hero took while carefully ascending the precarious precipices, Orpheus became more and more dubious of Hades' promise. The climber diligently labored-up the last treacherous stretch with his sad heart laden with doubt and despair. The darkness soon converted into a grayish mist, indicating that the weary minstrel had finally advanced close to the Earth's surface. The air was cleaner and more breathe-able, and as Orpheus inhaled the fresh oxygen, his brain realized that the entrance to the dreary, huge cavern was just ahead. Still, the musician's beleaguered mind questioned Hades' veracity."

"Now, Hector," Andromache continued her narrative. "Orpheus could not bear his heavy emotional burden any longer. Acting on impulse, in the ominous, nebulous light that belonged to neither the Land of the Living nor the Land of the Dead, the confused trekker veered-around, and his eyes beheld a thin misty shade at his rear, and quickly, the indistinct female specter with the beautiful face loudly cried, 'You really fucked yourself over this time, you stupid, dumb-dicked, virgin asshole'!"

"Orpheus frantically cried-out 'Eurydice!' But the faint female specter soon hazily crystallized, and then evaporated into nothingness. A slight echo of 'Farewell Orpheus' resonated throughout the deep, dark, vertical tunnel directly below his shaky feet."

"The disconsolate lover quickly gathered his sensibilities and hurried back-down the now-familiar, steep path which he had just laboriously ascended. The depressed lover's efforts were greatly thwarted by his extreme apathy, and by his overwhelming sorrow. This second time, Charon was deaf to the singer's prayerful voice, which lacked the innocence, and the romantic quality, of its first authentic presentation to the unhappy inhabitants of Hades."

"Stop trespassing where you aren't supposed to go," Charon warned in a bellicose tone of voice. "You must have a death wish, but if you want to achieve your fatal dream, you must honor tradition and go back to Earth and commit suicide like I had originally advised you to do."

"Shove your rotten oar all the way up your' stinkin' bony ass!" Orpheus angrily replied. "How in Hades do you manage to get into your house? With a goddamned skeleton key?"

"Fuck-off, you jerk-off mortal!" Charon vehemently yelled. "You should have more respect for the custodians of the dead!"

"Go home and work your skinny-dicked boner!" Orpheus screamed like a demented maniac. "Instead of white semen, you must shoot out pink marrow from your bony dick, if you aren't already impotent!"

"Finally, dear husband; Orpheus tried duplicating the original beauty of his song, but eventually acknowledged that his meaningless endeavor was a total failure. For a whole week, the glum singer sat upon the dismal banks of the bleak river, watching Charon transport doomed souls to their final resting places in Hades' black kingdom. The pathetic wailing of the morose *River Styx* canceled-out any cheerful love song that the depressed singer could muster. The swirling ghosts also ignored Orpheus's entreaties, and the frustrated musician finally realized that his sad intonations no longer had any tangible effect on his completely apathetic, inhospitable, now-alien, wretched environment."

"I guess I really pissed-away my one and only chance of reuniting with Eurydice," Orpheus sobbed and regretted. "I'm so dejected that I feel like slicing my balls off!"

"Disgusted and defeated, Orpheus rose from his sitting position and then trudged and stumbled up along the dark, steep path which he then knew so well. When the frustrated youth eventually arrived back to Earth, all bedraggled and begrimed, his lyrics and voice sounded both pitiful and hopeful. Orpheus could tolerate human company no longer, and the irate musician chased people away when the area natives came around to hear his exceptionally haunting melodies, along with sad love themes, that he kept *harping* on the lyre."

"In the end, the disillusioned lover met his ultimate demise. Women of Thrace were angered at Orpheus's refusal to play upbeat romantic melodies for them, so out of sheer contempt, the scornful bitches attacked, molested and attempted to rape the young man. And when he couldn't achieve an adequate erection, the crazy females choked and killed the unfortunate minstrel by shoving unsanitary sanitary napkins down his parched throat. Legends maintain that as the body of Orpheus smashed against jagged rocks in the *River Hebrus's* many rapids, the musician's waxen, dead lips faintly uttered 'Eurydice' all the way down to the *River Styx.*"

"Did Orpheus's spirit ever get to reunite with the ghost of Eurydice?" Hector asked Andromache.

"In the daffodil meadows of Elysium, Orpheus's specter met-up with the ghost of Eurydice, and since Orpheus no longer had a three-dimensional pecker, his shade used a daffodil stem as a vagina-insertion-device, which soon became known all throughout Hades as a 'daffy-dildo'! And where the main path in the complicated underworld network becomes particularly narrow, Orpheus's apparition goes first into the unexplored tunnel, and thereafter, his flat form admiringly looks back, and then beckons the spirit of its one true love, Eurydice."

"What a great myth!" Prince Hector enthusiastically congratulated Andromache. "It almost makes me wish that I was an Achaean!"

Just then, baby Scamandrius began crying in his cradle, which was hanging and suspended from a half-broken olive tree bough protruding through his bedroom window.

"I hope that our little whimpering wiener doesn't grow-up to become a freakin' hot dog like his wimpy Uncle Paris!" Hector snickered. "I wouldn't relish such a grotesque development happening one iota!"

Andromache handed the screaming baby to Hector, and Scamandrius shrieked even louder at being transferred from parent to parent, obviously frightened by his father's war helmet.

"Don't be distressed by the symbolism of impending future calamity," Hector imperatively related. "No Greek enemy can kill me before fate determines that my time of demise has come. And Scamandrius must think that my bronze helmet must be one of those bizarre goo-goo or zombie dolls sold in the downtown marketplace."

At that moment, Paris came hustling into the upstairs palace living quarters, wearing his battle helmet, and carrying his spear and shield. "Brother; am I too late or slow to resume participating in the battle? I feel rejuvenated and ready to engage in combat. Let's get our act together and make the scene!"

"Paris, you are a paris-site in both general appearance and demeanor," Hector intensely chided. "I can't find fault with the speed of your legs, but your Trojan will to fight and triumph are evidently lacking. It seems that you have the dream, but not the drive, in order to sufficiently survive vicious combat. The warriors in our camp often mention your condemned name in absolute contempt. It's up to your determination to salvage your reputation and to redeem our glorious family honor. Let's now return to the all-too-familiar Troad battlefield, and dually experience what whimsical fate has in store for us!"

Chapter 7

"HECTOR AND AJAX DUEL"

Emboldened with a desire to cancel-out his cowardice while again dueling with Menelaus, Prince Paris killed the Achaean lieutenant Menesthius, while *his* older brother Hector killed Etonius, who did not have a severe case of meningitis like Menesthius, brother of Buenosthius, did. As the latest battle raged upon the Troad Non-Fruitive Plain, Athena, on her daily route to lofty Mt. Olympus, peered-down and noticed that the warfare was swaying in favor of the more-motivated Trojans. In her haste, the gliding goddess nearly collided in mid-air with Phoebus Apollo, whose perceptive eyes were also focusing upon the killings being administered and led by Hector and Paris.

"Are you arriving near Priam's city to help the Argives pursuit of destroying Troy?" Apollo asked rival Pallas Athene while both were hovering above an active volcano. "Listen to my infallible rhetoric, Daughter of Zeus. We both need a brief vacation from this dumb-shit war nonsense. Let's temporarily forget our separate allegiances and cooperate in stopping the conflict for today. We can each seek satisfying our daily boredom, and again enjoy maneuvering our Greek and Trojan pawns upon our gameboards tomorrow!"

"Very well, bachelor, hen-pecked, chicken god," Pallas Athene chided. "Are you planning first licking some succulent female breasts and thighs, and then screwing some unfortunate mortal beauty queen? In terms of abandoning your Trojan loyalty and responsibility for one mere day, do you desire to leave it to beaver, or what?" Athena asked. "But honestly, Apollo. I also need a twenty-four-hour requiem from this nerve-racking war bullshit. I mean, like yourself with the Greeks, I'm getting tired of breaking Trojan men's balls and deflating Trojan woman's tits! Now then, addled archer god; what duplicitous trick does your miniature mind cunningly propose?"

"Yes, immortal virgin chick," Apollo replied. "I'll casually zoom-down to the battlefield and whisper some suggestive instructions into Hector's infected left ear, pretending that I'm the idiot's wimpy brother, Paris. I just love implementing this oddball impersonation foolishness on the gullible Trojans, who have the bodies of muscular weightlifters, and the minds of little toddlers! The only pleasure *we* have in escaping eternal monotony is by causing friction and conflict in the lives of those totally fucked-up Greeks and Trojans!"

And so, being influenced by Apollo's imitation of Paris's staccato voice, Hector yelled for the Trojan forces to cease their deliberate advance and to heed *his* plausible suggestion, which was to be offered to both ready-to-fight armies.

"Listen to me, Achaeans and Trojans," Hector screamed from his chariot platform. "Zeus had arbitrarily decided to not allow our current truce to prevail. So, to avert thousands of more good warriors from being slain, I propose an alternative solution. I will fight any Achaean to the death, and whoever wins *that* struggle for personal glory, the victor will claim the armor of the deceased, and his fallen corpse will be properly prepared for burial by the loser's pedophile priest. Now, who amongst you weakling Danaans will come forward and challenge me, Prince Hector of Troy, to single combat?"

Silence reigned supreme among the shocked Achaean ranks. Worried Agamemnon commanded that the major Greek captains confer and figure-out which warrior would valorously confront Hector in the proposed imminent duel. While that important captains' consultation was occurring, Odysseus's five psychopath lieutenants were engaged exchanging irrelevant gibberish in their own dumb-ass sidebar conference.

"I'll bet that Ajax is just as strong as the legendary Hercules," Eurdicisin opined to his four knuckleheaded, psycho-case companions. "When Ajax finishes with Hector, that is if Ajax is selected to represent us Greeks and kicks the arrogant prince's rear end, the Trojan heir won't know his huge aching asshole from the volcanic crater on top of Mt. Etna!"

"Old Nestor told me yesterday that he had had several past adventures with mighty Hercules," Eurshiddenme confidentially disclosed to his four peers. "And then the old fart from Pylos described to me in detail the acclaimed Theban hero's fantastic Twelve Labors. Listen Eurdicisin; I'll now tell you about those Twelve Labors of yore."

"What the hell are you talking about?" Eurdicisin defensively challenged Eurshiddenme. *"My* Twelve Labors? I have no fuckin' Twelve Labors. Hercules is the one who had the twelve difficult tasks to perform."

"You stupid-fuck!" Eurshiddenme screamed at Eurdicisin, violently shaking his clenched fist. "By the Twelve Labors of *yore,* I did not mean *your* non-existent twelve labors! I had meant the damned, historic Twelve Labors of Hercules!"

"Forget slumbering on the night desert sand, Eurshiddenme! Instead, tonight go and fuckin' sleep on a gigantic, shriveled-up apri*cot!*" exasperated and neurotic Eurdicisin defiantly countered his prime nemesis.

Unfazed by Eurdicisin's insolent demeanor, Eurshiddenme attempted to educate his apathetic audience of four concerning the fabled Twelve Labors of Hercules.

"King Eurystheus of Mycenae had assigned Hercules the task of performing twelve super-arduous labors in order to atone for his alleged egregious misdeeds," Eurshiddenme prefaced his narrative. "In his initial assignment, Hercules' first choked to death the vicious Lion of Nemea, the carcass of which the legendary champion immediately returned to King Eurystheus to keep as a coveted souvenir."

"Eurshiddenme; you aren't lyin' one smidgeon about that ferocious lion," Eurassisgras eagerly confirmed. "That cowardly King Eurystheus could never develop courage if he wore a dozen lion's skins during a wicked blizzard. I've heard where the royal moron has two ovaries for testicles!"

"The second superhuman task was to travel to a place called Lerna to kill the nine-headed Hydra that terrorized anyone who accidentally came close to its native swamp," Eurshiddenme continued his dull depiction while ignoring Eurassisgras's general lunacy. "Whenever a head of the dangerous Hydra was chopped-off, another one would instantly grow back in its place. But then Hercules seared-off each of the nine necks with a burning brand, so that the heads eventually could not sprout-out again. It was a pretty ingenious solution for a brawny guy like Hercules to creatively solve such a challenging dilemma, ha, ha, ha! Hercules had invented the surgical art of cauterizing! Ha, ha, ha!"

"Wow!" Eurcockisnum exclaimed. "Hercules had branded his reputation by cleverly branding the nine-headed Hydra! I'll bet that old Herc used the poisonous blood oozing-out of the writhing beast's nine headless necks to invent hydra-chloric acid!"

Showing rare admirable intelligence, Eurdshiddenme also wisely ignored Eurcockisnum's faulty conjecture and proceeded with his fairly informative account. "The third obligation to be enacted by Hercules was capturing a wild stag that had been sacred to the hunting goddess Artemis."

"Was the hart on its way to a stag party?" Eurballsourout uttered and laughed, much to florid-faced Eurshiddenme's utter chagrin. "I'll bet that good old Hercules had to hang-on to those antlers for *deer* life!"

Eurshiddenme pretended that Eurballsourout's outrageous words had been spoken on another planet. "The fourth detail was for Hercules to kill a great boar, and the fifth command was to clean the filthy stables of Augeas that contained thousands of ill-tempered horses and cattle possessing very loose bowels. What a nasty, smelly mess *that* terrible environment must've been! Hercules imaginatively used his great strength to change the course of two rivers, making the separate diversions flood right through the stables as if the smelly barns were common sieves."

"That wild fierce boar sounds just as unstable as the temperamental horses and cattle that Hercules had evacuated from their confined enclosures," Eurassisgras contributed to the rather zany dialogue. "It also sounds like the stables of Augeas had been drastically influenced by the coincidental confluence of the two rivers!"

"And the sixth demanding labor was to chase away a flock of huge predatory, carnivorous birds using *his* trusty bow and arrow. Say, guys! These unique labors are not only funny, they're quite interesting, too!"

"I feel like breaking your two legs so that you can do sit-down comedy on stage at King Priam's Palace," Eurcockisnum replied to almost-livid Eurshiddenme, and then the fucked-up lieutenant loudly guffawed. "I'm really happy to learn that Hercules was able to get the flock out of there!"

"The seventh mandatory labor was that Hercules had to journey to Crete and capture King Minos's legendary monster, the gigantic sharp-horned Minotaur, and then put the wild beast on an immense boat and transport it to King Eurystheus' palace back in Mycenae, which is now Agamemnon's bailiwick."

"It sounds like King Eurystheus is the real cretin who belongs living with the other asshole Cretans on Crete," Eurballsourout zanily remarked, amusing his three other lieutenant colleagues. "But I'm happy that Hercules had utilized a con-Crete solution to trap and deliver the formidable Minotaur."

"The eighth labor of Hercules was to kill Eurystheus' principal enemy and to disperse *his* rival's hostile man-eating stallions out of their stables. And the ninth tough labor was to steal and bring back the girdle of the Amazon Queen, Hippolyta, which the very renowned Greek hero had scrupulously accomplished using both charm and guile."

"Did daring Hercules also steal Queen Hippolyta's bra, dildo, and sanitary napkins, too!" Eurcockisnum further harassed Eurshiddenme, testing the speaker's tolerance limit. "Did Hercules give naked Hippolyta to old fart Nestor, so that the former Amazon Queen could perform nude lap-dancing at hoary Nestor's world-famous whorehouse!"

Getting extraordinarily peeved, Eurshiddenme decided it was time to conclude his recollection of the Twelve Labors of Hercules as divulged to him by the gaseous old geezer, Nestor of Pylos. "Look, junior jerk-offs! I don't need any exacerbation to my exasperation by your nitwit collaboration and corroboration! These wonderful fantasy stories, or should I say, 'extraordinary myths' that I'm expertly relating, are indeed absolutely intriguing," Eurshiddenme maintained to his zestful, don't-give-a-shit fellow officers. "Ancient people probably were totally bored with the mundane difficulties of everyday life, so the creative mortals invented this crazy, outrageous fiction, making-up what we today call mythology, in order to entertain and inspire the happy campers around campfires."

"Hurry-up with the last three labors," Eurballsourout insisted. "I have to take a huge dump, and I feel like my throbbing asshole is pregnant with triplets!"

"Okay, Eurballsourout. Don't shit your exposed balls off while your asshole is blasting-out volumes of insufferable diarrhea! Now then; the tenth major job was for Hercules to bring back the cattle of Geryon, and in the process, the exceptional hero formed the Pillars of Hercules, now Gibraltar (then Calpe) in Southern Spain, and Abyla in Northern Africa, with the wine-dark Mediterranean Sea flowing between the two landmark rock masses directly into the Atlantic Ocean."

"We're glad to know that Hercules finally got into the flow of things by skillfully using his giant rocks," amused Eurcockisnum expressed and then chortled. "And with the cattle of Geryon, it was lucky that Hercules had possessed a certain herd mentality!"

"In Hercules' eleventh labor, the amazing hulk had to retrieve and bring back the Three Golden Apples of the Hesperides, and also briefly had to hold-up the sky for the very demanding Titan known as Atlas, who had volunteered to obtain the rare golden apples from the north African magic tree. That's why those famed mountains are called the Atlas Range."

"What?" Eurdicisin euphorically exclaimed. "Hercules was the first official bandit in history who had invented the crime of hold-up! Ha, ha, ha!"

Eurshiddenme was then fully pissed-off, but chose to finish what Nestor had recently told him. "Finally, you four dipshits; Hercules had courageously trekked-down to Hades for the purpose of releasing the champion Theseus from the Chair of Forgetfulness, and as part of his assignment, the hero next single-handedly captured and brought the savage three-headed dog Cerberus up from Hades, and then proudly carried the vicious cur directly to King Eurystheus in Mycenae."

Before Eurshiddenme could vigorously punch his four dumb-ass listeners in their hyperactive jaws, the conference that Agamemnon had organized with his captains came-up with a plausible method to answer Hector's challenge of man-to-man combat to save thousands of lives on both sides.

"This is quite a thrilling match-up; a lethal white tornado against a killer black monsoon!" Eurshiddenme announced. "I'll tell you four imbeciles this terrific wager idea of mine. If Ajax wins, I get to receive three blowjobs from each of you. But if Hector wins, I'm lick each of your smelly assholes twice, for five minutes each time!"

"Why don't you suggest the same fucked-up, non-nostalgic notion to King Odysseus?" Eurballsourout boldly answered Eurshiddenme. "Our mercurial-minded boss will make you fart your liver right out of *your shittin' me* asshole!"

Old fart Nestor inserted the various colored stone lots into King Agamemnon's helmet, shook them up inside, and the first one to exit was that of the Great Ajax.

"I'm anxious to eliminate Hector from this sacred soil!" Ajax shouted with his raised right hand. "Now all Achaean warriors on the non-fruitive desert plain should pray to Zeus for my swift victory. For the glory of Greece, I shall prevail! Achilles may be sulking inside his distant Bireme, but the Trojans will soon know that we have many equally-deadly soldiers within our ranks."

The pair of combat champions approached each other as their respective armies stood in separate lines at a short distance. Tension was mounting as the anxious spectators anticipated the upcoming brawl.

Meanwhile, the pair of combatants slowly encountered each other upon the sandy Troad Plain. "Hector; I will make your hemorrhoids wish that they were asteroids," Ajax bellowed above the massive cheering being yelled by both opposing armies. "When I get done with you, you won't know your ass from your little-boy kid knees! Ha, ha, ha!"

"Let's not bandy silly words!" Hector firmly screamed back. "Ready yourself, Ajax, to go-down like a five-pound turd during one of your easier dumps. I shall throw my spear at you to commence the contest!"

Ajax's massive shield had been made of seven thick bull's hides, and an eighth innermost layer had been composed of dense bronze. The giant's defense had miraculously stifled the penetration of Hector's toss, and then, the Trojan's dependable shield had absorbed Ajax's speedy javelin fling. Each combatant pried loose their opponent's spears from their own shields and together, the pair wildly charged at one another. During the loud collision, the Achaean's spear (really Hector's spear) drove through the top of the Trojan's shield, grazing the warrior's exposed neck.

With blood trickling from his neck onto his hairy chest, Hector reached-down, picked-up a large rock, and threw the object at Ajax's stomach, but the heavy item merely bounced-off the giant's muscular frame. But then, in imitation of his illustrious opponent, with one hand Ajax lifted a hundred-pound-rock from the desert floor and hurled the circular sphere into Hector's bronze breastplate, sending the injured Trojan Prince flying onto the arid Troad Plain.

Seeing the ferocity of the ongoing clash, heralds from both sides dashed between the two participants. Trojan old coot Idaeus, gasping for air, and also seriously afflicted with dementia, nervously offered one of his better ideas.

"Ajax and Hector; it is obvious that Almighty Zeus loves both of you along with your mutual courage and your shared integrity. It is advisable that, since dusk is rapidly descending, that fighting between you two killers should be suspended for at least a day."

"Idaeus's idea is right," the anonymous Greek herald concurred with the Trojan old codger emissary. "Put your swords and spears away, to live to fight another day!"

The two awesome army representatives agreed to a temporary truce as recommended by the mentally-deficient emissaries. As tokens of honor and dignity, Ajax and Hector, according to established tradition, exchanged appropriate gifts. Hector gave his capable foe his treasured silver-studded sword, and Ajax gifted Hector his purple-dyed, putrid-smelling, stinking, sweaty loin-guard.

Both armies brandished their raised swords and screamed approval of the battlefield bartering, and Agamemnon arranged a massive feast to celebrate Ajax's fighting ability, and a similar event was simultaneously sponsored by King Priam to praise Prince Hector's heroism.

At Ajax's banquet, Nestor rose and addressed the principal Greek military brass. "Fellow Achaeans; I propose a temporary truce for both sides to clear the battlefield of the hundreds of warriors whose stench-laden corpses are rotting upon the red-stained desert. Let us allow sufficient time for the Greeks and the Trojans to gather their dead for proper cremation on recently-assembled funeral pyres, for the hungry buzzards are swooping-down and scavenging human flesh, which horribly violates both Achaean and Trojan religious culture."

With Agamemnon's consent, Nestor was dispatched to the Trojan camp, and the stuttering courier presented the funeral pyre truce to Hector and Priam, but Paris instantly objected to one of the ancillary conditions.

"I endorse old fogey Nestor's truce idea to mutually bury our dead, but I oppose the provision that I must surrender both Helen's gold and Helen back to Menelaus. I mean, okay, I'm willing to value love over mammon, so let the Greeks have Helen's gold, but I must keep the most beautiful woman in the world as a much-warranted, acceptable compromise."

The two armies agreed on the burial proposition, so funeral personnel gathered rotting bodies from the blood-stained desert sand. However, most of the corpses were so mutilated and maimed that many Trojans were burned upon Greek pyres, and a plethora of Achaeans were cremated upon blazing Trojan funeral pyres.

During the night hours, with Odysseus's guidance and supervision, the conscientious Danaans assiduously labored and constructed a sturdy wall, and an accompanying trench, between *their* vulnerable beach encampment and the distant city of Troy. However, Zeus and Poseidon were displeased that Agamemnon had not asked for or gained *their* permission to commence the fantastic-in-scope building project.

"The invading fools never prayed or sacrificed animals and wine to acquire *our* blessing to construct yonder wall," aggrieved Poseidon mentioned to Zeus. "That new Achaean wall makes the one that Apollo and I had cooperatively designed and built around Troy look like a project conceived by infants and toddlers."

"Why complain your childish grievance to me," Zeus answered his sea-dwelling brother visiting Mt. Olympus. "You have the power to destroy that wall at your own personal discretion, any time you desire. And Lord Poseidon; even though I haven't eaten a morsel of food for simple pleasure in over a week, my bowels are currently in an uproar, just like yours! I think that we both should stop farting-around and polluting the entire atmosphere!"

The interaction among the two gods made Zeus so upset that the Earth-shaker filled the night sky with tremendous thunder and lightning, and the frightening spectacle lasted until dawn the following morning.

Chapter 8

"THE GODS DON'T PARTICIPATE"

"Why are we clandestinely meeting fifty-feet underground in the horizontal secret LBGTQRMSV meeting cavern?" Eurballsourout wondered and asked his main shipmate Eurshiddenme. "If King Odysseus finds out, he'll suspect that we're gay faggots and have us demoted to lowly infantry status. Then we'll liable to be executed at sunrise by either the Trojans or our own Greeks!"

"Because, brain-dead asshole; it's my theory that the gods are greedy bastards and bitches who have definitely implemented a conspiracy against mortals," Eurshiddenme explained to his four dunce-like colleagues. "Their sinister method is rather simple and rudimentary. If Zeus and his family fear that the human race has the potential to overthrow their control over Heaven and Earth", Eurshiddenme lectured, "just like the Olympus gods had overthrown Cronus and the Titans, their furtive scheme is to always have humans fighting amongst ourselves, as is now occurring with the Greeks waging war with the Trojans."

"Your logic seems to make sense," Eurassisgras agreed, stupidly nodding his head in the dark. "With us lieutenants surreptitiously meeting fifty-feet underground in pitch blackness, we won't be surveilled by either the fickle and capricious gods, by the fucked-up Trojans, or by Commander Odysseus."

"So, what the fuck are you going to tell us down here in this spooky dark tunnel?" Eurdicisin asked Eurshiddenme. "Are you preparing us for the eerie Area of Atonement down in shadowy Hades? I'd rather have death by chocolate!"

"No dipshit!" Eurshiddenme bluntly replied. "I'm now going to tell you all about how the devious gods operate, even though they're not medical surgeons. I'm going to thoroughly review for your education the story of Epimetheus and Prometheus."

"We know all about Prometheus being a Titan, and being banned from Olympus because the kind-hearted god had given men the gift of fire, but who the hell was Epimetheus?" Eurdicisin queried.

Eurshiddenme divulged to his uninformed comrades that in the beginning, only male humans were created to populate the Earth. Then,

Zeus requested that the blacksmith god Hephaestus sculpt a statue of what a female of the race should look like, and then magically, have the lame blacksmith god convert the statue into Pandora, the *first lady,* who, in the future, never lived in any White Cave. Zeus then presented the voluptuous new female with a trunk-full of glimmering amber that had a lid adorned with flowers and pomegranates, along with clusters of prickly porcupine quills. The amber chest had two polished semi-circular golden snakes that served as handles.

"So, what?" Eurcockisnum objected. "All women have boxes, hairy ones at that! You mean to say that you called this meeting fifty-feet underground just to tell us that women have boxes?"

Eurshiddenme, used to such stupid commentary from his unacademic, hedonistic peers, continued with his Epimetheus story. "Check her out," Zeus commanded his eminent Mt. Olympus family. "For this new woman we have created is really the cat's meow that can make any impotent man have an instant erection and blast messy sticky ejaculations all over the damned place! She is indeed endowed with heaven's most magnificent treasures," Zeus imperially prattled. "And I can't wait to take away her virginity and pump the poop out of her snatcheroo, so to speak! Of course, I'll have to swallow some pride and shrink-down from fifty-foot-tall to six-foot in height, and my penis will have to contract from three-foot-long to a mere twelve inches in length, but I can live with that compromise, for at least a half-hour of sublime pleasure!"

"What did the gods name the beautiful bitch?" Eurdicisin curiously asked, before short-tempered Eurshiddenme continued his lengthy narrative to his four lethargic-but-comical compatriots.

"Her name will be Pandora," Zeus attested, "which means 'All-Gifted', including doing anything from exotic couch-dancing to administering good professional blow-jobs. But Pandora is mortal and not fit to be a permanent mate for a *Mt. Olympus* stud like you, Apollo, or you Ares, or me. "

"Then why have you tempted and teased us with her abundant charms?" Lord Hermes challenged Zeus's ambiguous statement. "Why do you make me want and lust for what I can't have, namely this gorgeous bitch that Hephaestus has just artfully manufactured?"

"Because Shit-head!" Zeus thundered. "I intend to send Pandora down to Earth and wed Epimetheus, Prometheus's not so down-to-earth moronic brother, who can only see and understand things *after* they have happened, and then it is too late to do anything remedial about them," Zeus maintained. "In this way, *we* can get even with that traitor Prometheus by cursing Epimetheus, along with all mankind, with the first woman. With the mortals preoccupied with sex and distrust, *Olympus* will now be safe from the challenge of human intelligence!"

"Way to go, Zeus Baby!" Apollo exclaimed to his fellow gods at the Mt. Olympus summit conference. "You're so shrewd and sly that you could even sell ancient grease to ancient Greece!"

"I get what you're implying," alert Eurballsourout piped-up in response to Eurshiddenme's recollection of mythology. "Prometheus had the gift of prophecy, knowing the future, and was fully aware that Zeus would punish him for compassionately giving mankind the gift of fire. But his twin brother, asshole Epimetheus, was in many ways like the five of us Greek dimwits. The poor idiot could not recognize evil danger until *after* it had been vividly shown and demonstrated!"

"Anyway," Eurshiddenme continued with his luminous account inside the dark LBGTQRMSV underground tunnel. "Zeus commanded Hermes, the official messenger god having wings on his sandals, and also upon *his* bronze helmet, to conduct Pandora to Epimetheus's gay village residence, which somehow had been spared being demolished by heterosexual Hephaestus's most recent violent sperm storm. "Tell the asshole degenerate Epimetheus," Zeus sternly instructed Hermes, "that the king of the gods extends *his* goodwill in the form of this enchanting bride, who is also an ultra-fine screwing machine, in addition to being a woman possessing a fantastic dowry being delivered by Hermes Express directly from *Mt. Olympus.*"

"So, how the hell was Pandora representative of women being evil as has always been believed?" Eurdicisin wanted to know. "Was she the first example of such a valid suspicion?"

Eurshiddenme gave Eurdicisin a dirty look inside the absolutely dark cave. "So, guys; Hermes delivered the first woman and dowry via *Olympus Hermes Express* to Arcadia, a pleasant northern region of ancient Greece, where the inhabitants' fun-loving and carefree descendants would eventually learn how to invent and play sophisticated pinball machine games. When the giant Epimetheus perceived what a knockout Pandora was, and soon learned that matrimony was her special assignment," Eurshiddenme emphasized, "the numbskull had three premature ejaculations during the day and four white dreams that night, completely obliterating seven innocent gay men's villages clear across the *Aegean Sea* and into Asia Minor."

"Even in the dark, I see your point, even tough points are for pinheads," Eurcockisnum contributed to the insane conversation. "Speak to us more irrelevant nomenclature!"

"Anyway," Eurshiddenme proceeded with his rather weird tale. "Prometheus's dumb-shit twin brother accepted his new bride along with her extensive dowry into his house, which was actually a primitive cave, because Epimetheus's dwelling had been destroyed by one of Hephaestus's catastrophic sperm storms originating from atop *Mt. Olympus*. Epimetheus soon wedded Pandora that day, without the services of any temple pedophile priest, and couldn't wait to get his noodle wet, so the demented ignoramus completely ignored Prometheus's prior warning about not receiving any possibly detrimental gift from conniving Zeus."

"What happened next?" intrigued Eurballsourout annoyingly asked. "Did Epimetheus get to pump the poop and sweet pussy juice out of Pandora?"

"According to geeky Greek mythology, as had already been alluded," Eurshiddenme explained, "Prometheus was clairvoyant and had the power of prophecy, but Epimetheus was a stubborn blockhead that couldn't see events until *after* they had happened. The following morning, the totally dense Earth inhabitant remembered *his* brother's statement about rejecting any gift from Zeus, but it was too late to repent about accepting the woman and about receiving the magnificent jewel-studded trunk. Epimetheus finally realized that the dowry Zeus had conferred upon Pandora had been designed to effectively break *his* balls and to sever *his* aching hemorrhoids. "Pandora, have you opened your box yet?" Epimetheus asked.

"Wow! I'm getting a boner just thinking about Pandora opening her box!" Eurdicisin vociferated to his four mates inside the dark cavern. "What the fuck happened next?"

"Of course, my dear husband," Pandora answered. "I opened my box eight times and you screwed the crap out of me eight times last night like a young stud in heat! I think you should change your name from Epimetheus to Big Dick-o-Pump!" Eurshiddenme told his four peers about the fucked-up myth. "Pandora; I had meant the amber casket Zeus had given you!" Epimetheus blushed. "Did you open *that* box?"

"Oh no, my dear, beloved spouse," Pandora responded. "I know right where it is, and am also eager to learn precisely what the unscrupulous *Mt. Olympus* immortals had placed inside it! I trust it's a wide array of new sex toys, along with a variety of pornographic drawings to stimulate *our* docile libidos!"

"Holy cow manure!" Eurassisgras hollered in the dark. "I think I just creamed my battle-loin guard and am about to crap my intestines into my already wet undergarment!"

Eurshiddenme ignored Eurassisgras's lunatic remark and resumed his lengthy exposition. "Pandora; please listen carefully to what the *Hades* I have to say!" Epimetheus emphatically indicated. "I have a suspicion that your chest contains some dangerous, evil secret that will haunt us and our accursed descendants throughout the decadent decades to come."

"I assure you, dear husband," Pandora idiotically replied. "*My chest* simply contains hard flesh and erect nipples for you to suck-on and fondle, and nothing else!"

"Damn it, Pandora! I meant *the chest* that Zeus had given you as a gift! Another word for a box is a chest! Learn the freakin' language, will ya'!" Epimetheus shouted at his beautiful, naïve and very gullible wife.

"Well, dear husband," Pandora defensively replied. "If *you* think that my box is my chest and that my chest is my box, then that's okay with me, as long as you keep licking and munching away at either! But when you decide to insert your erection inside my box," Pandora clarified, "make sure you don't try and shove it inside my sensitive chest!"

"Holy intercourse!" Eurcockisnum exclaimed. "I think that right now my tiny erection and my huge asshole are imitating Eurassisgras's dick and asshole!"

Aggravated Eurshiddenme decided it was time to conclude his interesting rendition of the Greek first lady who had been created by the very-cunning gods. "Pandora," Epimetheus stated. "As long as we keep that amber casket, or trunk, or whatever you want to call that box or chest that Zeus had given you, well wife, keep it shut and please, don't open the lid," the worried husband adamantly insisted. "Then the actual difference between a box and a chest really doesn't matter one fuckin' bit. Anyway, beautiful Pandora," Epimetheus continued his romantic discourse. "The hole in that amber box Zeus gave you is entirely too big and wide to screw. Not even *Atlas's* enormous fadorkenbender could fill-up that gargantuan cavity!"

"I promise you, dear husband, that I will never be overwhelmed by curiosity to ever open that amber trunk," Pandora pledged. "All I desire to do is to admire its magnificent external beauty!"

"Holy sperm cells!" Eurcockisnum bellowed in the dark. "I think I just ejaculated my balls and my epididymis right through my tiny penis hole!"

"Pandora was elated that her after-the-fact, dim-witty husband had permitted her to keep the amber chest, and the comely woman viewed it with pride the entire day. But after several centuries of staring at the dumb-ass amber container, Pandora wondered what its contents might be. The temptation to look inside the three-dimensional, rectangular chest had always been present, but Pandora was afraid that Epimetheus would become livid and *flip his lid* if she were to flip hers."

"This sounds like some sort of Greek soap-less soap opera," Eurballsourout complained. "Why not tell us about Ajax's singular ability to deter gents? Especially, Trojan gents!"

"When Epimetheus was out of the house inspecting the heavens for the next possible nasty sperm storm raining-down from *Mt. Olympus*, the tantalizing amber box again inspired temptation to reign supreme in Pandora's curious mind. The first lady of Greece laid her avaricious hands upon the delicate surface, lifted the squeaky latch, and slowly and apprehensively raised the lid. To her chagrin, a swarm of teeming, winged spirits ascended, and then flew-out of the accursed amber trunk, swirling like a typhoon around the cave, and then vanishing outside into the atmosphere to plague mankind for the remainder of *his* tenure on this despicable planet."

"I see your impeccable logic," Eurdicisin complimented Eurshiddenme. "The gods are all ballbusters who want to distract us mortals with stupid-shit wars, chores, bores and whores!"

"Well anyway, fellow lieutenants; Pandora swiftly closed the box with a loud jolt, but her futile effort was far too late to attain any satisfactory results. Tears of guilt and disappointment filled her blurry eyes, for Pandora had released upon the world all of the grief, diseases, woes and miseries that have afflicted the human race from womb to tomb, ever since the very beginning of antiquity. The first lady of Greece had initiated widespread melancholy to flourish upon the Earth!"

"What happened next?" worm-brain Eurcockisnum wanted to know. "Did Pandora's swollen clit suddenly get numb like my dangling dingle?"

"Epimetheus entered the nondescript cave all covered with sticky *Olympus* sperm from another Hephaestus semen storm that had also recently destroyed a neighboring gay village five miles away. "Pandora, what have you done? I told you not to play with your box while I'm not around!" the brother of Prometheus strenuously objected.

"I'm sorry for opening *my box*," the penitent wife cried and grieved to accomplished idiot Epimetheus. "But you got me so confused that I thought

I was really opening *my chest* instead. At any rate, our unfortunate doomed descendants are going to be royally screwed by Zeus and his vindictive *Olympus* family for at least the next ten thousand years!"

"It's all partially my fault," Epimetheus reluctantly confessed as *he* wiped some excess sperm juice from his thin scalp and thick hair. "If only I could be like my brother Prometheus," the doltish fool reckoned. "Then, I could avoid divine orgasms and avert evil surprises *before* the fucked-up events happen!"

"Wow! This is some sensational story!" Eurdicisin commended Eurshiddenme. "Now that I've creamed my loin-guard a second time, please get to the anti-climax!"

"And finally, Epimetheus knew exactly what those unleashed evil spirits represented: death, famine, pestilence, disease, work, sickness, murder, theft, jealousy, envy, pride, war, constipation, diarrhea, and even nasty venereal warts. Thinking that all of the spirits had escaped the amber dowry box's interior, the sympathetic husband asked his upset-yet-obedient wife to cautiously lift the lid to closely examine the chest's presumably empty, mammoth compartment."

"Now guys; only one timid, weaker spirit still had been occupying the interior, and the sprite seemed afraid to escape its singular confinement. But the remaining spirit was not a bottle of wine! As the last box occupant finally flapped its wings and fluttered upward, it then lamely ascended out of the most famous chest in history. Pandora and Epimetheus instinctively knew that the last spirit was abstract Hope, the only decent quality given by the gods for man to cope with all of the maladies and curses that had been packed inside the evil container."

"I hope you've finished with your exaggerated and very strange story," Eurballsourout indicated to Eurshiddenme. "I think that my ears can now see better than my eyes!"

"When Pandora noticed that Hope could not easily fly around the room and leave the cave like the malicious spirits had done, the wife of Epimetheus pitied the orphaned sprite, held it to her firm breasts, and nursed Hope to good health. Hope felt so content that *it* managed to eat right through Pandora's enviable nipples, and soon entered her warm heart, where inside women *it* has resided until this very day."

"That was a tremendous story!" Eurassisgras ecstatically told Eurshiddenme. "Now let's go up to ground level, kill a few stray cats, and enjoy eating some luscious pussy!"

* * * * * * * * * * * *

"Listen, my family," Zeus forcefully announced. "I'm ready to execute my dynamic plan into action. Let no god or mortal believe that he or she can oppose my indomitable will."

"We get the message," Hermes, the official Mt. Olympus courier replied. "Every vowel, consonant and syllable!"

"If any of you jealous idiots dare to plot rebellion against me, I'll cast you down to Tartarus where you can enjoy the shackled company of Cronus and his not-too-penitent Titan cronies. If all of you imbeciles held a separate length of my famed golden rope at one end, I could easily defeat your entire pulling force with a single, effortless tug."

"Father," Athena respectfully and anxiously stated. "Although some of us feel sympathy for Odysseus and the Argives, we promise to not directly intervene in the active Trojan War, but we'll only offer constructive advice to the intrepid, on-a-mission Danaans, but we'll provide no direct divine assistance."

"My child; I'll always value and try to satisfy your idealistic desires!" Zeus politely returned; and then the god of thunder and lightning promptly adjourned the brief parley, swiftly harnessed his team of white stallions, got onto his golden chariot, and rode his magnificent vehicle to the top of Mt. Gargaron where he would have an eagle-eye view of the Trojan Troad Plain.

Zeus held-up his golden scales of balance, with the Greek interest on the left and the Trojan perspective on the right-hand-side. Immediately, responding to the weight of Zeus's finger, the Achaean side tipped-down, indicating that the Trojans had been designated to win the ensuing battle. Several ear-shattering thunderclaps resounded and resonated throughout the Greek ranks, and the intimidated Danaans scurried in rapid retreat from the aggressive Trojan onslaught.

Diomedes halted his chariot and picked-up old and feeble Nestor, who had fallen to the ground when one of his chariot's horses had stumbled over a rock and had broken a leg.

"Zeus favors our avowed enemy today!" half-senile Nestor observed and related to Diomedes. "Let Hector brag and crow that he has scared your ass into abandoning the fight, and fleeing like a frightened mouse to your ship. Remember that tomorrow might see a reversal in fate, and that the widowed wives left behind in Greece could have some well-deserved vindication for the loss of their valiant spouses and louses."

Hector's speedy chariot pursued Diomedes and Nestor across the sandy plain, with the highly-focused Trojan prince yelling myriad expletives at his principal adversary, "Coward! Wimp! Jerk-off! Craven Faggot!"

The Achaean army had been trapped like corralled sheep inside the defensive wall that the Greek idiots had constructed the night before, and the fools were crushing each other in their futile stampede to escape the Trojans' fierce wrath.

Distraught King Agamemnon stood above the wall, shouting inaudible instructions that were indiscernible because of all the commotion occurring below: "Shame on you, Argives! You all claim and boast to be able to annihilate a hundred Trojans each, but now, you pussies wouldn't even be able to kill a colony of paralyzed chipmunks! Great Zeus!" Agamemnon hollered-up to the chief god. "I have offered to you superb burned animal flesh upon your altar! But I humbly apologize for sacrificing to you ram, sheep and goat meat, so I guess you can call me a muttonhead. So, please don't scream-down from High Heaven, 'Where's the beef'. Oh, Mighty Zeus: if we Achaeans cannot savor victory today on the toad, er, I mean the Troad, then please grant my army a successful escape to the safety of their rotting, anchored Biremes!"

Amazingly, Zeus heard and fathomed Agamemnon's sincere prayer, so the king god dispatched a huge golden eagle, with a helpless fawn clutched to its powerful talons, and the baby deer was mercilessly dropped and deposited directly upon the Greeks' sacred altar to Zeus.

Seeing Zeus's encouragement being provided from above, the Achaeans, led by dauntless and relentless Diomedes, did a one-eighty about-face and sprinted towards the astonished Trojans in a brilliant surprise-move tactic. Diomedes smartly yelled several promises to his inspired captains: "If you kill your counterpart Trojan officers, we'll then flawlessly sack Troy, and you soldiers will be rewarded with fine horses, the best used chariots, and a dozen highly-versatile, kinky prostitutes to keep you warm and comfortable each night in bed."

Thinking of all the female muffins that the lieutenants could munch-on and screw, the Greek captains performed brilliantly, and easily massacred hundreds of Trojan warriors. But then, amusing himself, Zeus tipped his golden scales of injustice to the opposite side with his right index finger, and the tide of battle quickly switched to the decisive advantage of Hector and his crazed minions.

'I will not assist the invading Achaeans and pacify Athena and Hera's egos until belligerent Achilles wisely decides to resolves his differences with greedy Agamemnon and returns to again fight the Trojans,' Zeus contemplated. 'All is fair in love and war from the mortal perspective, but all could be completely unfair from mine!'

In two short hours, darkness had enveloped the battlefield, and Hector abandoned his goal of forcing the Greeks all the way to their anchored ships, and then in contempt, arrogantly torching the Biremes and instantly cremating all of the mariners aboard.

Hector ordered his specialized soldiers to construct watchtowers on the Trojan side of Troad Plain, and have surveillance teams spy and report on any unusual Greek maneuvers and activities. "Tomorrow, at dawn father," Hector promised King Priam, "we'll attack the somnolent Greek camp and see who will push back whom: Diomedes or myself!"

That star-laden night, the familiar constellations shined brightly in the firmament, and thousands of Trojan fires burned near the hundreds of sturdy watchtowers, absolutely frightening the feces out of the now scared-shitless Achaeans.

Chapter 9

"EMBASSY TO ACHILLES"

Seeing his forces getting their' rear-ends becoming black and blue, along with their testicles punctured and pulverized, King Agamemnon called an unscheduled military council meeting for his senior commanders to develop a new crucial strategy in order to regain the essential services of Achilles and his Myrmidons to finally defeat the persistent Trojans.

"Generals; I see now that Zeus has betrayed me in favor of King Priam and Prince Hector," Agamemnon lamented and shared. "We'll never be able to sack the walls of Troy, because Almighty Zeus thinks that we're a bunch of sad-sack dirtbags. I propose that we should board our Biremes and sail for home in humiliation for unsuccessfully enduring our nine-year raid. We cannot fight against omnipotent Zeus, Ares, and Apollo, in addition to getting slaughtered by the ruthless Trojans, who I understand from our intelligence gathering, now intend to suffocate us with our heads, mouths, throats and nostrils smothered inside of tight-fitting, ribbed prophylactics."

Hearing the king's pessimistic lecture, Diomedes was disenchanted with Agamemnon's craven suggestion of abandoning the war after the Greeks had encountered so much adversity, and the young warrior was inspired to make a strong speech to contradict what *he,* the upstart, considered to be the Greek leader's unsound strategy.

"What the fuck's the matter with you, timid King of Mycenae? Do you have angry cow's disease?" Diomedes aggressively mocked Menelaus's brother. "Zeus may have given you dominion over men, but apparently, the Almighty Lord of Olympus did not allot you any emotional capital in the courage department. You may leave this struggle, King Agamemnon, like a small puppy dog with your tail between your legs, but I and thousands of determined Greeks will stay on task and plunder Troy; we'll capture Helen, and steal-back her immense treasure trove from Prince Paris. Even if everyone else in our contingent elects to follow your mortifying exit, Sthenelus, er, I mean my key man Stenny, and I, will remain until our last ounce of blood is drained from our Achaean arteries and veins!"

"Diomedes is positively right," Sthenelus declared in support of his immediate superior. "Many of the more-outspoken soldiers and army officers actually believe that you, King Agamemnon, are a silent, clandestine member of the non-macho Y.M.C.A."

"What the fuck's the Y.M.C.A.?" Agamemnon shrieked. "It sounds like some perverted Trojan propaganda nonsense to me!"

"The Abbreviation stands for 'Yahoo Masturbating Cowards Alliance," Sthenelus explained. "And I must admit, King Agamemnon; you definitely fit the faggot group's description rather perfectly."

Fearing dissension within the ranks gradually evolving into outright rebellion, old Nestor of Pylos spoke-up to add a degree of decorum and tradition to the escalating heated dialogue.

"Lord Agamemnon; let me add a new perspective to this fucked-up debate, for I wish to contribute an element of aged wisdom, mainly because I'm a wiz, and I certainly ain't dumb! You had been erroneous in judgment when you pissed-off Achilles by pilfering his cherished prize, the slave girl Briseis, which was the source of the dispute within our rank Greek ranks," Nestor articulated. "I recommend that you make adequate reparations to placate peeved Lord Achilles, to satisfy his distinguished honor, and to pacify his abnormal volatile temper. If you present to the son of Thetis some basic kingly gifts, I believe that Achilles will feel vindicated, will rejoin our crusade with a changed heart, and we will then easily be able to soundly trounce the devious Trojans, despite their notorious deployment of deadly prophylactics used as sinister suffocating weapons!"

Agamemnon bowed his head to acknowledge the elementary truth evident in old Nestor's words of experience, and the worried king confessed to his bevy of Argive generals that he had been wrong all along, and that the commander from Pylos was deemed correct in introducing a viable solution to the stalemate existing with stubborn Achilles.

"I'll gladly give Achilles seven chariot tripods; ten gold bars; three bars with accompanying restaurants; twenty copper cauldrons to distill rye whiskey; a dozen of my finest stallions in their 'hay day', not to mention the highly-coveted slave girl Briseis; and finally, I'll throw into the offer seven gorgeous lesbians imported from Lesbos, who naturally will teach Briseis all about female homosexuality, just to frustrate Lord Achilles's voracious and lustful heterosexual, virgin appetite."

"That's an excellent and admirable solution!" Ajax verified and commended Agamemnon. "If the gods permit us to sack and maraud Troy, Achilles, if he elects to lead us in our final hostile assault, will be able to sail for home with a cargo of jewels, gold, bronze, silver, and lesbian hussies, who don't have to worry about stupid bullshit such as reproductive freedom and dumb-fuck female slogans like 'my body, my choice'!"

"Do you have any other gifts to offer ill-tempered Achilles?" Nestor interrogated the Greek expedition leader. "How about some surgical equipment to creatively transform the seven voluptuous lesbian dolls into wage-earning, transgender, highly profitable male prostitutes?"

"Okay, Nestor," Agamemnon concurred. "Let's try this additional present I'm suggesting as an added bonus to give to Achilles. The Prince from Phthia will have the option to select one of my three ugly, obese daughters to marry, so that the mercurial-minded outlaw can become my principal heir and legitimate son-in-law, without any dowry being needed for Achilles to provide for me. All of this reward will be his, if only the obstinate idiot would relent and submit to my authority as high king of this sophisticated Greek invasion task force."

"Your shrewd solution with Achilles appears to be both rational and fair," Ajax complimented Agamemnon. "It sounds as Greek as the ideas of mother, gyros, and apple moussaka! Your obdurate Argive adversary will forget all about your quarrel with him over Briseis, and will soon be able to make a handsome profit by pimping the converted lesbians from Lesbos into money-making transgendered male hookers!"

Nestor was designated by Agamemnon to choose three other emissaries besides himself to approach Achilles's Bireme, which was anchored at the far end of the peninsula. Phoenix was selected for inclusion because the old codger had known Achilles as a boy, and had accompanied the lad out into the desert to catch and ignite on fire an indigenous bird into embers, just to see if the creature would reincarnate itself from the ashes to amazingly live another hundred years. Ajax was chosen next because the affable giant had once tossed Achilles to the top limb of a pine tree to prepare the teenager for future summit meetings, and Odysseus was the last representative of Agamemnon, since Achilles had always admired the King of Ithaca's skilled rhetoric and sagacious military strategies.

The four delegates left the Argives main camp and ambled two miles to the ships of the Myrmidons, the skilled soldiers of the affronted Achaean hero. The quartet, singing familiar Greco war anthems during their trek along the beach, found the disgruntled, leery champion idly playing his lyre, while dissonantly harping and carping off-key about being mistreated and bullied by cowardly King Agamemnon.

Achilles, with his main lieutenant, Patroclus, warmly greeted the "military truce entourage" into their modest officer's hut. A meal of meat and bread was hastily prepared, and the six acquainted men consumed their food and reminisced about past shared adventures and conquests. But then, sly and cunning old Nestor diplomatically changed the tone of the conversation to envelop the present dilemma involving the bitter debacle between aggrieved Achilles and tyrannical Agamemnon.

"Your noble father Peleus sent you off to war with the philosophy that power among mortals was the gods' discretion to give, but it was bestowed favorably only if humans respected the deities' whims, and controlled *their* fluctuating pride and arrogance," Nestor emphasized. "Now then, I encourage you, Achilles, to cease your ridiculous quarrel with Agamemnon and in so doing, master the art of courtesy to match your extensive knowledge of the science of war. I maintain that all of the Argives will admire your transformed desire to compromise with *our* Greek leader. I had heard your father often speak in public about the importance of utilizing words of tolerance. Have you forgotten *his* diplomatic genius?"

"Nestor is correct in his general assessment," Odysseus concurred with his revered elder. "Achilles, I now beg you; learn to become more moderate and conciliatory in handling your' oscillating emotions. Hector now has the Danaans with our backs against the sea, and his motivated forces might break through our vulnerable defenses tomorrow, and the Greeks might falter without your invaluable alliance and assistance. The Trojans will surely burn-up all of our ships as if we were helpless phoenixes out in the arid desert, and most of *your* comrades from various cities will perish and be incinerated while onboard. That horrible memory certainly will be ingrained inside your hassled brain until you arrive upon your deathbed. You'll be miserably haunted for the remainder of your days, Achilles of Phthia, by your tainted recollection of refusing to aid *our* joint and totally praiseworthy cause!"

Achilles was not-at-all impressed with Odysseus's summary of his relationship with the leader of the Greek invasion, claiming that Agamemnon was a slippery bastard who thinks one way, but maliciously behaves in an opposite manner. The aggrieved Greek warrior insisted that yellow-bellied Agamemnon had always treated cowards with the same regard as the egregious king rewarded his most loyal and audacious generals. The brave-but-egocentric hero argued to the four emissaries that he had successfully sacked and ransacked a dozen cities allied with Troy, and that after humbly presenting the treasures to Agamemnon, the king awarded Achilles a mere pittance of the booty, while keeping the bulk of the valuables all to himself. But when greedy Agamemnon deliberately stole Briseis away from Achilles's custody, then *that* very belittling embarrassment was more than the great warrior could either tolerate or accept.

"Agamemnon had raised a fantastic army of one thousand ships and fifty thousand soldiers, but for what purpose?" Achilles demanded hearing from his four guest ambassadors. "To retrieve Helen for the benefit of red-bearded Menelaus? Is Menelaus the only man who loves a woman? Didn't I love Briseis in a similar fashion? In my estimation, your King of Mycenae is a lying, conniving clown, and nothing more!"

"But the King has offered to you any of his three daughters in marriage?" Odysseus attempted to negotiate basic reason with Agamemnon's prime antagonist. "The King of Mycenae is indeed the richest royal personage in all of Greece? Are you going to pass-up *that* tremendous once-in-a-lifetime opportunity of being *his* main heir?"

"In truth Odysseus, I happen to value the abstraction known as love over the possession of physical treasure and property," quixotic Achilles idealistically answered. "And as far as the bastard king's three daughters are concerned, the trio of fat bitches all possess horrendous-in-appearance pachyderm skin. And also, two of the obese sluts look like female elephants lacking grotesque tusks, and the third hideous-looking, mammoth beast looks something like a pregnant hippopotamus that is about to deliver corpulent quadruplets!"

"Forget your incredible animosity towards Agamemnon for a moment," intelligently counseled wise Nestor. "For, Odysseus, Ajax, Phoenix's and my sake, won't you assist *our* Greek endeavor against Troy by joining our coordinated assault? In all honesty, Achilles; we four negotiators admit that we desperately need your indispensable allegiance!"

"If the gods in their mercy allow me to proudly return from here to my native Phthia, I'll easily find a good wife who could cook, sew, give good head, and screw like a rabbit. There are numerous, well-endowed, very pretty daughters of strong fathers living back home, and those stout yeomen staunchly guard the various towns and forts. I'll choose the one special woman whom I prefer best, and have her as my queen to help me rule over my father's kingdom."

"I deeply resent the way that you have nixed your mentor Phoenix," Nestor verbally lambasted Achilles. "But to cut to the chase, I am an avid student of child psychology, and I wish to learn the true reason for your unmitigated belligerence! Why are *you* so adamantly petulant toward the Greeks' arduous struggle against Troy and its allies?"

"My mother Thetis of the sea has told me of two separate destinies, depending on which decision or path I should pursue," Achilles almost-tearfully revealed. "First off, if I stay and fight here at Troy, I'll die in battle, but then, eternal fame and glory will be forever identified with my name. But secondly, if I return home from Troy to Phthia, my name will evaporate into nothing several generations later. But conversely, I will enjoy a long and happy life, adroitly reigning over my father's prosperous kingdom!"

"Are you saying that you value a long dull life over a short glorious one?" Odysseus challenged. "In my opinion, I would not make such a mediocre choice of destinies!"

"I believe that joy and love are more important in life than power and wealth!" Achilles austerely replied. "One cannot neither buy nor steal back honor and pride, which happen to be abstract qualities that Agamemnon has deceitfully pilfered from me. So, dear friends, my unsolicited advice to you noble men would be for you to voluntarily join me in sailing back empty-handed to our native lands with our mutual pride and our shared honor still intact!"

Phoenix then raised his right hand to his heart and solemnly pledged that Achilles was like his own flesh-and-blood son; the hundred-year-old geezer eloquently stated that the gods had cursed him to never have a child of his own; and then the neurotic curmudgeon declared that he would sleep the night inside Achilles's nondescript hut, and with his loyal troops, would set sail with the dissident fleet of Myrmidons in the morning.

"But before Odysseus, Ajax and Nestor leave these premises," hoary Phoenix commented, "I hope that you, Achilles, will learn to harness and control your haughtiness. I advise that you pray to Zeus and fear his many whims, so that the Greek cause can be salvaged without either you or I contributing to their ultimate victory. Everyone in the Greek camp is aware that Agamemnon had wronged you! And everyone in the camp admires your daring and skill more than *his* lack thereof. However, the King's generosity, regardless of his gutless character, is quite generous in nature, and Agamemnon has sent his cream-of-the-crop commanders to represent his extraordinary concessions. I would prefer that you, Achilles, settle this complicated matter with grace and dignity, rather than with the childish temper-tantrum that you've so blatantly exhibited. If you make a minor yield, I'm certain that all of the Achaeans, with the exception of cowardly Agamemnon, will treat and honor you as a god of Olympus!"

"I have no particular regard or consideration for the petty Achaeans' negative opinion regarding my proud behavior," Achilles snapped back. "I don't trust that rogue Agamemnon one iota. When the bastard stole beautiful Briseis from me, that was the final hair than broke the giraffe's spine. I here and now warn you gentlemen that if you take Agamemnon's side in *our* personal dispute, then in so doing, you also oppose me, and will have then become my avowed enemies."

"Nestor and Odysseus; I now comprehend that Achilles cannot be swayed or convinced to ever accede to reason," Ajax assessed and related. "Our candid words are, in meaning, mute to his deaf ears and his closed-mind. But Achilles; your colossal grudge will not budge an inch," Ajax insisted. "According to out ancient laws and traditions, even if a terrible murder has been committed, it is common practice for a brother, a father, an uncle, or an affected son to agree to accept blood money as a feasible compensation to settle a harsh wrangle with the murderer. But you, valiant warrior, have worked yourself into an implacable frenzy over one insignificant slave girl, even though Agamemnon, through our well-intentioned embassy, has offered you Briseis along with seven even-more-horny harlots besides. Why do you obstinately resist absolutely clear reason?"

"You speak the truth, big oaf Ajax. But when I reconsider and mull-over in my mind how that gutless son-of-a-bitch bastard had humiliated me in front of my peers, namely, the other Achaean generals, well, my blood still boils just thinking about the entire warped scenario."

Nestor, Ajax and Odysseus dejectedly paced back to the Achaean camp with the bad news that Achilles was beyond being unbearably obdurate. "The stubborn asshole evidently had been born with a stubbed-head," Odysseus evaluated and commented. "His noggin is harder than Hephaestus's solid metal anvil!"

"True," Ajax spontaneously confirmed. "Achilles's brains are more solid than rocks, and his dense skull is twice as thick as volcanic basalt!"

Chapter 10

"NIGHT-TIME FORAY"

"Eurshiddenme, why the hell are we again fifty-feet below ground in this fifty-foot-deep secret LBGTQRMSV tunnel that apparently isn't too secret if the four of us gabby lieutenants know about it," Eurballsourout asked his Argive superior. I mean, we four nitwits are undoubtedly narrow-minded dolts! But are you now trying to give us a type of dumb-ass tunnel-vision way down here in the dark?"

"Quiet idiot!" Eurshiddenme ordered, even though he was the same rank as Eurballsourout. "Down inside this horizontal hollow, even the shadows may have ears and mouths!"

"But why the hell are we down here?" Eurassisgras echoed Eurballsourout's inquiry. "Are you attempting to convert us into being condemned members of the gay, lesbian, transgender and tri-sexual community?"

'Listen assholes, and that includes you too, Eurdicisin and Eurcockisnum!" Eurshiddenme imperatively stated. "I finally figured-out how the gods, particularly Zeus and Hermes, operate when dealing with mortals who are humans, and with humans who are mortals. So that's why I specifically led you four insane asylum candidates down here to learn something relevant!"

"We could be in bed sleeping with our arms around our life-sized, straw prostitute dolls, so this better be worth our while!" Eurdicisin angrily complained. "Usually, Eurshiddenme; you don't know your ass from a hole in the ground, but now, quite apparently, you don't know a fuckin' huge dark tunnel from your damned diminutive asshole!"

"Hurry-up and tell us your loony bullshit story so that we can get back to having imaginary sex with our prostitute dolls, now that we're all half-awake! And your reason for being down here better be good, or else your butt will soon be poison ivy weeds!" Eurassisgras predicted.

"Well men; here's what I kind of finally figured-out," Eurshiddenme commenced with his wholly disheveled preface. "Although neither Zeus nor Hermes were ever down to Earth gods, the pair were having a serious conversation about how to evaluate humans down here on Earth."

"This is probably the last time I'll ever listen to one of your dumb-shit demands," Eurcockisnum grieved. "I'm always in the dark without ever before being down here inside this fucked-up, pitch-black tunnel!"

"We must show the crazy humans that we are essentially 'down-to-earth' guys once in a while," all-powerful Zeus reminded Hermes, the mischievous messenger god, as the two deities were ambling through a patch of forest in Phrygia. "I'm really fuckin' tired of watching those big-breasted Graces and Muses doing couch-dancing in my face. Now Hermes, let's try to act meek, meager and ordinary for a change, rather than hedonistic and fucked-up like we normally do! Sometimes, my dear Messenger, *we* must attempt setting a good example for those irascible assholes residing down here on Earth. The mentally-deficient numbskulls will hypnotically imitate our behavior as if they were ordinary, mimicking monkeys."

"I fully concur My Lord," Hermes amiably agreed. "So, it's nice that once in a blue moon we disguise ourselves as mendicant suppliants, and rub shoulders with mortal riffraff, just to see if the rabble lowlife still worships us. And don't forget, almighty Zeus; we have to shrink-down from fifty-foot-tall to *their* diminutive height before we fuckin' indiscriminately encounter any mortals; clever disguises or no damned clever disguises!"

"That's a great practical idea Hermes. You tend to have many pedestrian ideas when we walk together," Zeus commended and endorsed. "That way, as you have just so sagely suggested, our irritated and enlarged hemorrhoids will also shrink-down, just like our fifty-foot-tall bodies!"

"This story better get better, or you might never again see the sunlight on the other side of the grass, er, I mean desert!" Eurdicisin threatened. 'Truthfully, Eurshiddenme. You need to go to primary storytelling school and earn a diploma!"

"Stop being so impetuous and presumptuous! Let me' finish with the introductory characters and setting descriptions," agitated Eurshiddenme angrily retorted. "Now then; Hermes was indeed the most cunning and creative of the great gods. The winged-footed deity had suggested to his superior Zeus that the two should show-up in Phrygia, to investigate how receptive and hospitable the natives would be to *their* visiting-but-anonymous Olympus guests."

"You sound like a parrot constantly repeating yourself," Eurassisgras criticized the already-harassed speaker. "Pretty soon you'll be reiterating, 'My ass hurts! My ass hurts', hundreds of times, over and over again."

"Ya' know Hermes," Zeus indicated as the chief deity glanced at his pleasant peasant's garb that had instantly replaced his rich robe. "I want to see exactly how the mortals over here in Asia Minor are honoring my controversial Law of the Suppliants. If you recollect, all god-fearing mortals should…"

"Should give food, shelter and good cheer to traveling visitors, because luxurious lodges designated for travelers haven't been invented yet," Hermes interrupted his moody supreme boss. "According to *your* fine law, Master Zeus, all human itinerants must be treated with courtesy and dignity, even if they're wandering bandits, scoundrels, terrorists, or robbers; or else, the derelict homeowners not honoring your law will be visited by an earthquake, or perhaps a devastating tidal wave, or maybe wind-up having high-voltage lightning bolts flying up their targeted tender butt-holes."

"We'll wander through the pathetic land where other strange local gods compete for the humans' loyalties," Zeus summarized to his more jovial colleague. "Yes, dear Hermes. We'll knock on each door and request food and lodging, and if we don't get expected cooperation, then…"

"Then Phrygia will be destroyed out of *your* arbitrary spite, and the land will be left to the other fuckin' obscure, indigenous gods to fuckin' worry about," the immortal courier finished.

"For your lucky benefit, your myth is getting a trifle better," Eurassisgras, out of character, complimented Eurshiddenme. "At this rate, you might just make it breathing and living until dawn appears tomorrow morning on the eastern horizon!"

"At every stop, the two nomadic guests were savagely cursed-out, treated with belligerent insolence, and greeted with cruel defiance, and *that* hostile rejection had occurred at least three-hundred-times, for the outlandish natives were pragmatic pagans, heathens, and cynical atheistic realists. The obnoxious Phrygians generally worshiped sex and perversion, much more than the natives honored impractical, arrogant, and egotistical foreign and local gods and goddesses, along with the Olympus gods' stupid and inflexible laws, decrees, and bullshit edicts."

"Almost completely frustrated, totally mortified, and virtually out of patience, the noble dual *Olympus* travelers decided to try one more home before taking-out their mutual wraths upon the barbaric Phrygian cave and shanty dwellers. Finally, Zeus and Hermes arrived at a remote shack situated all by itself in the countryside, because the already-scorned husband and wife occupants had been evicted and ostracized from the nearest city's numerous ghettoes and barrios."

"I would rather have my bouncing balls pieced by a Trojan spear than to hear any more of your dumb-fuck drivel," Eurcockisnum protested to Eurshiddenme. "I can never get a decent erection whenever listening to your fake bullshit!"

"After Zeus angrily knocked on the shack's splintery door, the pair were greeted by a cheerful male voice and courteously invited inside the raunchy, ramshackle abode. An elderly, thin gent with a long grizzly beard, instructed the wayfarers to sit-down upon the only hard 'bench', which was normally reserved for unethical area judges and magistrates that occasionally showed-up at the old man's door cold and lost, asking for directions to King Midas's ornate palace, or how to find the nearest Phrygian cemetery."

"Where are ya' odd-looking strangers from?" the aged man's old-looking wrinkled wife asked. "We haven't had any visitors in these parts for over fifty years. As you already can tell, kind sirs, my husband Philemon and I live way out here in the god-forsaken boondocks, far beyond this accursed country's damned hinterlands and dangerous cities."

"What's your name old woman?" the omniscient Zeus inquired just for the sake of polite conversation. "I'll have to enter it into my secret black date book!"

"It's Baucis," the old dame answered. "And my husband Philemon's two unfortunate brothers, Philharmonic and Philanthropic, were both philosophical philanderers that died from phlebitis over in Philadelphia, that ghetto town between here and Egypt. Now guys," Eurshiddenme continued. "Philemon's two idiot brothers always treated rare visitors to their homes with indignity and with violence. And consequently, both of Baucis's fucked-up brothers-in-law were punished by the gods with clogged arteries and with super-clogged sperm ducts. "Shit, kind sirs," Baucis elaborated to the weird-looking guests. "Philharmonic and Philanthropic were both glad that they were about to die from blood clots, and not from excruciating painful sperm clots inside their rotting-away crotches!"

"Baucis and I have always been cooperative with the gods' capricious laws, ever since the dreadful demise of Philharmonic and Philanthropic," Philemon added to his wife's testimony. "And neither of us want our assholes cauterized by some errant high-voltage lightning bolts, or by some lacerating molten lava shooting and squirting-up our sensitive, withered anuses. That's why we so eagerly answered our door this afternoon," the old codger explained to shrunken-down guests Zeus and Hermes. "Ya' never know when a crazy pair of Greek *Olympus* wanderers will visit your humble dump for an unannounced, impromptu inspection, ha, ha, ha!"

"For the sake of our morale," Eurdicisin bitched to Eurshiddenme, "does this fucked-up story have a moral? Please proceed before my eyes close, and a number of *zs* start floating out of my mouth!"

"Do you two folks enjoy living way out here in abject poverty in the middle of nowhere?" Hermes curiously inquired. "If I had to live in a dirty shithouse like this one apparently is, I'd simultaneously contemplate blindness, insanity, starvation and a most-welcomed suicide."

"We are very poor as your keen eyes can determine," Philemon verified. "But Baucis and I have blithe spirits that rejoice whenever we recall and discuss the great sex life that we had shared six decadent decades ago. Our passion used to be hotter than the ashes and embers now-burning inside our modest fireplace," the decrepit husband explained. "Let me fan the flames on the hearth so that I may distribute more warmth for the four of us occupants to share. All I ever dream about, kind strangers, is growing and maintaining a nice stiff erection, and planting the throbbing mother into a young Baucis's wet pink love tunnel. Those fond memories perpetually haunt my flagging spirit. But unfortunately," poor Philemon continued his sorrowful monologue, "her honey-well now is dryer than the barren Phrygian desert out there, and even more regrettably, I haven't popped a decent load in almost a non-fuckin', pussy-pumpin', fuckin' century!"

"Now, my fellow lieutenants, I have to mention that Baucis's water kettle was beginning to boil and steam. Soon, the wife poured the container's contents into a pot of common cabbage, which had been selected from the couple's sparse garden. "*Let' us* be good friends and eat this boiled cabbage when it soon will be ready to consume and digest," Baucis suggested to her fully-amused visitors. "I'll stir the pot with a piece of pork that's hanging-down from that termite-infested, decaying beam up there. I stare at that fabulous piece of pork every morning, wishing that it was a young Philemon's hard erection ready for some important bed action. But alas, gentle guests; my aged husband now has a tiny rat's dick that looks like it belongs on a friggin' chipmunk!"

"Then guys; Baucis methodically set the table with her gnarled arthritic hands that shook and exhibited an advanced case of Parkinson's disease, and next the afflicted woman used a broken plate as a shim under one of the shorter bench legs, because the attached picnic table had contracted a nasty case of polio in its youth. And finally, the old domesticated dame set some olives, carrots, and turnips upon the rickety old table, along with several eggs that she had been saving for hungry area 'poachers'. Appalled Zeus and Hermes were then invited to sample the horrible food, and to flourish in the poor couple's genuine hospitality inside the dilapidated framed home that itself would have served a better purpose as winter kindling wood."

"Get to the essential theme and plot," Eurballsourout objected to Eurshiddenme. "I had seriously studied advanced literature in kindergarten, and your lackluster story is about as interesting as me committing suicide twice. And honestly, Eurshiddenme; your wholly mediocre unholy tale is akin to someone saying that sour dough tastes better than dildo!"

"Please accept this wine in wooden bowls. I apologize that its foul flavor tastes like sour vinegar," Philemon offered his incognito-but-neato distinguished guests. "I wish I had better vintage to offer you two weird vagabond travelers, and I hope my dirt-clogged ears do not hear any sour grapes originating from the lips of either of you two strange-looking freeloaders. I sincerely trust that you two peculiar-looking gentlemen are enjoying our heartfelt hospitality."

"This is the best damned fuckin' wine I've ever tasted, either being sober or drunk," Zeus commended his poverty-stricken hosts. "And may Dionysus bless your rural asses with a productive grape harvest in years to come. In fact, I believe that this rancid shit will kill every radical germ and bacteria thriving inside my whole friggin' body. And if it makes me piss vinegar," the king-god remarked, "then I'll definitely urinate into a decanter and celebrate you Philemon, and your wrinkled-faced wife, as both of you being real pissers!"

"Baucis and Philemon stared incredulously at each other when the pair noticed that no matter how much their' thirsty visitors and they drank, that the wine bottle incredibly remained full and undiminished in liquid volume. Then, the toothless host and the incontinent hostess stared at each other in utter astonishment, fully realizing that their gregarious guests were indeed visiting immortals of the highest magnitude. Both mortals dropped to their knees in adoration of the two traveling *Olympus* itinerants, apparently masquerading as common wayfaring bums."

"Kind sirs," Philemon timidly stated as the host's astonished eyes squinted and finally observed Hermes's shrunken winged sandals. "Baucis and I have a goose stashed-away that my wife would gladly prepare for you. I'll attempt to catch it if you would like to observe and be humored by my awkward frivolity. I mean, My Lords," Philemon stuttered and paused. "My whole pathetic life has been one vast wild-goose-chase in pursuit of wealth, pleasure, decent and indecent pornography, and other idiotic, sinful, earthly nonsense that you gods matter-of-factly enjoy all the fuckin' time."

"That's perfectly all right, old man," Hermes indulgently laughed. "We don't want to sit here all night and watch your quack wife suck-on your skinny bird. Just the thought of such a gross sight makes me want to split my gut while laughing my ass off, before vomiting my guts out! Geriatric sex would be too much raucous entertainment for my weak heart to ever endure," the great messenger god confided. "I might then become the first fuckin' giddy immortal to ever die laughing, and wind-up going to that very notorious University of the Dead, *Hades Hall*. Ha, ha, ha, ha!"

"It sounds like Philemon's aged dick is as big as Eurcockisnum's shriveled pecker!" Eurdicisin said and then laughed. "Call the army medical patrol because Eurcockisnum needs a stretcher, right now! This whole scenario is entirely too rich to tolerate! Ha, ha, ha!"

Ignoring Eurdicisin's mocking of Eurcockisnum's miniature manhood, Eurshiddenme proceeded with his wholly ludicrous narrative. "Zeus then said, you two mediocre and ridiculous senior citizens, who already look like walking zombies, have been wonderfully generous hosts to me and to my dear companion Hermes," the chief god sincerely declared with a thankful smile. "I shall prodigiously reward you two hapless adult dolts for your wonderful acceptance of a pair of wayward travelers into your pathetic abode, that doesn't even have an outhouse in which to take a freakin' healthy dump."

"What do you intend to do to the remainder of sinful Phrygia, Lord Zeus?" Baucis curiously asked. "Do I have to go through damned menopause again with the other transgender males and regular females? What a lot of bloody bullshit that messy business was!"

"The wicked inhabitants of your bizarre country shall be severely and *amply* punished for their blatant violation of my sacred laws, and also for their audacious mistreatment of Hermes and me," Zeus promised the elderly couple. "Those antagonistic and repulsive assholes will be deluged with the biggest catastrophe of their fucked-up lives."

"*Amp*ly punished usually means Lord Zeus administering high-voltage electric lightning volts up the old asshole," Hermes reminded his flabbergasted mortal listeners. "Your aberrant Phrygian countrymen back in the city and town ghettoes and barrios will then think that they've become ancient Ass-Searians! Ha, ha, ha, ha!"

"Look over there at yonder fireplace!" Hermes pointed his index finger and directed the quivering old couple. "Your goose is cooked! Ha, ha, ha!"

"This story better be getting to its dead end, or you will be, too!" Eurballsourout said to Eurshiddenme, even though the lieutenant's balls were out, but couldn't be observed by his three companions inside the dark tunnel.

"Zeus opened the shack's squeaky door, brushed some active termites from his hands, and escorted the other three occupants outside. Amazingly, the king-god and Hermes instantly shot-up to their normal fifty-foot-tall height. Baucis and Philemon trembled to their knees in sheer supplication of the show-off Olympus deities. And when the elderly couple stared in all directions, the two penitent paupers frightfully observed that a gigantic flood had just devastated Phrygia in all four directions of the knoll upon which their' deteriorating house had been crudely constructed eighty years before. The visibly distraught pair wept for their' old age, and cried-out loud utterances, vehemently protesting to the majestic, radiant gods that the elderly couple had not also been drowned in the terrible calamity that Zeus had maliciously and vindictively caused upon baneful Phrygia."

"And as the bleary-eyed old duo perceived their hands, feet and each other's faces, all of their ugly wrinkles had miraculously disappeared, and Baucis's visage was once again young and beautiful, and her rejuvenated slit hole was now a bright pink and sporting well-lubricated walls; and finally, her crotch again looked like a decent healthy brown bush."

"Now your obnoxious tale is finally reaching its climax," Eurassisgras commented with a sigh of relief. "Honestly Eurshiddenme; I hope that Philemon's body explodes into flesh fragments from having his erect pecker erupt in a wild, volcanic-type sperm orgasm!"

"Philemon looked-down and was delighted to see a large bulge sticking-out from his newly acquired, rich-looking, embroidered tunic. The two old farts immediately passionately embraced, lowered their newly-acquired young bodies to the wet ground, and wildly screwed like horny lions in heat for three consecutive hours. And while the two were euphorically humping and pumping and changing positions like there was no tomorrow, their decrepit old shack magically transformed from shambles into a splendid marble mansion, featuring a magnificent golden roof, with a large quacking, non-edible, silver goose at its summit.

"Good fucked-up people. I have sympathetically provided you with youth and with a fine home, simply because you've shown noteworthy respect for us, the disguised omnipotent gods," Zeus, the accomplished voyeur, related as he and Hermes ascended into the sky. "And I shall now form a shrine with large marble pillars, and send the two of you off to a distant future place called *Temple University* to study and learn to be my official priest and priestess in this fucked-up land of Phrygia, or what's left of Phrygia. And please remember, humble hosts," the supreme deity emphasized while partially hidden behind several cottony clouds. "All future incantations and chants to Hermes and me must be played and sung exclusively in the key of Asia Minor. Now, do you two raunchy, incompetent, lucky imbeciles have any further requests before my immortal, illustrious companion and I zoom back-up to eternal *Mt. Olympus?*"

"Why, indeed yes!" Philemon affirmatively answered and yelled-up with his hands forming a sort of megaphone in front of his now-vernal mouth. "I don't want to live forever and then have to be thoroughly bored to death like you two pedestrian immortal assholes obviously are! With that remarkable remark being truthfully said, I would prefer that once Baucis and I enjoy each other's company and our new-found prosperity on our second splendid chance at married life," Philemon solemnly indicated to Zeus and Hermes, "please grant that we may both die and be united as one soul immediately after the next miserable century commences."

"Zeus enthusiastically acceded and quickly and benignly granted the old gent's unusual request. Not one pilgrim, lost or otherwise, ever accidentally or purposefully visited the sensational white marble temple and accompanying pillared mansion during the next hundred years. After an eighty-year-tenure as appointed custodians of the recently formed temple, which was conveniently situated next to the exquisite white marble mansion, the second-time-around, the old odd couple finally, mutually and sadly, died locked in a tender embrace."

"Until death descended, the dumb-fucks did depart together," Eurballsourout concluded, breathing a sigh of satisfaction. "But I was hoping that Zeus and Hermes somehow had died and not those freaky mortals Philemon and Baucis."

"But instead of turning into gruesome bony skeletons, Baucis and Philemon had an unusual bark miraculously form around their human remains, and Philemon's body became an oak tree, and Baucis's corpse coincidentally transformed into a linden, so that remarkably, their symbiosis grew from the exact same entwined roots, because Zeus and Hermes were still *rooting* for the pair up on *Mt. Olympus.*"

"So, what does that fucked-up, bullshit story of yours actually in essence symbolically mean?" dumbfounded and befuddled Eurcockisnum asked Eurshiddenme. "It all sounds like a crock of phony-baloney religious propaganda to me!"

"It simply means that the great gods of Olympus are extremely fickle and unpredictable, but sometimes, the omnipotent nutcases may enter into your life unexpectedly, and in so doing, fortuitously confer upon you your deepest wishes and desires; that is, if you had faithfully and religiously worshipped and revered them in your prayers and in your sacrifices!"

* * * * * * * * * * * *

That night, Menelaus noticed Agamemnon standing atop the wall that the Greeks had constructed for the purpose of thwarting a direct, massive enemy assault on their campfires.

"What besides your two legs has you standing up there?" Menelaus asked Agamemnon. "Are you trying to get closer to the gods in Heaven?"

"I'm so damned depressed about the possibility that the reprehensible Trojans are about to raid and conquer our various camps, that the very thought of such a major catastrophe has me climbing the walls!"

"What should we do?" Menelaus asked his older brother. "Build the ten-foot-high wall ten-feet higher?"

"No, but my troubled mind has conceived a certain viable plan," Agamemnon shared his design with his red-bearded brother. "Immediately contact the army generals, and we'll have an important conference where I shall divulge my latest brainstorm to my key officers."

At the hastily-arranged meeting, Agamemnon addressed his already-dubious unhappy campers. "I'm worried that Hector and his fanatical Trojans are going to push our defenses back to the sea, and then set our anchored Biremes ablaze," the dejected King confidentially told him grim-faced commanders. "We should strive to cut the Trojans' feet off at the ankles, because I'm extremely concerned that they're about to kick our asses right off of our friggin' anatomies!"

"Yes, my sagacious King," Nestor agreed, nodding his aged head. "The enemy has become smug and complacent, and Hector and his lunatic minions need to have an element of terror instilled into their psyches. What particular action do you propose?"

"From what I can observe and rationally decipher, my dear officers, Zeus now favors Hector and Paris over us," Menelaus interrupted and added to the discussion in a melancholy tone of voice. "What sort of counter-stratagem does your' demonic character have in mind?" the King of Sparta asked the King of Mycenae, inadvertently reiterating Nestor's prior entreaty.

"I hereby command that I will select two of you subordinates to venture into the fringe of the Trojan camp and conduct a surprise foray upon the unwary enemy troops," the expedition leader ordered. "Now all of you dimwits raise your right hands, and I'll randomly chose one from amongst you as the raid's reconnaissance commander."

"I'll gladly volunteer for this crucial commando mission, and I would like to choose brave Odysseus as my trustful accomplice," Diomedes clearly declared. "The incomparable King of Ithaca is demonstrably shrewd in difficult battle situations, and my trustworthy comrade is always cool as a squash, er, I meant to say 'cool as an encumbered-cucumber'. And besides," Diomedes added. "Odysseus has the support and protection of Pallas Athene, and quite possibly, I might be shielded by her awesome powers, also! I would, without question or doubt, follow Odysseus through towering fences of fire, desperately searching for some old flames of ours!"

"No need for flattery and other associated phony bullshit," Odysseus chided Diomedes. "The evening is two-thirds expired, so let's get started on initiating our surprise foray."

The pair of spy-scouts stealthily set-out to the east on foot, and in an hour, reached the perimeter of the Trojan encampment. Every Achaean captain waited impatiently for news of what the enemy was planning to enact. Then, feeble Nestor, who had a severe hearing impairment, heard the galloping of horses approaching from the east.

"Is that sound my ears perceive Diomedes and Odysseus triumphantly coming, or is it the sound of Trojan chariots encroaching onto our beachhead?"

The two courageous scouts soon came into the view of the Greek's blazing torches, and the pair were immediately recognized by the jubilant, cheering Achaean generals.

"Where did you get such beautiful white stallions attached to this fabulous jewel-studded chariot?" Agamemnon marveled and asked his valiant spies. "Did they belong to Paris or Pandarus?"

"No!" Odysseus answered from his high position upon the chariot's platform. "These phenomenal steeds had just arrived from Trace, an enemy ally of Troy. Diomedes and I had confiscated them after entering a brief conflict with several inebriated Tracian guards."

"We killed a dozen of the intoxicated bastards along with their disoriented drunken king," Diomedes added as the murderer threw a guard's severed head upon the desert sand.

"And two heads are better than one!" Odysseus exclaimed as the Ithacan champion tossed a second guard's decapitated head at the sandaled feet of King Agamemnon.

Chapter 11

"THE GREEKS FACE DISASTER"

Eris, who had intentionally rolled the golden apple on the marble floor at Peleus and Thetis's wedding, which had initiated the famous beauty contest between Aphrodite, Athena and Hera, was again active in inspiring the Achaeans with new-found courage, and with using her great power of suggestion, compelled the vulnerable-minded Danaans to forget all about voyaging-back to their native lands. Motivated by Eris, also known as 'Strife' or 'Discord', the following morning the rejuvenated Greeks, led by compulsive Agamemnon, marched forward to battle the Trojans upon the Troad Non-Fruitive Plain.

Imitating his principal Achaean foe, namely Achilles, Agamemnon had organized the current charge against the enemy front lines, riding upon his stately chariot that was being pulled by two powerful gray horses. Stimulated by a massive adrenaline rush, the insane Greek leader had managed to execute a wicked assault that had successfully infiltrated the Trojan front line, killing and trampling several dozen disposable opponents who had been obstructing his soldiers' advance, dying with *their* failed efforts at defending a makeshift wooden barrier.

But during the incursion, Almighty Zeus, keenly examining the ongoing action upon his magical gameboard, dispatched the fleet-footed Rainbow Goddess, Iris, with a message specifically earmarked for Hector's ear. "Stay back, Hector while Agamemnon slaughters all unfortunate Trojans in front of you. Yell for your men to keep-on battling, and their horses to keep-on dancing and a-prancing. But according to Zeus's command," Iris softly whispered, "if and when the God of Thunder decides that Agamemnon should be injured, and subsequently speeds back to his lines in his jeweled chariot, then Hector, you should swiftly advance forward and drive the insidious invaders back to their anchored sleek black ships."

"Agamemnon managed to callously kill several lieutenants among the recently-arrived Trojan ranks originating from Thrace, but in so doing, the obsessed king received a hard spear thrust to his curiass, which to curious asses reading this chronicle, is located in front of the warrior's plated loin-guard. And although minorly wounded near his crotch, crotchety Agamemnon, pretending that he was Achilles, also suffered a second blow that had punctured the skin below his right elbow. With one quick swoop of his bronze sword, the Greek leader deftly decapitated the enemy soldier Iphidamas, brother of Givadamis, who as a result of losing his head, could no longer neck with either his wife or his slutty girlfriend, nor lose his head over any other whoring piece of ass.

Feeling dizzy from the extreme loss of blood, Agamemnon commanded Odysseus to continue the battle, as the possessed and injured king drove his gray horses and chariot back to the Achaean lines. Immediately, Hector, remembering Iris's message from Zeus, spontaneously swung into the fray, ferociously killing a dozen Greek warriors in his path.

During the frenzied melee, Odysseus's five zany lieutenants developed a unique survival plan where Eurshiddenme, Eurballsourout, Eurassisgras, Eurdicisin, and Eurcockisnum formed an irregular circle and began slamming and smashing their bronze swords against each other's raised shields, pretending to be frenetically parrying heavy blows against attacking Trojans.

"Hand me your knife," Eurballsourout demanded to Eurassisgras, "so that I can scrape its dull blade against my left wrist and create a minor gash. Then, I'll make another small cut above my right thigh."

"I'll do the same thin slashes to myself," Eusassisgras nervously answered his nutcase colleague. "These superficial cuts will be our scarlet badges of cowardice, er, I meant to say, 'of courage'."

"Let me have your blade after you're through harmlessly penetrating your epidermises," Eurdicisin requested of Eurcockisnum and of Eurassisgras. "But I gotta' make sure I don't sever any artery or vein!"

*"Suit your*self if you happen to slice through your thin skin too deeply!" Eurdicisin inadvertently punned. "I'm no damned surgeon, so don't expect me to sew your gashes back together! I mean, my mother had amnesia and never taught me how to knit-one, purl two! And quite frankly, I only know how to stitch together my flimsy loin cloth, but I never mastered how to mend a fractured femur or a fountain-like, hemorrhaging asshole with exploding hemorrhoids!"

"I think you four worthless dumb-dicks are totally daft!" Eurshiddenme assessed and exclaimed above the clamor erupting all around them. "You' stupid, weirdo shits must take hour-long meteor showers every damned friggin' morning!"

Diomedes and Odysseus, fully engaged in real combat, were unaware of the ridiculous ruse being perpetrated by the Ithacan king's nearby five stooge-like lieutenants, and the dueling dual Greek dynamos were dynamic killing machines, mowing-down Trojans with their trusty blades as if the enemy soldiers were thin blades of grass. But then Paris shot an arrow at Diomedes that grazed the Achaean hero's foot, which compelled the aggressor to challenge the craven Trojan prince to man-to-man combat.

But Odysseus's five dumb-dick lieutenants, still feigning dueling with imaginary Trojan warriors, stumbled atop a hill, and rolled and tumbled down the steep embankment, hitting into both Diomedes and Paris; the double collisions had knocked the prospective duelers plopping onto the desert sand. Becoming lost in the general frenzy and fog of war, Diomedes could not discover Paris's location, and vice versa, Paris had lost track of incensed Diomedes.

However, during the myriad in-progress altercations, Odysseus had been superficially wounded above the groin, immediately suffering a 'my groin' headache, as blood rushed from the champion's head down-toward his abdomen, thus making the Ithacan king very groggy and disoriented. "Which way is China?" delirious Odysseus loudly yelled to bewildered Menelaus. "I only wish that my five valiant lieutenants were here to rescue my embattled ass from the Chinese antagonists!"

Menelaus, demonstrating a degree of humanity and compassion, carried unconscious Odysseus to his chariot, but then Ajax, fiercely crippling Trojan after Trojan, grudgingly retreated back in the direction and relative safety of the Achaean camp. The colossal giant was soon joined by Odysseus's five conniving lieutenants, whom Ajax instinctively praised, after noting that the five mischievous scoundrels were bleeding from their wrists, arms and thighs.

"Did you brave fellows kill many Trojans today?" Ajax innocently inquired. "We need to steal a couple of their head-covering, suffocating prophylactics, and then figure-out the precise materials from which those bizarre smothering weapons are manufactured!"

"Too many victims to ever count on a common, unsophisticated abacus!" Eurshiddenme fibbed and alertly replied in regard to his slaughtering prowess. "Maybe tomorrow, our inimitable captain King Odysseus, will provide us with a competent statistician to keep an accurate record of our' combined total number of brutal slayings!"

"You men need to get a good night's sleep," Ajax boomed to the five inane, lying lieutenants. "Tomorrow you'll have to go into battle and get rolling again!" the massive giant inadvertently and coincidentally stated to Odysseus's main officers. 'I predict that tomorrow, our crucial battle will finally be downhill!"

* * * * * * * * * * * *

While the intense conflict was reaching its crescendo, Achilles was astutely watching the battle's termination from the stern of his anchored Bireme, all the while observing the Troad Plain with his personal bodyguard, Patroclus from Iolcus. "Look over to your right!" Achilles verbally indicated and pointed. "That apparently-wounded old coot looks like my elderly friend Machaon, riding in one of Nestor's chariots on fire. Go and see if my eyes are correct in their suspect visual acuity!"

Five minutes later, Nestor was preoccupied in his tent conversing with Machaon, with both Generals sitting inside the Pylos king's flimsy enclosure, drinking potent wine to restore their already-expended energy. "Welcome long-lost Patroclus!" Nestor politely greeted the new arrival. "Come into my humble headquarters and share some delicious vino with us! Let us merrily reminisce our past convivial camaraderie!"

"I cannot stay too long bullshitting with you two old farts," Patroclus unpatriotically apologized to doddering and dementia-stricken, feeble Nestor and Machaon. "Achilles has dispatched me to see if you, Machaon, had been near-fatally injured. Now that I've comprehensively evaluated the obvious situation, I believe that I should immediately return to my superior's headquarters, where Achilles and I are scheduled to receive from kinky-sluts quality head in his headquarters. What I mean, Nestor, is that our privates will no longer be private!"

"I don't understand the thinking of your fucked-up General Achilles," Nestor confided to the unexpected visitor. "Hundreds of his countrymen have been seriously maimed and wounded today; Odysseus, Diomedes and Agamemnon, to name just a few. Yet your boss Achilles is solely concerned with my healer friend Machaon, who has not been injured as badly as the others have!" Nestor maintained. "What the hell is your comrade waiting for? Is your superior waiting for our ships being all in flame with their crews inside being cremated and incinerated? Does Achilles wish to see our entire army being decimated and obliterated? If only I were a young stud again," Nestor genuinely confided. "I would first show the troops a tent full of naked whores; promise them to be rewarded with any kind of hot sex that they might desire, and then lead the ready-and-willing assholes into the center of the glorious fight!"

"Nestor is perfectly right in his thinking!" Machaon logically confirmed. "As an unorthodox doctor, I can verify that sex, either straight or gay, is usually the best motivational medicine! And also," Machaon eloquently elaborated. "I'm frantically afraid that the enemy soldiers are getting stronger and more muscular, and that we wimpy Greeks are becoming weaker in both strength and size. I believe that we should re-examine our consumption of meat, fruit, vegetables, milk, and grain, because in my professional opinion, in regard to dietary matters, my regiment needs a new nutritional regimen."

"Patroclus, do you recollect the morning when Odysseus and I came to your city to recruit your ass into this fucked-up war?" Nestor asked his fellow Greek. "We had promised you a toy sex doll to sleep with at night, and it has been generously provided to you. Now then; your mentor Achilles is half immortal, with his mother being the sea-goddess Thetis, and he was his mother's cherished fetus after being her precious embryo. But you, Patroclus, are a few years older than your arrogant commander, and hopefully, a few years wiser, too."

"What are you driving at, even though your obsolete chariot is parked outside?" Patroclus irately questioned aged Nestor. "Now then, old fart! When you were a much younger stud and were about to have hot sex, did you then also beat around the bush as you do now? Get to the fuckin' point, you wrinkly old pinhead!"

"I think that if Achilles stays stubborn and refuses to lead the Myrmidons into the fray, then you should step-up and do so, because I believe that you, noble Patroclus, are equally qualified in terms of courage and ability. If your master conveniently lent you his armor, then the apprehensive Trojans, thinking that you were your invincible commander, would stick corks up their asses to stop their diarrhea discharges, and automatically start dashing the other way!"

"Consider heeding Nestor's impeccable words," Machaon cleverly advised. "Knuckle-down, Patroclus, and put your finger on the basic problem! Our in-jeopardy lives are now solely in *your* hands, and not in those treasonous palms of your unscrupulous commander, your seditious, pithy, Achilles of Phthia!"

After ambling out of Nestor's headquarters in a rather-confused and addled state of mind, Patroclus encountered and addressed an old trusted acquaintance. "Eurypylus, you old goat. Is this the day that Hector trounces and defeats the Danaans? Are the Greeks doomed to imminent disaster? Will future generations be reading about the Argives' impending demise in their various library Archives? Will Pallas Athene lose her coveted virginity to her acknowledged hero, Odysseus of Ithaca?"

"There's no salvation, Patroclus, neither in this despicable war nor in our fucked-up religion!" Eurypylus tersely and succinctly answered. "But if you can render us even a tiny bit of marginal aid, without engaging in actual fighting, then your' welcomed assistance would be vastly appreciated. Confidentially, most of our best surgeons have recently been somewhat mauled and mutilated on the Troad," Eurypylus disclosed. "And I understand from hearsay, and it behooves me to say, that you possess certain healing ability that had been acquired from the reputable drug experimenter, Chiron the Centaur, who never horsed-around when it came to administering medicine and dispensing both legal and illegal drugs!"

"Friend, Eurypylus; you've somewhat appealed to my sense of national pride, so if no direct fighting is involved, out of sheer empathy for my fellow Achaeans, I shall accede to your benign request and help bandage the fallen wounded, and also as a bonus, I'll perform rudimentary surgery on several of your officers!"

While Patroclus was skillfully practicing his physician skills, the Trojans were attacking the Greek front line with tremendous ferocity. The Achaeans desperately fought-back out of survival necessity, but the dedicated enemy used ladders to clamber-up the long wall that the Achaeans had crudely constructed, and then tossed spears and small rocks at the targeted Argive troops below.

Ajax, after drinking three gallons of potent wine that had been 'deported' from Sicily, met and slayed his rival match, the giant Sarpedon, who had earlier drunk six gallons of 'deported' Sicilian wine. And so, the ensuing conflict reached its culmination, with neither side establishing any observable advantage.

Being inspired by Zeus, Hector lifted-up a five-hundred-pound boulder and flung the huge stone at the central gate inside the Achaean wall, and the enormous rock crashed through the wooden portal, with hundreds of screaming Trojans soon quickly rushing through the opening to confront the startled Greeks, who, including Eurassisgras, each soldier fearing that *his* tender ass was about to be grass.

Chapter 12
"BATTLE AT THE BARRICADE"

"Okay, junior jerk-offs. I have one more plume in my helmet than any of you deranged nutcases have, and that single feather makes me higher in rank than you four non-Cretan cretins," Eurshiddenme redressed his apathetic lieutenant peers. "This additional red plume is irrefutable evidence that you retards have to listen to me."

"So, why the hell are we again meeting down here in the forbidden gay, lesbian, trans-gender, tri-sexual dark tunnel?" Eurballsourout requested knowing. "Are we finally gonna' be initiated and indoctrinated into the LBGTQRMSV community? I'm not thoroughly-convinced that I want to go down that perverted-sex avenue!"

"No, asshole! I'll venture to guess that even Eurassisgras knows more about Greek culture and about our peculiar religion than you do. We're gathered down here this hallowed evening because I have to tell you that King Odysseus's Cunt Tree Shrine is not the only smelly, stench-laden cunt tree in Greece."

"Well then, where are the others?" Eurdicisin wondered and asked. "I could spend an entire day climbing its limbs and branches, just randomly fuckin' around! When this fucked-up war is over, if I'm still alive, I'll take an advanced course in tree-climbing at the Ithacan Arbor University!"

"Yeah! Good idea!" equally moronic Eurcockisnum piped-up. "If I could find one of those cunt trees out in the country, I might be able to overcome my erectile dysfunction and get my first hard-on since I entered puberty."

"All right, you mentally deficient dunces," Eurshiddenme evaluated and stated. "I'm going to tie the four of you' assholes together down here in the secret tunnel, because it seems that you four nutjobs have already spent your whole freakin' lives in the friggin' dark. Then, I'll stuff four separate gags into your individual mouths, so that I don't have to listen to your perverted prattle interrupting my scholarly mythological presentation. Now, if you four numbskulls keep quiet and cooperate, then I promise that I'll hire four highly-skilled prostitutes to give you extremely satisfying blowjobs that will blow-away any other fellatio that you fellas' have ever received at any state-sponsored bordello or brothel."

The four, empty-brained, ludicrous, sex-starved lieutenants quickly considered Eurshiddenme's intriguing proposition, and simultaneously agreed to be tethered together, and mutually gagged, to again mentally suffer through another obscure, dumb-ass myth lecture, in order to later be rewarded by four registered government hookers administering four professionally administered blowjobs.

"Okay men; I'll now commence with my little informative symposium," Eurshiddenme began his academic myth seminar.

So, *this* tale that follows is the contrived, convoluted myth that Eurshiddenme recounted and related to his gagged and tied-up peers.

"Oedipus did not have eight, strange-looking arms like his deformed ugly older brother Octopus had grown. Octopus had been violently discarded and hurled into the sea, where he and his descendants have been dangerous denizens, molesters and on-the-prowl predators ever since. Oedipus was the great-great grandson of a cad named Cadmus, who was a great-great pain-in-the-ass, who was so fucked-up that the gods decided that all of his degenerate future generations, including Oedipus, should be doomed to suffer great hardship and adversity to make them even more fucked-up than they already were."

"King Laius of Thebes, who liked to get laid but had a bisexual wife that inexplicably had cement formed inside her atrophied vagina, was the third ruler of that dysfunctional ancient Greek city after Cadmus had reigned in Thebes. According to his regal family's fucked-up tradition, the royal pain-in-the-ass King Laius had married a distant cousin named Jocastra. Soon, Oedipus came under the influence of Apollo's Oracle at Delphi, which was far worse than being under the influence of drugs, tobacco, and alcohol. The Oracle actually fucked-up Oedipus even more than his fucked-up genetics had biologically fucked-up both his older brother Octopus and himself."

"Apollo was the renowned Greek god of music, medicine, legal and illegal drugs, and also of truth or consequences. The indecisive deity communicated with humans through his famous Oracle at Delphi, a lesbian priestess with a clitoris bigger than all five of her tits put together. Hearing a rumor about free sex, Laius had gone to the Oracle of Delphi to get laid, but when the pussy-hungry king discovered that the priestess was a practicing lesbian nymphomaniac with a clit bigger than his own erection, the dipshit monarch reluctantly asked the Oracle to tell him his future instead of engaging in regular sex."

"Laius, you will die at the hands of your younger son after you throw Octopus into the sea for good riddance," the totally gay, demented priestess predicted. "And you gotta' admit; throwing Octopus into the sea is much better than pissing into a strong wind!"

"How could that be?" Laius incredulously challenged the Oracle's omniscient prophecy. "Octopus is more likely to kill me with eight arms, and my human-in-appearance younger son Oedipus has only two arms. How then am I to die at the hands of Oedipus? I mean, I could just cut his damned hands off by creating a new 'Hands-off edict' in my totally bizarre kingdom of Thebes!"

"Apollo says that it's your fuckin' problem to solve, Asshole!" the faggot lady Oracle told Laius, who was now doubly disappointed because he couldn't get laid with his gay wife, who had mysteriously formed cement in her collapsed crotch, and now the livid king had learned that his younger son was, in the future, going to murder his deserving ass, right-off the friggin' planet."

"When King Laius had tossed Octopus into the sea one October morning, Oedipus was only a baby, but still not old enough to join the Theban infantry. Laius realized that close genetics indeed did have certain physical and psychological repercussions, and that the famous Greek maxim 'Incest is best!' might actually be a blatant fallacy."

"The Theban King soon began to worry. 'Octopus was genetically defective and looked like an absolute miniature monster,' Laius lamented while glancing into his favorite mirror. 'And now Oedipus looks all right physically, but the rambunctious child might be a fuckin' crazy lunatic. I gotta' dispose of the insane little bastard before the future assassin eliminates my happy, privileged existence from this deplorable Earth! My mother had always warned me to stay away from gloom and doom fortunetellers! Sometimes, I wish I weren't such a stupid, asinine jerk-off'!"

"Laius handed to a faithful servant the complex baby Oedipus to carry-off to a secluded high crag that was so distant that area mountain goats had not yet even discovered it. The obedient servant tied the infant's feet together, but did not have the heart to leave Laius's second son on the lonely precipice to die."

'I can socially engineer my future better than that homosexual dyke Oracle's predictions can,' Laius thought. 'By Zeus, her goddamned clitoris was twice as large as my biggest erection! That freakin' gay Oracle was more of a freakin' freak than my ugly son by incest Octopus was!'

"Twenty years later, King Laius arrived at a very important crossroads in his life. The Theban monarch and his traveling entourage of bisexual bodyguards got into an argument with a young punk' hooligan over the right-of-way at an intersection that was devoid of any "Stop Sign". The pugnacious hooligan leaped-out of his souped-up chariot, accosted Laius and his four intoxicated bodyguards, and after a vitriolic argument ensued, the punk whippersnapper first beat the shit out of, and then allegedly slaughtered the five adults with his birthday-gift bronze sword. The young thug murderer happened to be Oedipus, and by slaying his father, he had fulfilled Apollo's pathetic prophecy that had been forecast by the lesbian' Oracle at Delphi."

"A false rumor circulated around Thebes that an army from the city of Athens had slaughtered Laius and his loyal bodyguards. The heavy gossip thus glorified the former despicable, wimpy Theban king as a warrior and a martyr. However, one of the bodyguards had not died and had only been critically wounded. A traveling fruit and vegetable huckster had stopped his oxcart at the intersection, picked-up the sole survivor, and transported the lucky asshole to the crowded marketplace stalls in Thebes."

"Now, no one in Thebes, not even the king's wife Jocastra, gave a flying shit about Laius's cruel death, because the city was then being besieged by a very great threat. A monster that was known as 'the Sphinx' had been terrorizing and killing any Thebans that dared venture outside the city's southern gates. The Sphinx had a lion's body, eagle wings, a woman's face, a female elephant's tits and ass, and a gigantic clitoris even bigger than the one the Oracle at Delphi had."

"The venomous creature clandestinely hid in waiting and halted any traveler it confronted by surprise on his or her way to Thebes. The Sphinx presented the apprehended trekker with a ridiculous riddle, and when the unfortunate traveler could not give the correct response under great duress in a one-minute time period, the horrible creature ferociously devoured man after man alive, first sucking and then eating their throbbing dicks, and then chewing-up and swallowing the remainder of their predestined, doomed bodies, flesh, blood, sweat, tears, piss, shit and all."

"After Laius's funeral and burial had occurred, the seven great gates that allowed entrance into, and exit from Thebes, were permanently closed, and the citizens began suffering from severe famine and pestilence. Worse yet; the horrid Sphinx had devoured most of the Theban men, and consequently, Jocastra and the other promiscuous ladies of the accursed city became even bigger lesbians in the absence of eligible males than the fucked-up Oracle at Delphi ever was."

"Soon, a total stranger with exaggerated physical features similar to those of the deceased King Laius arrived at Thebes. The newcomer knocked-down one of the wooden gates and egotistically entered the isolated city. The intruder was intelligent, intrepid, obnoxious, arrogant and audacious. The brazen adolescent introduced himself' to the usually apathetic Theban citizens as Oedipus the Fifteenth from Corinth, son of entrepreneurial King Polybus, who owned several fleets of chariot and oxcart taxi cabs."

"I am in self-exile," Oedipus told his biological mother Jocastra outside the regal palace. "The Oracle at Delphi had told me that I was destined to kill my father, which oftentimes is not a bad idea for acne-faced teenagers like myself to consider."

"So, why have you come to Thebes, young stranger?" Jocastra asked her itinerant son Oedipus, whom she never recognized. "Aren't you afraid that the voracious Sphinx will consume you? She has a fuckin' edible complex about men, ya' know!"

"I didn't want to kill my father Polybus," Oedipus lied to his biological mother, "because I am a strict practicing heterosexual, and it is a myth in Corinth that Polybus eats from a magical cunt tree out in the country. If I was to savagely kill my father Polybus, then I could not ever learn exactly where this magical cunt tree out in the country actually is located!"

"I have planted a similar tree in the center of my palace bedroom," Jocastra confided and informed Oedipus, presuming that her son was dead. "But only my lady friends and I are allowed to eat the delicious fruit of the womb from my own fabulous cunt tree, which is most-certainly not out in the country!"

"Oedipus set-out on foot to walk from Thebes to Corinth to locate King Polybus's famed mythical cunt tree out in the country. On his wayward escapade, the tragic hero encountered the wicked detestable Sphinx, who then presented her singular riddle for the itinerant wanderer to solve in one minute's time."

"What creature walks on four legs in the morning, two at noon, and three appendages in the evening?" the monster nefariously asked the hero. 'You have *one minute* minute to provide the correct answer, or you will be reduced to rice grains!"

"That's a rather easy riddle, Bitch!" Oedipus confidently replied. "The answer obviously is 'a man'. As an infant, the child creeps and crawls on all fours, all over the fuckin' place; in manhood, the adult male walks erect, with or without an erection; and in old age, an elderly coot walks with his staff, and if he is poor and doesn't have any goddamned secretaries, the codger walks alone with his fuckin' cane without his fuckin' staff. What do ya' Sphinx about *that* extraordinary bullshit, you dumb fuckin' cocksuckin', riddling man-eater!"

"Oedipus had amazingly delivered the correct response to the monster's cryptic conundrum. The Sphinx was so pissed-off that she killed herself by biting-off her giant, swollen clitoris, and subsequently, bleeding to death, and finally plunging off of her cliff."

"Thanks to Oedipus's exceptional mental dynamics, the Thebans had become miraculously saved from their wretched nemesis. The jubilant numbskulls transported their new-found champion into the city and gave Oedipus an outstanding hero's welcome. The happy revelers roasted the disgusting dead creature in ancient grease, meticulously carved-up the Sphinx's scaly corpse, and ate a sumptuous supper at a splendid barbecue and hot wings feast."

"At the merry All-Meat Banquet Buffet, the grateful citizens quickly elected Oedipus as their king, and Jocastra was pissed-off that she had to marry a young stud with a big dick, because it violated her avowed lesbianism, and also because his thrusting pecker would naturally force the concrete in her vagina all the way up to her windpipe when she would have to engage in straight incestual sex with her royal son. It seemed to Jocastra that Apollo's prophecy delivered by the Oracle at Delphi had been false, since Oedipus the Fifteenth was believed to be the son of King Polybus of Corinth, who claimed that he had secretly gotten a vasectomy at the age of six."

"Jocastra reluctantly allowed Oedipus to screw and sodomize her, and that's exactly how Oedipus became the biggest ball-breaking, and vagina breaking, mother-fucker in all history. That sinful, incest behavior inadvertently brought a terrible plague to Thebes, especially provided by Almighty Zeus. Men died from venereal diseases all over the place, and it didn't matter whether the fools were screwing their wives, their girlfriends, or sodomizing sheep, or ramming rams, during that fucked-up time of widespread peril."

"Herds of animals and orchards of fruit also inexplicably died during that terrible time period. It was even rumored that King Polybus of Corinth and Queen Jocastra of Thebes' dual cunt trees had dried-up, had shriveled, and then had regrettably expired. And those unlucky mortals that didn't die from sex diseases, or who weren't eliminated in the next locust invasion, were then also plagued by an atrocious famine. Oedipus felt guilty for ever living anywhere on the damned Earth, and possibly causing the devastating 'damnations' all over his damned nation."

"Oedipus was developing a mental complex about all of the disasters that were occurring in and around Thebes. The new king dispatched his Uncle Creon, Jocastra's older brother, who still liked scribbling inside coloring books, to the notoriously gay Oracle at Delphi to learn how the abominable plague and the formidable famine could be permanently eliminated."

"Creon returned to Thebes with meritorious news. The infallible Oracle, whose heart, as was already known, had only one auricle, publicly revealed that Apollo would lift the wicked curses only on one relevant stipulation. "Whoever had killed King Laius at the crossroads must be severely punished," Creon wrote with his favorite coal' crayon for all to see on a scroll of papyrus, and then the message soon appeared as distasteful graffiti all over the city's walls."

"I'm relieved, and I haven't even taken a decent shit!" young King Oedipus told Creon. "Surely, by virtue of the Oracle's sacred words, the men, or the individual, who had killed King Laius, must still be alive and can be captured and brought to justice. Then, Oedipus spoke to his disgruntled, pissed-off people from the palace balcony."

"Citizens and Assholes of Thebes: I see the writing on the wall. Let none of you *harbor* the killer of Laius, since Thebes is not located anywhere near an ocean, or anywhere near the sea. Don't give the anonymous murderer of Laius any shelter, including tax annuity shelters, animal shelters, or fuckin' fallout shelters. You are hereby officially directed to bar the anonymous shit-head from your homes and businesses. You must solemnly commit to bar the unknown asshole from your taverns. And most importantly, you must bar him from your pubs, saloons, and bars, and also from all your asshole bar associations."

"Laius's murderer is a villain that must be condemned, mocked, scorned, tortured and perpetually whipped and punished. And I, Oedipus, sincerely pray that the gutless, cut-throated bastard-assassin's dick rots-off, and that his balls should also become polluted, infected, and contaminated, requiring immediate castration."

"Oedipus then sent for Teresias, the hoary blind prophet, and at the time, the most revered of the three remaining decrepit Theban men. The soothsayer had once blindsided teenaged Oedipus while the prophet was trying to drive a runaway chariot along a narrow alleyway. According to ancient oral chronicles, Teresias's Theban mom was the very popular Mother Teresias."

"Hey Teresias, you old, dumb, blind fuck," Oedipus gregariously greeted. "Use your gift of prophecy to tell me the identity of the men, or man, that had evilly killed King Laius at the infamous crossroads."

"If I ever told you'," the very shrewd, old, blind savant cautioned Oedipus, "you'd be mighty pissed-off. You might first be inclined to beat the shit out of me, or maybe even go into a blind rage! The city residents don't call you Oedipus wrecks for nothin', ya' know!"

"For the love and mercy of vindictive, emotionally-unstable Zeus," Oedipus continued his query. "Who the fuck killed Laius? Tell me now, or I'll dig-up Mother Teresias, and have you screw her, you old, blind, soft-dicked mother-fucker!"

"Fools!" Teresias cleverly and enigmatically answered. "Idiotic fools disposed of the former king. Only Laius's smelly asshole has remained from the scene of massacre, and as you know, his anus has been on display at the Theban Proctological Colon Museum."

"I suspect that you were one of Laius's murderers," Oedipus impetuously accused the sightless prophet. "And I believe that you', old man, were having an affair with Queen Jocastra, and that you had violated the sacred moral precepts of your Mother Teresias by teaching my wife the secret formula for making cement."

"Those ugly words had greatly angered the aged soothsayer, who then communicated a certain grotesque truth to the adolescent King. "How's this for some concrete thinking, young Oedipus? It is *you* that are the murderer whom you seek! It takes a no-good-bastard to murder another no-good-bastard!"

"Oedipus thought that the elderly prophet had gone bizarrely insane, so the teenaged king ordered the mentally-deranged old fart out of the palace. "Disappear old man," Oedipus screamed. "And never come inside this palace again until you get your next hard-on, which hopefully, will be fuckin' never!"

"Jocastra had been eavesdropping on the loud conversation from behind a curtain, and the Queen had heard the old man's startling testimony to her young husband, and regarded 'the drivel' as absolute bullshit. "Prophets and oracles have limited knowledge just like we other mortals do," the disbelieving queen later ineffectively argued to her despondent husband/son/king. "And prophets and oracles are mere mortals, the same as we are, and twice as fucked-up, too!"

"Stop speaking in preposterous, absurd riddles, Jocastra," the youthful King warned. "You're beginning to sound like the insane maniacal Sphinx.

I made her commit suicide, and I'll make you do the same thing if you persist in bustin' my goddamned balls!"

"Oedipus, there's something salient I must now disclose," Queen Jocastra articulated. "The stupid priestess at Delphi prophesied that Laius would die at the hands of his son, so my deceased husband and I saw to it that you, our son, should be left alone upon a distant mountain peak to peacefully die with a dumb-ass yo-yo while playing rock the cradle. Then, my husband Laius was later murdered near the busy convenience bizarre-bazaar store, not far from 'Three Points', where the triple dirt roads intersect."

"When the fuck did that tragedy happen?" the young King asked his matronly-looking wife. "I hope I was not yet born!"

"Just a short time before you had arrived in Thebes!" Jocastra instantly answered. "There are too many coincidences to ignore!"

"How many assassins had performed the vile deed at the crossroads?" Oedipus interrogated his mother/wife/queen."

"Rumor has it that there were four felons in all," Jocastra replied. "All were killed but one. The surviving highway thief was picked-up by a traveling hawker, tossed onto the back of the huckster's fruit and vegetable oxcart, and then conveyed into the city."

"I must see and question that lone survivor, for only he knows the truth as to what had really transpired on that auspicious day," Oedipus forcefully demanded. "Send for the dirty old prick right now!"

"I shall summon the survivor," Jocastra promised her impulsive husband/son/king. "But what is the truth regarding this series of events from your perspective? I mean, I'm your damned wife, and I hardly know a thing about your past prior to your coming to Thebes. What do you think is actually your real friggin' ancestry?"

"I shall honestly tell you all that I know about my past," Oedipus contritely stated. "I had traveled to Delphi to consult Apollo's Oracle. A nobleman back in Corinth had divulged to me that I was not the biological son of King Polybus. I was totally pissed-off, because I thought that I would never inherit his fleet of chariot and oxcart taxis, and as a result, would never possess his mythical cunt tree somewhere out in the country. Anyway," the newly elected Theban King pontificated. "I was not about to apologize to Apollo for anything. The psychotic priestess at Delphi then told me a most horrible thing."

"That you had herpes, psoriasis, syphilis and gonorrhea?" Jocastra sarcastically and un-elegantly asked."

"The fucked-up Oracle foretold that I would kill my father, marry my mother, and would have children uglier than someone named Octopus, and even uglier than the lousy, hideous-looking Sphinx. I didn't want to kill eminent Polybus, so I left Corinth and journeyed here to Thebes."

"But you could've been a pillar of the community back in that other city," Jocastra theorized and then communicated. "You could have been a Corinthian column in that famous city!"

"Anyway, you dumb lesbian slut," Oedipus elaborated his narrative. "On my way from Delphi to Thebes, I came upon a man and his bodyguards at a crossroads."

"Near the busy bizarre-bazaar convenience store at Three Points?" his wife asked in amazement. "There's a gay and lesbian house of prostitution upstairs!"

"Yes," Oedipus reluctantly admitted as a one-time patron. "We got into an intense argument as to which one of us had the right of way. There was no 'Yield' or 'Stop' sign at the congested Three Points dirt trail crossroads."

"So, you became cross at the crossroads!" Jocastra criticized. "Like biological father, like biological son really happens to be a very true moral axiom! Some punk delinquent teen vandals must've stolen the damned traffic sign," Jocastra hypothesized and related."

"Anyway," Oedipus impulsively interrupted his mother/wife/queen. "The short-tempered man riding on the chariot platform struck me with his whip, and being a young whippersnapper myself', I killed the dumb cock-sucker, along with his goddamned pathetically weak attendants."

"Holy shit Oedipus! The one man that had survived the ordeal returned critically wounded to the city on the back of a huckster's oxcart," Jocastra informed her astonished-but-attentive son. "The drunken asshole reported that Laius had been assassinated by bandits attempting to get away with highway robbery. And I then wept for another five minutes, because my son reportedly had died upon a distant mountain peak, and now my bullheaded husband, King Laius, was also dead."

"Did you feel guilty about the murders? Had the fear of possibly killing your father drive you from Corinth?" Jocastra asked."

"No; it was my black horses and my chariot that drove me from Corinth, and then to Delphi, and then to Three Points near the busy bizarre-bazaar convenience store," Oedipus stupidly divulged. "The murder didn't drive me anywhere."

At that moment, an excited courier from Corinth coincidentally arrived at the Theban palace to deliver an important message. "King Polybus has died," the messenger solemnly informed Jocastra and Oedipus. "He died of a parched tongue, dry mouth, and arid throat while eating some dried-up fruit of the womb that had been growing upon a remarkable cunt tree out in the Corinthian country."

"I'm relieved that Polypus died a peculiar natural death rather than being killed by me!" Oedipus vociferously exclaimed. "My false guilt has now been eradicated. I now believe that I'm vindicated from being accused of committing the alleged vile sin of murdering my father!"

"Polybus was not your biological father," the Corinthian King's servant attested. "The King had raised you from childhood as if you shared his fucked-up genetics, but you were definitely not the son of King Polybus and his promiscuous wife Queen Omnibus."

"Well then, exactly how did I get into the King's hands?" Oedipus insisted on knowing. "Where and how did you, or anyone else, get to deliver me to the King of Corinth?"

"I know nothing of your true biological parents," the out-of-breath messenger from Corinth acknowledged. "But a wandering shepherd had found you freezing to death upon a mountainside while toying with a yo-yo in your rocking cradle, and then the merciful herdsman presented you to me. I soon donated you to King Polybus and Queen Omnibus," the loyal servant/courier indicated. "Dear Oedipus; I'm afraid to disclose that you are a mere red-blooded commoner; the son of impoverished mountain peasants, and an impostor to blue-blooded royalty everywhere."

"What kind of fuckin' bullshit is this story you have told?" Oedipus yelled in a fit of rage. "Are you joking, Jocastra? You falsely say fake news that I have been discarded by mountain peasant scumbag parents? I'll have you slain right this minute!"

"Jocastra's countenance turned whiter than a lily. Absolute horror radiated from her face. "Oedipus; don't pay any attention to this old senile Corinthian fuck. He's even more fucked-up than Teresias, and the asshole's dead matriarch, Mother Teresias. Everything this moron from Corinth has just told us has been imaginatively fabricated, except possibly the fact that King Polybus is dead!"

"Jocastra, you are claiming that my birth origin doesn't fuckin' matter?" Oedipus impetuously yelled. "You're a bigger bitch than the pernicious Sphinx ever was!"

"Say no more, you demented ignoramus," Jocastra admonished her son/husband/king. "My agony and my misery are now complete non-ecstasy! I must replenish myself and my damaged ego at my cunt tree in the center of my private garden!"

"The blind prophet Teresias then accidentally stumbled into the palace throne chamber, thinking that he had entered a public rest room to take a half-hour leak. The messenger from Corinth instantly recognized the chief Theban prophet."

"Oh, noble King Oedipus; that's the old fuck shepherd that gave you to me," the courier from Corinth stated. "He was a blind young fuck shepherd, though, at the time!"

"Hold your sacrilegious tongue!" Teresias balked as the revered soothsayer recognized the voice of his past acquaintance and distant cousin from Corinth."

"Teresias, did you bring me from Thebes to Corinth and place me on top of the cold mountain?" the shocked Oedipus asked his' chief-religious counselor. "If I were a woman cow-herder, I could've been a frozen dairy queen!"

"I must confess the truth, and get the whole fuckin' mess off my about-to-die conscience," the old blind prophet explained. "Your wife Jocastra is also your mother. She and Laius gave you to me. I didn't have the heart to leave you abandoned up on the frigid mountain, so I presented you to my distant cousin, who then orphaned you to King Polybus and Queen Omnibus."

"I made my father into dead meat. I made him into road kill!" Oedipus sobbed. "And today, I am also most-grieved upon learning of King Polybus's passing. But worst of all," Oedipus somberly concluded. "The good people of Thebes have been right on the money every time they call me a dirty mother-fucker! Indeed, I have been cursed by that son-of-a-bitchin' Apollo, and his deranged lesbian priestess, who had slyly tricked me into marrying my dyke mother!"

"The priestess's prophecy has been verified," Teresias confirmed. "You have murdered your biological father, and you have married your biological mother, who has turned from a bisexual into a practicing lesbian with a solid concrete love tunnel. You, Oedipus, have been adequately cursed by Lord Phoebus Apollo, and as a result, have been completely fucked-up your whole damned life!"

"Oedipus left the Theban throne chamber in a wild, raging state of mind. The young king searched the entire palace until he eventually found his mother/wife/queen lying dead in her private garden. "She's choked to death eating fruit of the womb from her cunt tree! Her throat is fuckin' clogged with black, brown, blonde and red pubic hair!" the teenaged monarch sorrowfully realized and muttered."

"Then, Oedipus's perplexed mind evaluated his entire life. 'I hate viewing and reviewing what fate has repugnantly presented me,' the Boy King regretted in despair. 'I'm going to blind myself and become a disciple of eminent Teresias. It is better to live life blind to its evils rather than see contemptible events happening before my very eyes every fuckin' day. What a lot of bullshit both eyesight and human life really are!' Oedipus mourned to his mirror-reflection in Jocastra's private garden water-pond, situated next to the deceased queen's now lethal cunt tree."

"So morally speaking," Eurshiddenme announced and concluded to his disgruntled and sleeping four gagged and tied-up, peeved listeners. "We foolhardy soldiers should piously pay homage to the gods of Olympus, and just as importantly, we should get our damned mendacious minds off of sex, which will only further destroy our already fucked-up characters. Instead, be celibate, my fellow lieutenants, and concentrate your vital energies on maintaining abstinence, and also on obeying Lord Odysseus. And while doing so, enjoy killing as many diabolical Trojans as we possibly can. We must religiously implement these vital moral lessons represented in the story of Oedipus to ensure the essential continuation of the human race throughout Greece."

* * * * * * * * * * * *

The Trojans again assailed the Greek barrier wall, but were repelled by the Achaean forces out of a desperation for surviving the escalating battle. The Danaans' recently-dug trench, situated before the wall. had effectively kept-out Trojan chariots, and every wounded enemy soldier, before the victim died in the deep ditch, was given mud inside his mouth, thus automatically contracting and dying from trench-mouth. Ajax fought like a berserk killer from atop the wall, spearing Trojans as if the attackers were trapped fish inside a barrel.

The great giant Sarpedon, Junior got into an urgent wrestling scrimmage with his Greek counterpart, Ajax, who astonishingly elevated the Trojan weightlifter upon his broad soldiers, put the enemy grappler in a dizzying propeller spin, and then tossed the hulking behemoth off the recently constructed wall onto three quickly-clobbered foes, who had been busily fighting with several Danaan warriors below.

"Nice going Ajax!" the giant's partner and comrade Teucer commended. "You threw Sarpedon, Jr. down to the desert floor as if he were a scrawny rag doll! Fearsome Sarpedon, Jr. will be immobile for quite some time. He's still lying upon the hot sand down there, and I don't think there's any crap left in his intestines with all of that brown-feces surrounding his abdomen and asshole! My eyes don't deceive me. The stationary ogre even has crap and sand inside his sandals!"

Hector became infuriated at witnessing the celebrated champion being so methodically knocked unconscious, so the livid Trojan prince lifted a second immense boulder, thrust it at high speed, and crashed the mammoth rock through the still partially-standing second gate in the Greek defensive wall.

"Almighty Zeus!" Hector shouted-up to the clear blue sky. "Thank you for making me stronger and *bolder,* with me easily hoisting-up and forcefully tossing this second five-hundred-pound boulder!"

Chapter 13

"TROJANS ATTACK THE SHIPS"

Zeus was satisfied that his strategy of allowing the Trojans to take the battlefield advantage was being successfully implemented, so the chief god was certain that no other residents of Mt. Olympus would dare to interfere with his plan to appease Thetis, in deference to her sulking son, Achilles. But as soon as Zeus sped-off to (nearby-Troy) Mt. Ida's high peak in his golden chariot, Poseidon, who had been surveilling his sky-brother's recent activities, used his supernatural influence, and rallied the crestfallen Achaeans, affording the newly-inspired warriors' divine strength to take the battlefront initiative.

Hector, who had been savagely slaughtering and decapitating dozens of Argive soldiers daring to raise their bronze swords, was suddenly stymied by the trio of Ajax, Odysseus and Diomedes, and although the three heroes were mildly injured, the Greek fighters were exceptionally motivated to contribute their combined talents in thwarting the Trojan prince's ambitious assault. The clamorous combat was fought within tight quadrants, so at times, Trojans were wildly stabbing Trojans, and Greeks were accidentally slashing Greeks.

Thirteen heroes on both sides were killed in the grueling battle, and many soldiers were incidentally maimed by their own comrades. Hearing the loud clanging and banging of swords and shields, Nestor left aching Machaon inside *his* tent and exited to investigate how the war zone was rapidly changing from one side to the other. The King of Pylos located Agamemnon taking an extended dump outside his tent, and the two plotters decided to visit Odysseus to see if the military guru could concoct some suitable battle scenario to advantageously stifle Hector and his minions.

The two vigilant kings found Odysseus sitting inside his modest tent conferring with his five zany lieutenants, who had that same afternoon been showered with praise by Ajax for "cleverly rolling down the hill" and knocking Prince Paris off his feet.

"I must commend you five stout-hearted men for your noteworthy bravery," Odysseus cited with a rare smile. "Keep-up the good work, and who the hell knows? Perhaps you'll all earn the privilege of being promoted to the rank of captain."

"Sorry to interrupt your impromptu conference," Agamemnon said to Odysseus upon entering the Ithacan king's tent. "The Trojans are beating our ranks back toward our black Biremes, and the wall that you suggested is not confining the enemy groups to their original positions. We must tax our brains and develop a new dynamic plan. Do you', brilliant savant Odysseus, have any novel ideas besides authoring a fiction book, once writing and alphabets are developed?"

"The well has run dry," downtrodden Odysseus confessed. "Perhaps my creative-minded lieutenants could describe a viable solution to our current dilemma," the Ithacan king stated, passing the buck to his subordinate five nincompoops. "What say you', Lieutenant Eurshiddenme? Give us a constructive plan of attack!"

"I say that we utilize this amazing flammable black substance my fellow officers have discovered that's spewing-up from below the Earth's surface," Eurshiddenme offered. "The substance burns very easily, and the men call it 'petroleum', or smelly, common oil. We've managed to collect several hundred barrels of the black liquid to run our bonfires, which are burning near our rudely-constructed watchtowers."

"And we could muster and have a hundred naked slave girls and a hundred nude, muscular infantrymen stand in front of the bug-eyed Trojan troops," Eurballsourout suavely recommended. "The heterosexual Trojans will chase after the hundred voluptuous naked dolls, and the homosexual gay jerk-offs will instantly pursue the nude and muscular, tanned, Adonis-like faggots."

"Won't the hundred Achaean vivacious chicks and the hundred nude, gay, Greek guys dash into the surf and possibly drown?" Odysseus skeptically asked. "The two hundred nude sprinters better know how to swim like sharks!"

"No, my king," Eurassisgras disagreed. "We'll artistically draw in the sand two similar-in-dimension rectangles, five-hundred-feet long, and two-hundred-feet wide. The two identical rectangles will be parallel to each other, and situated a hundred feet apart."

"How the hell are two rectangles going to stop the crazed Trojans from chasing after the hundred gorgeous girls and the hundred gay Adonis imitators?" Agamemnon challenged the five stooge lieutenants. "There better be more elaborate details to your dumb-fuck plan."

"The hundred barrels of oil will be spread around the entire perimeter of the twin drawn rectangles," Eurdicisin added to the oddball discussion. "And after the hundred naked chicks and the hundred nude studs run through the drawn rectangles, the hundreds of Trojan pursuers will enter the drawn-out areas. Then, our most-skilled soldiers will torch the surrounding oil, and the horny Trojans will be trapped inside the dual conflagrations with no possible escape from the rising fences of fire!"

"That's absolutely right," Eurcockisnum remarked and endorsed. "The tricked, sexually-aroused Trojans will be promptly barbecued, and their scorched flesh will be gratefully consumed by the numerous vultures and buzzards patrolling the late afternoon skies."

"If your ingenious plan, being converted from theory to practice, is a success," Agamemnon enthusiastically declared, "then you five stellar strategists will be swiftly promoted to the rank of captain."

The hundred naked bitches and the hundred gay, nude bastards quickly gained the attention of the sex-starved Trojans, who reflexively scampered after their two-hundred lures with great speed and dexterity. Upon reaching the designated rectangular traps, the two-hundred Trojans, sporting stiff erections, were instantly roasted by the blazing shafts of fire.

"You five saviors are like god-sent messiahs who have salvaged our already-battered Biremes," King Agamemnon happily congratulated Odysseus's sagacious new captains. "It's too bad that Hector wasn't involved in the spectacular chaos, or else, the hot-to-trot prince would've been incinerated into embers just like his pathetic comrades had been broiled and fried."

"That plan you've fabricated was absolutely incredible!" Odysseus lauded his five new captains. "The Trojans fond Sex Wish had transformed into the idiots' very fatal Death Wish! Ha, ha, ha! Remember this very important maxim, men; always think with your brains and not with you erect fadorkenbenders!"

* * * * * * * * * * *

Hera had perceptively noticed that Poseidon had been engaged in enacting certain mischief against Zeus's supreme will when the Achaeans had taken to the offensive, and the alert wife also observed that her moody spouse was idly resting and basking in the sun atop nearby Mount Ida. Hera then considered paying a visit to Aphrodite's luxurious suite atop glorious Mt. Olympus to have a much-needed summit conference.

"Spellbinding Goddess of Love and Beauty," Hera politely addressed her goddess counterpart, who obviously favored the Trojan cause. Brother and sister Oceanus and Tethys have been quarreling about trifles for some time now, and I absolutely loathe conflict and estrangement. Please lend me your wondrous Girdle of Desire, so that I may soften the pair's contentious relationship, and have harmony and tranquility again prevail amongst our extended family. The feuding twosome must be reconciled," Hera convincingly insisted, "and with your cooperation, *that* peaceful end to hostilities between the bickering siblings can and will be achieved."

"You speak and seek a noble goal, even though you and I are on opposite sides of the mortals' dumb-shit war," Aphrodite replied. "Now Hera; if your unusual request has nothing to do with promoting the Achaean cause, I shall lend you my coveted Girdle of Desire."

Feeling guileful, Hera zoomed-off to the Isle of Lemnos with Aphrodite's Girdle of Desire to communicate with Sleep, the snoozing and slumbering brother of Death. "Sweet Sleep. Sorry to awaken you from your loud snoring. But I must ask a favor of you, which is designed to guarantee peace among the immortals. As you are aware, my husband Zeus has chronic insomnia, and never fully receives the therapeutic benefit of enjoying deep sleep," Hera insisted, feigning both alarm and concern. "If you assist me in accomplishing my endeavor, I'll make sure that my blacksmith son Hephaestus builds you a magnificent golden throne equal to the one that Zeus sits his chubby ass upon."

"Listen, Hera. I once before tried that sleep antic with Zeus at your behest, and if it weren't for my mother Night descending and saving my butt from Zeus's wrath, I might have been condemned to the Black Pit of Tartarus on a non-reversible, non-rehabilitation sentence."

'Hurry-up and grant me my wish,' Hera impatiently thought. 'This tight girdle I've borrowed from svelte Aphrodite is chaffing the clit right off of my sensitive slit hole, and the friction is quite irritating. The friggin' too-small girdle that I'm uncomfortably wearing doesn't seem to be producing satisfactory results!'

Then, all-too-cunning Hera remained on task and resumed her cordial conversation with gullible Sleep. "Oh yes. I do remember now. But that situation you've recollected involving Zeus was much different than the current dilemma I wish to resolve. If I recall, Zeus groggily awoke from your influential sleeping spell, and his blurry eyes perceived Hercules shipwrecked on the Isle of Kos. Thank goodness your mother Night saved your ass from major harassment. But you didn't have your hemorrhoids explode as you had originally feared, and not one minor lightning bolt from my husband ever penetrated-up your vulnerable asshole!"

"Do you have any other gift besides the Golden Throne offer?" Sleep curiously asked. "I already have seven Golden Thrones situated in separate spots all over this remote island."

"I promise I will give you one of the beautiful Graces to have as your private valet, and also as your personal mistress, whom you could screw day and night in fabulous pleasure all the way to High Heaven! You'll no longer have to pop a white dream load into that magical inflatable doll of yours, and then have to clean-up the sticky mess every time."

"Yes, Hera," Sleep amenably concurred. "I've always desired to marry and have both conversational and sexual intercourse with lovely Pasithee, and now you present me with my strongest desire as a wonderful gift. Quite frankly, my fidgety fingers can't wait to explore Pasithee's passionate pink pussy-pit. Yes Hera; I shall gladly accompany you to Mt. Ida to send Almighty Zeus upon a marvelous fantasy adventure to visit old, reliable Mr. Sandman."

When Zeus saw Hera appear in his midst atop the mountain overlooking Troy, the chief deity became sexually aroused, and as the Thunder and Lightning god shoved and thrust his incredibly lengthy godhood deep into Hera's wet-pink love tunnel, magical Sleep induced Dreamland onto Zeus's subconscious libido, simultaneously saving goddess Hera from experiencing a painful, ruptured esophagus.

"Thank you for saving my partially-pulverized ass, and also my aching love tunnel from experiencing total destruction," Hera said to Sleep. 'Ah yes,' the goddess imagined. 'Zeus is now sound asleep and quite distracted from his involvement in pacifying Achilles's interest and ego regarding the dumb-shit Trojan War! Thetis's intercession has been neutralized!'

"Have no anxiety over your in-progress request," Sleep happily assured Hera. "Soon, your vindictive husband will be all relaxed, imagining in his calm trance either him chopping a hundred cords of wood, or him watching several thousand sheep slowly jumping over a high fence, one by one!"

* * * * * * * * * * * *

While Zeus soundly slept, and his impressive godhood had shrunk-down to three-feet in length, back on the Troad Plain, Hector and Ajax were duking it out near the Achaean ships, even though both combatants were princes and not dukes. The Greeks were pushing their disarrayed enemy back onto the Trojan side of the Argives' wall, throwing many of the resisters off the elevated platform and into the recently-excavated nearby trench, also referred to as "the moat".

Hector was the incensed aggressor, partially hitting Ajax in the chest with his sharp spear, but the thick leather cross-bands inside the Achaean's shield had deflected the impact of the sharp weapon's deadly tip. Then, responding to Zeus being fast asleep and unable to aid Hector's initiative, Ajax seized a large boulder and flung the heavy object at his main rival, striking Hector in his sternum, and sending the livid Trojan prince (stem-to-sternum) spinning in circles like a gay pole dancer on meth.

The Achaeans surged forward, simulating a colossal tidal wave, hurling spears, javelins, and a plethora of insults at the retreating Trojans, who had out of necessity, closed their ranks, forming a defensive circle around fallen Hector, whose body was lifted and carried to a nearby chariot that was not on fire. The Trojan prince had cold water from the Xanthus River splashed upon his face and body, and the son of Priam began coughing-up and vomiting large amounts of dark blood from his mouth and lungs, and also was heavily hemorrhaging through his nostrils.

"He's gone unconscious," the shocked commander of the rescue troops uttered. "His eyes are dull and his vision is growing dim. What we are witnessing must be what the local shamans say is a near-death-experience," one voice heard above the rest attested. "This is the first time I've ever seen Hector in a comatose and immobile state, lying prone in *this* terrible situation. I mean," the astonished warrior finished his remark. "Hector certainly battles like a maniacal wild cyclone, but that fuckin' behemoth Ajax violently fights like a fanatical white tornado."

Chapter 14

"THE BURNING OF THE BIREMES"

Zeus awoke from his abbreviated slumber that had been induced by Sleep, and immediately, the chief deity observed in the dusty plain off in the distance that Hector had been severely injured, and surmised that Poseidon had probably intervened during *his* brief siesta, and had mischievously aided and abetted the Greek forces. Exhausted Hera had also been napping on the Mt. Ida summit, and Zeus suspected right away that his conniving spouse had been involved in a secret pro-Achaean alliance with roguish Poseidon.

"Disobedient wife!" Zeus thundered and boomed. "Do you recall the last time you defied my orders? In anger, I hung you from the sky with anvils attached to your ankles? The other gods appeared on the scene and tried to rescue you from my experiment in learning about gravity, which I had incidentally and accidentally created centuries ago! But their efforts were futile. My addled mind tells me that I should viciously strike you down as if you were a tall timber; that is, if you weren't such a good piece of ass!"

"I swear by my entire heart and soul that I have never engaged in any conspiracy with Poseidon against you regarding the mortals' Trojan War," Hera uttered and then cried. 'It is Athena, Lord Zeus, who is the Argives' biggest non-athletic supporter!"

"Now begone with you, distrustful wife!" Zeus bellowed. "Go and find Iris and Apollo, whom I wish to consult in caucus. Thetis is also bothering me with her dumb-fuck favor requests, and it's about time that her crybaby son Achilles stops his persistent pouting and sulking, and returns to his participation in the war, which is now starting to bore me all-the-way to High Olympus!"

Several hours later, Zeus ordered Iris to locate Poseidon and direct the sea god to abandon his assumed allegiance to the Greeks, and to then thereafter, find Apollo, and state that Zeus commands that the archer god must assist Hector in regaining consciousness, and after attaining full cerebral and physical normalcy, promptly resume *his* mental obsession of devoutly defending Troy.

"Prince Hector, I have replenished your quivering quiver with a fresh supply of toxic-tipped arrows," Apollo, disguised as a vague vision, communicated to a still rather-dazed Hector. "Now, get your ass in gear and find some barbaric Greeks to maim and slaughter."

"Who the hell are you?" Hector interrogated the purple-hazed image. "Are you a rock-and-roll minstrel? I'm no fuckin' amateur meteorologist, but just a few minutes ago, I was almost perilously killed by Ajax behaving like a swirling white tornado."

"Sit-up now, Trojan prince!" the nebulous-in-appearance purple image sternly urged. "Your protector, Phoebus Apollo, will allow your acclaimed chariot to pass through the battered Greek wall!"

Hector rose-up from his knees, and stood above the baking-hot ground; the Trojan hero sprinted like a cheetah to his damaged chariot, and to the astonishment of his wide-eyed captains, sped forward to massacre any doomed Danaan who confronted his advance. With the assistance of Apollo aiding Hector, the Greeks instantly became intimidated, and the invaders hastily raced to the nearest outhouses to empty their smelly bowels. Apollo then collapsed the frail wall and its interior moat, thus allowing the Trojan chariots to easily chase the freshly-arrived Greeks to retreat and defend their anchored Biremes, because those new troops weren't among the panic-stricken Argives that were frantically scampering-back toward their stench-laden outhouses.

As the battle of the Argive ships ensued, Agamemnon took a moment to pray to Olympus, hoping that merciful Zeus would not permit Hector and his minions to overwhelm the moored vessels, and thus, emerge victorious in the nine-year-conflict. And during the culmination of the conflict, Odysseus's five newly-appointed captains, by virtue of their new-found high rank, were compelled to strenuously stay and fight in the escalating battle.

"This shit is nerve-racking," Eurshiddenme yelled above the active fray's noise. "I'd rather get my dick licked by Medusa the Gorgon than get my balls castrated by some berserk Trojan!"

"Fighting these swarming bastards is worse than receiving a bad blowjob from a homo Trojan having razor-sharp teeth!" Eurballsourout screamed above the ongoing sound of heavy metal against heavier metal. "If I survive this fucked-up war, I'll gladly get castrated and become a transgender priestess serving the fucked-up Oracle at Delphi!"

"I don't know which essential organ I'm going to lose first!" Eurassisgras's voice hollered above the surrounding clamor of bronze swords and shields banging and clanging. "I hope it's neither my precious scrotum sac, nor my cherished epididymis!"

Eurdicisin was the next captain to shriek-out a ludicrous comment during the intense melee. "Listen guys! I'd rather screw Queen Persephone's frozen-cold, icy sex tunnel down in dark Hades than die an insignificant death here upon this contemptible Troad battlefield."

"I refuse to die before I get my first erection," forty-two-year-old Eurcockisnum bellowed as he parried blows with a boy Trojan. "When the fuck am I going to ever experience the joys of puberty?" the fearful, disenchanted captain yelled above the disturbing noise and awesome clanking. "My pathetic limp dick has remained numb for over four lousy decades!" Eurcockisnum complained to his four disinterested and preoccupied, fighting colleagues. "If I'm ever lucky enough to survive this reprehensible war, I think I'm going right to the nearest butcher clinic and be transformed into a goddamned transsexual S and M instructor! I'd rather have two limp legs than a flaccid, limp pecker!"

* * * * * * * * * * *

King Priam's army was gaining the upper hand, and the weary Greeks were emotionally drained and physically exhausted. Agamemnon was becoming increasingly irritated that a mere several thousand Trojans could thwart fifty thousand supposedly superior Greeks upon the Troad battlefield. Only the king's huge animosity toward Achilles was greater than Agamemnon's mounting disdain for Prince Hector.

While the sounds and cries of carnage were discernible from far away, Patroclus was assiduously bandaging his old friend Eurypylus's wounds in a medical ward tent situated inside the Achaean main camp. But at the Bireme fleet that was moored along the beach, standing upon the stern, fleet-footed Ajax was defending his favorite vessel and jabbing at Trojans with his heavy, twelve-cubit-long pike, which was inflicting major stomach and abdomen wounds upon encroaching Trojan aggressors.

Hector was afraid that the Greeks would strip-away and confiscate as coveted trophies the armor of high-ranking Trojan brass, and then display the obtained prizes as special souvenirs from the masts of their anchored ships. The intensifying struggle near the Argive vessels raged-on, with every second revealing an eye for an eye, a tooth for a tooth, and a penis for a penis scenario. Although severely hindered by the devastating loss of life, both sides fiercely fought like male lions in heat, seeking dominance and possession of the ready-for-sex females in their pride.

"If your ship is burned and destroyed as is about to certainly happen," Hector screamed-up to the giant Ajax, "will you awkwardly walk across the deep wine-dark sea and arrive home on foot twenty years later? Zeus favors the Trojans in this wicked game of mortal death struggle! Your' end is near, Argives! Prepare to shake hands with your doom! I had always suspected that you were a piker, Ajax, and now, looking at your chosen weapon, I know for sure that you are!"

"Use your blazing torches to cauterize and seal the Trojans' assholes!" Odysseus loudly commanded his five new captains. "The enemy will wish that their butt apertures had been struck by Zeus's electrifying lightning bolts instead! Onward and upward, or some silly shit like that! Singe their' hairy assholes, I say!"

"You know Eurballsourout," Eurshiddenme said as the head captain scraped grimy sweat and blood from his right wrist. "We were better-off as inconspicuous lieutenants when we could easily hide and avoid battle and injury. Now that we're bona fide captains," Eurshiddenme regretted, "we're always expected to be constantly visible, getting our tender asses kicked in view of the perceptive eyes of Agamemnon, Diomedes and Odysseus!"

"I should've listened to my mother and committed suicide twenty years ago," Eurballsourout ruefully remarked. "She said to me: 'Eurballsourout! Your ugly, pimpled dick is out, too'!"

"Woe is me! Why the hell couldn't I be All-Powerful Zeus rather than being puny fucked-up Eurshiddenme!" the head captain disgustedly bitched to his four hapless-but-compatible subordinates.

Chapter 15

"THE DEATH OF PATROCLUS"

Drama was beginning to permeate throughout the camp of Achilles and his world-famous Myrmidons. Many among the ranks resented the fact that their eminent commander was openly denying them participation on the battlefield, simply because their illustrious general was involved in a picayune dispute with King Agamemnon over possession of a single captured slave girl.

"Patroclus, why are you crying?" Achilles asked his close friend and confidante who had just returned from the Achaeans' camp to his master's Bireme. "Are you magically turning into a fuckin' weeping willow tree, or what? Honestly; you're acting like a spoiled toddler who wants his doting mommy to pick-up his soft ass and carry his pouting mouth to his bedroom in order to be breast fed! Now then, I happen to have a rather erudite idea to convey to you, Patroclus. Why don't you take a long walk off a high cliff and evaluate your pedestrian ideas!"

"Brave Achilles; I am grievously sobbing for my Achaean friends who have been either wounded or killed in battle," Patroclus sorrowfully declared. "Odysseus, Diomedes, Agamemnon, Eurypylus, brother of Eurapylon, have all been seriously injured, all happening because you're a selfish dunce in continuing your petty squabble with Agamemnon over an unimportant slave girl's tiny tits and shaved pussy. From my perspective, that is also shared by a majority of your troops, you evidently lack basic pity and loyalty!"

"What the hell are you saying?" Achilles questioned and objected. "Don't you have any loyalty to me, your very competent commander? Haven't I brought you military discipline, honor and praise in the past?"

"You fear the oracle's announced prophecy, much to the detriment of *our* wounded and dying countrymen!" Patroclus accused his stubborn superior. "Kindly lend me your gleaming armor so that I can lead the caged-up Myrmidons into the heart of the heated conflict. Our troops are fresh, and being fresh, the irate soldiers even curse each other out quite frequently! I predict that the Trojans will flee like scared pigeons when their eyes see me wearing your armor, and the idiots will think that I am you!"

"You speak of past prophecy that has been spoken by weak and scared-shitless prophets," skeptical Achilles verbally parried. "Those feckless priests, priestesses, and oracles adroitly use religion as a mechanism to control the illiterate masses, and thus, make the public afraid of curses and plagues! Basically, religion is a form of cultural propaganda! Now dear Patroclus; I stay isolated here inside my camp solely for the purpose of punishing Agamemnon. It all boils-down to a matter of will grappling! My singular intent is to show the dirty bastard that he cannot defeat Hector and his maniacal Trojans without me and my valiant soldiers directly involved in the middle of the fray," the son of Thetis elaborated. "I'll concede to your general argument this one salient point: you Patroclus, should put-on my armor, but I caution your present boldness: once you've pushed the enemy back away from the moored Greek ships, cease your aggression so that you do not diminish my glory and sully my earned reputation among the Argives!"

"Will you ever again join the Argives in their nine-year assault on Troy?" Patroclus asked Achilles. "Or are you a shivering, petrified chicken as the popular rumor around camp claims that A-pollo is!"

"If and when the enemy approaches my beachhead and their encroachment jeopardizes my Biremes and my troops, then, and only then, will I feel compelled to fight for Greece. Now, my eyes see smoke rising in the distance. Several ships have already been set ablaze! Put on my invincible armor while I assemble the Myrmidons to prepare for combat. Patroclus; this is your shining moment of personal growth as a commander!"

The two-thousand-five-hundred muscular Myrmidons were quickly assembled and organized into five distinct marching groups, with five-hundred virulent troops within each designated division. Achilles stood high above the stern of his Bireme and firmly addressed his soldiers.

"Bold and audacious Myrmidons. You have been like hungry lions caged-up and ready to show the enemy how you are similar to the fierce carnivores. Follow Captain Patroclus into battle, and then slaughter as many Trojans as you possibly can. Don't return until you have your opponents' blood upon your spears and swords! And if you come across any food, steal it fast, even though I despise fast food!"

After the Myrmidons led by Patroclus marched in cadence from the aforementioned Greco-held beachhead in the direction of Troy, Achilles removed a solid gold cup from an inlaid chest that Thetis had especially given to her son to deal with any emerging crisis situation. Immediately, the renowned hero poured and offered libations to Zeus, and then drank seven lucky gulps of smooth-tasting wine from the chalice.

"Almighty Zeus. Protect my dear friend Patroclus as the inexperienced fool leads my veteran Myrmidons into the crux of the fight. My naïve captain has an abundance of valor thriving in his heart, and seeks glory and prestige under the protection of your invincible aegis. After honoring my trusty captain with victory, have Patroclus and my troops return safely back here, so that we may together savor his magnificent triumph."

The fresh Myrmidon warriors eagerly joined the battle, and buzzed around the Troad Plain like a frenzied colony of agitated hornets, swarming and making annoying bee sounds in their heightened mania.

"Just look at that teeming enemy activity!" Hector incredulously yelled to his loyal lieutenants. "There's Achilles over to our left, who has just entered the fight! And those fanatical swarming and buzzing wasps make me wonder why those fucked-up Achaean Myrmidons don't *beehive* like ordinary soldiers!"

Thinking that Patroclus, riding upon his commander's chariot, had been awesome Achilles, Hector became more-than-apprehensive, and immediately retreated back towards the city gates of Troy. Other commanders followed Hector's prudent example, but their heavy chariots and galloping horses could not climb the dug-out ditch's soft inclines, so many of the speeding teams toppled-over and could not safely make their active retreat back to Troy. Showing tremendous audacity, Patroclus and his vanguard violently killed a dozen Trojan officers as the unfortunate victims were clambering-up the steep banks of the recently excavated trench.

Seeing the bizarre confrontation unfolding, Great Zeus feared that his favored Trojan son Sarpedon would soon be smitten by Patroclus's lance, so the chief god informed Hera that he wished to whisk his bastard son away to Lycia before the highly-motivated Greek warrior would send Sarpedon's spirit swirling and spiraling-down to Hades.

"Husband, what the hell are you saying!" Hera chided her louse of a spouse. "This mortal man, Sarpedon, although half-divine, like other petty humans, has been born, only to eventually die. It doesn't really mean a rat's ass whether Sarpedon perishes now, or a mere century from now! If you save his ass from being annihilated, every god and goddess who has a dog in the hunt, so to speak, will desire doing the same for their favorite mortal champion. Let your valued child Sarpedon bleed to death from a sharp spear's penetration," Hera boldly suggested. "And besides, who the hell care's whether or not your half-god's tiny dingle ever penetrates any mortal whore's wet love tunnel!"

After Sarpedon's chest had been severely punctured by inspired Patroclus, Almighty Zeus, viewing the tragic event from on high, was greatly saddened, and the king of Olympus mystically blackened the sky over the Troad Plain at high noon, as the sound of clashing spears, swords and axes resounded across the neighboring plains and valleys, and soon loudly echoed throughout the nearby hills and mountains.

Still feeling disconsolate, Zeus assigned Apollo to dispatch brothers Sleep and Death to place Sarpedon's corpse upon a sturdy stretcher, and fly the hero's body back to his homeland for proper burial.

Soon thereafter, Apollo judiciously decided to enter the evolving fray and found ambitious Patroclus ascending an outer wall of Troy, after climbing-up a high olive tree and latching onto the high rampart's ledge. "Back-off arrogant Achaean!" the awesome archer god frightfully yelled. "I shall first break-off the limbs of your olive tree, and then I will break your fuckin' limbs and pull them off your deceased body as one would pull the legs off of a dead crab or spider!"

Being traumatized by Apollo's appearance and the archer god's numerous threats, Patroclus clumsily fell from the high olive tree branch and plummeted twenty-feet onto the hard ground below. Achilles's captain's unprotected behind was then wounded from behind by a well-thrown Trojan javelin, and then keen-eyed Hector confidently approached the writhing downed Achaean, and enthusiastically plunged his sharp-bladed spear directly into Patroclus's vulnerable mid-section.

"This is your moment of glory, Hector," the dying Argive captain hoarsely uttered. "With the help of Zeus and Apollo, you have temporarily triumphed, and I stress, only temporarily triumphed. A certain prophecy, however, will soon be fulfilled. Your remaining time on this planet is short-lived!"

"Just like your fucked-up superior, General Achilles," Hector answered and evilly laughed. "I too am a man of war and have no particular use for frivolous prophecies spoken by craven and feeble priests, by virgin-pussy priestesses, and by gutless, knee-knocking, pusillanimous oracles! The world is full of blood-sucking impostors; and prophets, priests, priestesses and oracles are the most successful bloodsuckers prospering on this fucked-up planet!"

Hearing the bad news about Hector killing Patroclus, Ajax stampeded into Agamemnon's tent to be the first messenger to tell the Achaean leader.

"Great Agamemnon! Brave Patroclus has been killed. All two auricles in his heart have been punctured!"

"Ajax, you pathetic asshole!" Agamemnon bellowed. "Do you think that I'm a stupid shit like you are! It's impossible for anyone to have two oracles in their fuckin' heart!"

Chapter 16

"THE FIGHT FOR THE BODY OF PATROCLUS"

"Listen guys, now that we're no longer lieutenants, I believe that rank has its privileges," Eurshiddenme haughtily lectured his four fellow captains. "I now have a spacious tent to hold meetings, so we don't have to worry about being caught conferring down in the gay, lesbian, transgender and tri-sexual horizontal dark tunnel."

"Okay about that!" Eurballsourout agreed and admitted. "But don't tell us any more cornball moral mythology lectures. I happen to enjoy committing mortal and venial sins as much as anyone else!"

"I'll level with you four dunderheads!" Eurshiddenme exclaimed. "I was once in the cemetery, er, I meant to say 'seminary', studying to be a priest of Apollo, and I know exactly how the archer god thinks and acts. And I see a definite parallel between a certain Apollo story and the recent demise of Patroclus!"

"Do you mean to tell us that you called this so-called military meeting to explain some immaterial mythology bullshit!" Eurassisgras strongly protested. "I suppose that the next thing you'll tell us is that the world is round and not flat! Flattery will get you nowhere, ha, ha, ha!"

"You dimwit! Your mind is as closed as a virgin's untouched pussy!" Eurshiddenme countered. "On the other hand, to you four nitwits, an open mind contains no brains inside."

"Do we again have to keep silent during your horse manure oration!" Eurdicisin wanted to know. 'Your softest words are like hard turds deeply deposited inside my earlobes!"

"Well, the more dumb-ass questions you ask, the longer the meeting will be," Eurshiddenme answered. "If you want to get back to your daily masturbation sessions, I suggest that you four dipshits remain quiet while I educate you about important moral and religious issues!"

"I see merit in your illogical rhetoric!" Eurcockisnum assessed and replied. "Hurry-up, Eurshiddenme, and get your fucked-up, sanctimonious presentation over with! Your holier-than-thou attitude leaves much sex to be desired!"

"Okay, garrulous dolts; here is my pertinent moral lesson for today. In the far-off land of Ethiopia, a punk teenager named Phaethon impatiently listened to his mother Clymene brag that *his* father was Phoebus Apollo, the Greek god of music, medicine, masturbation and the sun. According to exaggerated ancient renditions, every morning Apollo would mount his magnificent golden chariot and would commandeer four white stallions that flew across the sky from east to west, obviously dragging the sun on its daily celestial path from the eastern to the western horizon."

"A schoolboy friend that pretended to be a son of Zeus scoffed at Phaethon's claim that *he* was a bona fide offspring of Lord Apollo. Naturally, Clymene's son became incensed at his pal's malicious ridiculing."

"Look, asshole," the other boy scornfully hollered. "I am a son of Zeus, and my daddy can kick your daddy's stupid ass any fuckin' day of the whole fuckin' year. How do ya' like them fuckin' apples?"

"But my mother," Phaethon said, paused, and then reiterated. "But my mother has told me this truth that I am indeed Apollo's son, and that someday I might be able to perform comedy routines and revival music acts at one of my father's many theaters. As you know, Greek heroes like Hercules are born after a god of Olympus has sex with a mortal woman."

"Get a fuckin' life!" the other wise-ass punk suggested. "Phaethon, your mother is nothin' more than a goddamned kinky whore-turned-prostitute, and you're *her* illegitimate son! This lyin' story she's giving you is a lot of stinkin' *Mt. Olympus* bullshit! I know, because my mother's also a goddamned hooker, too! And I ain't no goddamned son of Zeus! And you ain't no goddamned son of Phoebus Apollo, either! That's all a bunch of speculative, self-serving horse manure!"

"Phaethon sadly walked home from nursery school for lunch in a mighty depressed state of mind. "Mom, tell me the truth," the boy requested. "Are you a goddamned whore or prostitute? Or is this weirdo story that I am indeed the son of Apollo actually true?"

"Son; you are indeed of heavenly birth," Clymene swore. "And if I speak falsely, may the gods punish my arrogance and make my hyperactive vagina atrophy. I strongly suggest that *you* journey to the eastern horizon and visit the temple of my handsome husband, Apollo. Ask *him* about *your* divine origin if you don't believe me."

"Okay Mom; pack my lunch, and I'll go and check it out. How do I get to India? I was never too good in geography and failed the damned subject last semester in toddler town nursery school!" the all-too-curious, slow-learner teenager asked. "I hear that India is the exact place where Dad's new marvelous marble temple is located."

"Just keep walking east for about a century," Clymene informed her impulsive son. "And hurry-up and get the hell out of here, because I have a wealthy client arriving in about fifteen minutes, and I need to wash my stinky crotch and freshen up a bit!"

"Apollo's Indian sun palace had columns of pure gold and glittering jewels that magically glistened and twinkled in the morning sunlight. The walls were made of rich platinum ore, and the ceiling of gleaming ivory. Murals of Earth, sky, sea and *Mt. Olympus* had been painted upon the walls of every chamber inside the splendid, colossal temple. Hephaestus had erected the fantastic edifice in tribute to Lord Apollo, who didn't know or care a shit about anything except music, medicine, masturbation, screwing beautiful mortal women, and tugging the hot sun across the sky the four separate seasons of each and every monotonous year."

"Phaethon cautiously entered Apollo's charmed sanctuary seeking confirmation of *his* true identity. The determined kid approached the radiant god imperially sitting upon his glimmering golden and jeweled throne, and the impetuous know-it-all punk soon had to cover his eyes for protection from the intense dazzling glare. The sun god was wearing a fabulous diamond-studded purple robe to complement his overall supernatural appearance."

"Oh Apollo, lord of the sun and custodian of its daily trek across the sky; I request of your excellence," Phaethon bullshitted, "that you please provide me some proof that I am indeed your mortal son."

"Who is your whoring mother?" the sun god thundered in a booming voice that shook the entire throne room, pillars and all. "I have screwed so many gorgeous mortals that I really can't remember all of *their* unimportant names."

"My mother is 'Tigress' Clymene, the finest prostitute in all of Ethiopia with the firmest set of knockers this side of the *Euphrates River,*" Phaethon boldly stated. "Do you remember her?"

"Wow, yes!" Apollo exclaimed. "How could I ever forget those fantastic tits she possesses? They were absolutely incredible, even for a little sucker like yourself! In fact, I'm getting a major hard-on just thinking about them!"

"Then *you* really are my father!" Phaethon eagerly screamed-out while thinking: 'Why you dirty mother-fucker'! That asshole son of Zeus ought to have his balls busted and ground into dog meat! The lying shithead!' Phaethon's diminutive brain internalized."

"Apollo beckoned for his bastard son to approach *his* stately-shimmering throne, so that the father could better admire the boy's strength and audacity. "You are indeed my son," Apollo informed Phaethon. "And *you* shall enjoy my genetics for the remainder of your years, and you'll have the stamina to screw at least sixty mature females a day, which comes to about three pussies an hour, if you don't sleep and decide to go non-stop. And to show you my appreciation of your surprise visit," the sun god continued in a booming voice, "I shall grant you any wish your little fart, er, I mean 'little heart' desires."

"Phaethon contemplated Apollo's promise for a full minute, and without giving the matter sufficient consideration, the dumb, overly-ambitious, proud kid blurted-out, "Please father, I beg of you; allow me to drive *your* exotic sun chariot across the sky for just one day to demonstrate to the world *my* true *Olympus* ancestry."

"But Phaethon; you don't even have a chariot driver's license yet!" Apollo objected. "You don't even have a goddamned learner's permit! I beg you, my son; do not attempt to surpass your limited bounds," the sun/archer god sincerely pleaded. "You're a mere aspiring mortal, and might suffer a mere mortal's fate unless you wise-up and make a more reasonable request! Not even Zeus could steer the flaming chariot without a week's worth of intensive lessons and flight training!"

"But Phaethon was adamant in his persistence, so Apollo had no alternative except to honor *his* promise to *his* and Clymene's son, and permit the impulsive idiot to attempt the impossible. "Never lose your grip control of the four powerful white horses," Apollo imperatively cautioned Phaethon. "And don't be distracted or lose your grasp on the reins when you get hit in the face by stenchy flying horseshit exploding out of the horses' smelly assholes. And whatever you do," Apollo continued, "never look down to Earth because that will make you as fuckin' dizzy as drunken *Lord Dionysus.* And my son, the horses' lungs are also full of fire, and if the animals turn their heads toward you, be careful, for the flames from their nostrils can singe the hair right off of your balls, and the flares might even set your hairy asshole on fire!"

"Apollo looked into Phaethon's eyes, which were bloodshot from the long trek to India from Ethiopia via a detour through, Russia, and then through ancient Palestine. Immediately, the divine father understood all was futile, and that persuasion was a useless tool to implement against the cocky teenager's obstinate insistence. "I hope you've already gotten laid many times, because otherwise, you're going to die a fucked-up virgin!" the sun god declared to his haughty, naughty, adventurous, over-zealous offspring."

"The scrupulous sun god accompanied his stubborn kid out the temple's platinum back door, where the fabulous golden chariot had already been hitched to the four immortal white stallions. "You still have time to change your mind," Apollo recommended, "because pretty soon, you won't have time to change your shit-streaked underwear! What do you have to say about it?"

"That's okay Pop," obdurate Phaethon reflexively replied. "I don't wear underwear!"

"The glorious sun god then applied some protective oil called 'suntan lotion' to *his* son's rosy face, so that *his* nose and chin would not be seared from the fiery sun's heat, or from the horses' hot breaths. "Take the shortest route across the sky, and whatever you do," Apollo cautioned the oblivious punk-dunce Phaethon, "don't deviate from *my* daily course. If *you* allow the horses to take charge of your responsibility, then you might as well commit suicide right now, because otherwise, you're as good as fuckin' dead!"

"Phaethon leaped upon the rider's narrow ledge of the heavenly golden chariot, and anxiously grasped and held the reins. The nervous white stallions snorted fire, and then stomped their hoofs in anticipation of their daily flight across the majestic sky. The chariot zoomed-off toward the western horizon, and after a minute of careful flying, the four imposing horses realized that the highly-skilled and experienced sun god was not at the helm piloting their present excursion."

"The chariot's intense speed was soon unbearable, and the task too overwhelming for any mere mortal to ever endure. Soon, the sun god's vehicle began to sway and vacillate as it meandered between constellations, planets, and the Earth and the moon, and then Phaethon became quite fearful, regretting that he had ever pleaded with his divine father to drive the sun chariot alone from horizon to horizon."

"The fire-breathing horses soon wildly ascended and erratically descended in abnormal flight patterns and zany oscillations across the morning sky, the magnificent steeds taking full control of the chariot from the alarmed and suddenly-frightened asshole teenager trying to do a god's job without proper training or practice."

'This excessive heat is intolerable!' Phaethon thought, 'and this hot horseshit smacking me in the face is far worse than any bullshit I've ever heard, or ever seen, or ever smelled! Alas, I'm being justly punished for being so fuckin' arrogant and so fuckin' stupid'!"

"As the fiery chariot swiveled, rocked, vacillated and then plunged toward the Earth, Phaethon frantically and desperately tugged and manipulated the reins. Finally, out of sheer fear of dying, the young rookie charioteer made a last-ditch effort to save himself from ultimate destruction."

"Amazingly, the beleaguered youth regained control of the seemingly-doomed chariot as *he* miraculously managed to reverse his *crash course* in sun pulling. The chariot astoundingly righted itself on a steady route, and the four white horses obediently responded to the courageous lad's loud commands. Apollo's impressive golden vehicle rose-up to a safer altitude, and eventually out of harm's way. Catastrophe had been temporarily averted."

"Then, just as Phaethon finally regained his cocky confidence and demonstrated admirable dexterity while vigorously piloting the heavenly, weaving, and bobbing chariot, an unexpected obstacle suddenly appeared before him. "Who the fuck is that idiotic asshole?" the stunned son of Apollo exclaimed as the confused lad crashed into Lord Hermes, zooming across the sky on an important errand for Zeus. In an instant, Phaethon blew-off of Apollo's flaming sun chariot, and crashed-down upon the Earth, deader than Patroclus!"

"That was a great story," thrilled Eurballsourout lavishly commended Eurshiddenme. "I'm almost-glad I listened to most of it."

"I agree," Eurassisgras concurred. "Even though it sounded like utter horse crap, the lesson taught is that we must obey those in authority, or else face the consequences of destroying ourselves!"

"When Phaethon ignored Apollo's advice, the kid placed his life in jeopardy on the wheel of fortune! What an asshole!" Eurdicisin added to the bizarre conversation.

"I suppose that the moral of the story is that we should never question the knowledge or wisdom of our superiors, just like Patroclus had violated the advice of veteran warrior Achilles!" Eurcockisnum concluded and shared.

"I hope you mini-minds enjoyed my little myth's moral," Eurshiddenme stated. "Meeting is dismissed!"

* * * * * * * * * * * *

Menelaus spotted Patroclus's body lying upon the hot sand, so the King of Mycenae wildly steered his chariot around in the direction of the corpse, in order to defend Achilles's armor from the avaricious Trojan officers who desired to possess the treasured item as a meritorious war trophy. Several Trojans approached the slain Achaean, but realizing that Menelaus had the reputation of being a superior killer, the timid armor robbers cravenly retreated to fight in a safer battlefield environment.

But not willing to make any concessions to Menelaus, Phoebus Apollo inspired Hector to consider pilfering Achilles's armor from Patroclus's chest as a powerful symbol of Trojan war supremacy. 'I'll proudly wear the gear of Achilles, and then both the Argives and the Trojans will fear my formidable existence. The breastplate formerly belonged to Peleus,' Achilles's father,' Hector considered. 'So, maybe after this fucked-up war is over, I can pretend to be Achilles's father, find the sea nymph Thetis, and screw the hell out of her salt-flavored love tunnel!'

Almighty Zeus, knowing from Fate that Hector's remaining time as a Trojan warrior was quite short, made Achilles's armor fit comfortably upon the haughty prince's shoulders. King Priam's older son then stood erect and addressed his silent vanguard, most of whom were from various cities allied with Troy.

"Listen to me, you parasitic vultures. The people of Troy have sacrificed greatly just to feed your hungry mouths during a time of horrible famine, as a result of this ass-backwards war!" Hector yelled. "Our horny women have also given you clumsy assholes quality sex, even during their monthly periods! Help me' force Ajax and his comrades back to the Argive ships so that I can then capture Patroclus's body as a trophy to exhibit with Achilles's purloined armor at the Trojan Museum of Unnatural History."

The two armies, in a struggle to possess Patroclus's corpse, battered each other with tremendous ferocity. To make matters even worse, Zeus imaginatively cloaked the escalating clash with a mystifying mist that was so thick that Trojans were killing both Achaeans and Trojans, and Argives were slaughtering other Danaans as well as enemy Trojans.

Meanwhile, Achilles was not aware of Patroclus's terrible fate, since the dense mist that had been generated by Zeus had clouded the stubborn warrior's view of the noisy Troad Plain. Agamemnon shouted an instruction to his brother Menelaus that the King of Sparta should send a speedy runner to inform Achilles that his "gay lover" Patroclus had been mortally wounded.

"Antilochus! Become anti-walking and dash to Achilles and tell the obstinate prick of Patroclus's demise, and also, that Hector has stolen his father Peleus's sacred breastplate!" Menelaus commanded. "Sprint quickly now Antilochus, before you get the runs, and shit your already wet loin cloth right off your skinny ass!"

Chapter 17

"ACHILLES'S ARMOR"

'What the hell's going on out there on the Troad?' Achilles wondered. 'It looks like a friggin' swirling dust bowl. And why are the Argives running out of the haze like scared rabbits? I have a dreadful premonition about all of this havoc; my mother Thetis had once told me that the best of the Myrmidons would be killed in battle! Dear Zeus; I hope that her prediction turns-out *not* to be true, and that Patroclus will be spared from Hector's sword.'

Antilochus, a dashing young man, sprinted from the inclement Troad toward Achilles's hut and then gasped and panted, "I have terrible news to convey. Patroclus has been killed by that ruthless bastard Hector, who has also greedily stolen your armor off of your Captain's dead body."

"Oh no!" Achilles moaned, falling to the ground and lying and sobbing face-up with his eyes shut; the Myrmidon commander's mind swimming in a totally hysterical, emotional state. Immediately after Antilochus had sped-off to tell other officers of the bad tidings, Ifavagina, a horny slave hostage, ran-over to the weeping and delirious General, raised-up her tunic, squatted-down, and positively enjoyed having the closed-eyed, whimpering Achilles licking and lapping her aroused clit and eager beaver.

'Different strokes for different folks!' Ifavagina gleefully imagined as the savvy sex kitten gyrated up and down upon unconscious Achilles' long-hard nose, which was rubbing against her ever-pumping engorged clit, and the sobbing General's foot-long tongue was massaging and licking the girl's crazily riveting genitals that were moving like a primitive piston. And then, Ifavagina reached the biggest multiple-orgasm of her whole whoring life. After the kinky slut's eighth pleasurable climax, completely exhausted, the promiscuous harlot arose to her feet and groggily wobbled and stumbled back to her slave-girls' tent.

Several minutes later, Achilles opened his eyes from his trance-like state, started gagging incessantly, and suddenly experienced a lengthy choking fit. The encumbered General reached his fingers down his throat, and was able to remove several hundred brown pubic hairs from his swollen larynx. 'This is all I need! A lousy hairy situation after learning the bad news about Patroclus being brutally killed by that scumbag Hector!' the confused General reckoned, as dumbfounded Achilles again examined the several hundred dark-brown pubic hairs in his palm.

Meanwhile, deep under the sea, immortal Thetis telepathically became cognizant of her son's overwhelming grief, so the sea goddess assembled her companion sisters, the Nereids, beautiful nymphs all, to share her grieving misery. 'Oh, my faithful Nereids. I'm so inconsolable. My son Achilles had sailed off to Troy, where the young adventurer was destined by prophecy to perish in battle after his friend Patroclus would die. Soon, my dear son will also have his demise, and his troubled soul, according to the prophet's words, will swiftly travel-down to Hades, where the mysterious god of darkness and Queen Persephone will have indisputable custody of my audacious Achilles forever!"

The Nereids, notorious denizens of the deep, accompanied Thetis through the tumultuous underwater sea currents, swimming like graceful dolphins until they and she parted company at the sandy shores of Troy. Thetis then employed her supernatural powers and located Achilles, who she found sitting-upon the ground and sniffing and obsessively smelling the palm of his right hand.

"My psychologically disturbed child!" Thetis whispered into Achilles's ear. "Always look at the brighter side of the storm. Zeus has granted your wish that the Trojans are winning the war, and that Agamemnon realizes that he has no chance of victory without your cooperation in bringing your brutal Myrmidons into the ever-vacillating combat zone. Why are you so distressed? You're too big and old to suck on your baby pacifier!"

"The Trojan prince Hector has slain my dearest friend, Patroclus, who is also my significant other," Achilles related to his sea goddess mother. "And to top-off that horrendous catastrophe, the obnoxious Trojan prince now wears my father's armor, which was given to your husband Peleus by Hephaestus when you two had married. Now, I wish that my father had taken home a mortal woman as his bride, instead of you, you conniving immortal bitch!"

"Oh, my Zeus!" Thetis exclaimed. "It had been prophesied by an anonymous oracle that once Patroclus would die, your fatal end would soon follow! If only Discord could be banished from terrorizing and plaguing mortals, then happiness could abound among humans."

"If only Hector could have murdered Discord instead of killing pure-hearted Patroclus!" Achilles hypothesized and declared. "Now Mother; I intend to go and hunt-down Hector and make the Trojan women weep as those in my camp are presently now doing over Patroclus's death. And don't try and stop me, no matter what the fucked-up pedophile priests and prophets predict, along with what the insane lesbian oracles think and say!"

"My son; Hector now has your armor, and without it, you cannot challenge the fierce Trojan and win any match in a death struggle. Stay calm and vigilant. I'll visit the blacksmith god Hephaestus, whom I know very well. He owes me a few sexual favors, and will gladly forge in his workshop a new bronze breastplate that you can proudly wear in combat, along with the finest shield, spear and sword."

Meanwhile, the Achaean pallbearers solemnly carried Patroclus's corpse, found near the deep trench that the Achaeans had dug, but as that somber funeral procession was happening, Hector attacked the moat like a ferocious tiger leaping upon its antelope prey, and fortunately, Ajax and his soldiers were able to successfully repel the attack and force the Trojans *to ditch* their assault.

Unarmed Achilles, in a moment of sheer madness, foolishly stood on top of the nearby wall and began hectoring Hector, persistently mocking, goading, and ridiculing his avowed enemy's alleged cravenness. But alert Athena cleverly cloaked the Argive General's head in her majestic Aegis, and a glowing halo appeared upon Achilles' crown that absolutely scared the shit and piss out of Hector and his burly, surly bodyguards.

The superstitious Trojans, being completely intimidated by the divine aura, pulled-back to the safety of the city's towering walls, and at the same time, the emboldened Achaeans sought shelter beside *their* recently-constructed ditch and accompanying wall, just as the eternal sun's warm glow gradually sank upon the western horizon.

The Trojans, all individually suffering from either severe diarrhea or chronic constipation as a result of Achilles' supernatural appearance, held a gathering of the minds where the prophet Polydamas, who had a multitude of sexy girlfriends, addressed the assembly, which included King Priam, Queen Hecuba, Helen of Troy, Prince Hector, and Prince Paris.

"Friends and colleagues," Polydamas began his oral commentary. "Here is what I argue is a logical plan for us to initiate. When Achilles held-back from entering the war over a minor squabble with Agamemnon, we had the distinct advantage in the conflict. But now, I dread facing the enraged Argive General and his formidable Myrmidons. If we confront him now, I foresee a terrible massacre of us Trojans occurring."

"Polydamas, what do you suggest?" King Priam asked.

"I wholeheartedly plead, especially with you, Hector. Let us retire to our beloved city and wait-out Achilles' crazed temper-tantrum. Out on the

Troad, our fatigued army is too exposed to *his* animalistic treachery. Our beleaguered troops can guard the city from the surrounding walls' high ramparts. Let's allow Achilles to exhaust his rage, and also fatigue his horses as the lunatic races his chariot in a wild frenzy around-and-around the well-defended city. The irate Phthian warrior will only experience perpetual frustration, and will then return sulking like a denied infant, back to his anchored ships."

"Polydamas, we used to see events and comprehend their nature in a similar fashion," Hector eloquently objected. "But now we're occupying opposite ends of the rainbow. If I interpret your words correctly, in your statement you desire that we should yield-back all the land that we've gained on the Troad by retiring our troops to the city, and that our brave soldiers should stay penned-up like slimy hogs and passive lambs, watching our wealth diminish like a hundred-year-old coot's limp dingle. I say to all my friends, Trojans, and fellow countrymen, that any intelligent person who is present at this meeting who endorses Polydamas's madness is both a traitor and an absolute coward."

"What say you, Trojans!" Hector vehemently challenged the council. "I say that tomorrow, we aggressively attack the Argives; Achilles or no Achilles! Our coordinated advance will dominate the Achaeans! And in conclusion, we'll let the gods determine which side will ultimately vanquish the other!"

With the influence of Pallas Athene, who had committed to side with Odysseus and the Achaeans, not one representative attending the Trojan conclave supported Polydamas's resolution, but instead, by virtue of shouting and raising their right hands, cast their votes for Hector's decisive plan of swift action.

Simultaneously, at the Greeks' somber encampment, a parallel strategy meeting was in-progress. Saddened by the loss of Patroclus, Achilles made an impassioned speech, with his oration's popular theme being that furious military action was necessary to avenge the well-loved hero Patroclus's death. The well-respected Myrmidon General ended his speech with the dire plea, "Someone give me a gold coin so that I may place it inside Patroclus's mouth. The coin will serve as a toll fee for the ghostly Charon to ferry my dear friend's immortal soul, stationed upon *his* barge, across the morbid, underground Styx River, with my dear friend's spirit being transported from the Land of the Living to Hades' dismal Kingdom of the Dead! Dear Patroclus: may you rest in peace among the colorful flowers growing in the Elysian Fields of Hades for all of eternity!"

Women attendants in Achilles' camp entered the funeral tent and washed the gore from Patroclus's corpse; oiled his skin, and administered perfumed salves to his open scarlet wounds. The champion's body was then gently lifted and placed upon a horizontal bier, and then covered with an immaculate white shroud, according to traditional custom.

Meanwhile, Thetis had arrived at the volcanic palace of Hephaestus and made an urgent request to the blacksmith craftsman, who was making wheels for the latest chariot models for Zeus, Ares and Apollo. The master of the flaming furnace was happy to see his unexpected visitor.

"Ah, wonderful Thetis!" Hephaestus warmly greeted. "I'll never forget the time when I had suffered Hera's wrath, and she flung me down from Mt. Olympus. I was but a mere toddler then, but your arms caught my plummet as I was about to plunge into the sea and drown. For your intercession, I am most grateful! What the hell can I do for you?"

After Thetis revealed that Achilles had lent Patroclus his cherished armor only to have it later stolen from the hero's dead body by Hector, Hephaestus, feeling empathy for Thetis's plight, labored for several hours manufacturing an immense shield having five layers of thick solid bronze, and the magnificent defensive item featured an intricate array of bold-relief images displaying Earth, Sun, Sky, Sea, Tits, Erect Penises, Stars and the Moon. And all twelve constellations of the zodiac, along with scenes of resplendent palaces, forts and castles, were also artistically etched upon the shield's majestic surface.

After lighting his forge to an extremely high temperature, the talented-but-lame blacksmith god next meticulously hammered-out upon his incomparable anvil several dozen silver arrows, and a javelin, a cuirass, gleaming shin greaves, and a marvelous bronze javelin for Achilles to use in battle.

Thetis graciously thanked Hephaestus for his prompt and deft assistance; then gathered together the recently formed armor pieces into her sea chariot, and like a predator eagle, swooped over to the distant Troad Plain to deliver the essential weapons and equipment to her still-grieving son.

Chapter 18

"RECONCILIATION OF ACHILLES"

"Well, Eurshiddenme, our pals Eurassisgras, Eurdicisin, Eurcockisnum and I have been really enjoying these dumb-ass moral lessons you're trying to academically teach us inside your new shoddy officer's hut," Eurballsourout praised. "Do you have another fucked-up myth that somehow corresponds with the recent death of Patroclus?"

"Yes, I concur with Eurballsourout," Eurassisgras agreed. "Your original bullshit now sounds like utter horse-shit, which is a step better and higher on the feces scale than your normal chicken-shit! Now Eurshiddenme, tell us a good moral to improve out general morale!"

"If and when we ever get back to Ithaca," Eurdicisin added to the ridiculous conversation, "Odysseus has said that he'll invite us to a big palace party over near his pool. The only problem is that his pool, which we've all been invited to swim-in, is a goddamned cesspool!"

"I had heard a strange rumor that Achilles is a bisexual who had Patroclus as his male Partner!" Eurcockisnum related to his whimsical comrades. "He might even be a secret member of the radical LBGTQRMSV community that Agamemnon, Menelaus, Menapauis, Odysseus, and Ajax have all condemned!"

"As far as I know, that's just only hearsay and not at all true," Eurshiddenme objectively answered. "The two friends always ate meals together, but only had a plate-tonic relationship!"

"But Eurdicisin is right in his blunt criticism of King Odysseus," Eurcockisnum contributed to the peculiar discussion. "I know from experience that visibility is not-too-good under the surface of the king's always-full cesspool! Now please, Eurshiddenme. We promise to remain quiet if you'll quickly divulge to us another one of your model-behavior myths!"

"Okay, guys. Before I had stupidly voyaged with King Odysseus here to Troy," Eurshiddenme confessed, "I was conscientiously studying to be a pedophile priest, and had to listen to major bullshit from the mouths of conceited professors teaching at the Ithacan Impostors Academy, and here's one of my favorite tales that I had learned while being a naïve student there."

"Some ancient Greek myths are popular because the people in them are fucked-up. Even today, people love gossiping and reading about others of their species that are complete assholes, just to make the gossiper or listener feel better about himself or herself. And even four thousand years ago, adults knew about what pains-in-the-ass' teenagers are like, and how the noxious punks' stubborn insistence that they are invincible often leads to predictable tragedy. When acne-faced, hormone-dominated kids think they know it all, then those know-it-alls either wind-up in the local hospital or in the community cemetery. Consequently, it is absolutely amazing that any of us survive those ugly adolescent years to eventually mature into wise adults. As it has been so aptly described, 'It is too bad that youth is wasted on the young'!"

"Now, my military friends, the inventor Daedalus was a genius from antiquity that dared to learn the gods' treasured secrets. The creative Greek was a master architect and engineer who had designed many extraordinary temples, amphitheaters, agoras, buildings, whorehouses, public projects and impressive co-ed' public restrooms. The experimenter was commissioned by the wealthy *cretin'* King Minos to oversee the construction of the Labyrinth, a complex series of underground caves and tunnels situated beneath the monarch's opulent palace on the island of Crete."

"I'll commit to building the Labyrinth for your personal honor and glory," Daedalus told Minos. "But I'll need a lot of foreign material to finish the job. Also, I need to bring along my royal, pain-in-the-ass, punk teenager to keep his ass out of trouble, and to teach the little thug how to value *constructive things,* so that hopefully, the blundering loser successfully makes it to adulthood."

"I know exactly what the fuck you mean!" King Minos concurred. "I need this 'a-mazing' Labyrinth built beneath my palace to keep my monster the *Minotaur* in a safe enclosure. The grotesque creature has got the body of a muscular man, and the head of a formidable bull. Every year, I plan to sacrifice seven young vestal virgins and seven acne-faced *bullheaded* male punks to the *Minotaur* inside my subterranean maze, just to get rid of the know-it-all bitches and the horny bastards, and also to appease the greedy gods," Minos related to the distinguished inventor. "Daedalus, if you're lucky, your horny, asshole kid might be one of the victimized, bullheaded, punk shit-heads to be sacrificed!"

"That's a deal!" Daedalus agreed, warmly shaking the king's already broken hand. "My son Icarus thinks he can do no wrong; the fool defies my authority, and always impetuously attempts taking the 'bull by the horns' when the frivolous asshole should be exercising mature patience and 'discretion', which does not rhyme with excretion."

"Your recalcitrant son Icarus sounds like the typical run-of-the-mill teenage jerk-off to me," King Minos surmised and agreed while examining his crushed right hand. "And Daedalus; I think that *'a minute' tour'* with the *Minotaur* ought to scare the living shit out of your wise-assed punk kid! Ha, ha, ha, ha!"

"After the intricate and complicated Labyrinth had finally been built for the king beneath his expansive-expensive palace, Minos loved its design and its confusing maze-like passages so much that the monarch decided to keep Daedalus on Crete, against the genius's will, to creatively erect other architectural wonders."

"Daedalus, I want you to engineer a great reservoir for Knossus," the tyrannical king insisted. "Since I am one of Zeus's favorite sons, it will be built to honor my omnipotent father, the founder of *my* city! Do I fuckin' make myself' clear?"

"I'd like to stay residing on your ugly, barren, arid, desolate island," Daedalus politely refused, "but I have to return to Athens back on the mainland and give my estranged wife money, or she has threatened me with divorce and with serious alimony payments that are certain to bankrupt my troubled ass!"

"Build me my damned reservoir for the taxpaying people of Knossus, or else, you'll most certainly be fed to the *Minotaur* along with your fucked-up, teenage, punk kid!" Minos boisterously threatened. "Get the message, you' delinquent, egomaniac, lowlife shit-head!"

"Daedalus intensively and extensively worked on the massive reservoir project for several years, but when King Minos had learned that the renowned architect had tried bribing sailors to stash Icarus and himself' inside a ship's cargo hull as stowaways, in order to sail to Athens, the Cretan cretin became incensed and mighty pissed-off. Minos had Daedalus and his insolent, know-it-all kid, locked inside a high stone tower situated upon a lofty cliff, overlooking the *Aegean Sea,* which gets older every single and married day."

"From his open-air window overlooking the sea, Daedalus studied the graceful seagulls zipping-around the towering cliffs, looking for human heads to drop their raunchy wet crap bombs upon. The inventor marveled at the birds' elegant flight patterns, as the eagles and vultures circled the stone tower, and the inventor envied the creatures absolute freedom, soaring, drifting, and majestically gliding all over the goddamned cloudless sky."

"Icarus, I have some friends on this island who are willing to smuggle bird feathers and wooden pieces to this tower," the father calmly explained. "We will make sturdy frames that will fit snugly over our arms and shoulders, and next, we'll cover them with feathers, and then fly-off of this Zeus-forsaken-island back to the mainland of Greece."

"Okay, I'll help you Pop," Icarus out-of-character complied. "But only because I need to get back to Athens to shack-up with my old girlfriend, and to escape the danger of that horny *Minotaur* predator, who is said to be gay in addition to being fucked-up. I heard that the big mother wants to screw young boys up the ass with his pillar-sized dick! Let me tell you Pop; I really don't need that kind of 'bull shit' happening to my young asshole!"

"Within six months, all of the necessary materials the accomplished builder had specified had been successfully smuggled into the stone tower, and Daedalus and Icarus diligently manufactured the two sets of wings, using thread and wax to attach the essential bird feathers to the flexible wooden frames. Soon, the determined conspirators had almost-completed their ambitious project."

"Remember Icarus," Daedalus reminded his independent-minded, aberrant son. "Don't fly too high or too low. Take the straightest, most moderate course back to the coast of Greece. Follow my stellar lead, and don't deviate, you fucked-up, young-punk deviate!"

"I'll do exactly what the hell I want," Icarus vehemently protested. "And that's all that I'll do, and nothing else. I know precisely how to use these stupid-ass wings without ever having the need for further education from attending *Hermes' Aviation School and Flight Academy!*"

"I wish you wouldn't have such a defiant *mercurial* personality!" Daedalus maturely and vociferously criticized his aberrant offspring. "If you fly too high and propel yourself too close to the sun, the goddamned wax on your wings will melt, and you'll swiftly plummet into the sea."

"Pop, the sun's gotta' be more than seven miles away from the fuckin' Earth, contrary to what you happen to think it is," Icarus argued. "And besides, once I had climbed a mountain and noticed that the higher that I ascended toward the summit, the colder the temperature got! I think you're trying to feed me a lot of nonsensical, superstitious, adult-mythological, non-scientific bullshit about the sun melting my wings!"

"And son," Daedalus proceeded while ignoring his son's arrogant and obnoxious comments. "Don't snafu yourself' and fly too close to the sea. Your wings might become damp and wet from the saltwater waves, and then you'll crash and splash into *Poseidon's* dangerous domain!"

"Pop, the word *don't* ain't in my friggin' vocabulary," the defensive, know-it-all knucklehead challenged. "Saying the damned word *don't* to a teenager is just like saying 'I dare you to fuckin' do it'!"

"The following morning, a light breeze accompanied the appearance of dawn, and the two plotters diligently prepared for their clandestine mission. The father and the son donned their portable feathered wings, and Dacdalus was the first to leap out of the stone tower's third-story open window. Icarus followed his father's steady example, and soon was also admirably gliding over the rugged mountain cliff, and heading out over the serene *Aegean Sea.* "

"That's the gods' *Hermes* and *Cupid* flying up there!" King Minos's chief counselor erroneously indicated to the astonished monarch. "Even without filing a flight itinerary, those two immortal chums really know how to wing it!"

"Minotaur shit!" Minos yelled and wildly cursed at his principal adviser. "Those nutcase idiots flying around up there are that stupid shithead Daedalus and his fucked-up kid Icarus, desperately attempting to escape my petty despotism!"

"Soon, Icarus became infatuated and enthralled with the extreme exhilaration of flying through the tranquil atmosphere. The excited youth had to test his physical limits zipping, looping, and zooming all over the azure sky in violation of his determined, steadfast father, who maintained *his* straight and narrow course in the direction of the distant Greek mainland."

"I can fly like the gods!" Icarus screamed in absolute delight. "I feel immortal! I feel invincible! I feel like jerking-off!" Icarus was rising and swooping all over the sky, frenetically attempting to gain control of his erratic path from Crete to the Greek mainland, after randomly experimenting with the thrill of flight."

"Daring Icarus evidently flew too high, and the intense heat from the glaring sun made the wax inside his artificial wings gradually melt. The unfortunate lad rapidly plummeted-down to Earth, instantly dying upon impact. The unperturbed and cautious Daedalus looked-back, shrugged his winged shoulders, and then continued his steady flight path to the Greek mainland. 'Father knows best!' Daedalus aptly concluded."

"Is the moral to your fascinating myth the dumb-fuck explanation that younger people like Achilles and Patroclus should always blindly obey the values, teachings, and statements of their parents and elders in authority?" Eusassisgras seriously asked Eurshiddenme.

"No!" Eurshiddenme tersely replied. "The trite moral to this esoteric myth is that a flighty personality will always lead to your demise! Now, my fellow captains; class is now officially adjourned!"

* * * * * * * * * * * *

Dawn predictably rose in the eastern sky, and Thetis appeared upon the beach where Archilles lay, conscientiously still guarding Patroclus's body. "Dear child; my son, please rest in peace, while Patroclus really and truly rests in peace! Sit-up, and let your blue eyes admire this inimitable shield that the blacksmith god has marvelously forged for you in his valley! No man has ever carried such fantastic protection into battle!"

The armor held by Thetis shone so brilliantly that the Myrmidon soldiers standing and bullshitting a half-mile away thought that the intense glare was from a more-miniature second sun that had been recently created.

"You're right, Mother!" Achilles readily agreed. "This shield is quite peerless. But if I now carry it as self-defense against the Trojan forces, the flies and maggots will most certainly land upon Patroclus's limp body and start consuming his exposed flesh!"

"In your absence, I will guard and preserve his corpse by inserting nectar and ambrosia into his lifeless nostrils," Thetis volunteered her specialized services. "It's too bad that I didn't think about shoving the nectar and ambrosia up your friend's nose before he ever engaged Hector on the Troad Plain."

At the Achaeans early-morning strategy session, Achilles apologetically addressed egocentric Agamemnon in front of the Argives' principal officers. "King of Mycenae; let us consider dropping our adversarial enmity toward each other, our lengthy quarrel just being in strife over a single slave girl. I hereby vow that I cease and desist my animosity towards you right now; that is, if you will sacredly promise to do the same towards me."

After a boisterous cheer erupted among the Danaan captains, Agamemnon told the assembled commanders that he too was willing to abandon his disdain, and eagerly welcome Achilles's alliance in savagely fighting Hector and his minions. "Folly has tricked both you and me, Achilles, and the conniving goddess, by the same name, had once hoodwinked Zeus himself," Agamemnon opined. "Then, the Almighty god cast Folly down to Earth, and mankind has grievously suffered ever since the appearance of that harmful female instigator, who perpetually aggravates all mankind with dumb-shit wants such as sex and greed. I'll reiterate the prolific offer that had been stated to you yesterday by Odysseus and his comrades, and upon your acceptance, the earmarked goods will be delivered to your Bireme later today."

"Alright then," Achilles firmly answered. "Let's not dither and dicker any further insignificant chicken-shit that's previously been disguised as serious bullshit! My body and soul burns and sizzles to avenge Patroclus's slaying. I'll not swallow a morsel of food, for I shall fast and make my soul holy by virtue of personal sacrifice! However, if the soldiers need to satisfy their appetites to make themselves stronger for the upcoming battle, then so be it! I crave not food, but instead, I hunger for the anguish and groans of moaning, dying Trojans, with my utmost contempt being especially for that reprehensible rogue, Hector!"

Odysseus departed the assembly of generals with an entourage of men to gather the gifts promised to Achilles by Agamemnon, which included seven chariot tripods, twenty gleaming bronze cauldrons, twelve splendid black stallions, and finally, seven skilled serving women highly-proficient at administering both fellatio and kinky sex.

"Should I include your slave girl Briseis in the count?" Agamemnon asked the leader of the Myrmidons. "Do you still wish to pump her pussy dry?"

"I no longer love or lust for Briseis. Instead, I now wish to screw another recently-arrived slave girl, the gorgeous Ifavagina," Achilles surprisingly revealed. "But no matter how I possessively stare at the girl's alluring body, she completely ignores my obvious flirting. Quite frankly, Agamemnon, I have forgotten all about Briseis and now would love to munch on and pump Ifavagina's love tunnel!"

"What did you say?" Agamemnon yelled in disbelief. "You brazenly say that you want to fuck my daughter, Iphigenia? Be careful with your loose words, Achilles! Your risqué business will soon become your risky business!"

"No, Agamemnon," Achilles angrily corrected the Achaean leader. "I want to screw the new slave girl Ifavagina; not your dyke daughter Iphigenia! But if a vagina comes my way like Ifavagina's vagina, then I might want to pork that new vagina as if it were Ifavagina's vagina!"

Then, Ajax wisely piped-up and interrupted the convoluted dialogue. "I hear from camp gossip that Iphigenia's vagina is hairier than Ifavagina's vagina, which is now, for some inexplicable reason, strangely almost bald! But I too have the hots for the new slave girl Ifavagina. I only wish that the bush-less bitch had a boner' to pick with me! Ha, ha, ha!"

Old Nestor laughed at the giant warrior's zany admission and declared: "Ajax; if frail Ifavagina was ever screwed by you, then Ifavagina's vagina would cease to exist. In my humble opinion, I think that Ifavagina would prefer being porked by a thousand-pound grunting and snorting wild boar in heat than be vigorously pumped and maimed by you!"

"True," Agamemnon verified. "Ajax; you are not only an existential threat to Hector and the rabid Trojans; you're also a lethal menace to every female in our camp who wants to get laid!"

Briseis finally learned of Patroclus's death, and rushed-out of her slave hut to mourn his passing. The slave girl knelt-down upon the lonely beach to pray and honor the young hero's shortened life.

'Oh, dear Patroclus; I modestly worship your former idealism and naivete. I never wanted to have sex with Achilles, but always wished to lay in bed with you! I know that you and Achilles had a secret bisexual nature, but now that you are dead, I must confess to Zeus, and all the gods, that Ifavagina and I have our own special relationship going, even though her pussy has somehow recently been denuded of pubic hairs. If and when Ifavagina and I ever luckily return alive to Phthia, we aspire to become entrepreneurial, and open a business to be called the Patroclus Gay and Lesbian Bordello, to fondly and respectfully honor your wonderful virgin memory.'

* * * * * * * * * * * *

Achilles was also lamenting the death of Patroclus as the Phthian heir donned his new armor that had been skillfully manufactured by Hephaestus. 'I think of all the dead I've known in addition to your friendship, and I know, dearly-departed Patroclus, according to foretold prophecy, that I'll soon be reunited with everyone deceased down in dark and dismal Hades,' Achilles lamented. 'I had thought that I would perish first here at foreign Troy, but you have beaten me into the hereafter. I care no longer for my future throne back in Phthia, nor do I ever think about all of the riches that Agamemnon has offered me for my allegiance to his and Menelaus's cause in this despicable war. All I think about is reuniting with your spirit in the swirling and mysterious darkness of subterranean Hades!'

Meanwhile, upon the summit of radiant Mt. Olympus, Zeus was asking Pallas Athene if the benign goddess had abandoned Odysseus and the Achaeans. "Go and imbue Achilles with nectar and ambrosia so that your new Greek hero will have sufficient power, stamina and energy in his limbs to successfully emerge from his impending combat with Hector. To tell you the truth, dear daughter, I'm beginning to like this defiant fellow Achilles myself!"

Achilles proudly mounted his chariot, which was hitched to Xanthus and Balius, two magnificent horses reputed to be divine in heritage. Amazingly, Xanthus spoke profound words to Achilles.

"Master; my keen extra-perception senses tell me that your prescribed doom draws near, despite your valorous intent to avenge Patroclus's death at the bloody hands of Hector, which most certainly has been inspired by interfering Lord Apollo. You're hearing this vital analysis right from the horse's mouth! Balius and I can only assist you in your quest, but we cannot save your ass from the encroachment of death, and we foresee your imminent rendezvous with King Hades and Queen Persephone! Stop being a stupid shit and go back and sulk inside your military hut!"

"Asshole equine!" Achilles rankled and yelled at the phenomenal talking steed. "I don't need to wear jockey shorts to comprehend that what you are commonly saying, I already am well-aware!"

Chapter 19

"THE GODS BATTLE"

As Odysseus's five lame-brained captains prepared to again confront the formidable Trojans in frivolous hand-to-hand, spear-to-spear combat, fastidious Eurballsourout asked his immediate superior Eurshiddenme for some moral inspiration and some fundamental rationale for fighting the "irrational war" for greedy King Agamemnon of Mycenae, and for equally avaricious King Menelaus of Sparta.

"Look guys," Eurshiddenme speculated and stated. "Here is the only moral justification that I can offer. If covetous people aren't punished by the gods in this world, then I submit that the violators will definitely find their deserved penance after death in gloomy Hades."

"I need more motivation to continue fighting for stupid-ass selfish causes," Eurdicisin added to the preposterous discussion. "Even if I receive a small sack of gold as my compensation for fighting for Menelaus and Agamemnon, that miniscule pittance will be meager consolation for my family if I get my balls castrated by an errant Trojan javelin, and as a result, can't sire any punk kids to raise back in Ithaca."

"Eurdicisin is right," Eurassisgras confirmed. "Agamemnon, Menelaus and Odysseus are tiny pawns on Almighty Zeus's gameboard, and even worse, we five assholes are minor pawns on Agamemnon, Menelaus, and Odysseus's less-important gameboard! No matter how you evaluate circumstances, we're being rooked by power-hungry kings and unfaithful queens. Don't worry, Eurshiddenme!" Eurdicisin cautioned. "We won't heckle you if you're sincere in your candid answer to us. But instead, give us some reason to die other than to become deceased for asshole narcissistic Agamemnon, for vindictive Menelaus, and for arrogant Achilles!"

"Yes; give us a good example that sinful dipshits playing with our frail fate will be punished in the end, either in this world or the next," Eurcockisnum begged Eurshiddenme. "I mean, I have low self-esteem to begin with. Give me some consolation for fighting for sex-driven royalty, when I suffer from chronic erectile dysfunction with my flaccid dingle, and also with me carrying useless barren testicles. Unlike Eurdicisin, I'm already impotent, and I don't need to be castrated by any fuckin' errant javelin in order to be sperm-less with a goddamned hollow-weenie!"

"Yes, I urge you high-ranking sir; tell us a decent story that will inspire us to fight and die," Eurassisgas requested of Eurshiddenme. "We promise to remain reticent and will try to relish your suspect rhetoric!"

"Well men; here's today's rendition as told to me by an about-to-die lesbian prostitute who had suffered from osteo-arthritis in her permanently stiff clit, and also from flat, punctured, deflated tits," Eurshiddenme prefaced. "Midas was King of Phrygia in Asia Minor, and most people living inside and outside Phrygia didn't give a fast fart about the egotistical ruler, or about any of his irrelevant, imperial bullshit. Despite the public's apathy about their royal guardian, Midas was extremely wealthy and very powerful, because he taxed his subjects to death and used their labor, and also their money, to break almost everyone's balls or puncture their tits. The emperor never took any crap from anyone, preferring to pursue his own foolish inclinations, making hasty and irrational judgments without the consent of his distinguished transvestite advisers, whom *he* thought were simply charlatans and demented assholes, instead of being harmless, deviant transvestites."

"One day Dionysus, the always-drunk Greek god of wine and frivolity, was traveling through Phrygia with his entourage of naked nymphs and retarded satyrs, who were creatures that happened to be half-man, half-goat, and fully fucked-up. Anyway, one member of the troupe was Salenus, an old, fat, bald-headed prick who was barely sober while nodding his noggin and seated upon his lazy donkey, which all of a sudden smelled some ass's ass a mile away in King Midas's royal stables."

"The donkey surreptitiously lagged behind, and then strayed from the caravan of merrymakers, who continued to party without even realizing that the old fat fart and his mount were missing from their elite company. The independent ass took Salenus's ass west, and an hour later, arrived at King Midas's incomparable rose garden, where Salenus's ass fell off *his* ass and tumbled into an *asinine* clump of thorny, asshole rose bushes."

"The King's alert gardeners discovered Salenus bleeding and laughing upon the ground, and the common laborers helped the comical, drunken idiot stagger to his feet and think of what words to say. Meanwhile, the good-natured gardeners searched in vain for Salenus's eight other asses."

"Where the fuck am I?" the chubby, bald-headed old codger inquired. "Who wants to fuckin' tickle my armpits and scratch my balls with both ends of an ostrich feather?"

"The notorious revels of hiccupping Dionysus had become common knowledge throughout Phrygia, and the alert gardeners perceptively recognized that Salenus was one of the wine-god's intimate colleagues. The landscapers wrapped a wreath around *his* neck, consisting of assorted flowers, along with assorted and discarded marijuana butts, and soon the various workers dragged his corpulent carcass up the palace steps, and gracefully dumped the intoxicated Salenus upon the marble floor. Greedy King Midas was then quickly summoned to royally entertain his new eminent guest."

"The King introduced himself to famous Salenus, who was still so inebriated that he believed *he* was speaking with a male prostitute in a nearby city ghetto. Midas was thrilled that one of Dionysus's close acquaintances had visited *his* opulent palace, and the monarch insisted that Salenus stay for a feast that would rival any that Dionysus himself had ever attended or provided."

"You must stay and enjoy my fine hospitality! I say hospitality because after you get done a full week of biological partying, drinking, eating, and screwing, you'll fuckin' wind-up in my royal hospital," Midas told the still-dysfunctional Salenus. "In this country, there is always feast and never famine! And when we run out of food, we suck on each other's genitals, and then merrily lick our sticky fingers."

"That's perfectly wonderful!" Salenus exclaimed, while groggily staggering-around and habitually hiccupping. "My throat, my stomach and my loins are all famished! Bring on the strippers, the switch-hitting lesbians, and the goddamned male couch dancers, you stingy, parsimonious bastard!"

"Much preparation and attention to palace detail was done for the impending celebration, with servants flitting-around setting tables, carrying wine jugs and baskets of food, and placing sweet-smelling, ancient aphrodisiac elixir at strategic places."

"A fantastic orgy followed, which lasted for ten whole days and nights, until all the male attendees ran out of sperm fluid, and all the women's hairy, pink honey-wells went dry. Lyres and pipes were played by female minstrels having their menstruals, so the musicians were exempted from participation in the orgy, and when not tooting-away, had to sit all by themselves at a designated "periodic table" where they had some "good chemistry and lousy biology" to share, while periodically taking their daily physics."

"Midas next conducted Salenus through the festooned halls to the King's favorite palace bath, where the two frolicked and toyed with each other like a pair of horny homosexual chimpanzees. Those flirtatious activities went on for another two whole days, until Midas collapsed on the mosaic tile floor from sheer exhaustion, and inebriated Salenus had drunk all of the dirty, scummy water from the hot tub, thinking and believing that it was sweet-tasting wine mingled with aphrodisiac elixir."

"Dionysus heard about Midas's wild celebration, and arrived at the King's palace to retrieve his wayward friend Salenus. When the god of wine learned of the wonderful hospitality Midas had extended to *his* "salubrious comrade", Dionysus promised to grant the illustrious monarch any gift *he* so desired, either reasonable or extravagant."

"The King's heart possessed many non-virtuous, negative qualities, such as lust, greed, pride, hedonism, and vanity. So naturally, *his* exploration of pleasure was predicated upon satisfying one or more of those particular self-destructive vices. Midas's mind was still-fatigued from all of the ten-day biological indulgence, along with the two-day private orgy with Salenus, so the king's selfish mind was now in total disarray; a facsimile of his obese, bald-headed guest's erratic thought patterns."

"King Midas's cerebrum envisioned the golden cups that his intoxicated revelers had dented and hurled upon the palace marble floors, and the ruler thought about *his* golden honeycomb that the famous Greek architect Daedalus had engineered for the king's honor. 'Those drunken, shit-faced imbeciles have ransacked my entire palace, have vandalized my cherished golden honeycomb, and have smashed or ruptured all of my treasured golden possessions,' the disenchanted emperor imagined and concluded."

"Dionysus," Midas answered the quasi-deity, who preferred reveling with scumbag mortals down on Earth rather than associating with *his* condescending, almighty, pompous peers on *Mt. Olympus*. "I wish to have golden statues of you and Salenus manufactured to commemorate your fine visit to Phrygia, and to pay tribute to your amusing friend's memorable stay ay my ornate palace." The King then realized a once in a lifetime very *golden opportunity*. "Therefore, Dionysus," Midas continued as the greedy bastard finally announced the true reason for his veiled plan. "Give *me* the power to transform everything that I touch into solid gold. This unique gift will protect me from gold diggers, from goldbrickers, and from itinerant *Golden Fleecers*. The Midas Touch will be like my own personal golden parachute, sheltering me from potential poverty, even though I don't know what the fuck a parachute is, let alone a goddamned golden one!"

"I suggest that you give the weird matter some more thought," Dionysus solemnly and soberly advised, while cautioning to his new acquaintance the importance of serious deliberation and rational discretion. "Don't do anything 'rash', for I have no ointment or lotion that can cure major skin irritations!"

"Kings of Asia Minor tended to be obstinate and stubborn after committing-to and announcing their intentions, so Midas was adamant about his innermost desire. "Dionysus, this is my grandest wish," the egomaniac selfishly maintained. "I would like to be conferred with the *Golden Touch.* Now, I insist that you keep your promise and afford me *that* particular luxury!"

"Okay Your Motley Majesty; you win the debate!" Dionysus replied and conceded, shaking his immortal head left and right to demonstrate his obvious skepticism and objection. "When Salenus and I exit your magnificent gardens, the *Golden Touch* will go into effect. But always remember, dear Midas," the god of wine austerely lectured. "The only things' that should be golden' are silence, sunrises, sensational sunsets, and your later years, you totally duplicitous idiot."

"Ten minutes later, Midas became so exhilarated from the official implementation of *his* new magical power that the emperor couldn't decide what object he should touch first in order to convert the item into solid gold. The covetous king chose a branch of a tall oak tree in the garden, located not far from the palace wall, and after Midas touched the tree's largest limb, its leaves slowly made a spectrum transformation from green, to yellow, and then finally to pure solid gold."

"These stellar leaves are better than the ones Daedalus and his son Icarus had manufactured inside the royal workshop!" Midas marveled and uttered. "They are worth a small fortune, and I have only begun to proliferate my already great wealth," the nutcase king laughed. "I can't wait to fuckin' touch the royal falcon and make it into a golden eagle! Ha, ha, ha!"

"Midas was now the greatest and most demented king in all the ancient world. He soon honored his next inclination, which was to stoop-down and touch his garden's well-manicured lawn, and the blades of grass instantly converted into strands of gold. The euphoric fellow next grabbed an ordinary stone, and the small rock astonishingly transformed into a lump of pure solid gold. The now-ebullient monarch next touched a familiar root crop vegetable growing in his private garden, and the nondescript object immediately turned into *twenty-four 'carrot' gold.*"

"The joyful King was extremely delirious upon contemplating his new-found ability. Midas playfully held-out his hand, and eagerly sprinted past a row of six white marble pillars, and after the excited gold-magician touched each separate one, the columns all magically changed into solid gold. The ecstatic ruler jubilantly hypothesized that he would make his entire palace into a beautiful gold edifice, but then, the royal magician considered that the six golden pillars were a nice contrast to the majestic white marble structure that rivaled any god's temple in either Greece, Egypt, Philadelphia, or anywhere else in Asia Minor."

"Then, crazed Midas had an inspiration. The enthralled king grabbed a golden delicious apple from a fruit bowl and held it up to his lips. 'This apple is already *golden*,' the gold collector mused. 'I wonder what will happen if I attempt biting into it'."

"The anxious King zealously bit the apple, and much to his dismay, chipped two of his formerly perfect-shaped front teeth. 'How stupid I was!' Midas acknowledged. 'I should've asked Dionysus to grant me the *Golden Touch* in just my left hand, so that I could use my right hand to eat, to write draconian edicts, and to fuckin' jerk-off. I must experiment more to evaluate the extent of this remarkable gift. Then, I should be able to ascertain whether it is or is not an evil, wretched curse masquerading in disguise'!"

"The regal King ordered his royal servants to set their master's table, and Midas amusingly entertained himself by converting the dishes, saucers, cups, and tablecloth into pure gold. The object-transformer accidentally touched the table, but then realized that it had been pure gold *before* he had acquired the phenomenal *Golden Touch.*"

"When Midas's chatty, gossipy servants had finally exited his personal dining room, the apprehensive king tampered some more with his newly-acquired special talent. He gingerly grabbed a slice of bread, and inserted one end into his mouth. The emperor nearly lost several incisors from *their* crunching-down upon the flat, solid metallic surface. The King suddenly became extremely terrified by his 'new damned and accursed power'."

'I will attempt biting, chewing, and swallowing a tiny morsel without using my hands!' the worried ruler theorized. 'If I just use my lips, I ought to be able to eat that second ordinary slice of bread on the table. Thank *Olympus* my lips don't fuckin' have fingers!"

"The frustrated King bent-over, and used his nose to move the slab of bread closer to his mouth. Then, the experimenter bit into the slice, but it too had become solid gold. Midas's emotions quickly shifted from disappointment, to anger, to shock, and then finally, to exasperation. "What the fuck's goin' on here!" the aggravated monarch yelled-out to his intimidated servants, who fearfully perceived their flamboyant master's petulance, and together hid behind the six golden pillars inside the botanical garden. "If only I had waited and thought the entire situation through," the King imagined and regretted. "Then, I would've wisely wished for the *Golden Touch* to only exist on the index finger of my left hand! Shit! Now I can't even finger Mrs. Midas's wet love canal! On second thought, that's not such a bad fuckin' idea!"

"Midas reached for a 'goblet' of wine, but soon the gold collector became aware that he could neither drink from nor *gobble it*. The liquid gold solidified inside his mouth and throat, nearly choking the incensed imbiber to death. In a fit of rage, the distraught king violently spit-out the solidified golden chunk, finally fully fathoming the futility of his extraordinary gift of touch."

"This is fuckin' insane!" Midas loudly exclaimed. "If I hold my dick while I'm taking a piss," the worrier orally considered while speaking to a wall mirror, "then my bird will turn into a fuckin' goldfinch, and my balls will transform into golden nuggets. Holy shit!" the emperor cried-out as he instantly experienced *social insecurity.* "And I'm still two decades away from my goddamned Golden Years! And if I feel or scratch my ass with the *Golden Touch*, my ass will become a *golden tush,* and I'll be shitting-out gold bricks that will scrape the feces right out of my corroded colon, and also clear out of my abused semi-colon!"

"Out of sheer desperation and extreme anxiety, the now-penitent ruler lifted his cursed hands up in the air and earnestly prayed, "Oh great and wise Dionysus. Forgive my terrible greed and my lustful need for perpetual ostentation. Please show me mercy by removing the *Golden Touch* that *you* have so generously conferred upon your humble suppliant!"

"A familiar voice descended from the sky and instructed, "Midas; you would've been better-off if you had discreetly requested a dozen additional assholes to complement the big one you already carry around with you. Go to the mountain of Tmolus', who as you know, was a minor god that had been punished by being transformed into a solid precipice. Bathe in the nearby stream," Dionysus's voice loudly directed. "And then the *Golden Touch* will be miraculously washed-away. And the next time a powerful immortal asshole like me offers you a special favor, make sure you have assessed all of the *goddamned* consequences. Show more prudence and less impudence, you' stupid, ingrate, fucked-up jerk-off!"

"Midas was very grateful to Dionysus for providing him with the appropriate solution to *his* terrible dilemma, but in his haste, the distracted king heeded the wine god's instruction, but unfortunately, ignored *his* sage advice. The possessor of the Golden Touch journeyed to the mountain of Tmolus, cleansed his entire naked body in the gentle shallow stream, and soon noticed that the sand at the bottom of the narrow river reflected a bright gold color that has been that exact particular hue ever since.”

“The Phrygian King was absolutely delighted to have been returned to a normal mortal existence. However, Midas still retained much of his former arrogance, vanity and greediness. The stubborn fellow soon resented, and then despised gold, as well as all of the other trappings associated with massive, limitless, decadent wealth.”

“Confused Midas soon became a quasi-environmentalist, appreciating the sounds of babbling brooks, along with singing meadows and whispering pines. The mentally-disheveled ruler often distanced himself from his splendid palace, from his gossipy staff, from his marvelous festivals, from his fancy embroidered robes and tunics, and from his fantastic harem of fifty horny harlots, all sporting hyperactive eager beavers. While partaking in *his* dedicated “communion with nature”, Midas coincidentally neglected the important political and economic affairs presently going haywire inside his burgeoning-but-chaotic empire.”

“Now, the satyr mini-god Pan had made himself a pipe to play, and it just so happened that the minor deity of amusement was cavorting-around in the woods near Mt. Tmolus. Pan delighted in playing his new flute when the woodland fellow wasn’t exercising, thrusting, or having his own impressive skin flute sucked on by some blind forest nymph that always craved oral gratification while providing sexual satisfaction in return. Hence, the well-endowed satyr had the appropriate nickname ‘Peter Pan’.”

“As a result of Pan giving his new flute a major blow-job because he had just received one from the aforementioned blind forest nymph, the beasts and the other creatures of the woods became very active and happy, making exotic sounds and enchanting dissonance, in addition to loudly farting all over the ‘Fuckin’ Forest’. Midas encountered Pan in the deep woods and requested that the goat-god continue playing *his* alluring melodies for hours and hours, until the chirping birds, the buzzing bees, and the squealing squirrels all developed chronic laryngitis and genital atrophy.”

“Phoebus Apollo, god of music and the lyre, will be proud of my new musical instrument,” Pan told Midas. “I’ll be glad to serenade you and the forest animals until my lips grow weary, or until the end of the world arrives; or until my dick falls off; or until the cows come home, or until whatever fucked-up event happens first!”

"But if Midas possessed one major fault in addition to his abundant greed, his vanity, and his arrogance, it was the fact that the king never learned when to keep his big mouth shut. "Great!" the idiotic emperor-turned-idiotic-naturalist answered the forest satyr. "I'll ask *Olympus* in a prayer that Apollo and *you* should compete in a musical contest, and that the honorable Tmolus will judge who is the more skilled musician. The pleasure of listening to the music will be much more satisfying than possessing the accursed *Golden Touch,* or even better than having a dozen additional assholes to crap out of!"

"Now naturally, Tmolus himself' was by birth a woodland deity, and would be biased toward selecting Pan while discriminating against Apollo's musical ability. The god of music's harmonies had a classical rhythm that edified the *Olympus residents,* that extolled Greek heroes, and that praised dignified, rational virtues such as justice, truth, honesty and generosity."

"But Pan's revolutionary music suggested emotional expression, along with freedom of thought, loose ethical and immoral human behavior, and the pursuit of basic physical pleasure. It was a competition between "mind and conscience versus heart and body," and Pan had the definite advantage as far as Tmolus was concerned, because Tmolus used to enjoy getting laid, getting blown, working his erect stick, and wiping his ugly asshole a thousand times a day. Hedonism appealed much more to Tmolus than intellectual activity ever had, so imaginative and creative Pan was destined to emerge victorious in his not-so-amicable rivalry with arrogant Apollo."

"But Tmolus soon discarded his favoritism for Pan, and also, his prejudice against Apollo. He awarded the coveted 'laurel wreath prize' to the god of music, being fully aware that Apollo was a dangerous *Olympus god,* and possessed far greater clout among the immortal "Powers That Be" than the less influential Pan had acquired. "I don't want to be a friggin' immobile mountain for all eternity," Tmolus said to a neighboring ridge named Cliff. "I don't even have hands or a throbbing dick to jerk-off with!"

"Midas, however, was not quite as prudent and as diplomatic as Tmolus had been. He too was biased in favor of Pan, and had completely shut and covered *his* ears when Apollo had been singing and playing his splendid lyre. The tyrannical king was quite spoiled, because in the past, when *he* yelled "Leap," his courtiers and servants would always request "How high"? And then the obedient subordinates would always habitually jump to the exact precise height that the dictatorial emperor had arbitrarily stipulated."

"No one has dominion over the way I think!" Midas selfishly muttered to his reflection in a nearby crystal-clear forest stream. "It's now time for me to speak-up for what is legitimately the forest god's triumph over that pompous *Olympus* loser Apollo!"

"The self-centered King of Phrygia came-out of his self-induced stupor and vehemently protested to the heavens that Pan had decisively won the musical competition, and not Apollo. Tmolus indignantly peered-down at Midas, wishing that 'the asshole should incinerate himself in a nearby active volcano's hot crater'. Perceiving Tmolus's rejection of *his* boisterous verbal appeal, Midas beckoned to Apollo, furiously criticizing the 'unfair judgment that had been rendered by Tmolus'."

"Go suck a wet one, you dumb fuck!" Apollo nastily retorted. "Oh, you fucked-up mortal King; you must most-certainly have defective ears," the archer god continued. "I now feel compelled to give *them* their true shape." The falsely victorious god' of music, medicine, literature and the lyre swiftly whirled-around, and then proceeded northwest toward venerable *Mt. Olympus,* thoroughly convinced that *his* final judgment pertaining to 'that asshole Midas' was far too lenient'."

"Midas raised his hands up to his long, furry donkey ears and screamed-out to the sky, "Great Zeus in heaven! I've been given an ass's ears. At least Apollo could've granted me a long donkey's dick to go along with these exaggerated furry ears!"

"Upon returning to his palace after his bizarre Mt. Tmolus and woods' escapades, Midas felt ashamed of his animalistic appearance, and wore a large purple turban to camouflage his abnormally large and embarrassing ass's ears. The Ruler attempted to explain to his perplexed advisers and counselors that wearing the purple turban was a privilege that only the King could exercise, and the chief consultants were happy to hear *that* dumb-shit proclamation, because no one in the court desired to look so horribly unstylish and unfashionable as the 'fucked-up eccentric Monarch' did'."

"After the King's hair grew so long that his tresses and braidy-bunches had to be sheared and trimmed, Midas summoned the services of the royal barber, who was also a royal gossiper, and a royal pain in the ass's ears."

"Cut and groom my straggly, shaggy tresses," King Midas sternly commanded. "And if *you* dare tell anyone of my secret ears, you'll have to sleep with the royal zoo's 'twelve dozen' female gorillas when the apes are all in heat. Can you think of any punishment more fuckin' *gross* than that?"

"The royal barber was tempted to relay the King's personal problem to almost-everyone the fellow saw or met, but *he* intensely feared he would be mauled and mangled by a hundred forty-four aggressive, sexually-aroused, affectionate, female gorillas. Consequently, the intimidated barber quietly bit his tongue so often that it was now two inches shorter than it normally would be. 'I don't know what's worse,' the barber painfully thought and anguished. 'Being emulsified by twelve-dozen, horny, female gorillas, or sleeping with my corpulent five-hundred-pound wife; that choice is really a very tough decision. I'll now have to seriously think about deciding which lousy option to pursue. The ugly gorillas are looking better and better in my mind every damned minute!' the neurotic barber concluded. 'And besides that, crazy King Midas also might get pissed-off at me, and send my ass all the way to a distant fabled place called America to fuckin' become, in the distant future, a Yankee clipper'!"

"In bed, the troubled barber tossed and turned, and his obese wife rolled over on top of him, thinking that the poor hair-cutter desired sex, when actually, all that *he* wanted was more oxygen. The paranoid barber even made mysterious noises and nebulous utterances in his deep-snoring sleep, and when *his* subconscious was about to reveal the King's awful 'donkey ear secret', in desperation, the diminutive barber would beg for more sexual gratification, and his steamrolling wife would accommodate his irregular request at least five times every single night, until the guy was steamrolled flat as a pancake."

"Feeling as flat as a table, one afternoon the bedraggled barber strolled-down to a distant meadow to take a leak in a waterlogged pond. When he noticed that no one was in the vicinity to observe his *private* behavior, the barber then stuck his head inside a groundhog hole to relieve his extreme tension, by then shouting profanities into the cavity. A belligerent woodchuck surfaced, quickly bit a chunk of flesh out of the bad-luck barber's scalp, and then burrowed back down to its dark den."

"I'll have to dig my own hole to get the necessary relief that I seek," the aggrieved hair trimmer said to himself. "I will not despair, despite my great apprehension! I fuckin' never want to be a goddamned Yankee clipper in that imaginary future fantasy place called America!"

"It required six minutes of assiduous excavation, but then the resolute barber finally accomplished his prime objective. Without hesitating, the hair-trimmer pressed his head inside the newly-created hole and bellowed, "King Midas has ass's ears! King Midas has ass's ears!"

"The excavated hole eventually filled-up with scummy stagnant pond water, and several weeks later, a colony of wild reeds began growing all around the cavity's circumference. When the thin reeds sprouted even higher, the growths rustled as the wind briskly blew between them. A court messenger happened to stop at the distant "pissing pond" to take a leak, and then *his* ears sensed a rather peculiar refrain. The young courier dashed to the King's majestic palace and alerted everyone he knew of the strange articulations originating from "an enchanted hole" down near the isolated palace swamp."

"A hundred or so curious imperial employees darted-down to the secluded pond area to observe and listen to "the most fascinating phenomenon ever". As the crowd gathered nearer to the hole that had been dug by the neurotic barber, the naughty reeds were melodically whispering and repeating, "King Midas has ass's ears, and King Midas's ass has ass's ears, too! King Midas has ass's ears, and King Midas's ass has ass's ears, too!"

* * * * * * * * * * * *

"That was a great inspirational story!" Eusballsourout excitedly commended Eurshiddenme. "King Midas is probably paying for his sinful greed down in Hades, as we speak. And his fucked-up kingdom of Phrygia was in Asia Minor, not too far from Troy!"

"And if we don't annoy the gods' fickle dispositions, we'll be rewarded in Hades by resting forever in the tranquil flower fields of Elysium," Eurdicisin constructively contributed to the myth's evaluation, "rather than being harshly punished for all eternity like Tantalus and Sisyphus in King Hades and Queen Persephone's dreadful Area of Atonement."

"Fuck toxic Agamemnon and Menelaus in pursuing their selfish ambitions here at Troy," Eurassisgras spoke-up. "If I can save my soul in the next world, if there is a next world, I'll behave myself now in this world, and then hope for the best!"

"I can identify with King Midas's curse. I'm glad that I'm not the only one who has had trouble with his dangling dingle, so let's proceed and go kill some deranged Trojans, and then luckily get killed ourselves," Eurcockisnum assessed and verbally concluded. "Maybe I'll be able to have a two-dimensional erection and a pair of virile testicles while whirling and swirling-around down in dark, lackluster Hades!"

"I think that we should collaborate in order to corroborate a viable plan of action," Eurballsourout pragmatically suggested. "If we can't become victims of homicide while fighting on the Troad, then perhaps we can commit mass suicide to escape this fucked-up war, and then take our chances as renegade spirits down in Hades!"

"I hope you ridiculous clowns enjoyed this morning's moral lesson!" Eurshiddenme remarked, before offering a brief prayer to Pallas Athene. "Let us not procrastinate in activating our new-found ethical campaign. Even if we lose this fuckin' Troad battle and get killed in the process, we'll die ethically knowing that we have morality and religion on our side!"

* * * * * * * * * * * *

In Zeus's resplendent marble temple atop Mt. Olympus, the all-powerful deity called an emergency session of his family for the purpose of reviewing current developments in the historic Trojan War.

"Some of you immortals have chosen to support the Greek side, namely you Athena, Hera, Poseidon, Hermes and Hephaestus, while on the other hand, you Aphrodite, Apollo, Ares and Artemis have come-out in support of the Trojans. Now mind you," Zeus emphasized and paused. "Even though you are immortal, and that nectar and ambrosia keep you that way, there is ample evidence that human-made weapons such as bronze spears and swords can cause you gods pain and injury, and perhaps if striking one of your vital organs, might even kill you! Nectar and ambrosia, and the immortality that those two ingredients provide, can only protect you so far!"

Several minutes later, Achilles went on a hostile killing rampage, and was weakly challenged by Priam's young son, Aeneas, who was swiftly whisked-away by Zeus, because the king god desired for the Trojan prince to escape from Troy and eventually establish a vast empire to the west. The intense battle raged-on, as the clattering of solid bronze weapons, and the accompanying clamor of screaming warriors permeated the air. During the melee, Achilles had violently knocked Hector to the ground, and the incensed maniac would have killed his avowed foe right then and there, but Phoebus Apollo quickly interceded and shrouded the Trojan warrior in a thick, mysterious mist, which effectively prevented berserk Achilles from gaining final sweet revenge for his beloved and fallen Patroclus. The leader of the fierce Myrmidons could not be appeased. Achilles remained furious about losing his most trusted friend, honorable-but-quixotic Patroclus.

Chapter 20

"ROUTING OF THE TROJANS"

Eurshiddenme, Eurballsourout, Eurassisgras, Eurdicisin, and Eurcockisnum paced at a short distance behind Achilles and his Myrmidons when Odysseus's head captain alertly spotted what appeared to be a shallow cave upon a low hill where the five mischievous Argives could easily hide and watch the about-to-occur conflict unfold from a distance.

Ten minutes later, Achilles and his forces were successfully driving the Trojans to the confluence of three rivers: the Scamander, the Salamander, and the zig-zagging Meander. The fleeing Trojans, fearing for their precious testicles, frenetically dashed into the Scamander, when the other half of the intimidated enemy darted toward the closed gates of Troy.

The avenging Myrmidon chief entered waist-deep into the river, and Achilles deftly slaughtered thirteen unlucky Trojans, and *his* following vanguard captured twelve other young enemy troops, and then expertly bound their hands behind their backs with thick leather belt-straps. The enemy hostages were to be taken to the funeral pyre of Patroclus to be executed as Achilles had earlier sworn to his soldiers, prior to the burial of the fallen Myrmidon hero.

But then, a garrulous Trojan named Lycaon, a son of King Priam, who Achilles thought he had killed in a previous encounter years before, appeared on the opposite shore and was surprised to again confront the Greek General face-to-face. Immediately, the Trojan felt a frantic need to supplicate himself.

"Spare me, great Achilles," Lycaon shouted out of sheer fright, yelling so loudly that Odysseus's five cowardly captains in the distant cave could easily eavesdrop his appeal. I shall not attempt to scam you, Great Greek, here near the Scamander. Instead, I beg you to spare my lackluster life. If you recall," Lycaon pitifully panted, "you had many years ago sold me for a hundred quality bulls. If you again ransom me now, my father Priam will pay three times *that* colossal sum! Almighty Zeus has put me into your hands, and I believe that our coincidental meeting is not of my volition!"

"It looks like Achilles has taken this enemy bullshitter by the horns and refuses to listen to some cornball bum steer," Eurballsourout laughed.

"Yes; it's deja-moo all over again," chortled a delighted Eurassisgras.

"Pretty soon that bullshit Trojan will be lying in the mud and soon becoming ground-beef for the buzzards!" Eurdicisin coughed and then snickered.

"It's way *past your* bedtime, Mr. Trojan! Stop cow-towing to Lord Achilles!" Eurcockisnum added to the zany litany of dumb-ass puns.

"Stop fuckin' *pun*ishing my ears!" Eurshiddenme ordered his four dunce-like subordinates. "We've all heard that kind of feckless bullshit pleading before, coming from other captured human cattle, that actually were begging Trojan chattel!"

But Achilles was drastically adamant about disposing of pleading Lycaon. "In the past, I had captured enemy prisoners and sold them to other nations as slaves. But Lycaon; that practice had been done before Patroclus had been killed by your sibling Hector. Even someone as strong and gallant as I will someday die! I say, pathetic Lycaon: this is your arrived-moment of fatal demise! Now, be voraciously devoured by famished fish seeking their next delicious meal!" Achilles's voice boomed as the impatient attacker thrust his bronze sword into the center of Lycaon's heart.

The river god Scamander naturally sided with the geographically-local Trojans. At that precise moment, Pallas Athene appeared upon the scene as a flat image at Achilles side, and the goddess mentally transmitted to the awesome hero's brain, 'Fear not, handsome warrior; Athena is on your side and has your back.'

Achilles heard a commotion and splash occurring behind him, and became exceedingly angry when he observed a huge Trojan wading into the three-foot-deep water to boldly challenge the avenger of Patroclus.

"Let us not bandy or banter silly words!" the newly arriving-warrior yelled his last sentence as Achilles's lethal spear entered the soldiers' chest and exited through the bragging Trojan's spine, and then protruded out his back.

Being pissed at the quick and sudden outcome of the short-lived duel, the upset river god caused a high wave surge to generate, which chased Achilles out of the cold water, rapidly pacing onto the steep bank, and then another two-hundred-foot sprint had the Greek General safely standing upon the hot desert plain.

"My mother Thetis told me that my fate was to die at Troy, but I prefer being killed by Apollo's silver arrows rather than merely drowning by means of a miniature tidal wave!" Achilles bellowed to the cloud-covered sky. "I'm not a clumsy toddler who accidentally slips into a local mountain stream."

166

At that moment, Pallas Athene again appeared as a flashing flat image at Achilles's side, and telepathically planted another brief message inside his vulnerable brain. 'Fear not, intrepid Greek! I assure that you will not become dead by drowning in river torrents!'

Noticing her special hero in jeopardy from a second even more massive tsunami about to crash onto the river bank, Hera, also favoring Achilles, spoke to her lame son, the blacksmith god Hephaestus. "Your unfaithful wife Aphrodite has aligned with her lover Ares against Achilles and the Argives. Follow my instructions carefully. Make the weak river god know the power of Olympus by having him suffer from formidable waves of spectacular wind-flames!"

"Hephaestus used his knowledge of forming fire and created a conflagration so immense that it cremated all of the Trojan corpses lying upon the river bank, and also upon the nearby plain; the blaze also parched trees, shrubs, weeds, cactus and wild desert flowers throughout the entire vicinity. And then, the fish submerged inside the heated river were also scorched and scalded, as the biased river god quickly surfaced and loudly pleaded for mercy.

"Stop this raging inferno, Hephaestus! I surrender and submit to your supreme authority! I withdraw from the fighting and wish to return to the river bottom in peace! Hera: I beg you; convince your crazy pyromaniac son to stop his wild activity! I now promise that I shall cease helping the Trojans wage their crusade against the invading Argives!"

Inside the nearby cave upon the hill, Odysseus's five Greek officers were observing and listening to the ongoing solicitation of the river god, crying and appealing to Hera and her arsonist son, Hephaestus.

"That bastard river god never before ran into a maniacal fanatic like Lord Hephaestus," Eurballsourout attested to his four colleagues. "The river god used to only have water on the brain, but now the fucked-up loudmouth has become a real hot-head!"

'True," Eurassisgras concurred with Eurballsourout's assessment. "Thanks to Hephaestus, the asshole river god is really in hot water now! Ha, ha, ha!"

"Achilles must really have the dumb-dick river god all burned-up!" Eurdicisin indulgently laughed. "The name of *that* river should be changed from Scamander to Hot Springs!" Eurdicisin added.

"We ought to throw some tulips and daffodils into the tremendous river inferno and have a fantastic florist fire!" coughed Eurcockisnum, nearly splitting his vibrating gut wide open.

"This is the river god's main claim to flame," Eurshiddenme indulgently jested. "That flammable river god is no longer quite as flame-boyant as he had been only fifteen-minutes ago!"

"Holy Harpies shit!" Eurballsourout exclaimed. "I used to think that all of this mythology nonsense was total fantasy, but after seeing the impressive, muscular blacksmith Hephaestus appear before my very eyes and almost-incinerate the bizarre river god, I'm *rapidly* becoming an avid believer!"

"Me, too!" Eurassisgras chimed-in. "I always thought that when our ancestors dug-up ancient bones and fossils, probably of incredible creatures that lived thousands, or perhaps even millions of years ago, that our predecessors had made-up fictional accounts of what kind of mythological animals those discovered bones and fossils represented; and then inventing imaginative creatures like Gorgons, such as Medusa, or like Scylla and Charybdis, or like...."

"The Sphinx, the Seven-headed Hydra, and Hades' vicious three-headed dog Cerberus," Eurdicisin academically added.

"Not to mention the smelly-fish-crotched Sirens, those big-breasted mermaids that sing and attract voyaging mariners' ships, and entice the vessels to crash into their jagged jetty; or even the legendary Cyclopes of yore could have been some real prehistoric animal instead of a mythological monster!" Eurcockisnum was inspired to articulate and then elaborate. "Or, perish the thought; even the very dangerous Chimera, or what about the legendary Kraken, supposedly terrorizing and killing innocent sailors navigating in foreign, northern waters!"

"Okay men; I'm glad you now see the merits of the mythology I've been futilely attempting to indoctrinate into your mini-minds," Eurshiddenme congratulated his underlings. "But on the contrary, those bones and fossils were not of prehistoric beasts as you've so falsely surmised, but actually those remnants and vestiges are of early mythology creatures that I've been inculcating into your miniature cerebrums. These excellent examples of mythology monsters are precisely why we must certainly obey, fear, and daily pray to the gods of Mt. Olympus, with our special homage starting with honoring Almighty Zeus and Pallas Athene."

* * * * * * * * * * * *

"Enough Hephaestus," beautiful Aphrodite demanded of her ugly husband. "You've completely scared the hydrogen and the oxygen out of the obnoxious river god. But don't violate Zeus's strict code of ethics. There is no need to further harm an immortal, even a minor one, like the insignificant local river god you've just terrorized, in defense of a mere mortal such as Achilles! Retire to your workshop, and who knows what might transpire later tonight? As you've often proven with me, your glamorous wife Aphrodite, opposites surely attract!"

Meanwhile, outside the gates of Troy, upon the Troad Plain, other gods were involved in their own rare disputes and imbroglios. Chauvinistic Ares threw his javelin at Pallas Athene yelling, "This is what the hell you get for motivating Diomedes to slash my exposed hand!"

The javelin deflected off of Athena's raised shield, so the favorite daughter of Zeus grabbed a large rock, hurled it at Ares, and the flung object hit the god of war in the helmet, and with its impact, knocked the contemptible bully onto the hard ground.

"That's for your overall stupidity!" Athena, a woman's rights advocate, yelled at the god of war, who was lying still and fecklessly whimpering like an infant upon the desert sand, almost unconscious. "Fuck with me one more time Ares, and you'll never fuck a mortal woman ever again! I guarantee it!"

Aphrodite zoomed upon the scene to render benevolent assistance to the fallen Ares, and Hera, noticing that development transpiring, and remembering Paris selecting Aphrodite over her and Athena in the beauty contest at Thetis and Peleus's wedding, the vindictive wife of Zeus instructed Athena to kick Aphrodite in the twat, and then punch the goddess of love and beauty's ass, lying flat upon the Troad Plain.

As Athena surveyed the damage done to whimpering Ares and to unconscious Aphrodite, the brave goddess hollered down to them: "Let all who decide to help amorous Paris and the rabid Trojans become as hapless and as incapacitated as you two defeated wimpy dumb-shits!"

Meanwhile, a short distance away, Poseidon and Apollo were about to slug-out their personal differences in broad daylight. "Just consider Apollo, how my brother, Mighty Zeus, compelled you and me to build these high walls surrounding Troy. Now, here today, we meet as determined enemies outside those same walls, and although it is not yet dusk, I intend to knock the living daylights out of you!"

"We are both immortal, Poseidon," Apollo objectively contended. "And I refuse to fight with you over the petty concerns and squabbles that prevail among mortal men. Let the asshole humans settle their own grievances without our direct involvement."

Artemis, the goddess of the hunt, was disappointed at her archer brother's recent exhibited cowardice. But the goddess of the bow and arrow was then confronted by Hera, who commanded, "Artemis; you kill deer and mortals efficiently, but don't you ever pretend that you can oppose me!" And with those imperative words, Hera lost her temper and beat the living and dead shit out of insolent Artemis.

Hermes was soon intercepted on the battlefield by the goddess Leto, the mother of twins Apollo and Artemis, whom Zeus had made pregnant. Hera had accumulative jealousy and contempt for Leto, and had cast the sultry bitch out of Zeus's white marble temple upon Mt. Olympus.

"Listen Leto," Hermes cautiously greeted his immortal female adversary in the ongoing war. "I've seen what the hell Hera has done to Aphrodite, to Ares and to Artemis, so if you don't mind, I'll pretend I'm a rabbit without a tail and hightail it the hell to a much safer place."

Now, all of the gods and goddesses had wisely decided to evacuate the oddball battle scene with the exception of Apollo, who stayed secluded inside the city walls to ascertain that Achilles would not destroy Troy until Fate had ordained for *that* destruction to happen.

At dusk, King Priam and Queen Hecuba surveyed the Troad Plain from the palace ramparts just above the Scaean Gate, and the royal pair witnessed their panicked army stampeding toward the narrow, open portals below.

"Hold the gates open until all of our soldiers have entered," Priam yelled-down, "and then bar and bolt the doors immediately to keep brutish Achilles and his prehistoric Myrmidons from entering and killing us!"

After the Troad battlefield had become clear and empty of the regularly clashing armies, Odysseus's five zany officers decided to evacuate the cave on the hill, and amble back to their camp next to the Ithacan king's Bireme.

Upon exiting the dark cavern, their noisy departure had aroused a huge brown bear that had been hibernating inside the hollow's narrow interior. The awakened carnivore growled at the screaming cowards, with the predator soon rushing to attack the shrieking intruders. Eurassisgras was the last to reach the cave's entrance, but the clumsy fool tripped over a misplaced tree branch and tumbled to the cave's rock floor. Amazingly, the uncoordinated asshole still was holding his spear upright, and as the agitated bear leaped into the air, the spear's tip penetrated the animal's underbelly, and most of the creature's guts were soon hanging out of its severed stomach. In a matter of seconds, the ferocious bear ceased breathing.

"Holy stenchy shit that's quickly plopping-out of Zeus's asshole!" Eurballsourout exclaimed to Eurassisgras. "You saved all of our lives from utter extinction. That fierce ursa was a definite existential threat to our cherished mortality."

"You'll certainly be celebrated as a spectacular hero back at camp!" Eurdicisin praised. "Even Odysseus will honor your sensational bravery!"

"Sometimes you get to eat the attacking bear," Eurcockisnum orally philosophized, "and sometimes the bear eats you!"

"If that vicious bear hadn't accidentally jumped upon your lucky spear," Eurshiddenme insisted, "then Eurassisgras, your ass would definitely have been grass if that beast had mowed you down! You were extremely fortunate to accidentally spear that bellicose beast in its soft belly with your trusty bronze weapon!"

172

Chapter 21

"DEATH OF HECTOR"

Odysseus's five colorful captains gutted the remaining organs from the deceased bear's underbelly and together, carried the animals' edible remains outside the cave's entrance. Eurshiddenme beckoned to and flagged-down a donkey cart that was in the area picking-up dead Achaean warriors lying upon the Troad Plain, to be later honored in a mass funeral service scheduled for that afternoon. The bear's carcass was casually tossed onto the back of the wagon, and the driver transported the former beast into the Argives camp, followed by the five zany hunters ambling behind on foot.

"I'm extremely proud of you brave men," Odysseus commended his stooge-like captains. "Killing that mammoth predator is equal to slaughtering five dozen charging Trojans!"

"It was not easy," Eurdicisin deftly prevaricated. "In fact, General Odysseus; the whole relentless fight was rather unbearable. But in the end, the five of us managed to triumphantly persevere."

"That's right," Eurshiddenme disingenuously fibbed and injected into the preposterous conversation. "Several hungry, feral male lions showed-up to greedily steal our fabulous prize, but we valiantly fought-off the cantankerous carnivores with our lethal bronze swords and spears. Honestly, Odysseus; the whole ordeal was rather frantic and life-threatening!"

"Well, you intrepid men are to be commended for your admirable audacity, and as an earned reward, I'll give you tomorrow off so that you can fully rest from your arduous experience," the Ithacan King praised his new-found audacious underlings. "But be prepared to engage the enemy after your brief hiatus from combat."

"Thank you, Sir," bozo Eurcockisnum replied, rather tongue-in-cheek. "Eurballsourout almost got his three testicles clawed-off, but then our comrade valiantly attacked the bear with his spear when the angry beast growled and stood on its massive two feet. The entire scenario was quite surreal!"

"Well, killing this enormous bear will be an inspiration to the legions of troops who will certainly marvel at your incredible accomplishment, and also fully appreciate your remarkable demonstration of Achaean valor,"

Odysseus lavishly congratulated his loony subordinates. "Surviving that terrifying, unanticipated rendezvous with such a dangerous creature is without a doubt an enviable badge of courage to be honored by all our amazed troops, and your illustrious achievement is obviously so outstanding that you men don't even have to tell me how many Trojans you've successfully massacred this cloudy afternoon!"

"Sometimes you kill the bear, but most of the time, the bear kills and eats you!" Eurassisgras impressively summarized and conveyed to Odysseus in a wonderful canard plagiarism of himself. "I only wish that there were four other ferocious bears in the general vicinity for Eurshiddenme, Eurdicisin, Eurcockisnum, Eurballsourout and myself to savagely kill, and later have a tremendous feast for a hundred or more famished troops."

The following morning, Hector stood alone outside the Scaean Gate to boldly defend Troy against on-a-mission Achilles in singular combat, in a crucial winner-take-all death match.

"Hector, my reckless son," King Priam shouted-down from the high wall overtop the citadel's main gates. "I implore you not to face that maniac Achilles all by yourself! That rampaging savage has killed so many of my sons, and I regret to publicly announce that I have no more sperm juice in my shriveled-up loins to produce any more fucked-up offspring."

"Listen to your beleaguered father," Queen Hecuba shouted-down to mentally-possessed Hector. "It has been prophesied that after you are killed and Troy crumbles, succumbs, and falls, Priam's feeble body will be torn apart by his own hungry hunting dogs near the bark of the historic barking olive tree."

"I care not for ordinary olive trees, or for the shallow words of senile old fuck prophets," Hector defiantly yelled-up to his petrified parents. "I care only about settling my score with Achilles!"

"But Hector," Queen Hecuba begged and pleaded. "Show more regard for your family, for your relatives, and for your besieged city. I had diligently nursed you with my tiny breasts when you were just a little sucker, and right then and there, I should've known your aggressive nature when you bit my nipples right off my chest without even having any damned teeth in your mouth!"

The passionate entreaties from Priam and Hecuba's lips went unheeded, and surreptitious Hector waited like a venomous snake huddled inside its lair for its human enemy to approach. 'I shall either save my countrymen and my city, or sacrifice my life and legacy in glory to the incensed

Achaean madman! This is my singular choice to decide now!' the Trojan champion reasoned. 'And to my devoted wife Andromache, it's now or never, my own true love'!"

"Hector, let's cut to the chase!" Achilles yelled as the Greek hero sprinted forward to encounter his worthy opponent face-to-face, and even though ice-making had not yet been invented, the Trojan prince suddenly got cold feet, turned-around, and hustled in the opposite direction, then being frenetically pursued by implacable Achilles.

Three times the pair dashed around the entire city walls, but then Achilles had a sudden brainstorm. 'I'll turn around, run in the reverse route, and I'll eventually again confront cowardly Hector face-to-face, since the scampering asshole is so frightened that he never turns-around to gauge my closeness in the chase. My gazelle legs are much faster than his rabbit's feet!"

During the superhuman sprinting event, Athena was active providing stamina to Achilles, and Apollo was supplying strength and endurance to the fleeing Trojan prince. But then, Almighty Zeus felt empathy for Hector's losing plight, since Priam's obdurate son had performed myriad sacrifices paying homage to the chief Mt. Olympus deity. "I've a mind to salvage Hector from Achilles's lust to avenge Patroclus!" Zeus uttered to Athena. "My heart has dual allegiances in this intriguing struggle!"

"What in Hades are you possibly thinking?" Pallas Athene challenged her omnipotent patriarch. "Fate has determined that what we are presently witnessing should materialize, and it is now in progress! According to prophecy, Achilles is about to butcher and maim Hector before the prince's alarmed parents appalled eyes, and all of the residents of Troy are irrefutably doomed!"

"I'll put an end to this bizarre death debacle right here and now," Zeus declared to Athena. "Hand me my scales of justice to decide a resolution to this dilemma! I'll arbitrarily put my finger on one side, and its weight will affect what blind Fate has already decreed!"

Zeus held-up his golden scales and placed his index finger upon Hector's left-hand side, which indicated that the unlucky Trojan would die with his losing side of the five-ton scale being pressed and lowered. But then, entering out of a dense mist, a Trojan ally sauntered-up to Hector and greeted his very surprised old friend and confidante.

"My brother, Deiphobus; you have come to give me aid and comfort as we both dually duel the crazed Achaean maniac!" Hector gleefully acknowledged. "Two against one certainly evens my chances!"

"Priam and Hecuba had begged me to stay upon the palace ramparts with them, but I could not witness you dying at the hands of the awesome Achaean champion. Oh brother; what a mess this is! Please take satisfaction in these propitious words: I pledge with all my honor and heart that you will not combat Achilles alone!"

"Achilles," Hector confidently greeted his avowed adversary, face to face. "We will now fight to the death, but I propose a bargain for you to consider, and for Zeus and his majestic family to also contemplate. If I shall be victorious over you, I shall strip you of your armor as a coveted trophy, but I'll not mutilate your body any further. I'll respectfully return your corpse to Agamemnon and to Menelaus for proper burial! Will you promise to do the same for my remains?"

"Fuck you, Hector!" Achilles stubbornly cursed and belittled his foe. "We are like rival lions from separate prides vying for dominance. No truce or settlement will exist between us! This is a wicked and desperate fight to the death, and nothing more!"

The combatants stood erect, twenty feet apart. Achilles hurled his deadly spear at Hector, but missed his aim as the Trojan swiftly ducked-down like a mallard paddling its webbed feet upon a pond and then dipping its head underwater. But then, Hector vigorously tossed his spear at Achilles, which deflected off of the inimitable solid bronze shield that Hephaestus had manufactured for Thetis to give to her son. The altercation had reached an impasse.

"Quick Deiphobus!" Hector shouted, holding out his empty hand. "Give me *your* spear to hurl at my obstinate opponent."

But Deiphobus was no longer present, and it was at that moment that Hector realized than Zeus, influenced by Athena, had played a cruel ruse upon his tricked psyche. 'Although I am aware that I'm fooled by an Olympus prank and am destined to die, let future generations tell and revere my glorious story!' Then Hector screamed, "Let's get it on, bastard Achilles!"

A mammoth two-opponent battle ensued, and after ten minutes of loudly clashing swords, Hector's chest was greatly pierced by Achilles's spear, and the Trojan warrior collapsed to the Troad's hot sand to utter his final words.

"The gods are watching your bitter wrath unfolding, and your time is coming soon. The sand in your hourglass, arrogant Achilles, does not match the sand upon this arid plain; and my hazy mind foresees Apollo and Paris gladly eliminating your petulant ass from earthly existence!"

Achilles triumphantly stripped Hector of his enviable armor, and contrary to the royal Trojan prince's wishes, the Phthian heir and his Myrmidon officers repeatedly slashed and penetrated the fallen hero's body with their sharp spears. Achilles, showing ultimate spite and rancor, then tied leather straps around Hector's bloody heels; attached the dead Trojan's feet to the rear of his colorfully-decorated chariot, and next proceeded to parade and drag his former nemesis around the entire walled city seven consecutive times.

Much to the horror and grief of Hector's wife Andromache, his parents King Priam and Queen Hecuba, Prince Paris, Helen of Troy, and the entire shocked residents of the whole damned city, Achilles ostentatiously displayed his vast contempt for his principal Trojan foe.

The one who suffered the most sorrow from Hector's horrible demise was his inconsolable wife, Andromache. 'That monster Achilles has callously and brutally abused my husband's body, which is no longer recognizable,' the sorrowed spouse uncontrollably sobbed and evaluated. 'I curse that I had even been born to have to suffer this inhuman emotional pain. And our only son, infant Scamandrius, being terribly unlucky through no fault of his own, being left an unfortunate fatherless orphan; and me a widow, *our* combined futures being helplessly wasted-away; a fatherless child and a husbandless spouse. My son,' Andromache contemplated and wept, 'will be shunned and ostracized by other inconsiderate boys, who will shout insults about *his* father's inability to save Troy, along with its many defensive bastions; the glorious city suffering immediate poverty and ruin. Scamandrius will be bullied and ignobly ridiculed by his ruthless peers, who will mock and chide my boy, saying that *his* incompetent father had failed Troy, and had made its tremendous wealth disintegrate into pitiful bankruptcy.'

"Thus, did aggrieved and melancholy Andromache sadly mourn, and at that mirthless moment in time, so did all of Troy weep with her.

Chapter 22

"FUNERAL GAMES"

"That bear meat we consumed last night was absolutely delicious," Eurassisgras declared to his four happy-go-lucky captain comrades. "Maybe within the next week, we can find another cave and cub a few clubs, er, I meant 'club a few cubs' to obtain some more tender protein."

"I've heard some gossip around the camp that Achilles is planning some exciting games and contests to honor Patroclus," Eurballsourout mentioned to his half-interested colleagues. "I was thinking about entering the javelin throwing event, but then I realized that I have a slipped discus in my lower back."

"When I was a kid, I used to be able to hit a bulls-eye in nursery school tossing a broomstick spear," Eurdicisin claimed. "But then I had a bad nightmare that the bull's eye was closely watching me, and that the bull was going to gore my tiny ass in a gory manner."

"I would voluntarily enter the archery contest," Eurcockisnum related to his four associates, "but when I shoot an arrow, my style is to bend-down, so if I pull the arrow too deep across the bridge, I'm afraid that I'll become even more bow-legged than I already am!"

"Say Eurshiddenme," Eurassisgras addressed his higher-ranked captain. "How about reaching deep into your mythology repertoire and telling us a good story that involves an athletic contest, perhaps even a racing event, to get us thinking about the upcoming Patroclus games. The guys and I will not interrupt your impromptu presentation, because we realize that you get your testicles twisted whenever we do!"

"Okay, you' junior jerk-offs, who only have calluses on your right hands," Eurshiddenme observed and related. "I do have a pertinent tale that matches-up perfectly with the athletic contests that have not yet been posted. Here it goes."

"A beautiful young girl, Atalanta, was a rapid-running speedster, and the daughter of King Schoeneus of Boeotia. Atlanta also was a highly-skilled archer who was desperately searching for a suitable *beau*. Although Atalanta was also very fast afoot, her dim-witted father King Schoeneus was not too swift."

"Atalanta had pledged to the Olympus gods that she would only marry a man that was a faster sprinter than she was. In fact, the girl was speedier and more fleet-footed than any naval *fleet* known to the ancient world. Young, horny, ambitious youths from all over Greece often arrived in Boeotia to race against the speedy doll, and each failed asshole left the city-state kingdom disappointed and defeated."

"King Schoeneus eventually got so pissed-off at all of the foolish parasitic gigolos showing-up in his isolated land, seeking fame and fortune, that the ruler made an explicit proclamation: "Any dumb-fuck jerk-off with a death wish that comes to Boeotia to challenge my daughter Atalanta to a foot race will be condemned to death at the hands of the official executioner, immediately after losing the contest." And then the volatile King Schoeneus turned to his beautiful daughter and said, "Atalanta; we need fewer male *racists* in Boeotia, so I made this special law to discriminate against the dirty, intruding, foreign bastards," the elderly, cantankerous, ill-tempered, totally soulless monarch preached to his lovely offspring."

"One fine morning, an impractical youth name Hippomenes arrived in Boeotia from an unknown *fishing village,* that actually knew how to catch sea bass, the remote, unidentified hamlet being situated on the other side of the vast mountain range. The happy-go-lucky young man was really a worthless, idealistic vagabond that appeared in the unhospitable country, only because his aimless aspiration in life was to wander all over the general topography without ever accomplishing a single damned thing."

"Why is everyone in attendance shouting over there near the pissed-off King?" Hippomenes asked a local resident. "Has a ferocious rogue lion maliciously scratched *their* tender balls, tits and fat asses'?"

"No, curious stranger; four young men have recently challenged the King's daughter Atalanta to a foot race, and when the dumb fucked-up aliens lose, they'll be promptly slaughtered by the royal executioner," the jubilant spectator disclosed to Hippomenes. "We Boeotians are basically cannibalistic and sadistic. We then, according to the King's new edict, will barbecue the four doomed losers' butchered flesh, and have a great picnic feast with lots and lots of delicious grilled meat! That's why everyone is cheering and prematurely celebrating their next nutritious meal!"

"Unlucky idiots!" Hippomenes answered, referring to the bold male challengers, and not to the carnivorous citizens of Boeotia. "How foolish the cocky assholes are to risk their lives simply for a permanent piece of ass along with the acquisition of great wealth," the critical wanderer commented to the excited bystander, while they both watched the four young men limbering-up their leg muscles for the start of the all-important 'life-or-death race'."

'This girl Atalanta must be a witch, a powerful enchantress, or a rich bitch with an ideal snatcheroo,' Hippomenes speculated. 'She might even be an evil sorceress, who possesses the ability to attract so many unfortunate distant young men to their deaths. This remote desert place Boeotia seems like a fool's paradise. I'm not so sure that I want my life abruptly abbreviated, simply over stupid things like money, prestige, power, good sex, and beauty.'

"Soon, the talkative and callow visitor observed Atalanta approaching, and his dingle began throbbing and bobbing under his orange tunic. 'That deadly witch is really a tough-looking bitch!' Hippomenes noted and rhymed. 'My blood-drained brain is so empty and light-headed that I feel like racing her myself right this very moment'."

"The trumpeters' shrill signal to commence the race gradually broke the naïve young man's highly-focused infatuation. On the count of three, the five contestants zoomed-off their starting blocks, but Atalanta soon moved-out into the lead with her gorgeous light-brown tresses blowing and waving over her shoulders in the morning wind."

"Hippomenes further evaluated all possible circumstances. 'I hope those four male participants lose the damned race! That way Atalanta will still be available for me to vanquish in a future sprint,' Hippomenes selfishly thought. 'I'll simply eat a pound of baked beans tomorrow morning and take-off like a falcon out of Hades, making a run to the first outhouse just beyond the finish line. But right now, I must admit, I've never attended a real-life human barbecue before,' the itinerant youth acknowledged. 'And strangely enough, I must confess that I'm enthusiastically looking forward to voraciously eating and licking other men's meat'!"

"Atalanta easily and deftly crossed the finish marker, and won the race by a wide margin. King Schoeneus placed a victor's laurel wreath on his athletic daughter's head, and announced to the boisterous crowd that a barbecued, high-protein meat smorgasbord would be set-up in one hour after the royal executioner', the butchers, and the chefs completed their particular tasks."

"The moody, fickle King looked-down on the throng and spotted the ever-plotting, lazy Hippomenes, while the almost-hypnotized traveler kept his eyes fastened on the very charming Atalanta's heavy breathing chest. 'These friggin' races are killing my military draft,' the highly-mercurial

King grieved and mentally weighed. 'That's four more soldiers I could've easily enlisted into my personal bodyguard'."

"But soon, the irritated King's daughter's attention turned toward the young newcomer, and the big-breasted girl immediately discerned that the lad would not be satisfied until he became un-mystery meat for a future 'Bountiful Boeotian Beef and Ale Barbecue'."

"Speak, oh visiting youth!" Schoeneus boomed at the thoroughly-entranced Hippomenes, who was busily admiring the King's daughter's firm tits and vivacious curves. "Tell us what brings you to Boeotia, as if we all don't fuckin' already know! Can't you get laid in your own fuckin' town, or what?"

"Your voluptuous, curvaceous daughter only races wimpy faggots to achieve athletic fame," Hippomenes arrogantly criticized. "She has not gone up against any man that has superior physical prowess like I possess. I am a son of Poseidon, the immortal sea god," Hippomenes boasted. "And if I lose and am executed and barbecued by you friggin' assholes, then my Big Daddy will seek vengeance by deluging Boeotia with a major tidal wave coming over yonder mountains, and efficiently and egregiously drowning all of you raunchy bastards and bitches as if your second-classed city was inhabited by a colony of filthy rabid rats!"

"You might want to re-think the possibility of actually losing a race," King Schoeneus gulped and whispered to his extremely talented daughter. "This young sucker seems to mean business, and I'm quite intimidated by his threat that we'll all suddenly drown out here in this desert community, right in the middle of fuckin' nowhere. I wonder if the fool has the wherewithal to do what he claims?"

"Don't worry, father!" Atalanta supportively answered. "I'll easily defeat his ass, and we'll just call his bluff about Poseidon being his father, and causing a major aquatic catastrophe! And if I am to drown to death, I can think of no person on this planet whom I'd rather do it with than you, Big Royal Daddy-o!"

"But the swift Princess, in her vulnerable heart, also didn't desire to see the young handsome visitor become the next-day' menu's barbecue entrée. "Brave, stupid, foolish asshole," Atalanta personally addressed Hippomenes. "Either Apollo, Hermes, or maybe even Zeus must be envious of your muscular physique, and each wants to see you aptly eliminated from the rolls of the living by voluntarily becoming 'dead meat'. I suggest that you not rendezvous with your imminent doom, and wisely retract your announced intention of racing me," the gorgeous girl begged. "When a simpleton such as yourself races against death and fate, the invincible almighty gods' opponent, namely me, always wins! I implore you', handsome stranger," the fair maiden continued. "Abandon your unreachable dream and leave Boeotia as soon as possible. The afternoon four-door-chariot to Corinth leaves in two short hours."

"No go, my fair lady," Hippomenes courageously replied. "For I shall enter tomorrow's race and wager my mortal life, just for the privileged opportunity to be your dedicated husband. I cannot live with sadness and cowardice, once I have gazed upon your slender beauty, and lustfully admire your firm, hard tits that stick-out from your magnificent chest like perfect dual female erections!"

"Atalanta fearfully stepped-away from her fascinating, fascinated challenger, bent-down to adjust her right sandal, and waited for her stern, psychotic, dominant father to answer the eager stranger's brazen remarks. Seconds later, the egomaniac King cleared his parched throat and gave the predictable response."

"Face your destiny at noon tomorrow, young fool!" the King definitively stated. "Prepare to meet your ultimate downfall, you outrageously covetous, wet-behind-the-ears neophyte! Tomorrow you fuckin' die!"

"Hippomenes left the belligerent King, *his* stunning daughter, and the fanatical barbecued beef banquet and ale crowd, and hurried into the woods to first vomit, and then take an extended dump, in that exact sequence. After the youth mechanically wiped his sore butt with dried leaves and prickly-painful tree bark fragments, the intrepid stud studied the sandy course upon which he and the swift girl would compete. 'Perhaps I spoke too prematurely without analyzing the whole situation properly,' the young fellow regretted. 'Maybe I'm even a bigger asshole than everyone actually thinks I am? A premature decision is almost as bad as a goddamned premature ejaculation'!"

As Hippomenes raised his eyes to the cloudless blue sky, the ambitious adolescent saw a remarkable heavenly figure drifting afar on the horizon, and then quickly moving towards him at breakneck supersonic speed. "Sacred *Mt. Olympus!*" the amazed and presumptuous youth gasped and exclaimed. "It's Aphrodite, goddess of beauty and love, come to give me guidance, confidence and a certain erection!"

"Greetings, dear Hippomenes," the almost-impeccable goddess saluted with her right hand raised over her head, showing an abundance of ugly underarm hair. "You have the stout heart of a *hippo,* Greek for 'horse', and a case of the *meanies,* like no other human presently alive on this whole damned Earth!"

"Then, you've come to succor me and give me strength and courage?" the lad inquired, as Hippomenes avariciously peered at the goddess's wonderful solid breasts. "I'm a little deficient in abstract qualities like love and beauty, so I often think with my blood-engorged penis, rather than with my brain-drained noggin that's devoid of fabled Type-O Negative red fluid."

"You must win the impending race and wed the King's comely daughter," Aphrodite insisted to her new-found champion. "Here, inside this scruffy bag my left hand is holding, are some valuable tools that will aid you in your current dilemma. I hope you find them practical, and figure-out how the Hades to effectively use each of them!"

"Hippomenes opened the dirty, blood-stained, goatskin sack and examined the weird array of objects stashed inside, while vivacious Aphrodite continued her rather odd discourse. The young champion conscientiously listened to the gorgeous goddess's authoritative and imperative rhetoric."

"I was just recently visiting distant Africa, and have taken three golden apples from the immortal tree that grows near the northern mountains, along with the sturdy thick foot-long branch that the golden fruit had matured upon," the goddess loquaciously explained to her chosen hero. "Since I am an immortal *Olympus* deity, I have a license to do what the Hades I like with complete impunity, whenever I feel motivated to act. And incidentally my dear mortal," Aphrodite orally proceeded. "Here is a little utilitarian gift from your sea god sponsor Poseidon; it's a small six-inch-long trident attached to a circular belt, fastened midway around."

"What am I to do with these wonderful-but-peculiar items?" Hippomenes urgently asked. "Sell the golden apples on the immortal bough, and use the trident as a fork during a future Boeotian barbecue?"

"That's where your noteworthy imagination is supposed to kick-in," the goddess impatiently-and-vaguely revealed. "Use your limited brain capacity, and implement the unique things in the bag, along with the souvenir trident in a creative manner. But I'll mercifully give you a good hint," Aphrodite declared out of pity for her new, favored champion. "Put all five gifts inside your tunic, and your essential clue is: 'Four to rod, and one to prod'! Get it, my favorite, thick-skull Earth asshole! 'Four to rod and one to prod'." And without providing any more helpful directions, the beautiful deity then *vanished into* thick oxygen, which hadn't adequately learned to diet properly, and therefore, naturally would have ordinarily been *thin air."*

"Four to rod and one to prod!" the inquisitive youth kept introspectively thinking and then repeating. "There's only one thing those fuckin' words, constituting a really dumb riddle, could possibly mean."

"The next morning, just before noon, Hippomenes first placed and next fastened the trident belt around his lower abdomen, so that the three-pronged fork would slam against his buttocks when he would run, and painfully "prod" the youth forward in his quest for the finish line. Then, the visitor to Boeotia ungracefully shoved and stuffed the long-branch and the three-attached, large golden apples down his girdle inside his tunic, making it appear that his genitals were ten times bigger than their normal, non-aroused size. Hippomenes then awkwardly walked towards the King's official starting line, as everyone in the gallery gawked, scoffed, jeered and pointed at *his* very exaggerated sexual and highly-visible, lower abominable abdominal apparatus.

'Look at his grand protruding dick and massive balls!' Atalanta thought in sheer astonishment, as the thoroughly-amused spectators all roared and heckled with laughter. 'With equipment like that, this city doesn't need any damned fire department to put out raging infernos!'

"And then, the angry tiny-pecker King Schoeneus, who didn't have the balls to do what Hippomenes had audaciously enacted at the starting-line, raised his imperial right hand for silence. "Hear me one, and hear me all. This gullible, idiotic, poverty-stricken youth Hippomenes seeks to gain my daughter Atalanta's hand in marriage by winning the upcoming foot-sprint against her. If the empty-headed fool somehow is victorious, and escapes the axe of the official royal executioner, then we'll all have to turn vegetarian this afternoon at the King's fruit and produce buffet, along with the accompanying ceremonial country salad bar!" the King reminded his peevish and suddenly irate subjects. "Let the dolt Hippomenes's death be a clear message to all other silly, frivolous youths that have the crazy notion to think that they can miraculously run faster than my talented, winged-footed little girl!"

"Then, determined Atalanta casually crouched-down in her regular starting position, but being encumbered by all of the paraphernalia stuffed inside *his* burgeoning girdle, poor beleaguered Hippomenes could only stand there and wish that the King would immediately articulate the numerical countdown to begin the race. 'Four to rod and one to prod!' the trustful, callow lad kept thinking over and over again inside his puzzled and befuddled mind. 'Four to rod and one to prod!' Soon, the familiar shrill-sounding trumpets were blown, and the King sanctimoniously gave the traditional three-number countdown."

"The young male challenger managed to maintain his initial dash side by side with his highly-skilled opponent, despite the handicap of having five uncomfortable objects jiggling-around inside his uncomfortable girdle. But about one-third of the way into the five-hundred-yard sprint, Atalanta began distancing herself from her tenacious rival. The girl then felt sorry for her inferior pursuer, so she slowed-down sufficiently for Hippomenes to run alongside of her. The princess's right hand accidentally touched *his* exaggerated crotch, and that unexpected wild sensation momentarily stunned and aroused the ordinarily very competent female athlete."

"Hippomenes instinctively used his innate intelligence, removed one of the three golden apples from under his tunic, and tossed it several hundred feet ahead, so that its falling would attract the attention of his spirited competitor. As the distracted young lady bent over to pick-up the priceless golden apple, the ambitious champion approached her behind from behind, and rammed the sturdy protruding tree branch into his rival's crotch, directly-up her butt hole, making Atalanta shriek with both pain and pleasure."

"The revitalized wannabe' champion removed his artificial dork from his formidable female opponent's tail-end, and then conscientiously continued sprinting towards the nearby finish line, with the six-inch-long trident repetitiously goosing and penetrating his severely-lacerated buttocks all the way. Atalanta got over her momentary, aberrant sexual deviation, and again hustled-back into the thick of the race. The fleet-footed girl was quickly catching-up to her inventive challenger, as Hippomenes neared the booing, jeering, incensed, carnivorous crowd assembled at the finish line."

"Much to everyone's disappointment, Hippomenes had won the race *by a rod,* or by a massive fake hard-on, and also had simultaneously won the right to ask for King Schoeneus's permission to marry *his* royal attractive daughter. When the chagrined King announced to the already-dissatisfied throng that a vegetarian buffet was to be served in an hour, all of the disgusted spectators belligerently pelted the royal asshole with pebbles, stones, and rocks, and then the agitated crowd angrily left the area in both miserable and disenchanted frames of mind to demonstrably boycott the lousy vegetarian smorgasbord."

"Then, ecstatic Hippomenes secretly reached-down into his girdle and removed the long sturdy branch with the two remaining golden apples still attached. He happily handed one of them to Atalanta, and romantically said to his prospective bride, "A golden apple a day keeps rabid cannibalism away!"

"Atalanta pulled-up Hippomenes's orange tunic, looked-down inside his pink girdle, and innocently-but-humorously exclaimed, "Where's the beef, you dumb-ass meathead?"

'That was a positively terrific story," Eurassisgras lavishly praised Eurshiddenme. "Speaking for my delighted comrades, we were all thoroughly impressed. I think you've satisfactorily made your four attentive listeners into devout athletic supporters!"

* * * * * * * * * * *

Two parallel events were simultaneously occurring as the Achaeans were lamenting Patroclus's passing, and the Trojans were sorrowing for their dead Prince Hector. Achilles insisted that a large funeral feast should be prepared, featuring butchered pigs, oxen, sheep, and rams, all roasted and barbecued over roaring pit flames. Getting ready for the grand banquet in honor of Patroclus, the Myrmidons all rinsed and scrubbed the dirt and blood from their arms and legs, but Achilles rested and dozed-off on the beach sand, without washing any of the grime from his corroded skin.

In Achilles' strange dream, Patroclus vaguely appeared, praising his master for honoring him with such a glorious feast. "My spirit is waiting upon the banks of the underground Styx, and impatiently hovering for the ferryman Charon to paddle his barge to this shore, and transport my soul to Hades and to Persephone's dismal Kingdom of the Dead. I only hope that my soul will be able to reside in the daffodil Fields of Elysium, and not in the Area of Atonement where the unhappy dead are doomed to an eternity of perpetual punishment. Once my body is burned upon my flaming funeral pyre, then I'll be able to finally hail Charon for my bleak river crossing into dark and mysterious Hades. And thank you, friend Achilles, for placing the gold coin in my mouth to cover the expense of Charon escorting me across the macabre Styx to Hades."

Achilles awoke from his subconscious manifestation and reached to embrace Patroclus's vanishing ghost, but the nebulous apparition evaporated into the thin air around it.

After the great feast had concluded, the following morning, Patroclus's lengthy funeral procession meandered around Troy's walls for the purpose of displaying Greek tradition to the astonished Trojan witnesses. Then, upon the beach near the Achaean camp, Achilles cut his long locks of hair and placed them inside Patroclus's joined hands. Upon the elaborate pyre built of massive logs and firewood, sacrifices to Zeus and his immortal family were sacredly consecrated, with dead hunting dogs, sheep, bulls, rams, hogs, and the twelve captured and recently-slaughtered Trojan youths lying prone beneath Patroclus in the gruesome mass cremation scene.

In the meantime, Hector's body lying near the Argives' camp was not touched by either wild dogs or buzzing insects, for the prince's corpse was shielded by Apollo, and also protected by Aphrodite, with the goddess applying nectar an ambrosia anointing the many gashes and wounds. In the distance, the roaring fire from Patroclus's funeral pyre leaped and danced high into the night sky in what appeared to be fences of flames, as the zealous Myrmidons sang and repeated in chorus, "Good, good, good, good libations!"

Daylight broke over the eastern horizon, and at noon, the Greeks, in honor of Patroclus, participated in the magnificent athletic contests in respectful commemoration of fallen Patroclus. Diomedes had won the chariot race with the beautiful white horses he had confiscated from Prince Aeneas of Troy. The fist-fighting contest was owned by the famed boxer Epeis; and Ajax and Odysseus's wresting match resulted in a tie decision, with both grapplers rolling around upon the hard sand, locked together in solid dual bear hugs. Showing remarkable stamina, Odysseus next was a favorite contestant in a footrace event, where the Ithacan King easily emerged victorious. Polypoetes of Thessaly, who only spoke in the words of many Greek poets, was triumphant in the shotput competition, and saddened Achilles came in second to Meriones in the close archery rivalry, shooting the wings off of a pigeon, which was acting as a sitting duck, the abused bird being tied to a high pole.

"Alright, worthy men," Agamemnon commanded and ordered. "The sporting games have officially ended. Let us now return to our separate huts, tents and campsites; for tomorrow, we'll again savagely engage the mendacious Trojans in mortal combat! Let's all get a good night's sleep, so that tomorrow, we can scurry out onto the Troad battlefield and win one for the fallen gipper, er, I mean, for the fallen Bireme skipper!"

Chapter 23

"RANSOM OF HECTOR"

For ten long nights, Achilles tossed and turned in his straw bed, not being able to soundly sleep. And each night, the lonely warrior ambled along the incoming surf until rosy-fingered dawn made her grand appearance upon the eastern horizon. Early that morning, the son of Peleus would drag Hector's corpse around Patroclus's mounded tomb, and then out of sheer frustration, leave the non-decaying body, which was still shielded and protected by Apollo and Aphrodite, lying face-up upon the hot and hard desert sand.

Seeing King Priam being insufferably miserable over Hector's demise, perceptive Zeus shrewdly dispatched Iris, Goddess of the Rainbow, to the Trojan monarch's regal palace to placate and advise the despondent ruler.

"Take heart," Iris spoke to the inconsolable monarch. "Zeus pities your great depression. I urge you to now venture into the Achaean camp of Achilles and offer him extravagant gifts. Bring along an elderly courier, for Achilles will honor Zeus's Law of the Suppliants and not harm old-age visitors who enter his military domain! He will perceive you and the aged herald as non-threatening encroachers! And take with you a sturdy wagon to carry your opulent gifts to Achilles as ransom for Hector's body, and perhaps to then transport your son's remains back to Troy for proper religious services and burial."

"But what guarantee is there that I and my aged herald will not be captured and killed by the ruthless Argive sentinels?" Priam asked his goddess visitor.

"Lord Hermes will guide you safely through harm's way to Achilles' hut, and the son of Peleus will greet you respectfully, for even he fears Zeus's retribution to anyone who violates the sacred Law of the Suppliants."

After Iris had vanished from the palace throne room, Priam told Queen Hecuba that he was going to visit Achilles to retrieve Hector's body in exchange for a sizeable ransom. The harried Queen answered, saying that her husband had gone insane for suggesting such a dangerous scenario to ever be attempted.

"Achilles has killed several dozens of you sons, and shows no evident shame or mercy. Husband; you jeopardize your life for considering direct involvement in such a perilous mission! Stay home with me where you know you will see the sun both rise and set tomorrow in its daily journey around the Earth!"

"If any Trojan said to me' what I have just said to you," Priam replied to his worried wife, "then I too would accuse the speaker of being crazy. But I had conversed with the anonymous goddess face-to-face, and I trust her words of wisdom. Now I shall call faithful Idaeus to accompany me to the Achaean camp."

Several other non-lackadaisical-but-adept servants were summoned to assist in gathering the treasure trove of gifts to be offered as ransom in exchange for Hector's corpse. The items included twelve extravagant jewel-studded robes; twelve full-length cloaks obtained from the palace cloak room; a dozen soft-fabric-but-rugged carpets; twelve linen capes along with a dozen matching tunics; ten Troy-pound bars of gold; six gleaming chariot tripods; four huge bronze cauldrons, and finally, a platinum partridge and a purple pear tree. All of those fabulous gifts were carefully loaded into the rear of the transportation cart, and Priam was at the reins of his own personal royal chariot, while senile Idaeus sat and controlled the horses pulling the wagon loaded with the expensive gifts.

As the melancholy king and the obedient herald approached the Achaean wall, an Argive sentry demanded that they halt their forward progress. "Let's flee while we can still get away!" Idaeus pleaded to Priam. "We can die only once in this pathetic life!"

"No, my herald! We must comply with the commands of the anonymous goddess who had appeared to me earlier this evening!"

"Where are you two old coots going so late at night?" the Achaean guard cautiously asked. 'Tell me the truth, and if I believe you, I shall allow you to safely pass through the locked gate into the Argives' camp!"

"I am Priam, father of slain Hector," the Trojan king all-too-honestly answered. "Those valuables in yonder wagon are to be offered to Achilles as ransom in exchange for my son Prince Hector's body. Tell me, kind sentinel. Has Achilles butchered my son and fed his flesh to wild hunting dogs?"

"No, King Priam! I think some gods' mercurial whims are truly at play. No maggots or flies have invaded your son's corpse. But every day, in his mania, Achilles drags Hector's remains around the mounded tomb of

Patroclus, who had been slain by the Trojan prince, as tribute to *his* dearest friend!"

"Benevolent guard; please take this golden chalice I'm holding as a deserved gift for assisting me with valuable information about my son Hector," Priam cordially requested. "You deserve some minor reward for your cooperation."

"Are you testing my loyalty, King Priam?" the faithful sentinel replied. "This golden cup is meant for my master, Lord Achilles, whom I both fear and respect. But now that I understand the true nature of your mission, I shall allow your chariot and your wagon to pass through the wall's gate. But first, I shall unbar the bolted door to ensure your safe passage into the Achaean camp."

A circular fence as high as a twenty-foot-palisade had been constructed around Achilles's modest hut, and a heavy beam acted as a bar that required three strong soldiers to lift in order to gain access to the Phthian heir's humble headquarters. A very tall figure stood in front of the obstacle and announced to Priam, standing upon his chariot's platform, "I am no mortal Achaean soldier. Instead, I am Hermes the Messenger, sent by Zeus himself to lead you inside to speak with sorrowed Achilles. Be sure to kneel at the gallant warrior's knees, and refer to yourself as being a father who has lost his beloved son, as Peleus would feel at losing Achilles. That sort of soap-opera melodramatic rhetoric will soften *his* heart."

Although the time of night was late, Priam courageously entered the hut and approached Achilles and his stunned generals, who were amazed to see an old man nervously encroach into their private conference.

"Who the hell dares to trespass into my residence? Are you animal, vegetable or mineral? You look older than the hills, and more-feeble than my wrinkled-faced and decrepit father, King Peleus!"

"Mighty Achilles! Hear my desperate plea. I am about the same age as your father, who still maintains a glimmer of hope that you will return to your native land alive. But my life has been riddled and cursed by ugly fate, for I am Priam, father of deceased Hector. Before this tragic war, I had fathered fifty sons with ten different women. Apathetic Ares has taken most of them away to reside as flitting spirits inside Hades' and Persephone's dark underground realm. Now my withered testicles are so soft that they soon will be tender-loins. It has now been twelve days since you had emerged triumphant in a tragic death battle with my dear son, Hector. Think of how your father Peleus would feel if he had lost you! I would like to pay you a king's ransom to retrieve my dear son's body for a proper religious burial. For you see, mighty Achilles, we are all victims of fate, and we must not violate Zeus's supreme will, or else suffer dire consequences."

"You must indeed have entered into my secured compound with the aid of some sophisticated god or goddess," astonished Achilles replied. "And I now believe that you are indeed Priam, aggrieved father of Hector and Paris."

"Fear the whimsical gods and their terrible wrath, dear Achilles, for we' are indeed mortal, and suffer *their* occasional anger and their volatile sensitivities."

"Zeus and his criminal family have no cares themselves, and must amuse their fickle desires by constantly manipulating us and frustrating our fragile lives," Achilles sagaciously answered. "Zeus has two jars sitting upon his mantel; one good and the other evil; and the all-powerful deity mixes ingredients from each, or from both, and the psychotic alchemist produces an outcome that his mercurial mood wishes at any given moment."

"Yes, most certainly, young handsome hero. Your father, like myself, had been blessed with wealth, glory and influence. Yet, he too is worried about losing his only son, and sorrows at the concept of *that* prospect ever occurring, if established prophecy does regrettably materialize. And here you are, fighting in a foreign land, all because greedy Menelaus of Sparta wants to retrieve his irresponsible wife from my stubborn son Paris, and take Helen back to Sparta against her will. Both you and I are unfortunate victims of such bad and selfish decisions of others."

"I pity you, King Priam; for you, like myself, have suffered excruciating emotional anguish caused by ignorant assholes. You have exhibited much daring in coming here, risking death, and showing me that you truly possess a heart of iron. I admire your conviction and your implacable sense of purpose."

"Oh, great Achilles; give me back my Hector, so that he can have a proper burial, and so that you can avoid retribution from Olympus for violating the mighty gods' sacred laws. Please accept my valuable gifts from my personal treasury, offered as worthy ransom for my dearly beloved son's corpse."

Remarkably, obstinate Achilles acceded to Priam's strange request, and then acting like a suave host, invited the herald Idaeus into his hut to warm by the fire, and next sent key personnel outside to unload the array of gifts from the transportation wagon, leaving only two shrouds as cloaks to envelop Hector's body for shipment back to Troy. Achilles then directed two skilled servants to thoroughly cleanse and wash the abused cadaver, and then wrap Hector's purified remains inside the expensive silk shrouds.

"Do not cry or weep, dear Priam," Achilles advised, "for nearby soldiers might hear your distress and report your presence to Agamemnon and Menelaus, who might warrant your capture and have you executed. But as long as you remain reticent, you are under my full protection and discretion."

An hour later, after Hector's corpse had been cleansed and adequately prepared, Achilles lifted the shrouded body and carried it to the cart that would be driven by Idaeus back to Troy before daylight.

"Before departing back to your palace, let us eat to consummate our fond bond and our agreed-upon firm resolution. You have astutely negotiated fairly and convincingly, King Priam, and I admire your wisdom, and envy your judgment."

"And likewise, I admire your courage and also your acute perception of reality," Priam complimented and returned. "I would like to sleep several hours before dawn shows its appearance to the east. Please provide beds for my loyal herald and me to rest until then. Your assistance and your empathy will be greatly appreciated."

"I will honor your noble intent," Achilles amenably replied. "The fighting on the Troad will not resume for nine days while you and your countrymen mourn Hector. And after your son's sacred burial, fighting will flare-up again when your grief and honorable intentions have been fully satisfied."

Then, Priam and Idaeus slept in a utilitarian back room while Achilles, still a virgin, slept with Briseis and Ifavagina, who were also recent secret lesbian lovers. In his light sleep, Achilles pondered that if avaricious Agamemnon ever learned of Priam's stay inside Achilles' hut, the Trojan King would have to pay at least three times the ransom that he had already provided to the already-rich Phthian heir.

Several hours later, dependable Hermes, exclusively assigned by Zeus, supervised Priam and Idaeus's safe return passage across the arid Troad Plain, with the pair easily accomplishing their trip back to the high walls of Troy. Priam's vigilant daughter, Cassandra, who possessed the gift of prophecy, was the first to see her father and his herald approaching the citadel's Scaean Gates. Soon, thousands of the city's residents and troops emerged from their domiciles to celebrate Priam's daring and accomplished venture into the camp of the Achaeans to successfully repossess Hector's body for decent burial.

Hector's remains were solemnly and somberly carried into the palace's temple sanctuary, where pitiful diriges were sung, mourning the intrepid prince's death along with acknowledging Priam's son's subsequent journey down to King Hades and Queen Persephone's ominous and mysterious Kingdom of the Dead.

Chapter 24
"THE TROJAN HORSE"

After King Priam had paid Achilles the extraordinarily handsome ransom for repossession of Hector's body for proper burial, and after Patroclus's death had been adequately appeased by Achilles and his' by-the-book Myrmidons, another terrible battle ensued on the Troad Plain where the hero Achilles was killed by an arrow shot by Prince Paris that had been guided by Phoebus Apollo, hitting the Greek archer in the tender heel of his right foot, which was the most vulnerable part of his anatomy, and hence, today's medical reference has evolved into commonly used nomenclature, "the Achilles tendon".

After noble Achilles had been born, his sea goddess mother Thetis had magically dipped his infant body into the Styx River, holding his inverted form by one ankle. Hence, the Greek champion was only vulnerable in *that* one heel, and that is precisely where devious Phoebus Apollo had furtively guided Paris's famous fatal arrow.

The *Trojan War* had taken nearly ten-long-years to fight, and the lengthy conflict was finally won when Odysseus, the notorious brilliant schemer and infamous ball-breaker, had two immense Wooden Trojan Horses constructed, and then had the best Greek warriors situate the separate structures outside the main gates of Troy, which was strategically located at the Hellespont Channel between Greece and Persia (now Turkey).

"How big does this Wooden Horse have to be?" King Agamemnon asked the designing genius Odysseus. "Give me a basic idea of its final dimensions and total weight."

"According to my schematic, the Wooden Horse should be at least ten-foot-wide, twenty-foot-long, and twenty-five foot high, and its capacity in its hollow stomach should be able to easily accommodate twelve-to-twenty of our best warriors."

"How about the approximate weight of this monstrosity?" the leader of the Achaeans asked Odysseus.

"I estimate it to be at around two tons, but that's without any soldiers hidden inside," the Ithacan king informed.

The Trojan army officers insisted that the Trojan Horses should remain outside the city gates, but the superstitious priests and priestesses had idiotically claimed that the Greeks had left the peculiar structures as respectful gifts to first honor and appease the gods, and second, as tokens of a final peace with Troy, and gullible King Priam foolishly had his guards drag the immense devices, which were built on large rollers, into the city proper.

The first wooden horse contained fifty horny, kinky Greek harlots that were instructed to exit down a hidden ladder at a designated time of night, and then directly proceed to flirt-with and expertly service free sex to the nearby, sex-starved Trojan guards.

While the aroused guards were humping and pumping the nymphomaniac Greek whores, a dozen of the finest Achaean soldiers had been confined and impatiently waiting inside the second more famous Wooden Horse's interior.

As a sidebar coincidence, Helen of Troy had approached the second horse and walked in a circle three times around it, and then raised her hand to curiously feel the recently-built equine's hollow underbelly.

Inspired by always-scheming Aphrodite, who had staunchly advocated the Trojan cause, Helen's melodic voice called-out, naming the best undigested Greek occupants among the concealed Danaans who were hidden inside the horse's abdomen, and Menelaus's stealthy wife amazingly spoke-up like an accomplished ventriloquist, sounding exactly like the voice of each soldier's Greek spouse.

Helen's estranged husband Menelaus was seething inside the horse's belly, sitting right next to clever Odysseus. Two of the fanatical interior combatants, Diomedes and the Spartan king, were eager to get-up and wildly charge outside the wooden wonder in response to their wives' voices, and all dozen heroes felt compelled to answer back their spouses' alluring beckoning from where the soldiers were sweating and huddling inside the artificial equine.

Diomedes and several others felt compelled to reactively scream-back imprudent replies to Helen's vocal imitations, but nimble-witted Menelaus and Odysseus held the others' destructive compulsions in check to preserve their secret mission from Trojan detection.

All of the scared-shitless Achaeans sitting inside the Wooden Horse's belly managed to keep their chatty mouths shut, except for fucked-up Anticlus, who was the only one about to raise his throat's vocal cords, and the imbecile had felt a dire death-wish to answer Helen's alluring summoning.

Odysseus instinctively and firmly clapped his hands upon Anticlus's mouth, and held the numbskull in a gorilla grip before then puncturing the stupid shit's already-abused testicles with a sharp dagger. In short, heroes Odysseus and Menelaus deftly kept their dual grips upon Anticlus's choked neck, and also upon the rogue's bleeding balls, until Athena again appeared upon the scene, and escorted Helen away from the second Trojan Horse, presumably being led to ultimate safety.

One by one, the dozen Greek heroes descended the concealed hidden ladder, and quickly killed the fifty Trojan guards while the preoccupied in-heat sexpots were busily screwing and happily climaxing inside the fifty insatiable, horny Greek harlots.

The hero Odysseus had ingeniously thought-up the stellar ideas of the dual *Trojan Horses,* basically because the perpetual schemer wanted to return to Ithaca and pump his old lady, Queen Penelope, whom the faithful, itinerant king had heard was being wooed by two-dozen or so totally-worthless suitors, walking around the rugged island with massive hard-ons. And thus, after inventing the infamous dual Horses, Odysseus was about to make the transition from the ten-year Trojan War to his incredible ten-year odyssey adventure, finally returning home to his native Ithaca.

HOMER'S ODD SEA ODYSSEY

Jay Dubya

Chapter 1

"GODDESS ATHENA VISITS ITHACA"

Brain-dead-but-awesome Ancient Muse, speak to me now of that intrepid hero who had wondered and wandered all over known creation after pillaging and looting the corrupt bordellos and brothels of Troy. This major mage explored many cities and citadels around the Mediterranean Sea, where Odysseus learned their unique cultures, and while sailing upon the treacherous waves, the brave explorer suffered many torments from mentors and tormentors alike, as the Greek mariner struggled to save his own existence and lead his crewmen (warriors and worriers) back home.

But though the courageous King of Ithaca desired to salvage his doomed sailors, Odysseus, swimming in his own frustration, could not rescue or salvage his rowers from either drowning or from being devoured by famished monsters. The obstinate jerk-offs all died from their own stupidity; the totally greedy and ambitious imbeciles. As a pertinent example, the avaricious dumb-fucks feasted upon the sacred cattle of Helios Hyperion, who was the jealous god of the sun. And so, the vindictive, small-dicked giant snuffed-away their slim opportunity of ever safely arriving back to Ithaca. So now, Athena, the well-endowed virgin daughter of Zeus, will explain to us the entire epic adventure of Odysseus, beginning anywhere her egregious mind wishes.

To supplement this lengthy poem's mystery that pertains to Odysseus, the other more-obedient Greek kings and warriors, including all those who had escaped being utterly destroyed while plundering Troy, were now safely returned to their island homes, facing no more wicked dangers from engaging Trojans in battle, or devastating threats from the unpredictable, and sometimes belligerent sea.

But regrettably, dim-witted Odysseus, who after two decades being separated from Ithaca, still-longed to be reunited with his gorgeous, sex-starved wife Penelope, and the plagued fellow was quite determined to reach his ever-deteriorating palace. Currently, in this wholly truthful account, the daring adventurer was being held captive in a hollow, dank cave by that mighty, sex-starved nymph Calypso, the immortal bitch being a hormone-driven, ignoble goddess, who vindictively desired to vicariously screw Odysseus every single hour of every single day as her enslaved, infidel paramour.

But as the various annual seasons progressed and advanced in succession, the correct year finally arrived in which, according to what the mentally-retarded main Olympian gods had once secretly ordained, the journeyman King was scheduled by Zeus's decree to venture back to his native home in Ithaca; not that the bad-luck-merchant would be free from troubles even there, especially among his horny, rebellious, straight and gay island residents. To add to the drama, most of the normally apathetic Olympian gods pitied troubled King Odysseus; that is, all except contemptuous Poseidon, the sea deity who characteristically maintained his disreputable anger against mortal, ambitious Ithacans. And to amplify the ongoing dilemma, the trident-carrying sea god did not relinquish in demonstrating his ruthless animosity until valiant and persistent Odysseus eventually, through sheer human determination, stubbornly reached his native island destination.

"What the Hades is my brother, Poseidon, King of the Sea doing, pretending to be a pathetic landlubber in Ethiopia?" Zeus (Jupiter) asked his don't give a shit Olympian family. "Does he have water on the brain? Is he learning to dance the Wah Watusi? Why is my wet-behind-the-ears sibling being so pedestrian, behaving like a very lost human ambler?"

"No, Father. Forget all about the Watusi! Our sea god relative, my uncle Poseidon, is learning the essential step gyrations from local African crab trappers as to how to expertly dance 'the Fish'!" Athena (Minerva) maintained. "Your just-mentioned account indicates that you're into the art of anachronism, and your ridiculous statements are living proof that you've been gloriously time-traveling into the decadent future."

But simultaneously, at *that* momentous moment in classic mythology, zany Poseidon was preoccupied and engaged in partying like Dionysus (Bacchus) somewhere in remote Africa; the sea-god's thrilling expedition taking him amongst the wild-and-crazy Ethiopians, with Poseidon's illustrious presence being a long way off from the magnificent temples atop sparkling Mt. Olympus. The other bored and intoxicated gods had already gathered inside the great white marble hall of their Olympian King, Omnipotent Zeus.

Among all the arrogant, self-centered potentates, the mentally-challenged father of gods and men was the first to address the obnoxious, insolent audience. In his immoral, immortal heart, Zeus was momentarily recalling the recent murder of royal asshole King Aegisthus. Insane Orestes,

King Agamemnon's celebrated son, had conveniently killed and butchered mentally unstable Aegisthus. So, with the deceased mortal ruler's memory kept in mind, Omnipotent Zeus now addressed his fully lethargic kin.

"It's excessively disgusting how these puny humans blame us kind-hearted gods for everything from their mild skin rashes to their lethal venereal diseases," Zeus lectured inside his mansion's radiant throne room. "The wily knuckleheads residing down on Earth falsely state that their abundant maladies originate from us innocent Olympians, when in fact, the pure truth is that the ludicrous nincompoops, through their own adulterous foolishness, bestow upon themselves harsh difficulties and consequences, most of which incidentally have not been officially devised by the reliable dictates of infallible Fate," Zeus unclearly emphasized. "Now then, my fellow Olympians; there was an absurd numbskull who had existed down on Earth named Aegisthus, but the sex-driven ignoramus selfishly possessed for himself the gorgeous wife of King Agamemnon of Mycenae. Aegisthus wound-up brutally murdering acclaimed Agamemnon, the pure-hearted son of all-too-kind Atreus. And then, Orestes, son of King Agamemnon, murdered Aegisthus, with the abominable assassination transpiring right inside Atreus's atrium."

"Father, what happened next in that ongoing saga of hate and murder?" insisted curious Athena. "It is my understanding that tragedy often begets more tragedy in continuous, redundant cycles among the devious mortals!"

"And to add more detail, my beautiful Daughter; sex-addict Aegisthus had maliciously butchered Agamemnon's corpse into tiny fragments, immediately after the renowned leader of the Greek navy triumphantly arrived home to the mainland from miraculously conquering Troy over in Asia Minor. That very deliberate kill and mutilation violation definitely was not prescribed by the potent whims of infallible Fate. Aegisthus knew all along that his vile and demented evil act would ultimately establish the idiot's total ruin. The morally deficient dip-shit was then soon butchered by Orestes, the deranged son of King Agamemnon, who, as you all know, had gallantly led the Greek expedition against Troy!"

"Did you have any personal enmity towards the slain Aegisthus?" Athena inquired of her Almighty Father. "Was the aberrant king on your personal elimination list?"

"I resented the fact that *that* weird-fuck mental case occasionally wore purple garments during important palace events, and as you're well-aware Daughter, purple is the chosen color of the gods and is limited to *our* use only," Zeus verbally related. "Other than that intolerable behavior of wearing the color purple, I conceded and allowed Eternal Fate to decide Aegisthus's final demise."

"Who gives a canine's crap about these miniscule, insignificant and mundane human affairs?" challenged the handsome chariot god, Apollo. "A deplorable human butchery enacted in imitation of a previous deplorable human butchering. Lord Zeus; in all candor, I have more nobility in my little pinky than does the brightest and best of that terribly deranged mortal species residing down on Mother Earth!"

"You are more than *a chicken,* Apollo, so stop acting like a foul fowl! So now, back to my history lesson," Zeus gruffly replied, resuming his lengthy exposition. "Yes, my inattentive heavenly family. That silly earthly fool, regal Aegisthus, has satisfactorily paid in full for everything he had deserved in the form of revenge. First, the power-hungry villain had viciously crushed Agamemnon's balls with a heavy sledgehammer. And next, the vile aggressor had painfully castrated the aged victim with his already-bloodied rusty sword!"

Athena, possessing gleaming eyes promptly answered Lord Zeus.

"Son of famed Titan Cronos (Saturn), and genetically inferior and brain-dead father to us all; you who rule on high from your high-chair, er, I mean throne; yes indeed, Father; I now understand the story. Thanks to Orestes's need for retribution, deceased Aegisthus now lies stone-cold dead, experiencing a personal destiny he had initially himself caused. May any other guilty man who does similar to what Aegisthus had evilly attempted also be quickly destroyed!"

A copycat murder!" Zeus interrupted Athena. "Aegisthus killed King Agamemnon, and Agamemnon's son Orestes killed Aegisthus in quite a similar manner!"

"But dear Father; my vulnerable heart remains tremendously tattered. I remain worrying about the fate of wonderful Odysseus; my very special, ill-fated, and extremely confused explorer, who has had to endure and struggle with a frustrating series of horrible disasters for so many years; my mortal champion's defiant activities are still occurring far away from his former friends, and also far-removed from certain often-visited amorous prostitutes. I adamantly believe that faithful Queen Penelope is unaware of her husband's adulterous conduct practiced over his twenty-year absence from Ithaca. Yes, Father; ten years fighting like a valorous Spartan against the Trojans, and ten years being punished by your cruel, heartless brother, Lord Poseidon!"

"Get to the point, Daughter Athena," Zeus angrily replied. "Or else, I'll gladly dry-up your virgin pubic love garden for all eternity! In *my* dominant Universe, might makes right, and quite apparently, Athena, I happen to control all of the might."

"Maybe so, Daddy. But you and Uncle Poseidon savagely punish ethical Odysseus while you completely ignore the other less-moral Greek inhabitants who constantly call you a dizzy dumb-dick and a flagrant fuck-head! Why are you so ambivalent? Can't you see that you are biased against certain mortals, but you tolerate multiple misdeeds from others?"

"Daughter; describe your defense of this primitive caveman Odysseus whom you so admire, while I still enjoy a degree of patience," Zeus nastily retorted. "Honestly, I have less patience than the average mortal physician does, ha, ha, ha! In the future, a low-intelligence asshole named Hippocrates will certainly envy my incredible patience!"

"Well, Pop. The itinerant King of Ithaca is now being held hostage on a little-known island; its topography being surrounded by the moody Mediterranean Sea," Athena informed the assembly of gods. "The extensive body of water forms the mythological ocean's naval navel. And there, Big Daddy, within the lush semi-tropical forest landscape, lives a voluptuous, minor goddess, Calypso, who intentionally prevents her disconsolate captive, my stellar hero Odysseus, who is being egregiously held against his free will, from ever escaping or leaving her rather obstinate authority."

"So, Athena, in a million words or less, what's so damned special about this very ordinary fellow, Odysseus, King of Ithaca?"

"I absolutely adore brave Odysseus," Pallas Athene adamantly answered. "My favorite hero yearns to once again see the smoke and pollution rising from Ithacan chimneys. And the weary victim's spirit presently longs to be immediately defeated by imminent death. Yet, despite *that* overwhelming, grotesque adversity, Great Olympian Almighty Zeus, your occasionally sympathetic heart does not adequately respond to the punished Greek King's incessant pleas and appeals. Now Father; did not Odysseus obediently and respectfully offer, in honor of your immense glory, spectacular sacrifices that had been exhibited upon Troy's arid desert plain, situated beside the moored Greek ships. If so, Father Zeus; why are you so fuckin' angry with afflicted and beleaguered Odysseus? Are your enormous hemorrhoids again acting-up, or what?"

Cloud-gatherer Zeus then answered his recalcitrant Daughter and cynically declared: "My beloved child. How could I ever forget god-like Odysseus, pre-eminent among all mortal men for his reputed intelligence and for his benign offerings to us immortal gods, *we* who hold dominion over wide Heaven and inferior Earth? But my vengeful brother, Earthquake-shaker Poseidon, the stubborn and powerful sea god, is still furious about *that* injured Cyclops, the monstrosity known as Polyphemus, the mightiest of the Cyclopes, whose singular eye Odysseus had violently destroyed during a brief physical encounter."

"But Father. Why is the ogre Polyphemus and his missing private eye so important to you?" Athena detected and asked. "It is true that Odysseus had made a spectacle out of the hideous villain!"

"Thoosa, the notorious and promiscuous sea nymph, bore ugly Polyphemus in childbirth," Zeus recalled and stated. "The minor deity was a radical daughter of that irresponsible Phorcys, who commands the restless deep seas. Sex-craving Poseidon, down in those dark hollow caves, often had twenty-four-hour daily social and physical intercourse with the sultry bitch."

"I wish that Thoosa should have had genetically damaged Polyphemus aborted," Athena sternly argued. "That Cyclops has been a menace to civilization, and also to any seamen who might get shipwrecked on the monster's formidable island. The death of all intruders and trespassers is the only special justice that vile Polyphemus ever administered!"

"The blinding of Polyphemus is the principal reason why Earthshaker Poseidon, father of the Cyclops, makes Odysseus futilely wander and squander his impotent life all over my creation, venturing from island to island," Zeus articulated. "But vindictive Poseidon has not yet released your hero, the hard-headed voyager. So, Pallas Athene, who doesn't own a palace; I insist on this strategy; come now, my subordinate Olympic family; let's together consider the King of Ithaca's eventual return, so that the perplexed leader can successfully journey back to Ithaca and reunite with Queen Penelope and his only son, Telemachus. I predict that Poseidon's notorious animosity will soon relent. My ocean brother can't successfully fight me, along with my allied Olympian family, all by himself; not with all of us aligned against his mounting wrath."

Athena, goddess with the sensational gleaming eyes, proudly and quickly replied to her father's monotonous oration.

"Son of Cronos and father to us all; your enviable wisdom vigilantly rules the stars and constellations of heaven above. Let's urgently dispatch the swift flying Hermes (Mercury), killer of Argus, as our personal courier, sending our messenger god over to the island of Ogygia, so that our trustworthy postman can quickly tell that fair-haired nymph Calypso of our firm decision; which is that bold Odysseus will now leave and complete his extraordinary voyage back to Ithaca."

"Well now, Daughter. Your solution must end, as usual, in a satisfactory, fairy tale conclusion," declared Zeus. "If your imaginative plan fails, and this witch Calypso does not cooperate, then I promise that I'll further punish Odysseus by having the addled blockhead shit out of his pecker and piss from his asshole. Or, in another scenario," Zeus threatened, "I might shoot a bolt of lightning up your favorite hero's fat rear-end and effectively cauterize his colon and also his large intestine. Then, your mortal champion could neither shit nor piss out of his sealed-up anus!"

"I'll deftly zoom-off to distant Ithaca and urge the King's son Telemachus to initiate action. I'll instill admirable courage inside the young man's heart," Athena informed, "so that the son of Odysseus will call those long-haired Achaeans destroying his property to assembly. Telemachus will then intrepidly address the bevy of covetous suitors, who keep on butchering his father's flocks of sheep, and also keep randomly slaughtering the King's bent-horned cattle. I'll soon surreptitiously send vernal Telemachus on a secret mission to sandy Pylos, and then off to Sparta, where the pure-hearted lad can learn all about his brave father's remarkable exploits along with his new-found journey home."

After Athena convincingly spoke, the gorgeous goddess gracefully tied her lovely sandals upon her dainty feet; the famed immortal, golden sandals, which reputedly carry Zeus's daughter as fast as stormy winter wind gusts across the ocean seas and over endless tracts of land masses. Athena raced-down from Mount Olympus's lofty peak, sped across the land and sea to Ithaca, and then just confidently stood there, at Odysseus's outer gate, located before the in-need-of-repair palace.

Standing erect outside the musty structure's threshold, the resolute goddess's right hand was still firmly gripping her gleaming bronze spear, imitating the general appearance of Mentes, a noteworthy foreigner who ruled the fierce Taphians. At her position before the dilapidated palace, audacious Athena encountered the egocentric suitors still pursuing the hand of enticing Queen Penelope, the devoted wife of King Odysseus, whose fidelity remained strong, despite her beleaguered husband being away for twenty long years.

Those narcissistic, competing troublemakers, all cowardly parasites, were obviously enjoying themselves playing ancient checkers, and arm-wrestling right outside the huge wooden entrance doors, and all the while merrily sitting-down and laughing upon soft, thick hides of cattle skins.

Little time was left for abandoned Queen Penelope to willfully surrender to gruesome reality, and agree to marry one of the malignant suitors, since her nomadic husband had been away from Ithaca for twenty long years.

Chapter 2
"STELLAR TELEMACHUS"

At the in-shambles Ithacan Palace, Telemachus observed Athena first, well-before the others males, the rabble consisting of dangerous and horny suitors. The attracted and distracted adolescent moved-up near the goddess's position and then softly spoke to her; the youth's inspired words seeming to have majestic wings, which instantly impressed his immortal Olympus visitor.

"My cordial welcome to you, most enchanting stranger. You must enjoy my humble hospitality. Then, after you have consumed some sumptuous food, you can tell me exactly what you might need."

After saying those polite introductory words, congenial Telemachus awkwardly led gorgeous Athena into his father's ramshackle palace's main hall. The youth courteously sat his vivacious visitor into a dust-laden chair, which twenty years earlier had represented a beautifully constructed work of intricate craftsmanship. Beneath Athena's golden sandals, the all-too-pleasant host rolled-out a utilitarian linen mat, and then set in place a flimsy footstool for his guest to rest her feminine feet. Beside her curvaceous body, the amiable lad drew-up a second lovely-but-archaic decorated chair for him to sit and squirm around while dealing with his pulsating erection. The boy's bizarre sexual fantasy was interrupted when a female servant entered the quarters and carried a fine gold-gilt jug, and soon proceeded to pour fresh water out into a silver basin, so that the new acquaintances could eagerly scrub and wash their sweaty hands.

"I'm sorry to admit that I cannot afford for you, kind lady, food, drink and golden thrones like those items enjoyed by the immortals, supposedly existing atop fabled Mt. Olympus," Telemachus apologized. "I sometimes myself imagine that I'm a god and an intimate friend of Hermes, Apollo and Hephaestus (Vulcan)."

"Your provisions are indeed adequate for little old me, a modest suppliant traveling around Greece under the protection of Almighty Zeus," Athena logically replied. And then the 'down-to-Earth' visitor considered further evaluating her freckle-faced host. 'This fucked-up junior jerk-off isn't even enough an intellectual challenge for me to waste my precious time. Telemachus probably doesn't even have signs of hair growing around his tiny dingle! I can't stand me shrinking-down to being a six-foot-tall human facsimile. I felt much more supreme and confident up on Olympus being my standard fifty-foot height.'

Beside the two oddball chamber-sitting occupants, the woman servant set-down an expensive, polished table. Then, the silent housekeeper carried-in newly baked bread and placed the loaf down before Telemachus and his immortal guest. The valet next laid-out a selection of spotted and speckled fruits, drawing freely on supplies that she had scrupulously kept hidden in a side storeroom, concealed away from the parasitic suitors' lustful scrutiny. A longtime palace carver sliced-up many different cuts of meat, and graciously provided slabs upon two cracked and stained plates. Then, the elderly, gray-bearded slicer abandoned his cutlery duties, left the room and found and brought-out tarnished golden goblets, as another lowlife herald entered the dismal area and served the pair sour wine.

Then, one after another, the conceited suitors sauntered into the vast dank chamber. The leeching slobs sat-down upon a variety of reclining seats and upon ugly, uncomfortable high-backed chairs. Available heralds, with nothing better to do, poured water out into mugs for everyone seated inside the enormous chamber, in order for them to wash their hands, and thereafter, laconic women piled assorted wicker baskets full of stale bread onto dirty tables, while young lads filled dull goblets up to their brims with putrid-smelling, cloudy red wine.

The suitors reached-out with their greedy hands to help themselves to the somewhat-diseased fruits that had been placed in front of the morally-bankrupt laughing assholes. When each and every scumbag had satisfied his vast need for mediocre food and sour drink, the freeloaders' degenerate hearts and tongues demanded something more in the form of lap-dancing and risqué song, lewd entertainment elements that the weirdo dregs regarded as the finest joys that the dreadful derelicts regularly associated with their marathon mooching habits.

Next, an enterprising herald handed a splendid lyre to Phemius, so the timid musician was forced to sing in front of all the ignoble scum-wagons. Upon the strange-sounding strings, the musical bard plucked the prelude to a romantic love song about a kinky royal queen lamenting having monthly menstrual and minstrel agony.

But then Telemachus, leaned his dandruff-filled head and scalp over, close to enchanting Athena, so that no other occupant inside the room could listen, and the want-to-get-laid youth murmured:

"Dear, kind, well-endowed stranger, and also my utterly attractive guest. These ruthless men here; yes, the deplorable freaks spend all their time like this, with disgusting songs and horrendous music. It's easy here for the depraved suitors, because the lazy, raucous shits gorge themselves on what belongs to someone else, and the fuck-heads devour my father's wealth with complete impunity; the dastardly creeps mock and malign a noble patriarch whose white bones may well be lying upon the barren mainland somewhere, vilely rotting in the pouring rain, or perhaps disintegrating deep inside the apathetic sea, being tossed around by uncaring waves. If these vermin in our midst ever saw my famous father returning to Ithaca, they'd all be praying to possess swifter feet, rather than accumulating more wealth in amassed gold, or finer clothing through excessive bullying." Telemachus paused to clear his raspy throat, and then continued to communicate his bullshit evaluation to Athena. "But by now, honored suppliant, I suspect that some evil fate much worse than mere acne has furiously killed blithe-hearted Odysseus, and for us, his dependents surviving here within his decrepit palace, there is no particular consolation; not even if some earth-bound immortal should arrive in this forsaken place and announce that my father will soon arrive. But tell me this information, well-mannered stranger, and please speak candidly. Who are your people? What city do you come from?"

'This especially naïve, young fool is even more of a dolt than I had originally suspected!' Athena assessed. 'I can tell by his gestures that this immature jester only desires to rape me and have juvenile sex, the rookie teenage dunce! That's all I need to have happening to me right now; his dumb-ass, over-excited, premature ejaculation shooting high into, and harmfully contaminating, my virgin vagina!'

Then Athena, goddess with the gleaming eyes, plausibly answered her new acquaintance:

"To respond to you, my suave gentleman, I will indeed speak openly. I can tell you that my common name is Mentes, a son of the wise Anchialus, who is the fearless king of the Taphians, who are highly-skilled rowers, and who absolutely love the oar. My dependable ship is securely docked in a berth some distance from your one-donkey town. But come, my eminent friend; speak openly, and tell me the irrelevant gossip that I request knowing," Athena urged. "What is this peculiar feast that I'm presently witnessing all about? Who are the mentally unstable members of this uncouth and sloppy gaggle of disheveled men, the freaks all appearing to be ridiculing you? And why do you need to be grotesquely exposed to all this colossal, belligerent mayhem? Is this a fucked-up bachelor party gone amok?" Athena wondered and asked. "Or, is it a raucous, low-budget university fraternity drinking fiasco? It seems clear enough to me, my callow host, that this vulgar event is no meal where each participant brings and offers his own fair share, and I can plainly observe with open pupils that the riffraff mob gathered here in this dreary room is guiltlessly acting in a totally insulting, overbearing, perverted way, while egregiously dining in a corrupt manner inside your unsophisticated palace."

Noble Telemachus then felt compelled to reply to Athena, anonymously pretending to be the unkempt philosopher Mendes: "Inquisitive stranger; since you've questioned me about the lunatic matter that your keen eyes perceive, I'll tell you the honest-to-Zeus truth. The house in which you sit was once well on its way to being rich and famous; at that time in the past, my father, kind Odysseus, was alive and active among his appreciative people. But now, the whimsical gods, practicing their malicious plans, have sinisterly changed all that phenomenal family history completely upside-down. The contemptible dwellers residing atop Mt. Olympus make sure that merciful Odysseus stays in obscurity, where nobody roaming this accursed planet can actually see him."

"Whose fault is responsible for this horrible chain of events that you cite?" Athena asked. "If I were you, I'd rather be a leper or a terminally ill cancer patient!"

"The mercurial gods, argumentative visitor, have not dealt with other men in a similar manner as the insane assholes have arbitrarily dealt with Odysseus," Telemachus maintained. "But it's not him alone who makes me sad and cry-out my frustration and disillusionment in utter distress. For now, the erratic gods have brought me more intolerable grief. All the best young men who rule the neighboring islands, Dulichium and woodsman Zacynthus, and that criminal Sameo, as well as those who lord *that* barren western land situated here in rocky Ithaca; indeed, my distinguished guest; those black-hearted scoundrels are all now wooing my mother and ravaging my soon-to-be-inherited house."

"Please describe your mother's unenviable plight?" Athena requested. "How is she ever enduring such mounting aggravation?"

"Queen Penelope is trapped within an unfortunate circumstance where, after twenty-years of insufferable unhappiness, she won't turn-down a marriage that she detests, but my mother can't bring herself to make the final choice," Telemachus explained. "Meanwhile, these mendacious suitors are disdainfully feasting on my home's assets, and the villainous rogues soon will be the death of me as well. These boisterous hoodlums are wickedly dismantling my father's august legacy, and bankrupting my mother and me in the process."

Those glaring and salient revelations divulged by Telemachus made Pallas Athena angry, and the livid goddess disclosed to her host:

"It's quite lamentable that your famous father Odysseus is still wandering all over creation when you and Queen Penelope need him here so much in Ithaca! Your mighty patriarch could easily lay his powerful hands upon these disrespectful suitors and strangle their annoying throats right out of their skinny necks! Listen now, besieged Telemachus, to what essential strategy I'm going to confidentially reveal to you," Athena beckoned. "Tomorrow, you must summon the encroaching Achaean suitors to an assembly and forcefully address the filthy bastards, dynamically appealing to the sympathetic gods of Mt. Olympus as divine witnesses. Next, Telemachus; imperatively direct the fucked-up suitors to go back to their shoddy, rented shanties. As for your sorrowed mother, Penelope, if her heart is honestly set on getting married to one of these garrulous dirtballs, then allow your' mom to return to where her compassionate father lives, for he's an imaginative savant of great abilities and of tremendous hidden, emotional power. Your understanding grandfather will smartly organize the intended marriage and arrange the specific wedding gifts, as many dowry contributions as befit a well-loved, slightly used, non-virgin daughter," Athena stressed. "Now, dear Telemachus; as for yourself, if you'll diligently listen, I have some super-wise, noteworthy advice. Set-off down south seeking fortuitous news concerning your father's fate, for Odysseus has been absent from Ithaca for so long. Some living mortal perhaps can provide you with tangible knowledge of his whereabouts, or you may fortunately hear a voice emanating from Lord Zeus, who often enjoys bringing mortals favorable news as a diversion from his eternal boredom."

"Well, kind stranger; who the hell do I have to see down south?"

I recommend, dear Telemachus, that you first journey to Pylos and eagerly consult with elderly and sagacious Nestor. After you've been there vegetating in Pylos, proceed in haste to Sparta and conscientiously confer with fair-haired, bullshitting King Menelaus, the last one of all the bronze-clad Achaeans to arrive safely home to the mainland after the ten-year Trojan War."

"Your thorough instructions seem easy enough to remember, suave guest. I'll be as cool as a cucumber when I vegetate in Pylos and Sparta. Do you have anything else of importance to convey?"

"Yes, Telemachus. I strongly suggest that you must not continue acting like a spoiled, feckless child; for indeed, craven son of Odysseus; the time has evolved where you're now too old to be weakly conducting yourself as an embarrassing, impotent wimp."

Prudent Telemachus, who in his ignorance actually believed that the traveling goddess was a genuine male cross-dressing transvestite, then constructively answered glamorous Athena:

"Stranger, you have been speaking to me as an authentic and caring friend, even though, before today, I didn't know your' ass from either Prometheus or Pandora. Indeed, you've spoken to me just like a father would advocate for his own disobedient offspring. And what peculiar wisdom you've just communicated! I'll always cherish and never forget your' fabulous counsel. But please come now," Telemachus attempted persuading. "Though you're eager to be off to yonder harbor, stay here for a while so that we can intimately learn about each other in a touchy-feely manner. Once you've enjoyed your naked bath with us both splashing-around in the nude, your fond heart, being a spectacular oracle with four auricles, will soon be fully satisfied. But since you insist on departing, I now instruct you, amiable stranger, to swiftly exit these premises with jubilant spirits, and be off to your awaiting ship."

"You demonstrate the fake valor of Apollo along with the brass balls of Hephaestus!" Athena shrewdly admonished. "I must confess, young and ambitious Telemachus, that you're a fast-read, unenviable, shallow-minded asshole!"

"Furthermore, anonymous guest; as a wonderful surprise, you'll be carrying with you an expensive gift that I wish to contribute to your safe passage home," the simple-minded youth stated. "The alluded-to object is something truly and positively magnificent, which will be my appreciative gratefulness to your sage guidance. In fact, the valuable item is a rather sentimental heirloom, dear guest; the aforementioned prize being the sort of present that a friend would often give to one whom he regards as *his* valued kindred comrade."

Goddess Athena, with the gleaming eyes thought, 'Wow! Perhaps it's a terrific wooden dildo without splinters, or maybe a carton of used, unsanitary napkins!' Then, the delighted guest visiting the ruinous Ithacan palace replied:

"Since I'm eager to depart this outrageous barn of yours that you preposterously describe as a palace, Telemachus, please don't dare keep me as a disenchanted hostage a moment longer. And whatever sensational gift

214

your heart suggests you'll afford me as your loyal friend, kindly present the designated merchandise to me when I eventually come back here to again visit your trashy dump. Pick me out something truly beautiful. I guarantee that your intelligent choice, son of King Odysseus and Queen Penelope, will earn you something desirable that will be even more worthy and stellar upon my return."

With that phony rhetoric being communicated, Athena with the gleaming hazel eyes, departed the decrepit mansion, and after exiting, flew-off like some wild famished sea bird in quest of its next meal. In the Ithacan lad's immature heart, the merciful goddess had inserted both necessary courage and strength. In the process, clever Athena had made Telemachus recall his father's fantastic audacity, which the hero often employed against impending adversity in the form of mortal enemies and insidious monsters. Inside his miniature, underdeveloped, cerebrum, frail Telemachus could vividly picture his apparently feminine guest, just as a sense of amazement suddenly invaded his vulnerable heart. In his wildest chauvinistic conjecture, the teenager envisioned his recent visitor as a cross-dressing god (and not a goddess). And so, the inspired youth moved away from his typical shyness and uncharacteristically mingled with the throng of antagonistic suitors.

The famous minstrel Phemius was currently performing his rehearsed tune at the Palace, as the demented two-dozen villains sat in silence, vaguely listening to the fucked-up lyrics. The phlegmatic vocalist was nostalgically singing of the return of King Agamemnon (brother of Menelaus), and his victorious Achaeans to Mycenae; that bitter trip which Athena had personally prescribed and guided when the weary warriors had sailed home from distant Troy.

Meanwhile, in her upstairs room, the daughter of Icarius, wise and devoted Queen Penelope, heard the minstrel's inspired military verses. The wife of Odysseus cautiously descended the towering staircase from her room, but her appearance below was not alone; two female servants followed Her Highness to the source of entertainment.

When beautiful Penelope reached the vicinity of the avaricious suitors, the Queen stayed beside the doorpost in the formerly well-built room, and a small blue veil across her face hid her attractive features. On either side of Odysseus's wife, her two attendants waited. With tears streaming down her cheeks (the ones on her face), sensitive Penelope respectfully addressed the popular singer.

"Clown show Phemius; you know all sorts of other ways to charm an audience besides your stupid propensity of masturbating in public, but right now, I'm specifically referring to paying homage to extraordinary actions performed by gods and men, which dumb-ass singers like yourself often celebrate. As you listlessly sit here, frog-throated Phemius, gently sing one of those monotonous Trojan War lyrics that I've just suggested, while these condescending suitors drink their putrid wine in absolute silence."

"You wish for me to sing a song of praise about the Greeks defeating the Trojans? Queen Penelope; the suitors might not savor such lyrics!"

"Don't keep vocalizing that painful song you've been chirping, which always breaks the heart pounding here in my chest, and makes my sensitive ovaries ache, for, more than anyone present within this dingy hall, I'm weighed-down with ceaseless grief and excruciating abdominal cramps which I cannot endure. I clearly remember, always, with such yearning, my dear husband's clean-shaven face and hairy crotch. Odysseus was a husband whose fame has spread like syphilis far and wide throughout Greece and central Argos."

Instead of Phemius replying, surprisingly, newly-sensible and inspired Telemachus answered Penelope and uttered:

"Mother, why begrudge this talented singer delighting us in any way. His mind should inspire him to adroitly activate his larynx in the manner he so chooses? One can't deny the minstrel his natural propensities. It seems to me that it's Zeus's lousy fault for all the horrible tragedies that affect men. Yes; the renegade chief god thwarts decent laboring men, limiting the success of each and every breathing mortal asshole, whatever the jealous god's supreme whim at that moment so desires. There's nothing exclusively inappropriate with this dissonant fellow's singing of the evil fate of the doomed Danaans, for brazen men instinctively praise the song which the idiots have heard most recently," asserted Telemachus, effectively articulating his newly-discovered adult independence.

"Where did you ever acquire your new-found courage?" Penelope asked her suddenly transformed son. "Have you visited Delphi without my expressed permission?"

"Your heart and spirit, Mother, should accept the literal interpretation of the disillusioned minstrel's song. Now venture-up to your rooms and keep busy there with your own favorite work, namely the family spindle and the fruitless loom. And instruct your more faithful servants to leave your preoccupied misery, and industriously attend to their separate duties. Talking politics is men's concern, and exchanging gossip is the matter of chattering women. Yes, Mother; your every focus should be on the safe return of your husband, King Odysseus, but his return should also be of special interest to me, since in this house, I'm now, by default, the only one who is in charge."

Astonished at her son's amazing mature speech, Penelope retired back up to her own chambers, keeping her son's strident nomenclature lodged deep inside her suffering heart. With her attendant women, the Queen climbed up the rickety stairs, veered in the direction of her private rooms, and there wept for her beloved missing husband, and his massive manhood, until gleaming-eyed Athena cast sleep upon the matron's heavy eyelids.

Inside the Ithacan palace's shadowy halls, the rambunctious suitors then started to create a loud uproar, with each jerk-off shouting-out his desperate hope to lie beside and then pork Penelope. Knowing their mutual, sinister motive, shrewd Telemachus boldly addressed the pernicious fuck-heads:

"You, frantic suitors of my precious mother's snatcheroo, who display such abundant arrogance, let us for now cooperate and together participate and delight in our imminent banquet. But I caution; there is to be no more exuberant shouting, for it is grand and more satisfying to the ear to listen to an excellent singer as accomplished as this ball-breaker, Phemius," Telemachus daringly maintained. "The minstrel's feminine, high-pitched, alto voice sounds like a god's perpetual orgasm."

"Where have you learned such defiant articulation?" a scar-faced suitor challenged. "You dare to defy us, even though you have no hair under your scrawny armpits!"

Telemachus completely ignored the wise-ass suitor and aggressively proceeded with his startling narrative. "But in the morning, let us all again assemble here, and sit our asses down for an important meeting. I will emphatically speak and tell you dumb-fucks, in a firm manner, to immediately depart my home."

"Why do we have to meet tomorrow morning to hear such nonsense when you've just told us what you plan to say?" the same egomaniac sarcastically vociferated a logical criticism.

Penelope's all-too-confident, recently transformed son was not distracted from continuing his stern narrative. "Listen shit-heads; prepare your un-delectable feasts elsewhere, and engage in dinners that eat-up your own possessions, and not mine. I recommend that you totally reprehensible freaks move your asses from house to house and from shanty to shack. If you think it's better, and would prefer that one man's livelihood should be consumed by your gross and parasitic nature, without paying any compensation in return, I'll simply notify the immortal gods to ascertain if mighty Zeus will devise, on my behalf, a suitable and devastating act of brutal retribution. And finally," Telemachus lectured. "I pray that if you' asinine retards are destroyed inside *my* palace, I wish that your instantaneous demise will not be avenged by any of your cowardly relatives or descendants presently living in and around Ithaca."

Queen Penelope's son finished his marvelous dissertation, much to the chagrin of his rather-shocked enemy audience. The gathered suitors all bit their lips, astounded by the youth's forceful language. Then, Antinous, son of heinous Eupeithes, summoned the wherewithal to answer the upstart:

"Telemachus; you who have yet to enter puberty. I suspect that the gods themselves, it seems, are decisively teaching you how to be a braggart by prompting you to deliver rash and dangerous speeches. I do hope that Almighty Zeus, the volatile son of Eternal Cronus, does not appoint your inexperienced testicles as king of this isolated and poverty-stricken island, even though this piece-of-shit eyesore we're standing in is your unavailable father's accursed legacy to you."

The repulsive suitors then switched their focus to performing intimate gay dancing routines, and to later singing faggot-related homosexual lyrics. The frenzied cabal of dumb-fucks entertained themselves until the darkness of evening fell under the New Moon. Then, each of the regurgitating perverts retired to his own downtown shack or shanty to vomit and sleep.

Telemachus casually strolled-up to his remote quarters, situated high above the wild courtyard vegetation. Enjoying a spacious view, and then on his way to bed, the lad's hyperactive mind was much-preoccupied about confronting the dastardly suitors the following morning.

Accompanying Telemachus, Eurycleia, the youth's personal servant who was suspected by area residents of being a devious pyromaniac, and was also believed to be an old flame of Odysseus, held two blazing torches. Of all the female household slaves, Eurycleia was the infatuated whore who had loved Telemachus most, for she had nursed him as an infant with her massive, flabby breasts. But now, the servant strongly desired to steal the adolescent's valued virginity.

Telemachus opened the doors to his grimy suite, sat-down upon his straw mattress, and pulled-off his soft tunic, giving the faded apparel to the scheming old harlot. Then, the horny, dry-crotched bitch left the room in a melancholy frame of mind, closing the door in despair by frenetically pulling its silver handle to express her stifled sexual frustration. Telemachus lay there upon his bed and deeply pondered, and several hours later, covered-up his gaunt form with a nasty-odor sheep's wool; the lad's foggy mind was reflecting-upon his upcoming exciting journey to Pylos and Sparta, which Pallas Athene had earlier proposed and described.

Chapter 3

"TELEMACHUS PREPARES FOR HIS VOYAGE"

As soon as rose-fingered early Dawn appeared upon the eastern horizon, Odysseus's one and only dear son anxiously jumped-out of bed and hurriedly dressed. The wacky kid carried a sharp sword hanging from his shoulders that he had won at a summer carnival concession, and gingerly laced-up lovely feminine sandals upon his shiny feet. At once, the new man-of-the-house asked the gay-voiced heralds to summon all of the long-haired, radical Achaeans that were aimlessly lounging-around to a scheduled assembly.

The heralds issued the call to meeting, and the Achaeans answered with shouts of "Fuck you!" But for some inexplicable reason, the loafers, all wearing sandals, gathered quickly for the announced parley. When the complaining rabble had quieted-down, Telemachus stepped inside the chamber and nervously convened the meeting. Among the crazed maniacs in attendance, heroic wrinkled Aegyptius, an old-but-revered curmudgeon, suffering from chronic arthritis, and also being a sight for psoriasis, was the first to speak.

"You other Achaean inhabitants of Ithaca, pay strict attention to the irrelevant cow manure I have to say. We have not held a general meeting or 'brain-dead conference' ever since that propitious day when dumb-ass Odysseus sailed-away from here with his twelve hollow-hulled warships. What captain has made us gather now? What's the puny punk's reasoning? Does the brazen novice wish to tell us that his father's defunct navy has bankrupt the land? Has this nincompoop Telemachus heard some female gossip about the Greek army's fate, and will give us false details about our vigilant soldiers' journey home, or is this impromptu seminar some other fucked-up, immaterial business that he'll bring-up and awkwardly attempt discussing with us?"

Inspired by Athena, Odysseus's emboldened son stood and spoke, talking first to Aegyptius, whose hyperactive asshole was having a major bowel movement:

"Old, feeble and doddering Aegyptius; the person who called the suitors to this decisive meeting is presently not far-off, as you will quickly comprehend. I did summon your asses to this room, and I'm proudly standing before your squinting eyes with knees that do not knock. For I'm now a mature individual whose brain suffers more mentally than you' miserly old farts ever will. But in all truth, I have no reports to reveal of our returning army pretending to be a navy, and consequently, no vital military details to pass-on to you morons; nor is there any other pertinent public business I intend to mention or discuss. The primary issue now is my own weighty need, for upon my household here, troubles have fallen like a thousand quivers full of heavy arrows, in a catastrophic double sense. Do you dimwits now fathom my rhetoric?"

"Who wants to hear your contrived bullshit?" bellowed a critical suitor standing in the rear. "Your expendable verbal crap smells lousier than Aegyptius's decaying, stinking asshole!"

But inspired Telemachus was neither thwarted nor discouraged by the vile invective and the obnoxious shouting that ensued. "First and foremost, I believe that my noble father Odysseus has possibly perished. Yes, the great archer, the spouse of Queen Penelope, who was once your privileged king, and also my kind father. And then there's an even greater prospective problem that persistently haunts my psyche, which will quickly and completely shatter this entire house. And my whole livelihood will be destroyed."

"Who gives an airborne shit besides Aegyptius, here, about your vulnerable psyche; about your father's fate; about your shoddy palace, or about your mediocre inheritance!" a second more-vocal suitor sarcastically hollered.

"Lazy and bellicose leeches," Telemachus firmly countered. "You are the deadbeat sons of those sailing champions possessing admirable nobility; yes, those mighty warriors, your patriarchs, under the command of Odysseus, might still be returning from Troy. But you, their ungrateful descendants, are constantly pestering my mother for her hand in marriage against her will. From past experience, I judge that you' disreputable dregs are not sufficiently brave enough to journey to her father for permission to wed."

"That fucked-up custom is obsolete!" yelled a third impostor. "Who gives a shit except Aegyptius? Ha, ha, ha!"

"Elderly, Icarius, Penelope's aged father, lives in his ancestral home, and is still fully capable of competently arranging a bride price for his treasured daughter, and then giving her to the rogue amongst you whom he likes best," Telemachus expressed. "Yes; the lucky asshole among you who pleases the old codger the most will get to wed Queen Penelope. But instead, you' leeching derelicts casually hang-around *my* house, day after day, butchering my cherished oxen; slaughtering my well-fed goats, and screwing *my* celibate sheep. You' disgraceful fucks are indeed dispensable liabilities to humanity. Your vile mouths keep-on feasting and drinking gleaming cups of wine without noticeable restraint or guilt, and without remorse, if I may add. You nauseating fuck-heads consume so much until you vomit all over my tarnished walls, and even regurgitate up to the tawdry high ceiling. My home is being demolished in a manner that is not right, ethical, or moral. You' pathetic scoundrels should all be ashamed of your scurrilous deportment."

Telemachus ceased speaking, and then surrendering to immaturity, threw the royal scepter upon the slate floor, and burst-out of the silent chamber, crying and sulking. Everyone seemed to momentarily pity the amateur orator, so all the dipshits seated in the assembly remained temporarily reticent and unwilling to give an antagonistic answer to Telemachus during his swift exiting from the chamber.

But Antinous, ready to exploit the opportunity, was the only one in the gallery motivated to verbally respond.

"Telemachus; you' conniving juvenile delinquent wannabe'; your boastful spirit is entirely too unrestrained. How you haughtily carry on, attempting to shame us into submission, since you so desire to blame your myriad failures upon us. But in your depraved and very disillusioned case, we amicable Achaean suitors aren't the guilty ones."

Telemachus turned and asked, "What the hell are you implying?"

"Your own dear mother, Penelope, is the cause of all our' woes," the loudmouth suitor insisted. "The Queen is an expert on how to use deceit to create emotional agony amongst us. It's been three long years now, and soon it will be sixteen terrible seasons since your devious mother began to deceive the hearts pounding within our Achaean chests, along with the blood pulsating inside our throbbing erect peckers."

"Antinous, even though points are for pinheads, get to the point!" Telemachus demanded before sobbing.

"The Queen gives false hope to each one of us; she makes fake promises to everyone, and constantly sends-out obscure and indecipherable messages to deliberately distress our eager egos. But indeed, Penelope's intent is different than her cryptic narrations. In her evil mind, your distraught mother has contrived another mischievous stratagem. She had a large loom set-up in her upstairs quarters and commenced weaving a mammoth tapestry, very enormous in dimensions. And your mother improvised her deceptive weaving thread, that was quite thin and non-binding. Then, Penelope had the unmitigated audacity to announce to us the following arcane twisted words: "Young men and old farts; those of you who are my suitors and tailors; since I feel that my wonderful husband Odysseus is now possibly dead, you must wait another while, although you are all keen for me to marry and be humped and pumped by one of you' horny bastards. But first, I must complete sewing a huge wall tapestry, for if I don't, my current weaving lessons would be fully wasted and done in vain. I'm sewing a tribute shroud to honor my father-in-law, failing warrior Laertes, for I've heard through the grapevine that a lethal Fate will soon strike Odysseus's father's lily-white ass. Then, none of the Achaean women dependent here, and in my employ, will be thoroughly annoyed with me because a man who once possessed so many riches, along with a most-fantastic fadorkenbender between his skinny legs, would lie in state without sufficient money to even pay for an ordinary sacred shroud."

"That bullshit is precisely what Penelope had stated," impetuous Antinous maintained. "I am not lying, because I am standing!"

Then, the fucked-up antagonist again clumsily quoted and paraphrased Penelope's lengthy commentary, but this time, his caustic remarks were addressed to frustrated Telemachus, who had just fully re-entered the palace hall.

"And Telemachus, our proud suitor hearts have mutually agreed about a certain practice performed by Penelope. And so, each day your obsessed mother weaves at her great loom, but every night the distrustful conniver sets-up torches in wall sconces and pulls her day's work apart. For three years now, your coy mother nefariously fooled us Achaeans with this devious unraveling trick. We positively trusted her. But as the seasons progressed and passed, the fourth year of delay had arrived. Then, one of her women who knew all the details spoke to us about her clandestine method, and we slyly surveilled and caught the Queen undoing her intricate weave."

"You fault my mother for being a perfectionist?" Telemachus instinctively argued. "You contemptible liar!"

"So naturally," Antinous continued his sarcastic commentary. "Becoming wise to your mother's scheme, we righteous and benign gentlemen compelled Penelope to complete the unscrupulous sewing enterprise against her obstinate will. The suitors now say this, so that you, naïve and quixotic Telemachus, deep inside your gullible heart, will fully understand as all Achaeans staying on this primitive island already know; send your mother back to her quarters to complete her impractical tapestry weave. Divulge to Penelope that she must marry whichever eligible wooer that her father Icarius decides and discloses. But we suitors are not returning to our native islands, or even traveling to someplace else like Persia or Africa; that is, not until Queen Penelope decides to marry a deserving macho Achaean of her own choosing."

Prudent Telemachus considered Antinous's testimony and then vehemently replied:

"Self-indulgent Asshole; there's no way I shall dismiss my charitable Mother out of this shabby palace, against her volition; Queen Penelope is the one who bore and nursed me inside my bed-sized cradle. As for my father, I've experienced valid dreams that he's being held captive in a distant land by a horny, promiscuous nymph. It would be hard for me to compensate for Queen Penelope, returning my mother to wealthy Icarius, with me providing a suitable reverse dowry, as I obviously would have to do if I stupidly sent her back to the greedy bastard."

"You previously said that you honored tradition," Antinous challenged Telemachus as the other suitors indulgently laughed. "Are you deliberately trying to be ambivalent?"

"Listen carefully, Antinous; if I did not pay the hoary loansharking prick compensation, then Queen Penelope's influential old man would treat me badly, and some observant deity on Mt. Olympus would initiate other troubles and crises, since my mother, as she ventured from this house back to her former protector, Icarius, her humiliating return to her father's estate would compel the dreaded and furious Furies to directly intervene in *our'* dilemma."

"More rhetorical bullshit," Antinous vehemently objected. "Utter religious nonsense spewing from your juvenile lips!"

"Jealous men like yourselves would automatically blame me for *their* debacle, too," Telemachus boldly argued, regaining his composure that had been inspired by Athena. "That's why I'll never issue such an insane, ludicrous order concerning my mother. But to you suitors I make *this* appeal. Just provide me with a swift ship and twenty veteran mariners, so that I can serenely make an arduous journey to sandy Pylos, and next to militant Sparta, just to determine if I can discover some accurate news about my father's highly-anticipated voyage home."

"What the hell would such a futile trip solve?" Antinous retorted. "More expensive daft delays?"

"If I hear from dependable sources that my father is still living and advancing towards Ithaca, I've concluded that my fortune could hold-out here in Ithaca for about one more year, although it's very hard for me to be frugal with you' voracious assholes sponging off of my ever-dwindling estate. Now, if I learn from Nestor and King Menelaus that Odysseus is dead and gone, I'll reluctantly return to my dear native land, build my father an extravagant tomb, and there perform as many funeral rites as are customarily appropriate. And after *that* responsibility is completed, or should I say that 'duty' is enacted, I will agree that my mother must choose a suitable suitor."

Telemachus strongly conveyed that specific declaration, and soon enthusiastically dissolved the meeting. The confused suitors slowly dispersed, each one going to his own ghetto house.

Soon thereafter, Telemachus walked away, pacing along the ocean shore, thinking about his many duties and obligations. Once the troubled youth had washed his hands in gray, stagnant salt water, the determined lad addressed a prayer to his personal mentor, Athena:

"Oh, hear me, you who yesterday visited my ramshackle mansion as a transgender god, and persuasively ordered me to embark from Ithaca in a swift sailing ship across the murky seas, with my designated mission to learn about my father's great voyage after being away from this miserable island for two decadent decades. My father's incredible success is what the selfish Achaeans are intentionally preventing from happening; most of all, especially with the horny suitors brazenly exhibiting and stating their evil objectives out loud."

As Telemachus solemnly and somberly expressed his prayer, divine, impeccable Athena appeared to him as an effeminate male, but this time the lad's immortal guidance counselor was looking and sounding just like the wise sage Mentor. Disguising her regular voice, the creative goddess spoke-out like an accomplished ventriloquist, with insightful words floating on heavenly wings:

"Telemachus, you must not procrastinate beginning that essential excursion I wish for you to make. I'm a grateful friend of your father's notable past, and I'm so much of an appreciative confederate that I will accommodate your *special needs* by furnishing a super-fast vessel, and as a tremendous incentive bonus, I'll personally accompany your simpleton ass as you visit Pylos and Sparta."

"What should I do?" Young Telemachus asked, his emotions mired in a quandary. "I've never ventured outside of Ithaca before!"

"Now then, young Fool; you must go home to your room, pack a few satchels, and politely mingle with the dumb-fuck suitors. I'll go through town and quickly round-up a non-inebriated crew of loyal, non-mutinous associates, all volunteer sailors with vital marine experience," Athena explained. "In a seaport such as impoverished Ithaca, I'll choose from the many leaking ships, both new and old, and select the finest, non-leaking tub for you to function as the captain, and when that ship has been made sea-worthy, and is fit to raise sail, we'll together launch it, with our currently unemployed mariners, out into the wine-dark sea."

Being motivated to commence his information-gathering expedition, Telemachus descended deep into the palace's storage rooms and instructed palace servant and sex-addict Nurse Eurycleia to locate some fancy adult toy supplies ready for his imminent voyage. The enthralled youth swore to the sex pervert, possessing the dried-up honey-well, to keep confidential secrecy about his impending voyage.

Telemachus next stridently marched down a dank corridor into the destitute dining hall, once more loaded to capacity with the hellish company of criminal suitors.

Then, sympathetic goddess Athena, with the signature glittering eyes, delved deep inside her suspect cranium and conceived a new-found plan. Looking like a facsimile of Telemachus, the sometimes-creative goddess roamed and traipsed all throughout the poor city endeavoring to organize a respectable sailing crew. To every crewman Pallas Athene encountered and enlisted, the recruiter-impersonator issued the same mundane instruction, which was to conserve the sailor's strength by not ejaculating the seaman's semen, and disclosing to each euphoric mariner to responsibly meet alongside the chartered ship at dusk.

Next, the crafty goddess, supernaturally disguised as Telemachus, asked Noemon, fine son of the blowhard Phronius, for his swiftest ship, and the penniless gambler was quite happy to oblige when the transvestite benefactor handed him three gold coins. Then, soon thereafter, the sun went-down on the western horizon, and all the cobblestone and gravel roads became dark. Using her awesome mental powers, Athena dragged the fast ship down into the placid harbor, and again exercising her magical Olympian faculties, the disguised goddess readily stocked the merchant vessel with substantial supplies, featuring all the utilitarian materials that well-decked boats usually have stowed on board. And finally, the immortal shape-shifter adroitly moved the ship to the port's outer edge. It was there at dusk that Athena's unrivaled cunning assembled that rag-tag group of unlikely companions. The goddess mystically filled their limited hearts with abounding spirit, renewing each man's ambition and self-esteem.

Next, in truly impressive military-like order, bright-eyed Athena imperatively commanded Telemachus to venture outside the decaying Ithacan palace and stand erect by the main entrance to the spacious hall. In her inimitable voice and radiant form, the lad's counselor somewhat resembled the political idiot, Telemachus' other mentor, Mentor:

"Telemachus, your well-armed companions are already sitting beside their newly fabricated oars, waiting for you to launch this historic expedition. Let us now be off, so that we don't delay this nonsensical, non-productive trip a moment longer."

With those magnificent words, Pallas Athene quickly led the way, and Telemachus followed his patron's fart trail. Then, with Athena ascending the plank and arriving on board ahead of him, Telemachus anxiously clambered on deck, too. The pair eagerly sat upon a sturdy bench at the "Pride of Ithaca" stern.

The experienced crewmen untied the stern mooring ropes, and then clambered on board the stellar vessel; each well-trained sailor moving to a plank-seat beside an oar. Bright-eyed Pallas Athene magically arranged a fair breeze for the shipmates to enjoy their labor, which constituted a strong West Wind blowing gustily across the wine-dark sea.

As the "Pride of Ithaca" majestically sliced through the rhythmic swells on its way forward, around the bow began the familiar great chorus of splashing waves. Then, all night long, and well beyond the sunrise, the majestic vessel continued sailing toward Pylos on its well-planned journey.

Chapter 4

"TELEMACHUS, NESTOR AND MENELAUS"

A weak week later, Telemachus had reached Pylos and was coolly welcomed and soon dismissed by Nestor, King of Pylos, and also the venerable dean of Pylos University. Nestor provided an ancient, wobbly-wheeled chariot for Telemachus to journey to Sparta, and the King/Dean sent his delinquent teenage son Peisistratus to accompany the Ithacan, just to have the little prick be out of his sight for several months.

"You mean I've sailed all the way to Pylos and you have nothing to report about my father's fate?" Telemachus bitched. "Not one bit of news, or even a rumor! What a freakin' bummer this is!"

"Look, naïve delinquent! Don't waste my valuable time. Now get the hell out of here. I'll have my sex-crazed son go joyriding with you and wish that you both never return! Hopefully, the wheels will come off the rigged chariot, and you'll both be hospitalized somewhere between here and Sparta!"

"What more important things do you have to do rather than granting me a short interview?" Odysseus's son wanted to know.

"I'm a hundred and twenty-seven years old, and right now, I have to figure-out how to die!" Nestor vehemently yelled. "Now hit the dirt road! On your way to Sparta, try yelling-up to the clouds, 'Apollo is a chicken! Apollo is a chicken!' and see what the fuck happens to you!"

Telemachus and Peisistratus, Nestor's leave-the-nest son, after taking three unnecessary detours and getting wildly lost each time, eventually arrived a month later at Menelaus's palace in Sparta, where a small feast was prepared for the two by the famous king and his beautiful wife Helen, who ten-years-before had been smuggled to Asia Minor by Paris, a Trojan prince. And thus, the re-capture of Helen by Menelaus was the principal cause of the Trojan War, with the aggressive Greek kings' combining their forces and sailing a fabulous naval expedition of a thousand warships and 50,000 soldiers to impractically retrieve the lustful whore. During the meager Spartan-type dinner, Menelaus and Helen talked about incomparable Odysseus's major strategy contributions at Troy.

Then, one of the men attending to the needs of Menelaus, faithful Asphalion, poured fresh water onto the visitors' hands and sticky fingers, and the traveling junior jerk-offs, Telemachus and Peisistratus, with the encouragement of Menelaus and Helen, ravenously reached for the week-old food that had been meticulously spread-out for their consumption. The Spartan King soon initiated the dinner conversation.

"Amuse me, callow son of Odysseus. Have you grown any amount of hair under your armpits?"

"No, King Menelaus," Telemachus modestly confessed. "But conversely, my skin has produced a thick blond tuft of hair atop my left shoulder, and also a dense brown fur patch on top of my right one."

"That's quite insignificant, and it doesn't add one iota to my overall empirical knowledge," the King commented. "Are you mature enough to eject a quantity of sticky, white juice from your erect dingle? I noticed that it required four minutes for you two visiting imbeciles to simply wash and scrub your palms!"

"Indeed, King Menelaus!" Telemachus exclaimed. "Young prepubescent Peisistratus and I had halted our squeaky chariot near a babbling brook just outside metropolitan downtown Sparta to take dual pisses. Then, I succeeded in shooting a volume of white fluid from my personal junk, but impotent Peisistratus could only blast-out erratic air blanks out of his semi-erect pecker!"

Queen Helen, showing a modest degree of mild mortification, covered her petite mouth with her right hand in response to the male bonding verbal exchange.

But Menelaus's wife soon regained her confidence and composure. Reputed to being a daughter of Almighty Zeus, the wily queen thought of something special that would allow the two adolescent guests to enjoy additional hospitality. Very discreetly and furtively, the Queen quickly dropped into the sour wine the jovial pair were sipping a potent drug that had the reputation of relieving men's pains and bothersome irritations, making the imbibers forget their many troubles. A drink of that powerful elixir, once mixed-in with potent wine, would be more intoxicating than the fabled African Lotus flowers. And the brain-addling mixture would guarantee that no man, or horny punk teenager, would let a tear fall upon his cheek for one whole day. Even if the consumer's mother and father had died during an earthquake; or even if wicked men brandishing sharp swords would be hacking-down the gulper's brother and his son, the killings would have no effect on the mesmerized drinker.

Helen had mastered the utilization of magical healing potions, like the aforementioned drug, which she'd obtained from Polydamna, wife of Thon, who came to Sparta from Egypt, where that heathen country, so rich in grain, produced the greatest crop of drugs and African aphrodisiacs. Many of these secret formulas, once dissolved, are quite beneficial, and many others are poisonous and lethal. Each person living in Egypt was rumored to be a quack physician whose knowledge of those potions surpassed that of every other human group, including the horny Trojans, who incidentally never practiced birth control.

When Helen had stirred-in the drug and ordered the dining room servants to again serve the tainted vinegar-wine to Telemachus and to Peisistratus, the King's devious wife rejoined the conversation and pleasantly spoke-up once again:

"Husband Menelaus, son of Atreus, whom gods both cherish and despise, and also you two mentally challenged nutcase sons of noble men; since both good blessings and bad omens are arbitrarily decided by capricious Zeus, you two dumb-dicks should now sit and eat this fast food with us. After that, your host, the local steak and burger king and I will together enjoy listening to your fascinating horse-shit stories."

"But I'm not here in Sparta to spin tales and myths to you two royal freaks of nature," Telemachus immaturely argued. "I'm here to learn about the fate of my adventurous Old Man!"

"Learn to conquer your glaring adolescence and strive be become more diplomatic," Menelaus cautioned Telemachus. "Become more contrite and less trite. Learn the difference between being adult and being a dolt! I do believe that you two royal assholes are both wet behind your ears and must endure daily an enormous flood of water on the brain!"

Helen felt compelled to interrupt her fearsome husband. "During our conversation, I'll tell you two smart-asses one ordinary thing I think is within the realm of being suitable. I'll not speak of, nor could I recite, everything about glorious, steadfast Odysseus. The famed Ithacan warrior managed to tackle immense hardships and dynamically thwart the Trojan enemies at every turn. But there's that time when the fucked-up Achaeans were in such distress, and undaunted Odysseus prevailed in his quests, and did so much for his erratic subordinates to survive, right in the homeland of those screaming, out-of-control Trojans, too! Enduring savage blows, and with your father's body being horribly battered, invincible Odysseus threw a ragged garment upon his wounded shoulders, so that the bigger-than-life champion looked like a mere ragged slave to the Trojans. Your father, Telemarketer, er, I mean Telemachus," Helen suavely corrected, "then ingeniously skulked along the main streets of that totally hostile city."

"Evidently, my father imaginatively concealed his Greek warrior status to the Trojans," Telemachus alertly remarked. "He had done the exact same thing to me when I was a kid, because I never knew what the hell he' honestly looked like, either!"

Helen then resumed her informative exposition. "Your father Odysseus sagely hid his own identity, slyly pretending to be a commonplace tinker, or a typical dreg, or even a vagrant begging for alms or copper coins. No Trojan there ever suspected his creative duplicity," Helen elaborated. "I was the only one in Troy who had recognized him, in spite of his terrific disguise. I questioned your father, but his skill in deception made my interrogation elusive. Still, when I escorted Odysseus inside King Priam's palace, I thoroughly bathed him in hot oil, rubbed his alluring manhood with myrrh, and helped him to dress after he shot a fantastic amount of sperm juice onto the high ceiling," Helen shared and ejaculated. "I was so enthralled with the size of his sexual apparatus that I instantly swore a solemn oath not to reveal to any Trojan that my mendicant guest was the great Odysseus of Ithaca; that is, until he'd reached the swift ships and the numerous Greek Army huts that had been constructed on the beach. During his massage, your incredible father told me all about the upcoming Achaean plans."

"About the legendary Trojan Horse? Was my father wearing jockey shorts, or his regular dependable diaper?"

"Don't be so impertinent! I'll get to that!" Helen chastised. "Then, soon after our chance encounter, your father's long sword slaughtered many Trojans, and Odysseus boldly returned to his countrymen, bringing to the craven Achaeans, a full report on the layout of Troy's main streets. Trojan women began to cry aloud when the Greeks invaded through the city gates, but I was fully glad. My heart, by then, had changed to ally with the marauding Greeks, led by my husband's brother, King Agamemnon of Mycenae. In my grieving heart, while still in Troy, I was sorry for that brief blindness that conspiring and untrustworthy Aphrodite (Venus), goddess of love, had brought upon my soul, when the intrusive troublemaker had mysteriously led me there, far from my own native land, abandoning my child, and my own husband Menelaus, who lacked nothing in terms of good looks and wisdom."

"Did you ever have sex with my father when you bathed his entire body?" Telemachus bluntly asked Queen Helen, while his acne-faced companion, drugged and drunken Peisistratus, sat there with his eyes crossed and his mouth wide open.

"Interesting question!" Helen of Sparta, formerly Helen of Troy, answered. "King Menelaus here is the only man who has ever penetrated my lush blonde-haired, pink-wet love tunnel. But I did administer really good oral sex to Odysseus, whose manhood was so huge that instead of me being deep throat, I suddenly choked and became deep esophagus!"

"What about your romantic relationship with Prince Paris of Troy?" Odysseus's only son and heir brashly requested knowing.

"That was just a foolish romantic fling, and nothing more," Helen replied after sighing. "Prince Paris had visited Menelaus's palace while on a political visit to Sparta. I recognized right away that the handsome fellow was very cute and attractive. But then Paris wooed and persuaded me to elope with him to Troy, and that stupid mistake of mine caused my husband and his brother Agamemnon to organize a major military campaign against Troy. Your father Odysseus was one of the Greek kings involved in the invasion!"

In reply to Helen's account of events, fair-haired Menelaus added: "Yes, indeed, dear wife; everything you say is genuinely true. Before now, I've come to understand the minds and plans of many crazed warriors. I've roamed many foreign lands, but these eyes of mine have never seen a man to match the exceptional integrity and dignity of your patriarch, King Odysseus."

"Then, Queen Helen; you're the cause of the fucked-up Trojan War. I'm glad to learn that fact," Telemachus revealed. "The Greeks weren't just greedy pirates and marauders sacking and plundering the city's wealth. But King Menelaus; please tell me more about my father's activities at Troy?" the young guest uttered before burping.

"How I loved your dad's chivalrous ball-breaking; his steadfast heart, and his remarkable fighting ability!" Menelaus frankly related. "And what about the things which that forceful man, your father, endured while designing and later stealthily contriving the infamous Wooden Horse? Achaea's finest men were crouching-down inside the large, fabricated structure, which in reality, omened a lethal fate to the dumb-fuck Trojans. Then, you, my spouse Helen, loyal to your immaculate heart, approached the marvelously constructed 'Horse', perhaps being instructed by some anonymous god who wished to give an inglorious defeat to the small-dicked Trojans."

"Did you feel trapped inside the horse's hollow stomach?" Telemachus obnoxiously asked and then loudly belched. "Were you about to suffocate or faint?"

"Look, junior jerk-off!" Menelaus vehemently yelled. "Stop farting out of your mouth! Show more discretion and culture, and give me sufficient time to accurately relate the entire weird sequence of events."

"I'm sorry for being so insolent and defiant," Telemachus apologized and soon hiccupped. "I value my tiny testicles, so I'll remain quiet while you piously smother me with your ludicrous and outrageous propaganda."

"So why are you lustfully staring at my breasts with such possessive eyes?" Helen asked half-intoxicated Telemachus. "Quite honestly, you look-like you haven't yet even learned how to work your stick!"

"My father always told me that I should study abroad, and that's exactly what the hell I'm doing right now!"

"And, where you walked, dear Helen," King Menelaus continued his boring litany, "noble Deiphobus followed the path of your enchanting footsteps. You deftly circled around the tall Wooden Horse three consecutive times, and then you raised your soft hand and felt the diameter of that hollow trap. Your melodic voice called-out, naming the best undigested occupants among the concealed Danaans hidden inside the horse's abominable abdomen, and you spoke-up exactly like the voice of each soldier's Greek wife. I was there, sitting inside with wise Odysseus, right smack in the middle. We heard your siren call, Helen. Two of us fanatical interior combatants, Diomedes and myself, were eager to get-up and wildly charge outside the wooden wonder, and we also felt prompted to answer back your alluring beckoning from where we were sweating and huddled inside the artificial equine."

"Then you and father weren't exactly horsing around?" stupidly joked Telemachus. "Were you and father wearing jockey shorts?"

King Menelaus totally ignored his young visitor's inane-absurd remark. "But fortunately, idiot Telemachus, perceptive Odysseus stopped us from entering imminent danger. Diomedes and I wished to scream-back imprudent replies, but your nimble-witted father aptly held our destructive compulsions in check. All of the scared-shitless Achaeans sitting with your father and me managed to keep their chatty mouths shut, except for that fucked-up scamp Anticlus, the only one who was about to raise his voice and who felt a death-wish to answer Helen's alluring summoning. Odysseus instinctively clapped his hand firmly upon Anticlus's mouth and held the numbskull in a gorilla grip before then puncturing the stupid shit's already-abused testicles with a sharp dagger. In short, hero Odysseus and I deftly kept our dual grips upon Anticlus's neck and upon the rogue's bleeding balls until Athena, I suspect, escorted you, Helen, away to ultimate safety."

Then, naive and intoxicated Telemachus belched again and replied in a dumb-ass stammer: "Menelaus, son of Atreus, and leader of the militant Spartans, and also truly loved by moody blues Zeus. That interesting Wooden Horse incident you've just described is more painful still; it could not save my revered father from bitter death; not even if the heart inside his hairy chest had been made of cast iron, just like his stomach. But come; send my comatose comrade and me off to bed, so that Sweet Sleep can bring us relaxing joy."

After Telemachus requested lodging for Peisistratus and himself, Helen instructed her servants to set-up mattresses within the drafty corridor and spread-out lovely purple blankets over the cushions, with rugs on top, and over those items some woolen cloaks. The women left the hall with blazing torches after skillfully arranged the beds. A drunken herald soon led the two inebriated guests to their appointed Spartan accommodations.

And so, the traveling Prince from Ithaca and his coughing colleague Peisistratus slept there inside the cold palace vestibule, which wasn't exactly a comfortable ancient Greek bread and breakfast scenario.

"You would think that King Menelaus would've had the courtesy to have his two guests sleep in Atreus's second atrium here in Sparta instead of us having to snore like muddy swine out here in this nasty corridor!" Telemachus complained and shared with his non-attentive, drunken companion. "On second thought, Peisistratus; we should be glad that we're not sleeping in the infamous Mycenae atrium death chamber."

The next morning, Menelaus arrived inside the chilly corridor and gave his two lethargic and groggy listeners a long account of his travels in Egypt, especially his adventures with the Old Man of the Sea, with the death of the lesser Ajax (who was an expert sword fighter who wanted to deter gents that were avowed enemies), and the king's lengthy speech also encompassed the death of his brother, Agamemnon, in Atreus's other atrium. Menelaus invited Telemachus to stay for several days longer, but the neurotic lad declined, futilely grieving of painful bed sores and of agonizing bedbug bites.

Meanwhile, back in Telemachus' crime-laden and rebellious Ithaca, the bewildered and agitated suitors gathered outside Odysseus's palace, enjoying themselves in recreation by throwing spears and discuses on level ground, with all the excessive arrogance that the raucous contingent usually displayed. The two men who led the worthless leeches, hostile Antinous and handsome Eurymachus, were sitting there smoking marijuana in the high weeds; the despicable pair, by far being the best of all the competing suitors. Noemon, Phronius's stuttering son, came-up to them to pertinently question Antinous.

"Fellow Achaean Antinous; I have a grievance to share. In our black hearts, do we truly know or not know the day Telemachus will be coming back from sandy Pylos? The punk fugitive had left Ithaca, taking a splendid ship, of which I am a principal investor, which I now need the vessel to make the abbreviated trip across the harbor to anchor at spacious Elis."

When Noemon finished his short spiel, the suitors were amazed at the boat owner's spunk. The eavesdropping buffoons had no inkling that Telemachus had traveled to Pylos, land of Neleus, and still had believed that the dim-headed fool was visiting the sickened flocks on his various squalor-laden estates. Antinous, son of Eupeithes, then spoke to the delirious throng of unhappy residents (from mainland Mycenae) that had been transplanted to insular Ithaca. Antinous was extremely angry, and his black heart was filled with intense rage.

"Here's the perfect depiction of the definition of the ugly word *trouble*", the head-suitor articulated. "In his overbearing way, that scheming, yellow-bellied snake Telemachus, with this ridiculous voyage of his, has now achieved significant success from recent reports I've received. And we permitted the dumb-fuck to venture-out to sea, fully believing that the motley cretin would never ever see his expedition through. So now," Antinous resumed his objecting rhetoric. "Provide me with a swift ship and twenty able, nautical comrades, so that I can watch and prepare for the asshole's eventual return. I'll set a surprise ambush as the simpleton traitor navigates his passage straight through the strait dividing Ithaca from rugged Asteris."

Antinous carefully selected twenty of the best-available remaining sailors in Ithaca. The crew marched-down to the shore and dragged a swift black ship out into shoulder-deep water, where the unhinged maniacs climbed aboard the vessel and sailed-away on the southern sea, all the while, contemplating and plotting the bloody slaughtering of unwary Telemachus.

Well out into the harbor lies rocky Asteris, where ships could easily moor and hide. The nutcase Achaeans impatiently waited there at Asteris and carefully organized their secret ambush of naïve Telemachus.

Chapter 5

"ODYSSEUS LEAVES CALYPSO'S ISLAND"

As rosy Dawn stirred from her bed beside Lord Tithonus, bringing light to superior eternal gods and also to inferior mortal humans, the occupants of Mt. Olympus were restlessly sitting in assembly, and among them, presided high-thundering Zeus, whose awesome power was supreme. Talkative Pallas Athene was reminding her immortal family of all the excellent stories depicting Odysseus's multiple troubles, and the empathetic deity was concerned for her favorite hero as the Ithacan King passed his days inside nymph Calypso's dark cavernous home.

"Father Zeus, let no sceptered earthly king be prudent, kind, or gentle from now on, or should you think about and consider my champion's consequential fate. Since you are immortal and supernatural, you're bored with life and only derive pleasure in torturing and humiliating trivial humans with your unfair power advantage. Let your ruthless brother Poseidon, instead, always be cruel and treat men with rancor, since few mortals in human civilization now have any fixed memory of Lord Odysseus, who favorably ruled his people, and was a kind and gentle father."

"Daughter; tell me more about this obstinate pawn on my gaming-board, this Odysseus," Zeus asked Pallas Athene. "Where on Earth is the charlatan at this moment?"

"Father, beleaguered Odysseus lies suffering extreme distress on that dreadful island where nymph Calypso is the sole authority. The immortal bitch keeps her captive as hostage by exercising magical force, and her helpless victim is unable to sail-away in even a hand-made timber raft. And now, some jealous, diabolical suitors are setting-out to kill his only son, whom the King of Ithaca fondly loves. The naïve adolescent has embarked way down south to Pylos and Sparta to gather news about his extremely exploited father."

Atop glorious Mt. Olympus, cloud-gatherer Zeus then firmly answered his distressed-but-beloved daughter.

"My overly concerned child; did you not concoct this ongoing bizarre Pylos and Sparta plan yourself, so that once the wanderer made it back to Ithaca, the mere avenger could take-out his animosity against those diabolical suitors? As for acne-faced Telemachus, you should use your granted skill to return him to his native land unharmed, and *that* easy task exists well-within your inherent power. If you act with dispatch, I assure you that the scumbag enemies of your insignificant Odysseus will quickly scurry back to Mycenae, on the Greek mainland, with the Ithacan King's vile antagonists voyaging inside a leaky merchant ship without ever achieving even minimal success at defeating your favored hero."

Austere Zeus next imperatively instructed Hermes:

"Swift-footed winged Messenger, Hermes. I command that you inform the fair-haired nymph Calypso of my firm decision that I must appease Athena, and that she should immediately release this Odysseus person from her custody, so that the brave King of Ithaca can use his ingenuity and courage to eventually arrive back home. However, the faltering, weak fellow will obtain no guidance, special assistance, or divine intervention from the gods, but his only viable option for escape is independently sailing-off upon a well-lashed wooden raft."

Once Almighty Zeus finished speaking, Hermes, the legendary killer of Argus, nodded and obediently obeyed his superior's imperial demand. At once, the messenger god laced-up his lovely golden-winged sandals upon his magnificent manicured feet; the eternal footgear which carried Zeus's private courier across frontiers as fast as stormy winter blasts of wind.

When the energetic messenger swiftly reached Calypso's remote island, Hermes rose-up above the violent violet sea, and easily drifted and glided onshore, until his flight conducted the golden-helmeted Olympian in proximity to an enormous cave; the residence of the fair-haired, promiscuous nymph, Calypso.

Hermes found the exotic nymph standing there, being comforted by a huge fire blazing above an enormous hearth. From far away, the smell of split cedar and burning sandal-wood spread like hypnotic aroma all across the tiny island. Calypso's enchanting voice was singing love renditions inside the colossal cavern, as the notorious, whoring witch/bitch moved in a rapid quandary all around; back and forth, before her cherished spindle loom. All around inside the unusual cave, contrary to conventional logic, wonderful cypress, oak, maple and alder trees were in splendid bloom, despite the lack of sunshine.

Long-winged strange birds were actively nesting inside the miniature deciduous forest, and owls, hawks, and chattering sea crows, who spend their time out on the water, also squawked and abounded. A garden vine, fully ripe and loaded with delicious-looking grapes, trailed and thrived in the dark shadows throughout the lengthy cave.

From four fountains, situated close to each other in a row, clear, clean water streamed-out into basins in various directions, and on every side of the natural enclosure, soft meadows displaying a variety of flowers spread-out in full colorful array. Even a major Olympic god, who lives forever, would be amazed to enviously gaze at the extraordinary spectacle, and Hermes's normally cold heart instantly filled with warm pleasure.

Lord Hermes marveled upon witnessing the entrancing entrance sight. But after the rare visitor's spirit had objectively contemplated *that* rather exceptional scenery with wonder, Hermes hesitated, but soon ambled inside the spacious cavity. And Calypso, that lovely goddess with the two-pound clitoris, when she saw the courier's heavenly face, was not ignorant of whom her unexpected guest was, for the Greek gods are not unknown to one another, even though the home of some minor immortal might geographically be far away from Olympus.

But Hermes did not find Odysseus inside the cave because the lion-hearted war champion sat lamenting, weeping and cursing upon the shore, his misery breaking his mental state with sorrowful tears and groans. As pathetic Odysseus's eyes looked-out upon the restless sea, Calypso was inviting Hermes to sit-down upon a lustrous, shining chair, with the nymph's immediate purpose having the courier explain the nature of his unanticipated arrival. Then, vivacious Calypso interrogated Zeus's only delivery service.

"My dear Hermes, honored and welcome guest; why have you come here with your golden wand, not the one between your legs, but the one held in your hand. You have not been a visitor before to this remote porno haven. Tell me exactly what concern is on your mind. My heart desires to perform whatever you request, and I hope it's munching on sweet pussy, or us turbulently getting laid like two warthogs in heat."

After that brief introductory speech, Calypso carefully arranged an exquisite banquet table laden with ambrosia, then mixed-in red nectar, the combined formula, the secret food of the gods, that when consumed together, allotted and guaranteed the supernatural, immoral beings, total eternal immortality.

And so, the messenger god, famed mythological killer of Argus, ate and drank the wonderful elixir. When his meal was over and the mixture had comforted his famished intestines and pacified his throbbing erection,

Hermes stated his answer, speaking to Calypso with these rather urgent words:

"Enchanting Calypso; you're indeed a renowned goddess of wonder. Since you've questioned me, I'll tell you the truth as I know it. Almighty Zeus has commanded me to fly here against my flexible will. My superior says that you have here under your jurisdiction an ordinary man, more unfortunate than many others, who had fought for nine crucial years around King Priam's immoral city. In the tenth year, the Greeks had destroyed and plundered Troy, and soon left Asia Minor to return home to their various towns, villages and cities. Now, Almighty Zeus is commanding you to send this unfortunate fellow, Odysseus of Ithaca, off your fucked-up island as soon as possible."

The Olympic gods' great messenger tersely announced those declarative words and quickly departed the premises with a limp dingle bobbing nowhere. The regal nymph Calypso, once she'd heard and fully comprehended Zeus's stern decree, dashed-away to find great-hearted Odysseus, who still was a dashing old man who was not dashing anywhere. The witch's sprint soon engaged her already-married hostage upon the shore, sitting upon a rock in a heightened melancholy frame of mind, all alone by the thundering sea waves.

The well-stacked, dazzling nymph no longer gave his abused soul joy. At night, Odysseus slept beside Calypso inside the immense cavern, as the hostage was forced to do; not of his own free will, although she herself was capable enough to screw his ass all the way to High-Olympus. Moving-up close beside her despondent captive, the lovely goddess, daydreaming about Odysseus pumping the poop out of her during animal-like intercourse, gently spoke to her depressed prisoner:

"Poor man, against my obdurate will, you'll spend no more time grieving on this desolate island, wasting-away your meaningless life. My heart agrees that the time has come for me to send you off into oblivion. So, come now; cut long timbers with a dull-bladed axe I shall provide, and construct a large, primitive raft. Build a deck high-up on it, so that your nautical craft can topple upside-down during a torrential sea tempest. Your improvised raft can carry you across the misty and dangerous sea. I'll reluctantly supply your floating timbers with all the food, water and red wine you'll need, clueless idiot, to adequately satisfy your nautical wants and needs."

The lovely-but-saddened, sex-starved nymph finished speaking, and then quickly led her human slave from the shore with a distraught mental attitude. Odysseus followed in her mud-laden, barefoot steps as the minor goddess and the Ithacan King entered the nymph's vast hollow. The famed wanderer sat-down in the same chair from which Hermes had recently risen, and the kinky nymph set upon the fine table a smorgasbord of sumptuous food and potent drink, the sort of delectable morsels and beverage which mortal humans generally consume.

Calypso grabbed a wooden chair and took a seat opposite godlike Odysseus, and her eunuch male servant entered and placed ambrosia and nectar, the secret edibles that made the gods remain immortal, right beside her lustful grasp. The pair of diners reached-out to partake of the other tasty foods that had been spread-out for their culinary satisfaction.

When Odysseus finished consuming his traditional appetite for ordinary meat, fruit, and wine, beautiful and divine Calypso was the first to speak after his regular meal. Starting with preliminary small-talk, the conversation gradually changed to the subject of the nymph's actual modus operandi.

"Admirable Odysseus; I'd love that you satisfy my deepest fantasy and vigorously pump the poop out of me upon yonder mattress. My overwhelming lust for having wild sex with you still dominates my total immortal soul. I can't get laid with any of my fifty-three eunuch servants, who obviously don't have the balls to screw my gushing wet, pink honey-well. Forget me getting laid by you, mortal Odysseus. I can't even get marmalade on this boring and depressing, fucked-up desert island."

"Immortal Calypso; all of these difficult and lonely months I've stayed with you inside your massive cavern, and I had to listen to your cornball singing when you made me shrink my body under your low-set bar and dance the fuckin' Limbo and not the Calypso, which I really preferred doing all along," Odysseus opined and replied. "I mean, gorgeous, eternal chic. How low can you go, without raising the fuckin' bar!"

"Nobly born mortal son of Laertes; yes, you, resourceful Odysseus, now still wish to get back to your own lackluster native land without delay. In spite of every nuance, I wish you well as you stubbornly return home to endeavor changing the current squalor of your former luxurious palace into its former magnificence. If your heavy heart recognized how much distress Fate has in store for you, before you ever reach your miserable homeland," Calypso emphasized, "you'd elect to stay here and keep this homely cavern with me. My hot pussy craves your marvelous tool, which I admire when you take a piss, even with your fabulous pecker being limp."

"I respect your sexual addiction," Odysseus commented, "but I have more drastic family concerns plaguing my mortal and inferior brain than merely desiring to frenetically pump your fantastic ass into yonder mattress. Now Calypso; do you have some sort of irrefusable proposal for me to evaluate? You sound very much like my deceased great-godfather. Do you have a tremendous offer to propose that you believe I can't refuse?"

"Well, Odysseus, here's the full agenda in a nutshell. You'd never die on this island, and every day, you will enjoy mad, passionate sex with me for all eternity. I have the ability to make you immortal, even if your obdurate will dictates otherwise. I realize that your limited spirit yearns to be reunited with your earthly wife, Penelope, who after twenty years of separation from you, your aged spouse now features a smelly, dried-up cunt. I can boast that at present, I'm far more beautiful than she is, but in terms of basic logic, it's simply wrong for mortal women to ever compete with an impeccable goddess such as myself in either form, libido or beauty. I've just thoroughly described my distinct advantage over your middle-aged wife? Handsome man; do you not now discern the wisdom of my keen observations? Speak to me."

Resourceful and clever Odysseus then rather explicitly answered Calypso's curious entreaty:

"Mighty sex-starved goddess; I promise to manufacture a functional dildo for you to use after my departure from this hellhole island you call home. Please do not be angry with my final decision to leave your benevolent custody," the captive king explained. "I myself know very well that Penelope, although intelligent, is only mortal, and not your match, either to look-at, or for she and me to fuck like minks as if there's no tomorrow. Although my wife is quite attractive, she is no rival to you in either stature or in beauty. But sad Penelope, just like myself, is a human being, and quite obviously, you're a fantastic and well-endowed goddess. You'll never die or age, but my spouse and I certainly will someday kick the pottery. But still," Odysseus insisted. "I wish, every moment of every breath I take, to return to my home that's probably now overloaded with tiny-dicked freeloaders who want to screw my wife's nasty, dried-up love tunnel. The fucked-up assholes only have the wherewithal to think with their tiny dicks and not with their miniscule brains!"

"You skillfully argue your case like Zeus himself would advocate!' Calypso maintained and complimented. "Do you not wish to become immortal like myself? I have the ability to provide you with that wonderful secret!"

"When I analyze your general deportment and tremendous loneliness, Calypso, I pity your chronic boredom and monotony. Those elements are the debilitating curses of enduring immortal existence, and of suffering eternal emotional grief. There are no life-threatening challenges in your existence, but on the contrary, I wholeheartedly value limitations and obstacles, which represent the thrill and fun of living through. Even if out there on the treacherous, wine-dark sea, some obnoxious god breaks my balls and rips my anatomy apart, I'll persevere and continue pursuing my lofty goals and dreams. I assure you, dear goddess, that I'll assiduously persist in my striving for civilized fame and fortune."

"Then Odysseus, you are refusing my offer of immortality? Why do you prefer death and being with aging Queen Penelope to living here with me forever on my pleasant island?"

"Who the hell wants to live forever without any hurdles to overcome, or any hardships and impediments to conquer? Look, Calypso. The fun in life is dealing with the problems that life offers to humans. What mortal wants to be bored forever, which is a terrible curse persistently annoying the gods? Beautiful Goddess: you know not the challenges, the hardships, and the difficulties that humans experience daily. Believe it or not, those are the things that make human life interesting. The heart beating inside my mortal chest is quite prepared to bear any affliction inflicted by either Zeus or Poseidon. I've already had so many perplexing physical troubles and mind-boggling riddles sent by those two Olympian bastards," Odysseus insisted, "and I've labored so hard through formidable ocean waves, along with wicked Trojan warfare. Let what's yet to come materialize before my eyes, so that I can resist their rather precarious advances."

Just after role-model Odysseus dramatically finished his fantastic oration, the familiar sun went-down upon the western horizon, and the sky grew dark as pitch. Both the mortal man and the immortal goddess slowly ambled into the vast cavern's inner chamber and lay-down there to obtain their mutual nightly sleeps. Although Calypso really never had to eat, rest or sleep, the nymph enjoyed vicariously pretending to be Queen Penelope.

As soon as rose-fingered early Dawn appeared in the eastern sky, Odysseus quickly dressed himself in a tunic and cloak, and the disappointed nymph adorned herself in a long white shining robe along with a lovely woven, see-through, dress. Calypso gathered the ordinary tools that brave Odysseus would require for his departure, handing him a huge axe, the instrument, made of a double-edged bronze blade, with the object possessing a finely-crafted shaft of durable olive wood. Next, the sorrowed nymph provided her former hostage with a polished adze, whatever the hell that piece of fucked-up equipment happened to be. Then, in a dejected and dismal state of mind, Calypso slowly escorted her about-to-be-freed captive along the familiar path down to the edge of the island, where tall coniferous trees grew, alongside alder, poplar, and oaks that seemingly reached and touched the upper sky.

"The dry wood from these most excellent trees will afford you the material you need to build your means of transportation upon the wine-dark sea," the goddess sadly lectured. "Whatever floats your boat, Odysseus. Whatever floats you boat, er, I meant to say 'raft'," Calypso reiterated and corrected.

Once the frustrated nymph had shown her human companion the location of those towering trees, inconsolable and utterly bored Calypso, returned back to her cavern home with her head crestfallen. Odysseus then aggressively began cutting and chopping the appropriate trees to obtain the best woods needed for his upcoming, strenuous voyage. The adamant fellow worked incessantly and as quickly as he could, and amazingly, took-down twenty trees in one afternoon.

Calypso, feeling sincere compassion inside her lonely emotional state, brought her Platonic lover an auger (not an augur), so that her dedicated-to-duty masculine protege could bore the timbers, deftly fasten them to one another, and tighten the beams with provided pins and ropes. After that job had been completed, the industrious king fabricated a functional mast with a yardarm fastened to it, and then the on-the-task amateur craftsman carved-out a long steering oar, acting as a rudder, to effectively guide the raft. Calypso, again returned from her shadowy cavern and brought her fantasy lover woven linen to weave and produce a viable sail, which the industrious craftsman manufactured very skillfully under her magical guidance.

On the assembled sail, the prospective mariner tied bracing ropes and sheets. Then, fatigued to the point of unbearable exhaustion, the weary builder levered the flimsy raft off the slanted beach and dragged his gaudy creation down to the shining sea.

By the fourth day of the mortal enterprise, expending incredible toil, the problem-solving artisan had completed all of that required arduous work. So, on the fifth day, beautiful Calypso gingerly bathed her prized mortal, and then administered a memorable, exaggerated farewell blowjob; dressed her "male doll" in sweet-smelling clothes, and took Odysseus to the place of his raft, ready to leave her secluded island, and against her wishes, probably to never return. The gorgeous goddess had stowed on board the flimsy wooden platform sacks full of dark wine, fresh water, and plenty of nourishing guacamole.

Calypso also handed Odysseus a small urn containing six ounces of aromatic pussy juice, to both inspire and remind the evacuee of his lonely island goddess acquaintance, and of his distant grieving, heartbroken wife. The goddess, through her awesome powers over nature, afforded her hero a warm and favoring wind, and Lord Odysseus was quite happy as the ancient mariner masterfully set his sails to catch the stiff breeze that Calypso had provided.

The mixed-feelings hero sat beside the steering oar, and used his reputed skill to guide the raft smoothly out of the tranquil harbor. Sleep did not fall across his eyelids as that night, the self-appointed navigator perceptively watched the constellations: the Pleiades, and the late setting Bootes (which erroneously reminded the raftsman of Calypso's solid boobies). In sheer desperation, Odysseus's voice boomed-out to the night sky, "Shake, shake, shake; shake shake, shake; shake your Booties, shake your Booties!" And next, the on-a-mission raftsman was viewing Ursa Major, the Great Bear constellation, which men call "the Wain", always turning in one place like a confused, spinning, fucked-up Ithacan suitor.

The vigilant helmsman's keen eyes perceptively kept a vigilant acknowledgment of Orion, the only star cluster that never takes a bath, or even a decent meteor shower. In regard to the volatile ocean, kind Calypso had told her male companion to keep the star Orion to his left as his course drifted-away from her island across the burgeoning, foreboding sea.

The courageous adventurer sailed for ten days upon the restive water, and then, safely for seven more, and using elementary arithmetic, on the eighteenth day, shadowy hills miraculously appeared, where the land of the Phaeacians, like a large shield riding upon the vacillating misty sea waves, lay very close, according to Odysseus's severe glaucoma condition.

Poseidon watched Odysseus sailing across the choppy waves, and the envious sea-god's spirit grew enraged, and his massive testicles suddenly became swollen. So, the spiteful nutjob's angry head actively communicated with his own angrier heart:

'Something's gone radically wrong in this uncanny scenario!' Poseidon conjectured. 'More than likely, my asshole brother Zeus must've changed what he was planning for this bizarre dumb-dick Odysseus, while I've been far away partying and enjoying mermaid lap-dancing among the Ethiopians. For now, the diminutive mortal's primitive raft is drifting hard by the land of the Phaeacians, where he'll temporarily escape the great non-nostalgic sorrows which have come over him; and so, inevitable Fate's will shall aptly ordain,' Poseidon evaluated. 'But still, even right now, I think and believe that I should further punish and pulverize this asshole's insolent defiance, so that the meager shit-head receives his well-deserved fill of troubles.'

Then, the contemptuous sea god seized and waved his magic fork and easily drove the separate sky clouds together. Utilizing his awesome three-pronged trident, Zeus's erratic brother stirred-up the formerly passive waves into a turbulent frenzy. The sea-god's anger and fury brought-on blasting tempests from every kind of stormy wind, concealing land and sea with gloomy clouds and wicked downpours; so soon, darkness fell from heaven, soaking and drenching vulnerable earthly inhabitants all over the globe. And East Winds clashed with South Winds, while West Winds, in a rage, smashed straight into ornery North Winds, until all living upon planet Earth got wind of what the fuck was happening.

Odysseus's fragile knees buckled and gave way, with his defeated spirit falling into a doom and gloom mode, and in great distress, Poseidon's nemesis cried-out, standing upon his vulnerable raft, addressing his tormentor and the sea god's invincible trident. "Fork you. Poseidon. Fork you! I'm facing a horrible disaster, a veritable twelve chariot crossroads' collision!" Odysseus imagined and yelled skyward. "How is all this unbearable adversity going to end-up for me? I'm afraid that everything that the bitch Calypso had predicted has now materialized as ugly truth, especially when she told me that while out to sea, before I arrived safe and sound back to my native land, I would experience more than my share of demanding troubles along with formidable obstacles."

As the weary rudder manipulator uttered those all-too-honest words, a massive wave charged forward like a ferocious incensed bull, swirled all around the unprotected raft, and then, from high above, crashed-down with a tremendous thud. Odysseus let go his grip upon the steering oar, and his body flipped into the raging sea; his plight being a long distance from the wildly bouncing raft. Fierce gusts of howling winds suddenly savagely snapped the mast in half, precisely along its middle.

Then, astute Athena, Zeus's empathetic daughter, thought of something rather phenomenal. The goddess blocked-off the pathways of every wind but one, and soon mentally ordered all of the gusty East, West and South blowhards to stop, and the compassionate goddess deftly checked their combined force. Being roused, the swift North Wind broke the waves in front, so that divinely-inspired Odysseus might yet make contact with the people of Phaeacia, men who loved the oar, and who cherished avoiding death while defying Fate.

"Oh Fate!" Odysseus loudly screamed to deaf ears in high heaven. "That was definitely the worse blowjob I've ever had!"

So, for two solid days and two whole nights, the ancient mariner floated and swam upon the tossing ocean waves, his vanquished heart being saturated with countless thoughts of welcomed death. But when fair-haired Dawn gave rise to the third morning, the intense wind died-down, the tempestuous sea grew calm and then still, and everything again seemed to be copesetic. Odysseus was raised-up by a large swell, and as the weary swimmer quickly glimpsed ahead, his eyes could see a land mass close by. Poseidon's human foe kept rapidly doggy-paddling until the sea god's human rival reached the mouth of a fair-flowing river, which seemed to him, the exhausted swimmer, the best place to stumble ashore.

There were no rocks upon the sandy beach, and the desolate place appeared sheltered from the accommodating North Wind. From hazy memory, Odysseus recognized the familiar, flowing river from an archaic map still-imagined and etched deep inside his cerebral recall. With both knees bent, the fatigued castaway let his strong hands fall, because the sea had crushed his heart along with his grip. All of the mortal's weatherworn skin surfacing his entire body (including his treasured scrotum sac) had become swollen from his intense ordeal. The defeated king lay there upon the pure white sand, out of breath, virtually an ungrateful escapee from drowning.

Close by the tiding water, the sea-survivor crawled-about, and finally discovered a place featuring a wide-open view. So, the discarded raftsman crept-forward like a curious animal on the prowl, peering-out beneath two bushes growing from a single source. One of the shrubs was an olive tree; the other a wild thorn. Alert Athena then poured-out much-needed sleep across the fellow's eyelids, so now the exhausted trekker could find necessary relief, a quick respite from his persistent troubles.

Odysseus's final thoughts before shutting his heavy eyes and slumbering into complete rest were, 'I may be a disillusioned fool, but who the fuck wants to live forever in a state of perpetual boredom! Fork you, Poseidon! Fork you!"

Chapter 6

"ODYSSEUS AND NAUSICAA"

While much-enduring Lord Odysseus soundly rested, lying in his new beach environment, being overcome with weariness and welcomed sleep, Athena flew-off to the land of the Phaeacians, to their principal city, and vaporized her form inside the palace of the king, Lord Alcinous. The goddess's prime objective was to cunningly arrange a safe journey back to Ithaca for brave Odysseus. Zeus's daughter moved into a wonderfully furnished room where a comely young girl slept, just like an immortal goddess, in both form and loveliness.

The slumbering teenager was Nausicaa, child of great-hearted Alcinous, whoever the hell he was. Like a frantic wind gust, Athena slipped-over to the young girl's bedside, stood there beside her head's brown tresses, and lowly whispered in the girl's ear. At that moment, the goddess's appearance mystically changed to look like Dymas's daughter, a young lesbian girl of the same age as her frequent companion mate, Nausicaa, whose heart was well-disposed to her cherished friend. Utilizing that clever disguise, bright-eyed Athena softly uttered:

"Nausicaa, how did your mother Queen Arete bear a girl who is so careless and who keeps a room so unkempt? Your fine clothes are lying and strewn-about upon the dirty floor, here untended. Soon enough, you'll have your wedding day, when you must dress-up in expensive robes and give the apparel, while standing nude, to your wedding groom, as is your country's ridiculous tradition. You'd better be a bisexual, or else you'll suffer an unhappy future being penetrated by a stiff penis every hour of every day for the remainder of your marriage!"

'Who the fuck is whispering in my ear?' Nausicaa thought in her deep sleep. 'I already have one fucked-up lesbian girlfriend, and the last thing I need is a second annoying bitch!'

"You know," Athena, in needless disguise, mentioned. "It's little things like tidiness that help to make a worthy reputation with *our* people, and also please your honored mother and father. But apparently, you don't give a tiny rat's turd about anything that requires self-discipline. At daybreak, let's together diligently wash-out the wrinkled clothing. Early this morning, politely ask your revered father to provide you with a commonplace donkey cart and his best mules, so that you can carry the bright covers, the heavy robes, and the family sashes to the distant laundry rocks. That use of the donkey cart would be better than carrying your burdensome load of garments on foot, because obviously, the dirty washing tubs are located some distance from the town."

When rose-colored Dawn on her golden throne arrived and woke fair-robed, lazy Nausicaa from her extended slumber, the fat girl was curious to learn more about her rather-peculiar dream. So, the spoiled brat sped through the house, located her apathetic father, and against her selfish nature, lovingly spoke:

"Dear favorite parent; can you kindly prepare a high wagon with quality sturdy wheels for me to use, so I can carry my fine clothing out and wash my abused garb on the distant riverbank? My attire is lying in a heap inside my room, all dirty upon the grimy floor. And as is your fine habit, it's appropriate for you to wear fresh-washed garments on your person, so I intend to imitate your fine example, especially when you're meeting with our city's leading politicians while legislating impractical laws in council."

"Why Nausicaa," her distracted father answered. "What has inspired you to abandon your sloven ways? I'm both shocked and stunned by your willingness to finally act responsibly!"

"You have five worthless sons living in your house," the seemingly-transformed daughter declared. "Two are married, but three are young assholes still unattached, and the lazy dolts always require freshly-washed clothing when they go-out dancing and romancing at the downtown strip clubs. All these are matters I must seriously think about. Now Father; I plan on washing the entire household's clothing down at the river basin."

Nausicaa declared those unusual matters because she felt ashamed to remind her father of her own happy thoughts of possibly getting married to a transvestite male. But the parent fully understood all that related bullshit and replied, saying:

"I have no objection to your unorthodox request of providing my strongest mules for you, or any other things you so desire, as long as you marry a man with a donkey dick and a huge bank account. Go on your way and get pregnant with carrying sextuplets, for all the hell I care. I need to get you, and the massive aggravation you engender, out of this fuckin' home as soon as possible. At your disposal, my slaves will get a four-wheeled wagon ready with a high box frame attached on top."

Once the elderly patriarch announced that concession to Nausicaa, the king called-out to his domestic slaves, and the fearful jerk-offs enacted exactly what their owner commanded. The obliging dumb-fucks prepared a smooth-running wagon exclusively designed for dun mules; the laborers led-up the animals, and then yoked the tamed mules to the improvised cart.

Nausicaa, pretending to be an adult, brought her fine clothing from her room, and the spoiled brat situated the various items inside the polished wagon. Household slaves gathered and packed the other dirty attire into the awaiting donkey cart. The girl's impressed mother, Queen Arete, loaded on board a box containing all sorts of tempting high-calorie foods that would instantly fatten-up the already-corpulent three-hundred-pound, spoiled-rotten teenager.

The conscientious mother then included some rare delicacies, too, and generously poured some month-old vinegar into a goat skin for her obese daughter's personal consumption. The still-mesmerized girl awkwardly climbed onto the wagon. Soon, employing a clatter of hooves, the king's mules moved ahead, carrying discardable clothing along with the dream-influenced girl, who was being accompanied by her regular attendants, who also were devout lesbians, dancing nightly at the popular downtown strip clubs.

When the jolly traveling party eventually reached the stream of the fair-flowing river, the giddy gay girls gathered-up the clothing from the wagon, carried the garb in their arms down to the murky stream, and then trampled and stomped the disposable apparel inside the often-used washing trenches, each motivated bitch trying to work more quickly than the others in order to later go behind the nearby beach shrubs and munch on each other's hairy bushes.

Once the aberrant teens had cleansed the clothing and scrubbed-off all the pussy juice and semen stains, the gay gals laid the laundry-out in rows along the shore, placing the garments where deposited waves beat and surfed upon the rugged coastline.

When the aroused lesbian chicks had bathed themselves and rubbed their curvaceous nude bodies well with greasy black oil, obtained from inside the ground, the young dames ate a meal beside the river mouth, waiting for their clothes to dry in the sun's warm rays. Once the naughty hussies had finished consuming their food and actively eating each other's crotches, Nausicaa and her perverted attendants, still naked from the neck down, removed their head scarves to more effectively play catch with an immobile sea urchin that had lost its will to live.

But when the spoiled princess threw the substitute beachball, Nausicaa accidentally missed her prospective target, and the quilled sea animal landed near the deep, swirling river.

The pissed-off attendants shouted sharp, dissonant protests, incidentally rousing Odysseus from his powerful slumber.

'That loud screaming is evidence of massive trouble occurring in this alien country,' Odysseus's brain hypothesized. 'What the fuck are those insane imbeciles shrieking about? Are these felines violent and untamed monsters without any sense of civilized justice, just like the mythological Cyclops? Or are the sirens simply hostile to random strangers? In their mini-minds, do the bitches fear the gods? Some young woman's shouts just rang-out around me; I don't need this weird shit; they're probably fucked-up nymphs like insane Calypso, who are living along steep mountain peaks and by the local river springs and grassy meadows,' Odysseus's skeptical brain assessed. 'Forget these raunchy, hysterical, emotional female dumb-clits! Could I somehow be near rational men possessing logical human speech? Well, come on now; I'm going to have to find-out this weird conundrum all by myself.'

With those all-too-nebulous thoughts, Odysseus crept-out of the thicket. In his strong hands, the veteran wanderer snapped-off a leafy branch from a nearby bush to hold across and conceal his impressive, naked groin area. Then, stepping forward, the slightly-embarrassed itinerant king emerged from the thicket, moving just like a stealthy mountain lion relying on its own cunning and strength. That's precisely how clever Odysseus was making his way out of the brush to face those fair-haired, lesbian girls, whom his instinct believed to be warlike Amazon fanatics.

The pathetic castaway, being mostly nude, was in dire psychological distress; but, caked with sea brine, the trespasser was an absolute fearful sight to the chatty lesbians, when after also being startled, Odysseus dropped his foliage camouflage and thus exposed his limp, foot-long, dangling dingle.

The delirious servants ran-off in fear, and anxiously crouched-down here and there among the jutting sand dune and beach cactus, thus piercing their delicate assholes along with their sensitive, dipshit pubic lip slits. The only one who did not rush-away was Alcinous's appalled and hypnotized only daughter.

So, the recent visitor to Phaeacian shores quickly used his legendary acumen and spoke to Nausicaa with soothing language, but the lesbian girl stood motionless and stared wonderingly at Odysseus's awesome, dangling fadorkenbender.

"Oh, you divine chubby beauty queen; I come here as a harassed and bewildered suppliant seeking your pity. Are you an exotic goddess, or an erotic mortal being?" the eccentric castaway praised. "If you're one of the gods who hold status in wide heaven, I think that you most resemble huntress Artemis (Diana), daughter of great Zeus, by mere virtue of your loveliness, your stature, and your oddball portly shape. If you're human, and since I'm a confirmed fibber who often prevaricates, I insist that your parents are thrice-blessed, and thrice-blessed are your shit-eating brothers, too, if you're lucky to have any male jerk-offs in your family," Odysseus wildly exaggerated.

"Your Greek sounds like absolute geek to me," Nausicaa criticized. "What's that salami hanging between your legs? It looks like pregnant pepperoni!"

"In their warm hearts, your lucky parents must glow like candles with pleasure for you always, when their delighted eyes see a child, such as yourself, moving-up into the adult phase of the life dance. But the happiest heart, more so buoyant than all the rest, belongs to the lucky groom who, with his stellar wedding gifts, will lead you home to merrily feed your hungry black cat," Odysseus stupidly joked. "These eyes of mine have never gazed upon anyone like you, either fruitcake man or vegetable woman. As my gaze marvels at the magnitude of your fantastic pulchritude, I'm gripped with ethereal wonder."

"What the fuck are you talking about?" Nausicaa yelled back. "A farting asshole makes more common sense than your phony lingo does!"

Odysseus was not deterred by his listener's brash criticism. "In Delos, I once observed something like this awkward situation," the nervous King of Ithaca proceeded with his peculiar narrative.

"Are you a recently escaped mental patient?" Nausicaa asked. "Your words sound stranger than strange!"

"A palm-tree sapling had grown beside Apollo's sacred altar in Delos," the sea survivor continued his recollection. "I had ventured there, with many others in my illustrious company, to attend a religious pilgrimage, but Fate had planned for me so many forthcoming Zeus-forsaken troubles. But when my eyes noticed that very special shrine, my understanding became quite astonished," Odysseus explained to the disinterested girl.

"Are you one of those nutcase greenies I often hear about?" Nausicaa asked. "The environment is perfectly okay without you' idealistic assholes and your destructive ideas ruining my general happiness!"

"I had never before perceived such a lovely tree springing from the Earth," Odysseus continued his boring monologue about his experience in Delos. "And, fair damsel, that's how I'm amazed at your fabulous facial and physical appearance; I'm lost in wonder, and very much afraid to clasp your knee. Do you perform oral sex? My conscience will not permit me to get laid with a hefty heifer, but I desperately need a decent blowjob."

"Listen to me, you dumb-ass mendicant randomly deposited upon this country's coastline," Nausicaa lividly replied. "Tell me some more fascinating bullshit so that I can get colitis and shit all of the constipation out of my anus hole."

"A great distress has recently overtaken me," Odysseus, still naked, proceeded to articulate. "Just yesterday, my twentieth day afloat upon the savage sea, I had miraculously escaped the wine-dark wrath of enraged Poseidon and his devastating Trident. Before that encounter, massive waves and swift-driving storm winds carried me from Calypso's Island of Ogygia to where I stand right this moment. And now, another anonymous, demented god has tossed me onto shore here, so that somehow, I'll suffer a litany of mysterious hardships in this strange location as well," the plagued traveler attempted to explain.

'You're so full of shit that you must have more than one asshole!" Nausicaa suspected and stated. "I guess, at least three!"

"For you see, fair young lady. I don't think my progression of problems will end right now. But, divine area queen, or whoever the hell you are, have bountiful mercy on my unenviable circumstance. You're the first mortal I've approached, after so much grief, and I do not know any prominent people living in your seemingly barbaric land."

"How can I render assistance?" naïve Nausicaa asked. "Do you need a good spanking? I sometimes randomly practice sadism and masochism, you know!"

"Kind child; help me by showing the direction of the nearest town. Give me some oily rag to throw around my personals, perhaps some useful wrapping you had brought for the clothes when you came here to wash," pleaded Odysseus. "As for you, despite my lack of heavenly influence, may the whimsical gods grant everything that your heart and ovaries desire. May you achieve a serene husband with a massive dingle, a luxurious mansion, and mutual harmony and melody with the two of you singing in your temple choir."

Skeptical, white-armed Nausicaa then replied:

"Mentally challenged Stranger; you don't seem to be a wicked or perverted heterosexual. Olympian Zeus himself gives happiness to both bad and worthy men, each one receiving just what Zeus desires them to deal with. But now you have reached our backwards land and primitive city. Despite our inferior education system and obsolete culture, we are aware of the gods' Law of the Suppliants, and we feel especially obligated to render aid and comfort to all visitors to our land who seek food, clothing and shelter before resuming their stupid-shit travels," Nausicaa divulged. "I'll gladly show you directions to the town, and I'll tell you the name our country bears, for we are the isolated Phaeacians, residing in antiquated Phaeacia. As for me, I am the daughter of the national criminal-politician, King Alcinous, and unfortunately, Phaeacian power and strength depend upon his warped brain and his reprehensible judgment."

When Nausicaa abruptly finished speaking, the naughty daughter of King Alcinous and Queen Arete called-out to her fair-haired attendants, still practicing sixty-nine in the dense beach bushes.

"Stand-up, you proud lesbians. Have you run-off because for the first time, you've seen a grown man's dangling dingle? Surely, you don't think he is our well-endowed contemptible enemy? So, girls, give this stranger adequate food and drink. Bathe his foreign ass and testicles in yonder river; select a calm place which offers our guest some nice shelter from the blustery wind."

Nausicaa briskly finished dictating the specific instructions to her obedient gay servants. The entire company stood-up in the bushes and called-out their mistress's command to one another. The garrulous troop took Odysseus aside and escorted their sandy guest to a sheltered spot, and two at a time, performed quality fellatio on the very happy fellow. In fact, one of the more proficient and talented servants, identified as Connie Lingus, was able to perform true to her name.

Then, after thoroughly enjoying their new-found pleasure, the gay dolls set-out appropriate clothing for the sea survivor to wear; a cloak and tunic; and next the bitches gave their new friend a gold flask full of smooth olive oil so that grateful Odysseus could wake-up oily the next morning. The blithe contingent advised the displaced king to bathe in the flowing river in order for his massive erection to shrink-down to its normal, limp, foot-long length.

When the castaway had washed himself all over and rubbed-on the soothing oil, Odysseus dressed into his newly-acquired clothes. The young girls gazed at him in wonder, imagining what it would feel like having his long, thick manhood penetrating their eager-beaver vaginas.

Without further delay, Nausicaa and several of her lesbian companions climbed-up onto the donkey cart, and then the driver shouted-down:

"Get-up off your ass now, muscular Stranger, and venture into the town. I'll show you the way to my wise-ass, er, I mean my wise father's house, where, I assure you, you'll get to meet all the finest jerk-off power brokers of Phaeacia. You seem to me to have a sophisticated, cultural background, so I suggest that you urgently act as follows. While we are moving through the countryside, past many farms, and past bulls and cows copulating in their muddy pastures, walk fast alongside my faithful attendants, directly behind the stubborn mules and the antiquated wagon. I'll cautiously lead the way from my position on the driver's bench."

"Can't I sit inside the wagon with you and enjoy the scenery much more?" Odysseus protested. 'I didn't grow a donkey dick simply by walking behind a primitive donkey cart, you know!"

"No, you totally ungrateful suppliant!" Nausicaa rather sternly reprimanded. "You'll walk past a fine olive grove to meet and communicate with the goddess Athena. Don't ask me how I've come to know this esoteric bullshit! The grove, situated near the road, is planted next to a clump of popular poplar trees. There's a dysfunctional fountain, with lush meadows abounding all around it. My father has a fertile vineyard at that remote place, within a mile's shouting distance from the town. I know all of this absurd family vineyard nonsense simply because I heard it through the grapevine."

Nausicaa then decisively cracked her shiny black whip, striking the docile mules, and quickly left the area of the flowing river. The donkey wagon moved briskly forward at a rapid pace. Using her judgment and noteworthy skill, the girl steadfastly and slowly drove ahead, so Odysseus and her talkative servants had to trot forward and keep-up on foot. Just at sunset, the contingent reached the celebrated grove, wholly sacred to Pallas Athene. Odysseus sat-down there and quickly made a prayer, appealing to great Zeus's daughter for assistance.

Chapter 7

"ODYSSEUS AT THE COURT OF ALCINOUS"

Lord Odysseus, who had endured so much tribulation, prayed there at the groovy grove, while two strong mules transported Nausicaa and her entourage back to her father's palatial home. Then, after successfully lighting a fire and offering a sacrifice of a dozen overripe oranges to Athena, Odysseus got-up from his knees and set-off on foot for the designated town, finally making his way to erudite King Alcinous's splendid mansion. The Phaeacians, men with dense eye cataracts who were celebrated for their armada of merchant ships, did not see the new pedestrian's approach into the tranquil city, mostly because Pallas Athene would not permit such observation or surveillance to occur. In her heart, the radiant goddess truly cared for the besieged Ithacan King, so Zeus's daughter defensively cast around her favorite mortal hero a mysterious, mystifying mist.

Above the high-vaulted home of pusillanimous and self-serving King Alcinous, there persisted a fabulous radiance, as if originating from the sun, or the then-visible moon. Bronze walls extended-out well-beyond the threshold in various directions, funneling into resplendent inner sanctuaries.

The entire architecture exhibited an eye-appealing, azure blue, enamel cornice. Gold-plated doors blocked the main entrance from trespassers, especially door-to-door-salesmen, from entering into the well-constructed edifice. The bronze threshold boasted silver doorposts set inside, and the closed portal featured a silver lintel. The handles were of glimmering gold, and on both sides of the entrance door stood solid gold and silver dogs, ageless, immortal creature representations that would not grow old, created by the lame blacksmith god Hephaestus's matchless artistry; the sensational animal statues were specifically designed to symbolically guard and protect the magnificent palace of great-hearted Alcinous.

Lord Odysseus, who had endured so much adversity, stood there and gazed-around in awe. When his heart and eyes had sufficiently marveled at the superlative entrance, the wary visitor, with the help of Athena, moved like a vapor quickly past the threshold, further into the mansion's interior.

The long-suffering King of Ithaca, his form still enveloped in the camouflaging mist that had been poured around him by the benevolent goddess, proceeded through the central hall until his invisible feet came to where Queen Arete and King Alcinous were preoccupied, alternately arm-wrestling and judo flipping. With both his tanned, muscular arms, Odysseus embraced the knees of Arete, who immediately enjoyed a major orgasm as the rush of adrenalin within her system enabled the Queen to easily defeat her husband, with his right-hand slamming and severing-in-half the table being utilized. At that wonderful and outstanding moment, the miraculous mist surrounding the castaway dissolved in a totally magical fashion, and Odysseus's appearance became visible to Nausicaa's slightly-embarrassed royal parents.

All the old-fart Phaeacians who were witnessing the arm-wrestling competition were struck dumbfounded, as the stunned politicians intensely gazed-upon the newcomer, their shallow minds overcome with wonder at the sight of the intrusive alien. Odysseus then made the following unique entreaty:

"Arete, daughter of godlike Rhexenor. I've come to you and to your husband King Alcinous, with my hands embracing your skinny kneecaps, in supplication to you and your benign mercy. I am an exhausted wanderer who has undergone much terrible hardship for ten-long-years all around the volatile Mediterranean Sea. And to those hoary spectators here, I also beg your undivided indulgence."

"What's going on here?" King Alcinous exclaimed. "How did you get through the locked security doors?"

"May the gods grant your other guests happiness in their personal lives," Lord Odysseus proceeded with his introduction, ignoring King Alcinous's concerned inquiry. "May each individual in attendance within this chamber generously pass on abundant riches within their households to all their blessed children, illegitimate bastards and horny bitches, too. And furthermore," Odysseus bullshitted. "May all you noblemen present in this huge room receive the finest honors and awards given by the richer residents of your most excellent city. Please rouse yourselves to heightened pity to help me travel home to my faraway kingdom of Ithaca; for me to get back quickly to my native soil, so that I might right the great evils that prevail within my traduced domain. For a long time now, I've been in great distress and away from friends and my nuclear family, people that I dearly love."

When King Alcinous heard those rather extraordinary words, the gullible asshole stretched out his hand, reaching for Odysseus, not ever suspecting that His Majesty could be successfully being duped by his wise and crafty, uninvited guest. The dim-witted host raised-up his visiting suppliant from the hearth, and asked Lord Odysseus to relax, and later, when the guest had gathered adequate strength, review for the monarch's pleasure his extensive tale of woe. Then, royal Alcinous called-out to his herald:

"Pontonous; please prepare wine in the mixing bowls, and then serve large portions to all people assembled in this hall, so that we may pour libations out to Almighty Zeus, who loves lightning, thunder, tidal waves, blizzards and nasty hurricanes, for Poseidon's brother accompanies all pious suppliants to our isolated island, and allows them to suffer immensely in their separate struggles."

Once Alcinous completed those imperative sentences, Pontonous meticulously prepared fifty-gallons of the honey-sweet wine, and poured-out the precious drops for libation into every extended cup. The gathered connoisseurs mumbled, grunted, and gulped, after falsely making their traditional offering, and quickly chugged-down their fill of the very rare and absolutely delicious wine, the moochers immediately demanding seconds and thirds.

Then, sinus congested King Alcinous addressed the rowdy, drunken revelers:

"You ridiculous Phaeacian government counselors and esteemed kindergarten administrative leaders, pay attention to me, so that I can verbally enunciate the concepts that the heart pounding inside my chest commands. Now that all of you have finished drinking and exchanging irrelevant anecdotes, I advise that you drunken corrupt bastards all return to your individual domiciles and get some much-needed rest."

"When can we have more wine?" an intoxicated old coot loudly asked. "I might not live to see tomorrow!"

"In the morning, we'll summon an assembly with even more of our senile elders in attendance, and we'll entertain this implausible stranger here inside my palatial home, and also sacrifice choice offerings to the apathetic Olympic gods. After that ritualistic travesty is completed, we'll think and assess how we intend to send this scruffy castaway off and away from our responsibility, so that this discouraged stranger, with us escorting him to the docks, without further pain or effort, may reach his native homeland, no matter how far distant from here that little-known, son-of-a-bitchin', insignificant island may be."

Antinous paused for a minute, evaluated how his speech was being received, and then proceeded with sharing his non-dynamic commentary.

"Meanwhile, this itinerant fellow, who ironically calls himself 'No Man', should not suffer additional harm or trouble, despite the fact that many of you dangerous dunces would take pleasure in assassinating the bullshitting asshole right here and now. After his return to his obscure land, 'No Man' will more-than-likely undergo explaining all those imaginary things he has so far described, including being given a thorough psychological examination to be performed by the local witchdoctor, or by the most available regional oracle on duty. Destiny, along with the dreaded spinning Fates have wickedly woven fantasies into the thread of this man's most complicated mental fabric, and we must wonder why this dumb-fuck ignoramus was ever born into this horribly deplorable world. However, if a deathless verdict comes-down from heaven, then gods are planning something different than my miniature brain can essentially theorize."

"The gods are indeed unpredictable," Queen Arete chimed-in. "As unpredictable as common earthquakes, typhoons, tsunamis and volcanic eruptions!"

"So far, the evasive and unpredictable gods occasionally show themselves to us in their true form, when we cleverly offer-up to their statues a well-received sacrifice," King Antinous lectured. "The divine deities sometimes invisibly dine with us, sitting in the very chairs where we park our fat asses upon. If someone traveling all by himself meets those immortal entities that we fearfully worship, the singular gods often don't hide their true identities, because we are close relatives of their genetics, just like the Cyclopes and the wild tribes of Crazy Giants that reside in caves all over the fucked-up Mediterranean. The only major difference between the Olympians and us is that the dirty knuckleheads have mastered the secret of what constitutes nectar and ambrosia, and we stupid earthly shits don't even have a partial clue concerning the nature of that special magic formula. Nor don't we comprehend what the fuck the nectar and ambrosia concoction really is, or even where the two elusive ingredients causing Olympian immortality can be found."

Resourceful Odysseus then answered the confused monarch:

"King Alcinous; you should not concern yourself about what you've just proclaimed, for I'm not like the immortal gods who hold wide heaven; with the exception of the eternally punished Titan known as Atlas, *that* commentary of mine is meant figuratively and not literally, neither in form nor in shape. In truth, I'm both frail and mortal, just like your dimwit senile politicians seated in this vast room happen to be."

"You dare to insult our integrity?" a farting elder challenged. "Finish-up with your jargon before I shit my diaper a third time! You mentioned Atlas! Why the hell didn't you cite the punished Titan Prometheus, also!"

"Indeed, Phaeacians. I could recount a much longer and detailed story when I have mustered the strength to do so; I'll articulate a gruesome tale enumerating all of the tragic hardships I've had to suffer from the ever-vacillating and capricious gods," Odysseus elaborated. "But first, allow me to peacefully eat my dinner, and although my tortured mind is in great distress, my stomach is extremely famished. For there's nothing more shameless than an unhappy growling belly, which compels a man to seriously think about his indispensable biological needs, even if one's spirit is enduring harsh excruciation; yet, a man must eat first, and reveal descriptions and explanations after."

"Well then, when can we hear your entire story?" King Alcinous demanded knowing. "I hope it's much better and more intriguing than your lackluster preface!"

"Kind Phaeacians; when dawn appears, I will relate my myriad calamities to you. Then, after hearing my incredible, lengthy adventure, you can stir yourselves to send me, in my miserable state, back to my own soil, in spite of all the arduous hardships I've clumsily endured. If I can see my goods, my properties, my slaves, and my large and high-roofed mansion again, then I'll be content to let life end. But I've been away from all of those abstract images for twenty-long-years, and my confused mind conceives all of those matters as perhaps vague, imaginary, contrived; a pauper's many illusions. I presently appeal to your generosity and respect, humbly urging your kindness under Zeus's supreme Law of the Suppliants!"

Once Odysseus finished orating his philosophical elucidation, the naïve, doddering idiots in attendance all approved and applauded his incredible words, and, because the itinerant had spoken so well and so directly to the point, every drunken asshole seated inside the enormous hall of Antinous agreed that their peculiar guest should be assisted and escorted upon his incomparable journey back to his native Ithaca.

Chapter 8

"ODYSSEUS IS ENTERTAINED IN PHAEACIA"

The following afternoon, King Alcinous addressed his chief government officials and clumsily stuttered to the distinguished-but-corrupt Phaeacians:

"Listen to my review of recent developments, you risk-taking Phaeacian counselors and leaders. I'll tell you what the heart in my chest says, even though the organ has no throat or voice-box. This wayward stranger here, a fellow who yesterday described himself as 'No Man', I do not personally know. I believe that our guest is a world wanderer who might be conveying to us the truth about his voyage here. No Man is asking us our cooperation and mercy to help him to be sent away, back to his uncharted native island, and our inimitable visitor wishes us to grant him his unprecedented request under Zeus's Suppliants Law. So royal officials, let us act as we have never done before with anyone else, and assist No Man to diligently continue along on his intended journey."

"If the weirdo stranger identifies himself as "No Man', is he some kind of female, or transgender, or neuter, or perhaps a tri-gender?" Queen Arete asked her regal husband. "Does the drifter ever use the pronoun 'he'?"

"No man arriving at my palace, including 'No Man', stays for very long, grieving about not getting back home," Alcinous explained to his inquisitive wife. "I'll make my position on this major agenda matter quite short and sweet. If any subject or topic ever unnerves and disturbs me, it's a groaning grown man crying his tear ducts right-out of his bony skull. I mean, we have to get rid of this 'No Man' character because taking care of him might be the start of a debilitating welfare system; an unnecessary tax burden on all of us businessmen!"

Alcinous spoke and soon led the smaller-sceptered regional kings in discussing the very strange matter. A herald was dispatched to find the missing forgetful singer so that the committee's decision could be captured in both song and history.

Meanwhile, fifty-two hand-picked young men were inanely assigned to scamper-off to the city's distant shore. Once the selected sailors had reached their appointed merchant ship, the chosen crew dragged the black vessel out to deeper water, set the mast and sails in place inside the boat, lashed the rowing oars onto their leather pivots, and then hoisted the standard friendly white sail. That being done, the fledgling mariners moored the ship well out to sea, and then upon completing that elementary task, returned to the great home of King Alcinous. Luckily, the singing minstrel had by accident remembered his scheduled gig and found his way back to King Alcinous's palace.

Hallways, corridors, and courtyards were full of dubious residents; the assembled dunces forming a massive crowd comprised of both young and old curious dolts. On their behalf, Alcinous had his regal butcher slaughter eight white-tusked boars, two shambling oxen, and twelve prized sheep.

Those twenty-two prodigious carcasses were carefully skinned and dressed, and then the palace chefs prepared a spectacular banquet for all present to partake. In the interim, the neurotic herald entered the premises, accompanied by the pompous, blind singer, a performer who was particularly loved by the melodic demigod Muse, above all other effeminate male sopranos. The herald, Pontonous, next brought-in a silver-studded chair with a circular hole in its center, which served a dual function of being King Alcinous's favorite seat, and also his favorite hopper.

After the rowdy congregation enjoyed their heart's fill of food and drink, the minstrel Demodocus, inspired by the immortal lyric critic Muse, sang about the glorious deeds of Greek warriors, especially about Odysseus and Achilles, son of Peleus, who had lost his life after his exposed heel/tendon had been lethally penetrated by a sharp Trojan arrow.

When the last morsels of the great array of meat had been consumed, the noble Phaeacians ventured outside upon the expansive, well-kept lawn, and the young men participated in a number of difficult individual competitions. Odysseus astounded all of the local athletes with his superior skill in throwing the discus across the city and embedding the heavy orb into a distant high mountain peak. After the preliminary games had terminated, Alcinous called for a large gathering, where the jovial Phaeacians could demonstrate their unique dancing ability, along with chanting a medley of oddball musical renditions.

Nine incompetent officials, who regularly specialized in organizing each detail of the absent-minded king's meetings, rose from their seats, smoothed-off a dancing space, and then marked-out a circumcised circumference. The hoarse herald stepped-up to the circle, and the raspy-voiced announcer was carrying the clear-toned lyre for fretful vocalist Demodocus to slowly strum.

Around the acclaimed singer stood a dozen pre-pubescent boys in the first bloom of youth; small-peckered, but relatively skillful dancers, whose dainty feet then stuck to the semen-laden, animal blood-strewn, recently-consecrated dance floor. Odysseus marveled at how rapidly those young boys in leotards could move their prancing feet, despite all of the recently ejaculated semen and disgusting dropped animal blood under their sandals.

The minstrel struck the opening chords to his complicated song, and sang about how Aphrodite had been married to the ugly blacksmith god Hephaestus; how the fair-crowned Aphrodite, goddess of love and beauty, lusted for the war god Ares; how in Hephaestus's own volcanic, lava-laden, subterranean abode, Aphrodite and the ugly blacksmith god first had secret sex, and how Ares, the god of war, gave Aphrodite many gifts, while the hostile war deity disgraced the marriage bed of Lord Hephaestus, forcing the goddess of love and beauty to give-up her private business, the very lucrative Aphro-dite Diaper Service.

But then, the trouble-making sun god Helios's spying observed the unlikely pair (Ares and Aphrodite) making love, and the tattle-taler hurried at once to tell disfigured Hephaestus of the illicit love affair. When the god of the forge heard the unwelcome news, the lame listener went to his underground foundry, angrily turning copper and tin over deep inside his furnace, and in a matter of hours, Hephaestus had creatively forged a heavy-duty net that neither mortal nor immortal could ever break or loosen. And the ensnarled victims of the net would have to stay immobile and inactive at the blacksmith god's constant, peeved discretion.

When, in his wild rage, Hephaestus had finished the encumbering snare, designed to trap and incapacitate Ares and Aphrodite, the livid personage entered into the honeymoon room, which housed his and Aphrodite's marriage bed, and the vengeful lame blacksmith adroitly anchored the metal netting around the high bed posts. The crazed lover next hung loops from sturdy ceiling beams above, the net being as intricate in design as the finest possible spider's web.

Once the livid, red-skinned anvil hammerer had set the whole snare in place above the honeymoon bed, according to the minstrel's song, Hephaestus loudly announced to Mt. Olympus that he would be taking an unscheduled trip to Lemnos, a well-built citadel that was his favorite retreat.

Seeing his immortal rival depart to Lemnos, wily Ares rushed over to Hephaestus's below-ground dwelling, eager to again have passionate adulterous sex with fair-crowned Aphrodite. The goddess of love and beauty had just left the presence of her father Zeus, and was sitting-down upon a soft-cushioned lounge chair. Ares charged inside the underground dwelling, and anxiously grabbed Aphrodite by the hand.

"Come, my dear; let's go together to bed and make insane, hog-snorting love together. Hephaestus is not home, and I'm hornier than Hades, both the god and the place. No doubt your hideous-looking husband has gone to visit Lemnos and communicate with the pornographic Sintians; yes, those evil creatures who speak like barbarians and who sloppily and ravenously eat luscious pussy like demented cannibals."

To lustful Aphrodite, having sex with Ares seemed quite delightful when compared to having any kind of intercourse (including verbal) with Hephaestus. So, the in-heat duo raced-off to bed and lay-down together. But then the metallic net that had been craftily fabricated by Hephaestus's great skill collapsed around the horny adulterers, so the immortal sinners could not maneuver their limbs, shift their bodies and genitals, or even move their smelly bowels. After a while, the trapped twosome finally realized that neither of them could possibly escape their very tight, confining entanglement.

Upon his returning to the screaming scene of marital infidelity, Lord Hephaestus stood inside the bedroom doorway, and gripped by ascending rage, the jilted husband yelled-out a dreadful cry to lofty Olympus, shouting to all the bored and disinterested gods: "Father Zeus, and you other narrow-minded, so-called sacred gods who live forever; come witness what has transpired within my modest volcano residence. Ares, the destroyer of cities and civilization, is quite handsome, having healthy limbs, while I had been born deformed and grotesque. I'm not to blame for my hideous appearance that has even frightened Medusa the Gorgon, and has made the snakes jump like grasshoppers out of her terrible, dandruff-infected scalp."

Sensing a dire emergency, the gods quickly gathered inside the bronze-floored Mt. Olympus Whorehouse Temple. Earthshaker Poseidon arrived, and speedy Lord Hermes, too. The archer and golden chariot god Apollo was the third to answer Hephaestus's call of anguish. But the female goddesses were all far-too-modest, afraid, and ashamed to participate in indicting fellow female Aphrodite, so the ravishing beauties stayed at a distance.

Hermes attested that Ares's misdeed should be punished, and Apollo agreed, saying that Hephaestus was a more important deity than was Ares because the abused blacksmith god had constructively made all of the swords, shields, sandals, helmets and other valued materials for the other key Olympians.

So, in conclusion, according to the minstrel's recollection, the male gods honored the shared statement between Hermes and Apollo, and soon thereafter, everyone on Olympus returned to their normal, everyday monotonous activity, while the punished war god was forced to spend several future peaceful centuries aimlessly ambling about the lackluster streets and alleys of a foreign city called Buenos Ares.

Then, Lord Odysseus, originally disguised as and professing to be "No Man", was cordially requested to address the relatively enthusiastic gathering:

"Mighty Alcinous, Queen Arete, and most distinguished officials among all men in this unparalleled land; you claimed that your dancers were the best in the known world, and now, indeed, what you have indicated is indisputably true. When I gazed at the effeminate faggots, er, I mean 'talented boys' dancing with the stars, I was lost in wonder, thinking that I'm watching a pack of graceful human gazelles having queer aerial sex in full motion."

At Odysseus's exaggerated and phony words, powerful King Alcinous felt a great delight, and at once commanded strict imperatives to his Phaeacian master sailors.

"Leaders and counselors of us illiterate Phaeacians; listen intently, even though there are no tents in this room in which to hear any fuckin' thing being mentioned. This remarkable Stranger possessing 'No Name' seems to me to be a rare mortal specimen exhibiting an uncommon wisdom that evidently transcends life itself. So, come now; let's give him our offer of friendship, as is only right and proper," Alcinous insisted. "As we all know, with the exception of eminent 'No Man' here, twelve honorable kings are rulers in our land and govern it inefficiently, and I myself, of course, am the lucky thirteenth, making us a unique baker's dozen. Let each one of us loyal patriots donate a fresh cloak and tunic, newly washed, and a money-exchange talent of pure gold for the benefit of our honored guest's departure from our jagged shores. All of this civic duty we should put together very quickly; our immediate preparation is to be rendered so that this nomadic stranger has his honorable gifts in hand, and meanders-off to dinner and wine with a joyful heart."

All those adult dolts present in the large room agreed with Lord Alcinous's stupidity, and consented that the thirteenth king's proposal should swiftly be executed, and not "No Man". Then, every one of the pecker-head aristocrats assigned a personal valet to find and bring forward the castaway's redundant clothes and money presents to be used at sea.

As the hot sun went-down in the western sky, the splendid gifts were carried-in and taken to Alcinous's spacious meeting room by worthy-unheralded heralds.

Nausicaa, whose incomparable fat ass was a horrendous-looking gift from the gods, stood inside the exit door of that well-built hall and stared at Odysseus, feeling a genuine sense of wonder. The portly teenager was compelled to utter winged words to him:

"Farewell, fair Stranger with the lengthy, impressive dangling dingle. Once you have successfully returned to your own distant country, I sincerely hope you'll occasionally remember me, since you owe me your fuckin' life."

Then Odysseus, presently masquerading as that fantastically resourceful fellow "No Man", candidly replied to the obese lesbian girl's audacious opinion.

"Nauseating Nausicaa, daughter of great orator King Alcinous and laconic Queen Arete; may Hera's loud-thundering husband, Zeus, grant that I see the day of my return when I eventually arrive at my native land to reclaim what is rightfully mine. There, I will pray to your happiness all my days, as I would to a god. For you, fat girl, your solicited sacrifices indeed saved me my beleaguered life; for I'm a traveling man, who has made a lot of stops, all over the known world!"

Completing his perfunctory remarks, Odysseus finished speaking and casually smiled. Then, the honored guest sat his ass down upon a soft chair right beside gas-farting King Alcinous, as Demodocus, who was inspired by the god Apollo, resumed singing his story at the point where the plundering Greeks, having burned their beachhead huts and ascended on board their well-oared ships, were sailing-off, away from Troy.

Magnificent warriors, led by glorious Odysseus, were furtively hidden inside the already-fabled wooden "Trojan Horse". City guards had hauled the massive structure inside the gates near King Priam's Palace, their "impregnable citadel". While groups of idle soldiers sat and conversed around the huge artificial equine, the guards were confused about exactly what they should do with the weird "gift from the gods". Three quite very different options existed in making their final decision.

The first was to split the hollow, wooden stomach apart with pitiless bronze swords. The second choice was to drag the heavy structure over to the distant cliffs and push the Wooden Horse from the heightened rocks into the sea. And the third method of disposing of the eyesore monstrosity was to let the awesome artifact stay inside the city gates and be worshipped as a superb offering to the Olympian gods. The impressive object would serve as a wonderful shrine that would assuage Zeus's notorious anger against mortals everywhere. And that third decision is precisely what the indiscreet fools finally agreed upon, for it was their ultimate fate to be totally obliterated once the military clowns had pulled within their city walls the gigantic Wooden Horse, inside which lay hidden all the finest Greek heroes. Obviously, Troy was doomed to inevitable death, collapse, and historic devastation.

Then, after reviewing his popular song version of the demise of Troy, the bard Demodocus proceeded to sing about how the bold Achaean warriors had left their hollow hiding place, lowered their bodies upon a rope hanging from the horse's interior, and easily overpowered the drunken guards, thereafter opening the city gates and allowing thousands of Greek soldiers to swarm into doomed Troy and wildly plunder the wealthy Asia Minor metropolis.

The bard maintained that the hero Odysseus, in a similar fashion to Ares's quarrel with the ugly blacksmith Hephaestus, went to the home of Deiphobus, where, the ferocious King of Ithaca engaged in a most-horrendous fight. The Greek swordsman emerged victorious, thanks to assistance received from Pallas Athene, who truly admired her champion's integrity and courage.

Odysseus, still role-playing the assembly scene as anonymous "No Man", was moved to sob and weep as the wayward warrior recalled his participation in des*troy*ing Troy by designing and inventing the legendary Wooden Horse. But "No Man" kept his tears well-hidden from the oblivious Phaeacians; that is, all except Alcinous, who, as the respected city leader sat there beside anonymous "No Man", and the King was the only individual sitting in the mosquito-infested chamber who had perceptively noticed his esteemed visitor sobbing and weeping honest-to-goodness sighs.

So, the observant lucky thirteenth king spoke-out, firmly addressing his "Old Salt" Phaeacians, ardent lovers of the sea:

"Listen to me speak, you lunatic Phaeacian counselors, and you listless lethargic leaders. Let talented Demodocus now cease from playing his clear-toned lyre, for the song he's singing does not please all his listeners in attendance at this exceptional conference. Since our godlike minstrel was first moved to sing, as we were dining like starving gluttons, our visiting guest has been in emotional pain, and his mournful sniffling has never stopped. 'No Man's heart, I think, surely overflows with grief in his recollection of the falling of Troy. Some of you might suspect that 'No

Man' is sorrowed because his people had been allied with the Trojans, but I'm inclined to truly believe the reverse, opposite scenario."

All of the gathered city noblemen, like typical, low intelligence politicians, enthusiastically applauded King Alcinous's supreme words. The thirteenth ruler didn't hesitate to continue his extraordinary oration.

"Please tell me your actual name, 'No Man'. What do your people call you inside your residence: your mother, your father, and the assumed others in your' nuclear family. Explicitly, reveal to us dumb-dicks assembled in this chamber of your country and of your people, and of your city, too, so that a sea-worthy Phaeacian ship can transport you there, using what available maps we've acquired to chart your passage."

"I promise to tell your assembly everything," pledged Odysseus. "Gosh; I truly wish I knew everything, but I don't! But I shall tell you some-things I remember!"

"And now 'No Man', divulge to us all the pertinent information, and calmly speak the truth. I learned in pre-school that the word 'travel' is derived from the word 'travail'. Where have you journeyed and where have you visited while suffering-through your perpetual wandering?" Antinous asked. "Before I recommend that you be provided a ship transport back to your native island, I demand to know what other fucked-up countries have you toured? Please describe to us all of the people and all of their well-built towns you've personally experienced in your abundant adventures and near-death misadventures; whether those cultures are cruel, unjust, and wild, or if the other unknown places you've visited welcome strangers, and if the inhabitants fear the same gods as we do within their mortal hearts and souls."

Chapter 9

"THE LOTUS EATERS"

Resourceful Odysseus then replied to Alcinous:

"Lord King, most renowned of local men; I say that there's nothing that provides one more delight than when joy seizes entire groups of drunken men who sit in proper order within a massive hall; feasting, farting, belching, and enjoying the lyrics of a talented minstrel. Indeed, fine tables have been presented throughout this stately chamber, laden with bread, fruit and meat," Odysseus commended. "All these provisions transpiring as the well-trained steward draws wine out of the ten-gallon mixing bowls, moves around, and pours the tasteful liquid into our empty cups. To me, this stellar arrangement seems the finest thing there is that is practiced among mortals."

Odysseus paused for a moment to organize his next thoughts into rational speech. "But now gentle noblemen, or should I say 'noble gentlemen'; your hearts and minds want to ask about my plentitude of grievous sorrows, so I, a grown fellow, can weep and moan more than I had done before. What phenomenal exploits shall I tell you first? Where do I stop? For the heavenly gods have given me so much accumulative distress," Odysseus further related. "Well, I shall begin my preface by telling you my actual birth name. Once you know my true identity, if I escape the painful day of impending death, then later I can welcome you into my kingdom as my honored guests, though I will then be living in a once-majestic palace that is far away from your' more-than-mediocre island."

"Cut the dramatic bullshit," an intoxicated Phaeacian bellowed. "Who the fuck are you?"

"I am the famous Odysseus, son of Laertes, and well-known to all Greek-related civilizations for my deceptive methods and for my accomplished skills. Proudly speaking, my reputation stretches all the way to Heaven, and also down to Hades. I lived in my palace in Ithaca, land of both sunshine and moonshine."

"Everyone in this immense hall has heard of Odysseus," a second unconvinced attendee boomed. "How the hell can we know that you aren't a quack impostor?"

"From far away one's eyes view a scenic mountain there on Ithaca; thick with whispering trees that hold no secrets. Mount Neriton, and many islets lying around its summit, exist close together. It's a rugged landscape, and the fruits and vegetables grown in the hard soil nurture fine young warriors. But now, avid listeners, I'll speak of the unhappy journey I've encountered, which mercurial-minded Zeus, allied with Fate, with the cooperation of that bastard sea-god Poseidon; yes, the three supernatural entities arranged for me a series of very traumatic events when I attempted to return to Ithaca immediately following the ten-year Trojan War."

"How did you manage to piss-off those vindictive deities?" a third listener asked. "You must have a death wish ascending to the tenth power!"

"From plundered Troy, my twelve ships with fifty men rowing on each, were carried by the strong southern wind to Ismarus, land of the bellicose Cicones. My six-hundred warriors raided and destroyed the primitive city, killed many of the fanatical cavemen, seized and screwed their crotch-diseased screaming women, and captured a trove of treasure, which my attentive subordinates eagerly divided-up."

"Then the stories that claim that you Greeks were pirates and looters appear to be absolutely true," a fourth critic yelled. "Why the hell should we trust a plunderer?"

"Don't jump the octopus!" Odysseus sharply countered. "Being democratic, I took great pains in requiring that each soldier should receive an equal share of the booty being distributed. Then, I gave orders that we should speedily leave the accursed land on foot, and fearing retribution from the fickle gods, we evacuated in haste. But my greedy crew was quite foolish. The dumb-shits did not listen to my savvy commands. The stupid fucks drank too much wine, and on the barren, shell-laden shoreline, the zany assholes slaughtered many bleating sheep, as well as wildly shambling the native cows having twisted horns."

"I've heard of these Cicones," King Alcinous interrupted. "Those nasty fucks would eat their own young if hungry!"

"Anyway, the remaining fierce Cicones set-off around their island and gathered-up their nutcase neighbors, barbaric tribesmen living further inland. There were more of those crazed cannibals than there were Cicones, and it is my opinion that the fucked-up cannibals were more awesome and ferocious than were the fucked-up Cicones."

Odysseus ceased speaking for a moment, took a deep breath, and then continued describing his exciting monologue to his captive audience. "As I was about to mention, the dual enemies of wild Cicones and their neighboring wilder cannibals, reached us in the morning, attacking thick as falling leaves, showing-up right near where my' own mother ship had been anchored. One of my more ignorant disciples yelled in defiance at the cannibal aggressors, 'Eat me!' And that's exactly what the hell the hungry, primitive mother-fuckers did. My warriors threw our lethal bronze-tipped spears at the fucked-up cannibals, and the rambunctious idiots began munching and chewing on those weapons, also."

Did you capture any of the perverted cannibals and take them back to Ithaca to be exhibited in a zoo?" King Antinous asked.

"No, dear King. But thank you for disrupting my series of thoughts," Odysseus politely answered with a smile. "While morning lasted, and when that sacred day gained age, we Greeks held our ground and beat the boisterous son-of-a-bitches back into the adjacent forest. But as the sun moved to the hour when oxen are normally unyoked, the very insane, dumb-ass Cicones broke-through our established outer defense perimeter, overpowering a dozen or so valiant Achaeans. Of my well-armed companions, six men from every ship had been killed in the savage melee. The rest of us frantically made our escape, avoiding the dual clutches of invincible Death and Fate."

"How many rowers does one of your boats require?" objectively asked Queen Arete. "Tell us the general name of your twelve warships."

"Two rows of twenty-five on each side," Odysseus informed. "The warship is called a Bireme. My remaining warriors hastily boarded our twelve Biremes and frantically rowed-away from there in a total frenzy. Our hearts were full of grief at losing many of our loyal comrades, though the survivors were happy and thrilled that we had cleverly eluded death ourselves. Cloud-gatherer Zeus then stirred-up the turbulent North Wind to rage against our under-manned dozen vessels."

"How did Zeus get wind of your location?" asked and accidentally punned Alcinous.

"Zeus knows all, and you can't keep any secrets from his omniscience," Odysseus replied. "The cyclonic gusts had produced a howling storm, with its pestering rain and swirls concealing both land and sea. And as darkness swept from heaven down-upon us mariners, every rower aboard my captain's ship was so scared that he emptied his kidneys dry."

"Your story is a real pisser," commended a fifth now-fascinated attendee. "Frankly, I'd be too pooped to pee!"

"Nine days of extremely fierce winds drove our Biremes far away from the charted land of the Cicones, and we floated in the dull doldrums across the fish-filled sea. And on the tenth day, we landed where the infamous Lotus-eaters live. These drug-happy people feed-upon the plant's delicious fruit, which has the ability to put humans into a deep trance, where they refuse to continue their journey, and only wish to stay and eat more Lotus flowers."

"I could use some Lotus flowers right here on Phaeacia," King Alcinous remarked. "I often feel a need to escape reality. Nausicaa is enough to drive me to overdose!"

"Unaware of the flowers' potent drug-addictive properties," Odysseus proceeded with his oration, "we waded ashore and carried fresh water back to our vessels. Then, my companions quickly had a meal by our swift boats, and several began sampling the very palatable Lotus flowers. We laughed and exchanged short stories and tall tales, enjoying our recently confiscated food that had been stolen from the Cicones. But I noticed that the crewmen who had experimented and eaten the Lotus flowers were no longer present amongst our company," Odysseus communicated to the totally fascinated Phaeacians.

"What happened next?" intrigued King Alcinous wanted to know. "Did you establish a chain of apothecaries or drug labs on other islands?"

"No, Idiot King," Odysseus vehemently replied. "I then sent some of my most capable comrades out to glean vital information about the missing crewmen who had eaten the sweet Lotus food, thinking that the flowers were a fine aphrodisiac that allowed the crewmen to get laid among the island's numerous harlots and prostitutes. I carefully chose two of my best sailors to act as spies, and being of a distrustful nature, I sent a third messenger to spy on the initial two spies."

'Three assholes and better than two," a sixth Phaeacian hollered from the rear. "But quite honestly; I'm just happy having two functioning parallel assholes inside my' rear-end!"

"Anyway," Odysseus resumed his bizarre recollection. "The three assholes left at once and soon engaged the Lotus-eaters, but did not marry them. The tribesmen were rather friendly and had no thought of killing my spying companions, but the village witchdoctor gave my dumb-shit spies sample Lotus plant flowers to eat; an exotic fruit, sweet as honey, which made any man who swallowed the seeds lose his desire to ever journey home, or bring back word of the flowers to us, who did not dare venture into the local village. My fucked-up spies were even more fucked-up because the moronic dunces then wished to stay and idly linger there amongst the unmotivated Lotus-eaters, who in fact were immature, idealistic Flower Children, who were uttering absurd jabberwocky such as 'Make love, and not war'!"

"These Flower Children sound like they're more fucked-up than we are!" laughed King Alcinous. "They might have even been naively singing in chorus, 'Give peace a chance'!"

"And so, dear Phaeacians," Odysseus began to summarize. "Feeding on the alluring plant, many of my foolhardy troops were eager to forget all about their homeward voyage to Ithaca; all about their families and kinky whores, and slutty girlfriends."

"Do you have any Lotus flowers for me to sample?" Antinous asked the semi-annoyed speaker. "I need to mentally escape the weight of my heavy government responsibilities, along with my three-hundred-pound lesbian daughter, nauseating Nausicaa."

"No, Dimwit!" Odysseus angrily answered the airheaded King. "Now, please allow me to continue my fantastic story. I, and my undrugged soldiers, forced our companions, the tearful derelict buffoons back onto the awaiting ships, dragged their asses underneath the rowing benches, and tied the frivolous fucks to the different Biremes' oar locks. Then, I issued orders for my other trusty comrades to embark and sail-away as quickly as possible with the utmost speed, in order to facilitate our rapid departure from that rather enticing land."

Chapter 10
"THE CYCLOPS"

"My mariners sailed-away from that dumb-shit island with heavy hearts, and a day's rowing later, our small armada reached the country of the Cyclopes, a totally crude and lawless cabal of ruthless one-eyed giants. The uneducated dumb-fucks don't grow any crops or plants, Lotus, or otherwise, by hand; or plow the Earth, but the tribe of stupid-assholes puts their entire faith and trust in the ever-vacillating, immortal Olympic gods."

"These Cyclopes sound a lot like us!" King Alcinous exclaimed. "There must be dumb-shits all over the world!"

"And although the lackadaisical bastards never sow or work the land, but still, every kind of vegetable and fruit magically springs-up out of the soil for their satisfaction, mostly in the form of wheat and barley, along with rich grape-bearing vines. And Zeus provides the cave-dwellers with sufficient rainfall to enable the various crops to mature and grow all on their own. The isolated tribe lives in rudimentary mountain-top caverns, without any council to make community laws and moral decisions."

"Sounds like Nausicaa belongs on their fucked-up island," Alcinous evaluated and stated. "I suppose that lesbians are taboo there, too!"

"Each of the one-eyed Cyclopes establishes his own family laws for himself, for his own wife, and for his children, and the entire culture, or lack thereof, shuns all civil dealings with each other, and also, ignores all contact with the outside world."

"I've heard of this primitive tribe you're describing!" Alcinous remembered and related. "The story goes that an eye doctor was once unfortunately stranded on that formidable island. The cannibalistic tribe sacrificed his ass to the Rainbow Goddess Iris, just before attaching the doomed physician to a hand-cranked, rotating barbecue rotisserie!"

"Now, King Alcinous, after a week of listless drifting at sea, my crew of 'don't-give-a-shit' sailors arrived at the island of the Cyclopes, giant lawless hermits that lived in virtually inaccessible mountain caves. The Cyclopes were illiterate, and never read about themselves in en*cyclope*dias. The mammoth, one-eyed idiots never planted crops or plowed their fields because the assholes were basically lazy, worthless, and indolent shit-heads. And worst of all, the immortal giants reputedly ate men, but ironically, were not homosexual, but generally celibate, and incidentally, to my knowledge, never ate pussy, either. Although immortal, the race also consumed wild grapes, wheat and barley that grew without any cultivation. That was their basic problem. The Cyclopes lived without cultivation, neither agricultural nor even cultural cultivation. But Lord Poseidon always provided the heinous creatures with ample nectar and ambrosia, conveniently stolen from Mt. Olympus. The Cyclopes voraciously ate the nectar and ambrosia, not knowing what the foods actually do!"

"Humans should keep an eye out for these vicious monsters when voyaging the sea," Alcinous realized and stated. "Perhaps even keep two eyes out would be a better approach!"

"However, in all due respect, King Alcinous, the Cyclopes did learn how to make grape juice, mixing it with semen to have a nice white froth resembling *head* on a cold mug of beer. This outlandish concoction the Cyclopes drank morning, noon and night, so each of the one-eyed monsters always had what looked like a milk mustache showing above his upper lip that in actuality, really was a 'semen cocktail' mustache instead'."

"Inform us more about the Cyclopes civilization, or lack thereof," Queen Arete asked the guest storyteller. "My moronic husband can't understand that if he kept both eyes out for the Cyclops, then my spouse would also be blind!"

"As had been alluded, the Cyclopes had no laws, no councils, no judges or courts, no government, no schools, no Bingo halls, and no legislatures, so in many respects, the ogres were much better off than fucked-up civilized men were. Each Cyclopes was a government unto himself', and the dangerous assholes never helped each other and were often arrogant, antagonistic neighbors. As a result, each Cyclopes had to live a good distance from any others of *his* species; otherwise, the loose society would self-destruct within a year's time. I make no reference to any female Cyclopes, but I have to believe that women existed among that peculiar colony of one-eyed creatures, simply in order to reproduce the idiotic race, evolving from generation to generation."

"What happened when your mother ship landed there?" interrogated a Phaeacian listener. "Did you receive a crazed, hostile reception?"

"Now, I observed that a fertile islet that remarkably wasn't pregnant had been situated about a half-mile from the lawless Cyclopes' Island. I commanded that *my* twelve ships be anchored off that smaller wooded territory, and my guileful mind planned on raiding a cave or two on the larger island to do what we ancient Greeks knew best: pilfer, plunder, pillage, and possibly pedophile little nude, unwary boys and girls."

"Were there any grazing animals to steal?" a second Phaeacian asked. "You suggested that these barbarian Cyclopes had a certain herd mentality."

"Yes; there was a multitude of goats grazing upon the smaller wooded island. The Cyclopes were too stupid to invent or build boats to sail the half-mile distance to bag the wild goats, and the imbeciles were too ignorant to ever attempt to learn how to swim, or even how to wade across the shallow harbor. Fresh water streams abounded on the 'goat island', but the dumb-shit Cyclopes were content living in misery on their less abundant, larger island, and killing and eating their fellow uncivilized cavemen whenever the opportunity presented itself, or whenever the food supply ran short."

"Odysseus; please continue with your very fascinating story," the Phaeacian King instructed. "I'm especially intrigued with gory details involving one-eye monster tales!"

"This looks like a fine island to beach our ships and to search for food and water, I told my second mate, Eurballsourout. We're now safe, as long as there are no fucked-up, hostile human residents dwelling here."

"Don't bother me when I'm trying to flirt-with and feel-up your first mate!" Eurballsourout, the second mate answered me. "Eurshiddenme is really pretty well-endowed!"

"Are you shittin' me?" I challenged Eurballsourout."

"No; my friggin' name is Eurballsourout," the second mate replied. "Eurshiddenme is your goddamned first mate! You oughta' know that common-knowledge bullshit by now!"

"I suppose that when no women are available over the course of many months, men are inclined to become horny homos!" the second alert Phaeacian listener spoke-out to me."

"Now then, most eminent King and Queen. That first morning in the uncharted area, *my crew* and I left the other eleven ships to explore the smaller island for food and water. The troop carried their spears, and bows and arrows, and divided into three *bands* that sang and danced to mediocre Greek folk songs. It was hard labor shooting the wild goats while singing and doing ancient Greek versions of *vaudeville*-type dance routines, so finally my men quieted-down so that the fags were able to stealthily sneak-up upon their intended prey and quickly zap them."

"Altogether, kind King, the hunting expeditions had killed a hundred and eight goats, and then the merry men from all twelve ships feasted, drinking sacks of wine they had stolen from the Cicones, a city of imbeciles *they* had recently marauded and plundered. The Greeks had obtained the 'sacks' of sweet mellow wine when the marauders had thoroughly *sacked* the entire city. Then they 'ran' away. That's how the soldiers had effectively *ransacked* the victimized Cicones' one and only town. But my macho warriors managed to kill most of the village people!"

"From the smaller island, my men could see the campfires glowing inside the Cyclopes' caves, a half-mile distant. I called a military council meeting the next morning to organize a raid on the unsuspecting, dumb-ass Cyclopes, who all didn't care a tiny shit about the outside world, or give a damn if they or anybody else lived, starved, disintegrated or died."

"Stay safe here on this magical island," I had instructed my other eleven crews earlier that morning, before I and *my* vanguard from *my* ship paid a visit to that larger, inhabited land situated over yonder. "I want to determine if the natives are uncivilized savages, or cunning and detestable civilized barbarians like we are."

"Now your story is getting to a climax," a Phaeacian sex pervert in the back remarked. "What happened next?"

"My special bodyguards and I boarded a sleek commando landing vessel, and after loosening the hawser ropes that had been used for mooring the boat, the team clandestinely rowed to the land of the Cyclopes, with visions of committing theft by looting, if random experimental conniving and ordinary trickery failed. After anchoring our landing boat in a remote harbor that was obscured by rocky cliffs, our hit squad of daring attackers furtively climbed-up the steep mountain ridge to an area where we could clearly view an unoccupied cave."

King Alcinous cautioned his councilmen to stop asking preposterous questions, and stated that the idiots should just sit and evaluate Odysseus's spellbinding testimony. "Queen Arete and I will be the only ones allowed to ask questions from here on out," the restless monarch announced. "Now tell us everything your brain recalls from paragraph-to-paragraph!"

"Look at the size of that chair inside that hollow up there!" I lowly marveled to my first mate. "Whatever creature lives there must be as big and as tall as Zeus himself'."

"Yes, Captain," agreed Eurshiddenme, my needed-to-be-castrated first mate. "The monster's dick is probably longer and larger than any of us are tall and wide. The salami on that huge fuck must be a real monstrosity!"

"The cave dweller might not be a human being at all!" Eurballsourout, the second mate, speculated and opined. "He might be half-beast and only part human! The asshole might be even more genetically and mentally fucked-up than we are!"

"Listen men! If you enter into that tall cave, some of you might never see your wives or your children again!"

"The crew-members all looked at each other and shrugged their brawny shoulders. None of them desired to ever want to see their fat ugly wives, or their bratty, parasitic kids ever again, and would gladly die first in a dark cave on an unknown island at the hands of a cruel, indiscriminate brute/monster."

"Listen to this next part, patient Phaeacians. I had selected my twelve 'best men', none of whom were ever in any wedding party, to accompany me the last hundred-feet up to the ominous hollow. The guests' had brought along a goatskin filled with sweet-tasting wine, which had been given to me by Maron, a priest of Apollo, after I had threatened to castrate Maron if *he* did not present a favorable gift of tribute. I often practiced receiving fabulous gifts by intimidation and by extortion."

"Upon reaching the Cyclops cave, the single-eyed monster was not inside, but instead, was out shepherding his hungry flock. My neurotic scouting patrol bravely advanced inside, leaving mounds of wet crap all the way from the entrance to a hundred-feet inside the dreary, dismal cavern."

"Look at those racks loaded with cheese," I whispered. "And the resident of this horrid place has more lambs, hoglets and kids than his pens could ever contain. He must certainly be a very prosperous fellow on this apparently forbidden island!"

"And look," noted Eurballsourout, my second mate. "His pails and bowls are as big as we are, and filled to the brim with milk and whey."

"Get out of my *whey!*" I exclaimed as I stuck my cupped hands into a shoulder-high bowl, and then voraciously drank some of the richly delicious dairy product. *"Whey* to go, Odysseus!" moronic Eurballsourout praised.

"After that trivial verbal exchange, dear King Alcinous, the men then begged me if they could steal some cheeses and a kid each, but I strictly commanded them to just take the cheeses and not get involved in any complicated, felonious, illegal, time-consuming kidnappings."

"Men, we are humble guests in the owner's house," I declared, "so according to *our* customs and tradition, our host should present us with gifts under the Law of the Suppliants. If you recall," I sanctimoniously lectured, "any strangers visiting a person's home while traveling through a distant town or village is to be extended hospitality and generosity. I say we *not* steal the cheeses! Let's wait until the *big cheese* gives us his cheesy cheeses under the protection of almighty Zeus and his Law of the Suppliants."

"I say your logic is really fucked-up," the first mate criticized. "Why should we risk injury, or maybe even death just because *we* honor *our* dumb laws and our fucked-up traditions?" Eurshiddenme adamantly indicated. "I say that this bigger-than-life creature that lives here might not favor us, or honor our asshole laws, gods or traditions!"

"If he's more fucked-up than we are," the second mate emphasized, "then we are undoubtedly in for a very long day, that's for damned sure!" Eurballsourout observed and opined. "Has anyone brought along any knitting needles, yarn and a rocking chair to passively pass the friggin' time away?"

"Now, King Alcinous, in the dark, dank cave my men lit a fire, and then sacrificed some cheeses to the gods before they ravenously ate like blackbirds any of the remaining ones themselves. Some of the soldiers became restless and picked their noses, twiddled their thumbs, squeezed various pimples, and scratched their itchy balls."

"Why do we sacrifice these good cheeses to the gods when we could have stolen them and eaten the pieces ourselves!" the first mate questioned. "Sometimes, we really do some stupid shitty things!" Eurshiddenme perceptively concluded."

"Because, Dip-shit!" I yelled back. "There might really be gods up on *Mt. Olympus* that might be offended if *we* didn't think of *them* first, before considering *our* own selfish, biological needs. And if we start getting our asses kicked by the creature that lives here in this putrid-smelling cave, we might require the emergency services of some supernatural intervention in a fuckin' hurry!"

"But still," the second mate challenged. "If there really aren't any gods on *Mt. Olympus* to be pleased by our offering, then we will have wasted all of that lousy burnt cheese for nothing!" Eurballsourout stubbornly argued. "And besides, what Greek god in his or her right or left mind would ever desire burned cheese that is no longer cheese anyway? You tell me that answer, Captain Asshole! Who the hell wants or needs evaporated or cheesy burnt cheese? A skinny mouse about to die, perhaps?"

"I never thought of that stupid bullshit," I reluctantly admitted. "But who's willing to take the risk if your supposition is wrong? I mean," I philosophically explained. "When's the last time you had one of Zeus's shocking lightning bolts shot-up the center of your smelly, hairy asshole?"

"Great Zeus! I really never thought about such a dreadful consequence!" the second mate exclaimed in a terrified tone of voice. "I don't need to be divinely juiced into reality by that kind of electrifying experience!"

"Merciful King Alcinous," Odysseus proceeded with his lengthy narrative. "An hour later, the horrible Cyclops finally entered his cave, accompanied by an obedient herd of bleating sheep. The monster carried with him a big load of firewood to light near his wooden supper table, still loaded with bowls of whey and slabs of goat meat. The hideous-looking giant flung the heavy timbers onto the ground, and the impact sounded like a wicked clap of thunder, almost scaring the entrails out of the us Greek trespassers' unlucky thirteen rectums."

"Now Phaeacians, the gargantuan Cyclops then used a wooden rod to drive the remainder of his ewes and she-goats inside the cavern, leaving the horny male goats and the rambunctious rams outside to gaily screw one another, rather than penetrate the females of their own species now trapped inside the colossal cave. Then, the ugly fierce behemoth, demonstrating the strength of two-dozen strong, healthy men, rolled a huge stone in front of the cave's entrance, preventing any of the domesticated creatures, along with us Greeks, from escaping to the outside."

"We're trapped inside this freakin' hellhole!" I softly whispered to my frightened crewmembers. "Who says a 'rolling stone' gathers no moss!"

"I think it was the minstrel Mik Jagged that once said *that* weirdo idiomatic expression, and he's the lead singer in a major 'rock' group back in Mycenae!" My first mate aptly replied. "Jagged's quite notorious for inventing silly, meaningless, bull crap aphorisms like *that* hackneyed cliché."

"Quiet Asshole!" I uttered a little too loudly. "Quit farting out of your mouth! That big jerk-off might overhear your zany, nauseous comments!"

"The men's ridiculous conversation echoed throughout the cavern, and soon distracted the Cyclops, who was about to piss a hundred gallons of urine onto a sidewall of the already-stenchy, foul-smelling cave."

"Strangers or Intruders; who is foolishly speaking so loud over there that a deaf person could hear your annoying drivel?" the Cyclops asked in a booming voice. "Are you A) traders, B) rovers, C) soldiers, D) thieves and trespassing pirates, or E), a combination of all of the above?"

"Well, King Alcinous and Queen Arete; we intruders were scared out of our wits until I mustered sufficient courage to address the towering, malicious ogre. "Kind Sir; we are Achaeans returning from the vanquished city of Troy," I proudly began. And Zeus's supreme will has detoured our armada to your beautiful land. We have come in peace!"

"Oh yeah!" bellowed the grotesque one-eyed giant. "You' trespassing dumb-fucks say you have come in peace, but you will soon *not* leave in scattered pieces, after I rip you' puny dirtballs to shreds! Ha, ha, ha, ha!"

"I beg you, Lord," I pleaded with my mouth continuing a little 'bolder' from me, fearfully hiding behind a boulder. "Please show some fear of Zeus's wrath, and demonstrate some respect for the almighty *Olympians*. We have come to your cave as suppliants, under the protection of Zeus, the travelers' god, and the avenger of all foreigners and legal and illegal aliens journeying in distress, while wandering along the world's highways, or sailing upon the high seas!"

"Well, King Alcinous; then the monstrous Cyclops laughed lustily and disrespectfully answered: "Stranger; *you* are certainly an ignorant dolt coming to this land so naively. I fear not your asshole gods, and I mock their impotent vengeance," the monster insisted. "I'm much more potent that any of your timid, weakling gods, and I shall now show my great animosity toward you and your absurd laws and customs," the one-eyed brute boasted. "And if your midget god Zeus were to appear in this cave right now, I would pull-down my animal furs from my torso and then directly shit on *his* pointed head while the feckless bastard is standing erect next to me. Ha, ha, ha, ha!"

"You speak quite haughtily for a fellow who merely lives in a friggin' cave!" I idiotically ridiculed my new-found adversary. "For the amount of advanced culture *you* have developed on this wretched island, you must sleep, shit and jerk-off all day long for how much progress you have achieved since the ancient dawn of mythology!"

"The Cyclops didn't like being harassed and chastised by a mere six-foot-tall man, so the deformed Titan figured he would stall for time so that the giant could capture and kill me, his egocentric, intrepid tormentor. "Tell me brave Intruder," the big bruiser replied. "Where is your ship anchored? Is it around the inlet, or is it moored straight off the land?" the frightening monster asked as *he* began systematically searching and sniffing around, attempting to trace the exact location of the little wise-ass mortal that had been mercilessly berating him."

"Well, Your Highness, King Alcinous. I knew that *I* had to think quickly, but I was too foolish to realize that the Cyclops didn't give two flying turds about anything an Achaean king would say. The reprehensible stalker only wanted to discover the location of my voice's origin, and then exterminate the antagonist's vocal cords, along with any targeted companions that might have recklessly strayed into *his* domain."

"Poseidon, awesome god of the sea, forced my ship to crash upon the rocks at the south end of this miserable, forsaken place," I creatively lied. "And the boat is so severely shipwrecked that neither my friends nor I will ever be able to repair the extensive damage to the hull! Thanks to Zeus's mercy, my crew and I have evaded the jaws of death!"

"The formidable Cyclops stretched his grimy, vile hand into the dismal shadows, his fingers reaching behind a prominent boulder, and the ruthless brute clutched two of my' paranoid, crouching crewmen. The creature easily picked-up the pair of warriors into the air, and then smashed my petrified bodyguards' skulls against the rock-solid floor, splitting-open their craniums with their worm-like brains oozing-out. Then, showing no compassion for human dead, the pagan Cyclops ripped each of the two soldiers' limbs from their torsos, just like pulling the legs off a dead crab, and without even heating the fresh meat inside the crackling fire, the fearsome fiend disgustingly gobbled-up the chewed flesh, and spit-out the bones from the victims' appendages."

'Wow!" bellowed King Alcinous. "This story has plenty of thrilling action adventure! I don't know what I'll involuntarily do next: piss or shit my tunic, or maybe begin writing a really tragic play!"

"The eleven human witnesses to the cave carnage knew not what to do except gasp in horror at the totally despicable, cannibalistic act we had viewed, and solemnly pray for the souls of the dearly-departed, who were now also the dearly-separated and the dearly-consumed."

"Then, King Alcinous and Queen Arete, when the carnivorous Cyclops had filled his tank-like stomach, and after he had washed-down his meal with ten gallons of whey, the creature further exhibited his great disdain for trespassing Greeks. The god-sized barbarian lied-down on the ground in ankle-deep sheep shit, resting among squealing goats, and soon dozed-off like a satisfied bear that had gorged itself' with a winter's supply of fat and protein."

"Well, my royal friends and Phaeacian guests; I was profoundly motivated to grab his five-hundred-pound sword and drive it deeply into the Cyclops' inhuman heart, but then my better judgment considered something rather salient. I understood that I was not strong enough to enact that bitter revenge, even with the help of my petrified warriors. Even if I were successful at killing the evil monster by thrusting *his* sword into his evil heart, then surely *me* and my remaining men would never be capable of moving the enormous stone away from the cave's entrance in order for us to exit. So, I instructed my soldiers to simply sit there all night long thinking 'Fuck! Fuck! Fuck!' a hundred thousand times each until shafts of light filtered through the circumference of the cavern's blocked mouth, signaling that morning had finally arrived."

"I'm really enjoying your bizarre story," King Alcinous's wife, Queen Arete, yelled-out. "Listening to your tale is better than watching a massive, in-progress sex orgy!"

"Well, Queen Arete; the Cyclops arose from his deep slumber and then brushed some of the excessive sheep and goat crap off of his fur clothing, and also from his arms, legs and face. The ruthless villain again ignited his woodpile, milked his ewes and goats, and then remembered that he had human trespassers hiding somewhere within the cave's confined perimeter. The disgusting dick-head gathered-up two more of my personal bodyguards and thrust their heads onto the cavern's rock floor, dashing-out their brains with pints of blood squirting into the air in all directions. Then *he* breakfasted as he had supped, licking his fingers that were coated with layers of human blood and smelly sheep shit."

"He just ate two more of my men!" I panted to my' knee-knocking companions. "He's a lawless fanatic!"

"The giant is too uncivilized to even be a homosexual," Eurshiddenme, my gay first mate regretted, "because the Cyclops just doesn't suck dick. He swallows the man's pecker along with the rest of the victimized person in one tremendous gulp! What a fuckin' pitiful waste of humanity!"

"The primitive brute then rolled the huge circular stone back against the cave's sidewall, allowing his ewes and his goats to venture-out into the sunshine to graze and be screwed by the lustful rams, and any other animals of different species waiting outside. Then, the monstrous hulk adroitly rolled the huge rock back from outside the cave as if the twenty-ton object weighed only twenty-pounds. Finally, my shrewd brain had time to plot a plan to defeat the extremely treacherous, unethical foe."

"Let's slice his balls and dick-off and barbecue them over the fire!" mate number one intelligently recommended. "I haven't sampled Greek meatballs in over twenty years."

"No, Asshole," I emphatically disagreed. "This Cyclops doesn't have any wife or kids, nor does the ugly bachelor bastard want any of those fucked-up headaches. His penis and testicles bring him no natural pleasure except maybe by means of masturbation! Boy, I'd hate to be splattered against this solid rock wall by one of *his* prodigious ejaculations!" I neurotically exclaimed. "I hope that's not a *coming* event!"

"Well then, we could pierce his jugular vein with our spears and have him fuckin' bleed to death!" Eurballsourout, my second mate, smartly suggested."

"No, Jerk-off. That would be too damned messy!" I objectively countered. "The merciless brute might have some unknown, contagious venereal blood disease that might kill us a month from now. And besides," I proceeded and argued. "If *he* moves and we miss the jugular while attacking his neck from both sides, we might accidentally pierce his earlobes, and then the berserk giant might get the idea of wearing two of us as decorative earrings. I can't take *that* chance. And furthermore," my machine-mouth elaborated. "We could never roll that immense stone back and be able to escape from this fuckin' cave. We must decisively punish the gargantuan asshole without killing him!"

"This tome is absolutely great!" King Alcinous complimented. "Please continue."

"I brazenly disclosed a nifty plan to my perceptive subordinates, who wholeheartedly endorsed the proposal after I promised the nine remaining idiots that each one could screw Queen Penelope and munch on her delicious, wet, pink pussy-hole upon their safe return to Ithaca, which *I* naturally believed was quite highly-unlikely to ever really happen."

"The Cyclops kept a great club the size of a ship's mast lying next to one of his sheep pens. I boldly instructed my remaining men to use their swords and cut-off a ten-foot-length of the massive staff, and then carefully shave-down the head until it was shaped into a hard, sharp, wooden point. The beam's tip was soon charred inside the fire as phase one of the 'stake-out' had been satisfactorily completed."

"The mighty Cyclops eventually returned from outside, and after re-entering the dismal cave, again rolled the tremendous stone to effectively block the entrance, keeping us from escaping. The giant next snatched-up two more of my loyal men, and heinously snacked on them just like the horrible animal had done with the other four unfortunate victims."

"That Cyclops must've been one hungry dude just getting off a big weight-loss diet!" King Alcinous commented. "What the fuck happened next? Is it now eye-for-an-eye time?"

"Well," I said to my remaining apprehensive crewmen. "We started-out with unlucky thirteen, and now we've been dwindled-down to a mere lucky seven. Just think men," I eloquently revealed. "This is really to your advantage because now with six men dead, you'll all have more time shafting Queen Penelope, day and night, and chomping on her sumptuous wet pink vagina upon us victoriously returning to Ithaca."

"Boss," said Eurshiddenme, the gay first mate. "We would stand more of a chance of living after drinking a five-gallon jug of hemlock mixed with arsenic than ever having the pleasure of either screwing your beautiful wife, or lapping and buttering-up her moist muffin! And anyway, I would only sodomize Penelope if she's a goddamned practicing lesbian!"

"Showing magnificent, steadfast courage, King Alcinous, soon my aching feet stepped forward with my trembling hands carrying a large bowl filled with the delicious dark wine that the priest of Apollo, Maron, had maron-ated and given me. "Here kind sir," I cleverly offered. "Sip some of this splendid wine I had originally brought to your fine home as a gift, as is the custom of travelers seeking Zeus's protection. My illustrious host; I request that you please drink man's rich beverage to wash-down the taste of man's rich flesh!"

"Well, gathered royal Phaeacians, the heinous Cyclops accepted the bowl and drank-down its fabulous contents, never before tasting wine, because the oversized asshole had never learned how to ferment liquid from grapes and then produce the wonderful substance. "Er, da; that drink tasted very good!" the hideous one-eyed giant conceded. "It tastes much better than grape juice, or even better than pussy juice, I believe. This flavor indeed tastes like the mysterious nectar and the ambrosia that my father Poseidon occasionally provides. I think it is definitely the drink of the gods that will indeed make me even more immortal than I already am!" Cyclops erroneously generalized. "Give me some more, so that I may live beyond all eternity! Ha, ha, ha, ha!" the drunken beast chortled like the demented lunatic that *he* truly was."

"I instinctively filled the huge bowl three more times, and the dumb-fuck Cyclops greedily consumed the fine, smooth-tasting wine, saying that he had never tasted such a wonderful elixir-type laxative. And then, the inebriated ogre asked me outright, "What exactly is your name, oh generous stranger?"

"My damned name is 'No Man'," I wisely answered. "And my mother, father, friends and enemies all address me by that terrific title. I hate my friggin' name with a passion!" I falsely exaggerated. "So Cyclops, watch exactly how you verbally use your smart-assed *No Man*-clature!"

"You're more fucked-up than your fucked-up gods are! Do you know that observable fact, wimpy No Man?" the Cyclops bellowed until the giant nearly started a serious landslide, or a turbulent earthquake outside the cavern. "You're so funny you ought to do standup comedy in an amphitheater without any damned seats! Ha, ha, ha, ha! You should suck a red rooster's red cock, you little cock-sucking dick-licker! Ha! Ha! Ha! Ha!"

"Odysseus, watch what you say to this horrible, ungodly thing!" Eurshiddenme, the first mate cautioned me. "This atrocious creature does not honor any laws and respects nothing that *we* value! Not even pussy or homosexuality!"

"That's right!" Eurballsourout, the second mate concurred with Eurshiddenme. "This big lummox respects 'no man', either gay or fuckin' straight!"

"That's precisely my goal," I honestly replied. "This big, oversized jerk-off is gonna' learn to respect No Man!"

"Then next, oh King Alcinous; the cruel fifty-foot-tall oaf' temporarily cleared his groggy head and declared: "I'll eat all of No Man's comrades first, and then save *his* tender skin and tiny dick for last. This is the gift I shall give to No Man in exchange for this savory wine from your fucked-up priest's vine! This juice is for Zeus!" the crazy pea-brain laughed and rhymed, as *he* held his half-full bowl up toward the cave's curved ceiling."

"Well, Queen Arete and noble husband. After the repugnant giant bragged and again sarcastically mocked Zeus, my chief deity, the intoxicated Cyclops tumbled-onto, and then sprawled-upon the cave's dirt floor, stoned out of his mind, which indeed was a very mini-mind in proportion to the enormity of *his* total anatomy. The drunken monster became quite animated, and then while lying there, soon belched-up a gallon of wine along with the semi-digested flesh of his last two consumed humans. He next spit the essence of his guts to the posterior area of the mammoth cavern, and the horrible debris splattered onto the faces of the seven remaining Greek survivors."

"I hope he barfs his intestines out and then goes into a deep sleep," I told my loyal men as the not-from-Crete cretin wiped the repulsive vomit from his arms and from his cheeks. "This uncouth Cyclops is gonna' pay for his insolence to our values, and for his defiance of our gods, I insisted!"

"How's he gonna' pay?" Eurshiddenme challenged. "They ain't got no friggin' money system on this freakin' freak show island of demented freaks!"

"I meant that the Cyclops is gonna' be punished for committin' cannibalism and for doing sacrilegious things in excess. Hubris will sentence this impudent, fat, barbaric asshole to a deserving fate," I bluntly asserted."

"This over-inflated shit-head thinks he's a god, so let's smash him with the stake right in his fuckin' *temple!*" Eurballsourout candidly suggested.

"No, Eurballsourout!" I strongly objected. "I have a much better idea to implement!"

"Well, King Alcinous, after the Cyclops finally stopped vomiting all over the damned place in his deep sleep, myself and the remaining crewmen lifted the wooden beam that we had hidden under three-foot-deep sheep and goat dung. The remaining intruders and me, their itinerant captain, again heated the charred tip inside the blazing fire, and after rotating the pole for a full ten-minutes, until the searing beam sizzled inside the roaring flames; then, inspired by Pallas Athene, the enraged entourage ran forward and violently thrust the red-hot spike directly into the center of the Cyclops' single eye!"

"Take that, Shit-head, since you think you are such hot stuff!" Eurshiddenme yelled at his avowed enemy."

"Now, your eye will be a real eyesore!" Eurballsourout frankly added insult to injury."

"The center of your eye has now become one of my *pupils!*" my tongue and throat gleefully shouted. "Now you can't keep an eye out for us any more, you dumb bastard!"

"Yowlllllllll! Owwwww!" the enraged Cyclops thundered as the brute was rudely awakened from his drunken slumber. "Hey; I can't see a goddamned fuckin' thing! What's this odd hissing sound coming from inside my eye?" The retard hideously screamed, as the giant twisted and then yanked the sizzling, flaming timber from the center of his scorched and blinded eye."

"Other Cyclopes in the vicinity heard the noisy racket and were curious what the source of the clamor might be. Three of them gathered outside the cave and yelled inside to their awesome, bellicose neighbor."

"What is the matter Polyphemus? What is bothering you? Did you accidentally ejaculate a ten-pound load backwards into your balls, or what?" a somewhat concerned Cyclopes yelled inside the still-closed cave entrance."

"Polyphemus, what has happened? Did you accidentally crush your dick on a rock while slamming-down your enormous sledgehammer?" a second inquisitive giant hypothesized and hollered inside."

"The still-delirious and drunken Polyphemus boisterously shouted from the cave's interior: "No Man is killing me! No Man has fuckin' killed me!"

"Surely Polyphemus, no man is capable of killing a fearsome giant like you," a surprised and amused neighbor replied from outside. "You must be hallucinating. *No man* has the strength or the force to do you any significant harm!"

"Listen fuck-heads. I need your goddamned help!" the wounded and distraught blind giant vehemently answered. "I tell you, neighbors. No Man has attacked and blinded me! No Man has fuckin' attacked and blinded me!"

"Well then, Polyphemus; if no man has attacked or blinded you," the first mountain cave resident concluded, "then what the fuck are ya' complainin' about? Stop annoying us with such bad, illogical, nonsensical riddles! Everyone knows that one puny man can't assault and blind a fifty-foot-tall jerk-off like you! It's just not fuckin' plausible!" the amused Cyclopes neighbor chided. "Just fondle and flog your log, pop a big load, and go the hell back to sleep! See ya' tomorrow, ya' big pouting crybaby!"

"No! Stop! Listen to me!" Polyphemus screamed and shrieked like a berserk maniac. "No Man has blinded me! Do you hear me? No Man has fuckin' blinded me!"

"Why don't you do something constructive like committing suicide!" a third voice remarked from the cave's exterior. "Goodbye Polyphemus; you dumb, melodramatic, thespian fuck! You can't stage a comeback! Ha, ha, ha!"

"Good stuff!" King Alcinous commended. "Please get to the big climax without squirting nasty sperm juice all over my face!"

"Well King, my remaining men laughed incessantly at the blinded Cyclops's very apparent frustration. The clumsy, injured giant sat with his back leaning against the rock wall, regretting that he had been born with only one eye in the center of his head, and now was blinded for the rest of his accursed tenure on our ass-backwards planet. But, as you already know, my stellar reputation has been renowned for inventing clever solutions to difficult dilemmas, and I still had to devise a viable method of escaping the cave and its blocked entrance."

"It was now daybreak, and time for Polyphemus to rotate the incredibly huge stone and allow his ewes and goats to leave the cavern to graze, to screw, and to shit in the sunshine. The big, hulking, blinded bully sat at the cave's entrance and felt in front, on top, and in between the evacuating animals to ascertain that 'No Man' escaped *his* intensive feeling. My eyes keenly scrutinized the blind giant's careful practice, and my creative brain planned a stratagem to counteract the wounded creep's predictable habit of search and seizure."

"Dear King and Queen; my head pondered and meditated, knowing full-well that a poor decision would cost me my life along with the lives of my remaining bodyguards. Quite ingeniously, the following morning, my keen vision found some leather straps, and I tethered together teams of large sheep in groups of three. Each of the anxious warriors crawled under the body of the center sheep and fastened his legs inside the straps, holding on to the middle animal's fleece with *his* bare hands."

"The hungry, healthy sheep rapidly rushed-out into the sunshine to feed. The vengeful Cyclops meticulously felt the fronts, sides and tops of each set of three sheep passing-by his tactile inspection, but not once ever suspecting that the conniving Greeks had escaped the cave under the belly of the center sheep in the groups of three that passed by."

"As my set of three sheep finally made it to the cave's entrance, the Cyclops reached-down, felt the top of the center animal and declared, "My favorite, most-treasured sheep. Why are you last to leave today? You are usually the leader, the proudest of my flock!"

"Well, dear Phaeacians, my heart was pounding so loudly inside my chest that I feared that the blind Cyclops might detect the abnormally distinct, loud beating. Right when I, being extremely petrified, started pissing myself', the Cyclops delivered some additional sentimental monologue."

"I know kind and faithful animal," the horrible monster verbally proceeded, speaking to his favorite sheep. "You must feel badly because you sense that your master can no longer see. No Man has blinded me, and I must make retribution and kill the dirty son-of-a-bitchin' scumbag. I know that if you could talk, you' pathetic beast," the Cyclops affectionately stated. "You would tell me exactly where my cunning adversary is hiding. I would crush his bones with my bare hands; then collide his head with the walls, and next impact his skull with the solid rock floor, spilling his brains all over the fuckin' cave until there is not an ounce of blood left in his petty, rotten, human arteries!"

"When I finally escaped the cave, I carefully freed myself from the underneath straps, and then assisted my men in being un-tethered from the center sheep in each set of three animals tied together. And with the attitude of genuine plunderers, we ecstatic Greeks led the sheep and goats in a bizarre parade down to the anchored ship, where the remaining crewmen accepted the pilfered animals aboard."

"This is an astounding tale that you've depicted," praised King Alcinous. "Please advance to the conclusion."

"Then, Your Highness; I told my well-disciplined commandos not to weep for their deceased comrades, for their cries of mourning might be discerned by Cyclops's sensitive auditory perception. I still feared that the horrendous freak might be capable of doing significant damage to my ship, despite Polyphemus's most recent blindness handicap."

"When the vessel lifted anchor and quietly sailed a hundred-yards out into the clear-blue harbor, my throat and mouth garnered enough courage to spitefully and scornfully address my blinded enemy. "Cyclops!" I haughtily yelled-up at the top of my lungs. "You have sinned against omnipotent Zeus and against the sacred laws of *Mt. Olympus.* You have rightfully been punished for the evils that you have egregiously committed, and you suffer for the outrageous disrespect you have demonstrated toward guests in your land, and toward *their* gods and customs!"

"The furious giant lividly grabbed hold of a nearby mountain crag and flung the heavy object in the direction from which he believed my explicit taunting had originated. The Cyclops's heave landed and splashed in the shallow harbor, and came within a breadth's length of destroying the ship's stern. An enormous wave surged, and then propelled the vessel back near the island's desolate beach. I tacitly signaled to my crew to row and not to speak or yell, for then I dreaded that the desperate avenger would become even more provoked, and manage to get lucky with another mountain peak toss, and successfully sink the Bireme with a broadside hit."

"That idiot almost demolished my ship and murdered my crew!" I realized and admitted. "I'm glad we had blinded the savage bastard, and I'm also happy that it is now time to relish the taste of sweet revenge!"

"The oversized asshole has thrown one boulder already and has driven us all the way back to the friggin' shore line," Eurshiddenme accurately protested. "So please, Captain; don't antagonize him any more until we are outside his throwing range!" the first mate implored his sometimes all-too-arrogant captain."

"I hope I will be still-born in my next life because I never want to experience any more fucked-up misadventures like this one!" Eurballsourout told Eurshiddenme and me."

"Cyclops!" I stubbornly bellowed and challenged when the vessel was officially three-hundred-yards or so out into the harbor. "If anyone asks you who had taken your eye out and blinded you, tell that asshole that it was Odysseus, King of Ithaca, son of Laertes!"

"The Cyclops then recalled the essence of an old prophecy told to him by the soothsayer Telemus, son of Eurymus, who had predicted that a man named Odysseus would handily blind the despicable bastard during a major dispute. But Polyphemus was expecting to confront a hundred-foot-tall *Adonis* kicking *his* big fat ass on *his* own turf, and not a little runt like me, the Ithacan King getting the job done under the alias of No Man."

"Come back Odysseus," the Cyclops hollered-out to the deaf sea, "so that I, the son of the vengeful sea god Poseidon, can give you gifts to take back to Ithaca. Come back, and I shall treat you like the royalty you really are!"

"Go fuck yourself', you' big cock-sucking asshole!" I defiantly screamed as loud as I could. "Do you think me half as stupid as yourself! You are just as blind to truth as you are to sight, you dumb, no-eyed fuck!"

"Then, vengeful Polyphemus cupped his hands to his mouth and grievously shouted skyward. "Oh, great Poseidon; hear my plea! If I am indeed your son as everyone on this fucked-up island claims that I am, see to it that Odysseus's shipmates never make it back to Ithaca alive! Let all of his scumbag mariners perish, and let Odysseus return home as a passenger in a foreign ship and discover his house in disarray, and later finds his wife pregnant with another man's triplets!"

"Poseidon heard his distraught son's vile plea, and so the rambunctious sea god yelled-back to his begotten son, "You stupid shit! I am the god of the sea, and I rule all the oceans from underwater with my trident as my royal scepter! Why are you praying up to heaven when that is Zeus's fuckin' domain!" the sea god loudly reprimanded his orphaned offspring. "Now, I know why I no longer visit you and your shit-eating Cyclopes' friends anymore! What a fuckin' waste you', they, and your whole asshole island are! Your land ought to sink into the friggin' sea and be swallowed-up in its eddying maelstrom!"

"Well, men," I announced to my crew of hardy rowers. "Poseidon has now disowned his own blinded son, but the fickle god has promised to kick our vulnerable asses good in future episodes and adventures."

"We're all going to die because of your insolent aggressiveness, and because of your inflexible impudence," Eurballsourout complained to me, his noble-but-imprudent king. "And if we never had sailed to that forbidden island behind us, we would not now be cursed and abused by the ruthless sea-god, nor would we have lost our colleagues to that terrible, blind, sore-loser monster, pouting and whimpering up there!"

"You're absolutely right," Eurshiddenme readily agreed with Eurballsourout. "And Captain; thanks for earning us *our* forthcoming execution from Poseidon as retribution for blinding *his* damned ugly freak of a son. And as for you," Eurshiddenme continued. "My King; your punishment will be the greatest of all! You will have to live for at least twenty more years in Ithaca after both Eurballsourout and I are fuckin' luckily dead and gone. Our spirits will be resting in the Elysian daffodil fields planted in the good sector of *Hades,* while you're still alive trying to fuckin' govern your majorly screwed-up kingdom."

"You're absolutely right, Eurshiddenme," my raspy voice glumly acknowledged. "For I am the one who is really cursed at sea, and later fated to be doomed in Ithaca by having to live through the bulk of Poseidon's wicked wrath!"

"Fabulous story; Bravo brave Odysseus," King Alcinous stated. "Admirable tale! Now I definitely believe that you are indeed the legendary hero of the Trojan War, who is rightfully celebrated and heralded throughout the known world!"

Jay Dubya

Chapter 11

"AEOLUS"

"We next sailed and reached Aeolia, a fucked-up, floating island, where the nature-wizard Aeolus lived, who was the son of Hippotas, whom immortal gods inexplicably hold dear. Around the airborne mass runs an impenetrable bronze wall, and towering cliffs rise-up in a sheer facade of solid rock. Aeolus's twelve children live there in a crystal palace, six talkative daughters as well as six full-grown, blowhard sons. Aeolus, who preferred incest to regular marital tradition, gave the six daughters to the six zealous sons in marriage, and the empty-headed freaks-of-nature are always enjoying gluttony at outrageous and garish banquet feasts."

"Now King Alcinous and Queen Arete. my small fleet reached the splendid palace, and for one whole month, the blow-hard windbag Aeolus entertained me, always asking immaterial questions about every existing academic topic: about Troy; about our Greek Argive ships, and about the great expedition returning back to Greece. I described in detail the entire sequence of events from start to finish. When, for my part, I asked to take my leave and told the pseudo-intellectual Aeolus to send me on my damned way, the flamboyant fuck-head surprisingly denied me nothing and actually helped me get my ass out of there."

"Please review your full visit with Aeolus," Alcinous requested. "I promise that you'll be able to depict your gripping tale with only minor interruptions about certain nuances."

"Well King, the avid prankster gave me a bag made out of thick ox-hide, dense skin flayed from a corpulent plow animal nine years old. And wily Aeolus tied-up the odd gift with ultra-thick hemp. The sealed bag contained all the winds that blow in all directions from every conceivable hemisphere and latitude, for the son of Cronos had made the disreputable clown Aeolus the official Keeper of the Winds, and the dumb-shit could calm or rouse the seasonal elements with real gusto, as his silly, juvenile whims wished."

"Now, listen to this, you Phaeacians. With a bright silver cord, the notorious jester, as a gesture of friend*ship*, tightly lashed that seemingly innocuous bag inside my hollow ship's hull, so as to stop even the smallest breath or breeze from escaping that one-of-a-kind air-tight goatskin container. After receiving the unique windbag from the hoary windbag, my accommodating host provided my twelve ships with a bland West Wind to carry my victorious, stout soldiers on our merry way home to nearby neighboring Ithaca."

"What happened next?" Alcinous asked. "Did you take a crash course in meteorology? Did the goatskin bag look anything like your old bag mother-in-law?"

"For nine consecutive sunny days and cloudless nights, our pilots steered our smooth sailing course, and on the tenth, we all cheered as we glimpsed sight of our native land. Our victorious fleet came in so close to the distant coast that our eyes could see the conscientious workmen who assiduously tend the beacon fires on the shoreline. But then, much to my detriment, sweet Sleep overcame my body and mind, both of which mutually surrendered to incredible exhaustion. All that time, my reliable hands had gripped my lead ship's sail rope."

"Honestly, dear King and Queen; I'd not let go of the gift, or pass the bag on to any muscular shipmate. I didn't want to gamble on him, or any other stressed-out colleague, falling fast asleep before my reputable vigilance would, so that we'd get home more quickly."

"Were Eurshiddenme and Eurballsourout still with you?" Queen Arete wanted to know. "I think that you should've donated the useless services of those two pecker-heads to that weirdo Aeolis."

"I'll get to those two incompetent ninnies soon enough. During my lengthy boredom, and while I was feigning sleep, I deftly eavesdropped on a nearby private conversation. "It's not fair. Everyone adores and honors our ambitious King, no matter where the hell he goes, to any city, barn, or garbage dump," Eurshiddenme softly mentioned in a whisper to equally fucked-up Eurballsourout. "The scuttlebutt circulating on board is that avaricious Odysseus is presently transporting a colossal stash of gold and silver loot, but those of us who've been passengers on the same trip to and from Troy are coming home with empty hands and empty wallets," Eurballsourout answered and then added. "And next, the mutinous conniver stated to his potential colleague-in-mischief the following nonsense: "That impractical joker Aeolus, because he's a valued friend of our money-hungry Captain, I understand that the aged windbag has willfully presented our ignoble monarch with other extravagant gifts as well. Come on, comrade; let's see how much gold and silver Odysseus has stored in yonder bag."

"Now, patient audience; as the jealous subordinates talked like this in confidential tones, in the final analysis, my companions' envious thoughts prevailed. The hateful pair used sharp-bladed knives and managed, after great effort, to untie and open the strongly-knotted bag. All Hades broke loose as the incarcerated winds rushed-out in unrivaled turbulence. Wicked torrential storm gusts seized the mutinous assholes, swept their rebellious torsos off the deck and out to sea, catapulting their mutinous anatomies far away from our temporarily visible native land."

"That's what happens when subordinates go overboard with pursuing their strange ideas," Alcinous inadvertently punned. "Their excessive greed just blew them away!"

"At *that* pivotal point, I instantly woke-up from my deleterious trance. Deep inside my pulsating heart, I was of two alternative minds: I either could jump overboard and drown in the swirling currents, or I could just keep striving to simply exist in unproductive silence, while regrettably remaining among the still-breathing; and while suffering *that* lousy fate, I felt that I was being manipulated like a dumb-ass marionette by the dual adversaries of Poseidon and Zeus. I stayed there onboard and persevered, contemplating the magnitude of my mammoth ordeal. Covering-up my tormented head, I just lay there upon the drenched deck, while our battered twelve ships, loaded with my thousands of jealous, whimpering companions, were driven by those wicked wind blasts and blown all the way back to Aeolus's fucked-up island."

"I see," commented Queen Arete. "Your stormy departure from Aeolus wasn't exactly a breeze. What occurred next?"

"In immense frustration, I disembarked and set-off for Aeolus's splendid home, and my search found the laughing ignoramus feasting like a famished caveman with his dominant wife and obnoxious children also snorting and guffawing. So, I angrily entered the well-constructed estate and sat-down at the threshold, right beside the thick doorposts. In his underdeveloped heart, the weather-control freak was seemingly amazed at recognizing my surprise reappearance. Feigning sincerity, the satirical shit-head busted my balls and asked me:

"Odysseus; why have you returned to my generous hospitality? Can't you live without enjoying my amusing company? I took great care in sending you on your way so that you'd arrive safely back to Ithaca; yes, if I vividly recall, back to your elusive native land."

"That non-digestible, fake horse manure is what the comic jerk-off articulated. Pissed-off to the hilt with a heavy heart and clenched fists, I impolitely answered the dick-head."

"My foolish and about-to-be-pummeled phony comrade; your non-funny antics and semantics, aided by your nefarious ally, malicious Sleep, have greatly harmed my public reputation throughout the civilized and uncivilized world, and I'll be perpetually maligned and ridiculed by goofball bards, poets, politicians, along with numerous cornball philosophers, especially in every part of Mother Greece."

"I'll bet that your serious threats scared the humorous funny-bone right out of the old windbag's arms," laughed Alcinous. "You were going to beat the shit out of the bad humor man."

"But Aeolus," I uttered with a frown. "I'll give you one more chance before I kill you and send your unfunny, black spirit across the River Styx, where the cheerless Charon will take you to see Hades in his dark Kingdom of the Dead. Now then; you must immediately repair the damage that's mocked and insulted me among my talkative shipmates, and I believe that *that* ability is indeed within your air-supply power. If you do not comply with my urgent demand, I'll persist in violently strangling your skinny throat and neck until shit and piss come out of your mouth and nostrils instead of un-comical words, bad breath, and stinking exhaled air!"

"Then, I mercifully released my lethal grip around his seven gulping throats, and after the zany fuck-head choked incessantly for five-minutes, I allowed the trickster another five-minute-period for the professional buffoon to gasp and rectify my faltering reputation among my crewmen."

"So, you administered to Aeolus a rather breathtaking experience," chuckled King Alcinous. "Your bold threat apparently sucked all of the oxygen out of the room!"

"Oh, dear friend, Odysseus," the droll nutcase prefaced. "Of all living mortals, you are the worst example of humility and modesty upon Mother Earth, and your obdurate demeanor is despised and resented by both Poseidon and Zeus, whom you always try mocking and imitating. So, Mr. Hot Shit! You must with dispatch leave this enchanted island with the utmost of speed, and evacuate as if your erratic rectum and testicles are shooting-out poisonous volcanic lava and toxic hyperactive lightning. It would violate all sense of what is morally right if I helped-out, or guided on his way a man of your low-caliber ilk that the blessed gods must absolutely loathe. So, Odysseus, I austerely advise that you promptly leave my luxurious estate before I eliminate your ass from human existence with a powerful northern snow blizzard, along with a series of incredible avalanches, immediately followed by an unearthly blowjob administered by

Medusa the Gorgon, who will then turn you dick, epididymis and balls into solid stone."

"Look here, Aeolis, you A-holeis!" I madly exclaimed. "Just summarize what the fuck you really mean! I don't like the general atmosphere prevalent in this fucked-up dining room!"

"In a nutshell, Odysseus; you're futilely debating with me this minute issue back here in peaceful Aeolia because the deathless gods absolutely despise your trite, human, smelly ass for maliciously blinding Polyphemus, son of Poseidon."

"Well, Aeolis; just remember that my sailors have gotten wind of what the hell you've done, and if we are blown-back here one more time, I will personally cause you, you old-fart windbag, your old bag wife, and your dirtbag kids to all be viciously slain and brutally beheaded."

"Then, King Alcinous and Queen Arete, with me being sick at heart, my ships sailed on further, but my rebellious oarsmen on all twelve Biremes were perturbed, weary and worn-down from so much futile rowing, since I had lost many of my mariners to the animalistic cannibals on the isle of the Cicones. Because we'd been such preposterous fools after leaving Troy, there was no breeze evident to facilitate our swift return to Ithaca. Our Biremes kept going in circles for six whole days and nights, operating against Fate, whose mind was in allegiance with both Poseidon and Zeus. But me still being in favor with Athena, and possibly also with Zeus's wife Hera, that vague hope gave my faltering heart moral conviction to persevere and continue onward on my very unenviable odyssey back home."

Chapter 12

"THE LAESTRYGONIANS"

"On the seventh auspicious day at sea, we came to Telepylus, great citadel of mythological Lamus, the important-but-retarded lame King of the Laestrygonians, who as a society, didn't know how to either spell or pronounce the name of their fucked-up people, nor did the illiterate shits care one iota, or give a tiny scintilla of a fuck about learning anything academic. After slowly drifting into a picturesque harbor, featuring sheer high cliffs on both sides, and jutting headlands, all facing one another, extending-out past the seemingly tranquil-but-empty channel. However, the narrow, shallow entrance to the empty dock was quite small and hazardous."

"Sounds like a picturesque paradise for a thriving honeymoon resort?" King Alcinous prematurely noted.

"Dear King; on the contrary; that fucked-up place would be my last resort. The dunces that lived there hadn't yet learned how the wipe their diarrhea asses. All my eleven other Bireme captains brought their curved ships up and moored them as if my inexperienced navigators were trained professional merchant marine pilots. Much to my amazement, everything appeared calm and bright around the scenic vista, despite the apparent evidence of no human activity. But for honoring some alien instinct, I anchored my black Bireme all by itself just outside the haunting harbor, and I had my skeptical crew-members tie and secure my abused warship right against the distant forest land, tethering the battered vessel to a colossal boulder. I climbed the nearest steep cliff on my chaffed knees and just stood there, gazing-about on a rugged outcrop, assessing the general environment, while perceptively looking around, wishing that I owned four eyes. But my poor vision observed no particular evidence of human labor, or any sign of agricultural earth plowing, and my impaired pupils perceived only random puffs of smoke rising and wafting upwards from the distant hills, which at that moment in time, made my weak spirit fume."

"Being somewhat worried, King Alcinous, I assigned and sent four of my intoxicated comrades to learn what the indigenous inhabitants were like. The neurotic scouts left the ship's safety and soon arrived at a smooth road, where wagons were apparently used to haul wood to the town from the prevailing high mountain slopes.”

“Outside the antiquated city’s gates, the dispatched surveillance contingent encountered a young girl collecting water, a noble daughter of Antiphates, a rather senile asshole Laestrygonian. My vanguard captain asked the preoccupied, disinterested young hussy who ruled the native people, and who the hell the residents were.”

“The deaf and dumb, twelve-foot-tall, pre-pubescent future whore, who probably was incapable of screaming-out wonderful cries of pleasure while bring raped by a maniac pedophile during sexual intercourse, quickly pointed out her father’s secluded home. My reconnaissance explorers carefully advanced and reached the ramshackle, oversized shanty, and found the hoary gent’s whoring wife, who looked more-than-likely to be an immense, mute woman wrestler as her sole occupation, and the wretched, abominable bitch was as humongous as an obese mountain peak, too big for even Polyphemus to throw at me.”

“Kind of makes me glad I live in somnolent Phaeacia,” Alcinous evaluated and concluded. “But we have more than our share of imbeciles wandering around, talking trash, ambling-around in our garbage-strewn streets and alleys!”

“Naturally, my scouting party was horrified and frightened by the twenty-foot-tall woman, who claimed that she was a mere midget on the island. The wife called her husband, strong and primitive Antiphates, who was attending a cantankerous government assembly, and the forty-foot-tall meathead quickly arranged a dreadful death sentence for all of my designated spies.”

“The horrendous-looking monster, displayed shark-like jagged teeth, and the hideous creep viciously seized one of my most-trustful shipmates and prepared to make a meal of him in gross imitation of the lawless Cyclops. The other three trekkers from my ship jumped-up, ran-off through the nearby forest, and frantically scampered back to my anchored vessel. The leader of the group sprinted fast because the other three spies were only dashing young men. Antiphates then raised a huge nerve-shattering cry that loudly reverberated throughout the seemingly abandoned city.”

“Your three soldiers were lucky to escape the ogre’s greedy clutches,” Lord Alcinous determined and declared. “You would think that Lord Zeus would cruelly punish that brazen violator for not honoring the sacred Law of the Suppliants.”

"Once the few idiots with decent auditory perception heard his ear-shattering call, the mighty Laestrygonian giants poured-out from all conceivable directions, thronging and shricking indiscernible syllables in countless numbers, and the only recognizable utterance emanating from their enraged lips was the one-syllable expletive 'Fuck'!"

"I suppose that their simple language communications contained more colloquial vocabulary terms than standard civil vernacular nomenclature," eggheaded Alcinous theorized and commented. "But sometimes, the more words existing in your language, the more stupid everyone sounds!"

"Well, Your Imperial Highness; from high cliffs above the harbor, the lunatic barbarians hurled a flurry of thousand-pound boulders down upon us. The clamor originating from the anchored ships was dreadful. My soldiers were being destroyed, and my other vessels in the fleet were smashing into one another, with those huge imposing monsters spearing my men as if they were helpless fish, and in the process, capturing and stealing new gruesome meals for the giants to consume."

"Naturally, those brave soldiers who remained at my side, attempting to shield their heads and testicles from the tremendous onslaught, all blamed me for being the cause of that disaster, and every other earlier debacle that had occurred."

"Ungrateful, rebellious fools!" Queen Arete decided and said to Odysseus and her husband. "You can't make chicken salad out of chicken shit, that's for damned sure!"

"While the determined and inhuman behemoths were slaughtering the bulk of my besieged sailors, who were trapped and being brutalized in that deep, narrow harbor, I grabbed my sword, pulled it from my thigh's scabbard, and cut the cables on my isolated, dark-prow ship, yelling and ordering to my crew, "Let's get the fuck out of here while we still have a smidgeon of time left to hurriedly get the fuck out of here!"

"The petrified and almost-paralyzed rowers hustled to their separate stations, sat-down quickly like they all had emergency cases of vertigo, and their powerful oars churned the passive water with their hued blades, with everyone aboard excessively afraid of being mauled, maimed, mangled and mutilated. My soul was somewhat-relieved as my ship left the raucous giants, all angrily clamoring atop the high cliffs above, as we thankfully were moving swiftly out to sea. But I was immensely grieving when my brain realized that the other eleven ships, along with their' crews, had been stranded in the perilous harbor, and all had been totally destroyed. My vessel, carrying the remnants of my seditious crew, was the sole Bireme to fortunately escape and survive that rather fucked-up, totally atrocious catastrophe."

Chapter 13
"CIRCE"

Lord Odysseus recited the following comprehensive account to King Alcinous, to Queen Arete and to the spellbound Phaeacian committee, who agreed to allow the Ithacan King to speak without the general assembly asking any further idiotic questions.

"Our remaining ship sailed-away from the assaulting giants, weighing-in with heavy hearts about the great loss of blood and treasure, until our sole Bireme reached the island of Aeaea, home of that dreaded goddess, fair-haired, thick-bushed, magical witch Circe, whom I suspected had brought our only ship, out of twelve, safely to land inside the harbor, which incidentally provided fine anchorage. Some benign god, I speculate that it had been Athena, was guiding us through a perilous ebb tide, and when I find-out who the hell rendered us assistance, I'll pay appropriate homage. Weary and recuperating from our recent wounds and injuries, my warriors disembarked and laid-up in that spot for two days and nights."

"As soon as rose-fingered early Dawn appeared, I quickly organized a meeting and addressed my low-spirited, shabby crew: "Shipmates; let's quickly put our tanned heads together without using glue to see if there's some practical scheme that our inferior brainstorming can devise about obtaining adequate food and shelter."

"I meticulously climbed a rocky crag, which was always my favorite hobby, and from that vantage point scoped-out the verdant landscape. Aeaea was an island with dark blue water surrounding its circumference, and featuring gentle, shallow, aqua-blue water next to the sandy beach."

"The semi-tropical terrain appeared to be low-lying and flat. Through the dense brush and tangled jungle vegetation, I did see some smoke rising in the middle of the island, and that observation prompted me to regretfully remember the fucked-up smoke being emitted from chimneys in the land of the fucked-up maniac giants."

"I considered and evaluated my new environment. Rising smoke meant some sort of human activity, and since this was not a desert setting, the thick vegetation indicated that the island received ample rainfall. I also surmised that there must have been a good variety of fruits and vegetables growing in abundance, but then, I wondered if the resident inhabitants were gay or mental retards."

"That's exactly what I soon stated to my ship's restive sailors, who were pissed-off at me for being responsible for so many deaths and general loss of treasure. But their spirits fell into a greater deep-dive emotional abyss when the aggregate of paranoid idiots remembered what the delirious Laestrygonian king had done to our other eleven Biremes and their now-dead shipmates; not to fully mention the loss of some key warriors at the hands of the mighty brute Polyphemus, that man-eating, blinded, uncivilized, loud-farting, fucked-up Cyclops."

"I split-up my well-armed comrades into two separate groups, each with its own leader. I commanded the first platoon, and godlike Eurylochus I had assigned to lead the second squad."

"When brave Eurylochus's lot fell-out, the scholarly graduate of the Ithaca Military Academy set-off with twenty-two anti-Odysseus companions, all in tears because of my questionable leadership and faulty decision-making, leaving the rest of us behind to grieve about my questionable leadership and my faulty decision-making ever since my battleships had left Troy."

"In an open forest clearing, Eurylochus and his surveillance team found Circe's dwelling of polished stone, an edifice having fabulous views in all four directions. There were mountain wolves and lions roaming around the property, but I suspected that the carnivorous predators had all been bewitched by Circe's wicked pharmaceutical potions. But the ordinarily dangerous animals made no expected attacks against my second squad of encroaching warriors."

"The creatures stood-up upon their hind legs and fawned like domesticated puppies, aggressively wagging their long tails in seeking to be lovingly petted. Just as dogs will beg for scraps and morsels while desiring attention and approval around their master's feet, especially after the pet's owner arrives home from a barbecue feast, that's how the docile wolves and sharp-clawed lions kept purring around my alarmed fellow Greek intruders, who were positively terrified just gazing in astonishment at those rather peculiar-but-tame beasts."

"My suspicious comrades stood-by fair-haired Circe's gate and heard her sweet voice singing about having sex with all of them inside her outhouse crapola, as the entrancing witch spun a pastel fabric back and forth upon her rotating loom, weaving a huge, immortal tapestry, which was the sort of artistic material that gifted Olympian goddesses, along with Queen

Penelope would imagine and create. Circe's intricate pattern-design appeared to be finely woven, quite luminous, and most-beautiful in terms of quality."

"My discourteous exploratory personnel started critically shouting-out, calling the alluring witch 'Bitch', 'Whore', 'Harlot' and 'Hussy'. Circe quickly ceased her weaving and came-out at once from her forest residence, opened the bright doors, and suavely asked her sex-starved critics to eagerly enter. In their juvenile folly, and honoring their throbbing hard-ons, the dumb-shits all anxiously went inside the gleaming mansion."

"Eurylochus was the only member of his scouting patrol to stay outside, since my captain was a homosexual who found heterosexual sex quite anathema to his gay value system. Also, the distrustful son-of-a-bitch believed that sexy Circe might be tricking his porno-lusting subordinates. The gorgeous witch led the twenty-two dick-heads inside and sat their asses and stiff erections down upon comfortable stools and chairs; then, the crafty sorceress made her surprise want-to-get-laid guests drinks of cheese, barley meal and yellow honey stirred into Pramnian wine. But with the tempting food, the scheming whore surreptitiously mixed a potent drug, so that the affected soldiers would lose all fond memories of country, family and home."

"When the stupid-ass trespassers had drunk-down the specially concocted formula, Circe took her magic wand, waved the object at the men's un-magic pulsating wands, and then inexplicably teleported the fools directly into in her outside pig-pens. The twenty-two dumb-shits suddenly had bristles, heads, and snorting voice-boxes, just like oinking hogs, and their bodies now resembled corpulent swine. However, the transformed soldiers' self-oriented minds were just as human as before the dumb-ass fools had entered the witch's premises. Inside their pens, the pigheaded ignoramuses wept like infants suffering from painful colic spasms."

"Circe threw-down some feed in front of them: acorns, beech nuts, and rotten fruit, and the twenty-two deceived dupes greedily ate their lousy meal very voraciously, while simultaneously shitting and wallowing in the pigsty-pigpen's deep mud."

"My Lieutenant, that nitwit Eurylochus immediately sprinted like a scared antelope back to our swift black ship, bringing an incredible report of his companions' pigheaded fate. I slung my large, bronze, silver-studded sword across my bleeding shoulder, grabbed my dependable bow, and hurried-off to confront gorgeous and enchanting Circe."

"Next, dear Phaeacians; as I was rapidly moving through the sacred groves on my route to Circe's abode, I recalled that I had heard from fanciful traveling bards that the bitch was not an amateur charlatan, but rather was a minor goddess and accomplished chemist, highly skilled in formulating many magic potions. I halted my frantic forward hustle when my eyes espied Hermes of the Golden Wand, taking a healthy piss in the dark woods. The startled messenger god looked like a handsome young man experiencing the first growth of hair showing upon his face, under his armpits, and around his tassel-like dangle; that special innocent, adolescent age when youthful charm is at its majestic height. The courier god gripped my hand with his, which was still wet with urine, and then informatively spoke."

"Your fuck-head shipmates, now over there outside Circe's slop-dump, have been penned-up like swine inside narrow, feces-laden stalls. Dumb-ass King of Ithaca; are you intending now to set your lame-brain sailors free? Confidentially, I don't think you'll ever make it back to Ithaca all by yourself; if you trespass and encounter Circe. I assure you, like your crew, that you'll remain there in a stench-filled enclosure, being held captive with your aberrant pig underlings. But come, haughty Odysseus. Heed my sage advice. I'll keep you free from harm and save you from being stored in one of the witch's many hogsheads. Take the remedial medicine I'm now providing you, and continue onward to Circe's house of chaos. The secret ingredient will protect you, and will also keep your penis safe from any venereal diseases this day might bring. The sex-starved witch will not have the power to cast a neutralizing spell that will be able to counteract the medicine I'm offering. The potent herb that I'll provide you with will not allow Circe to challenge the Olympians' superior science."

"After that irrational statement had been communicated, the Killer of Argus pulled a magical plant out of the ground, offered a tablet from one of the thin branches, and explained the pill's exceptional features. Its roots were black, the flower milk-white, and it truly smelled like shit. The gods call it 'Moly'."

"Holy Moly!" I replied, a trifle too disrespectful to all of the vindictive Olympians. "I'll try this preventive protection, even though I abhor taking drugs, either uppers or downers!"

"Then, fleet-footed Hermes amazingly left the forest, and his three-dimensional form almost-instantly vaporized into a fine mist as the god's physical anatomy blended-in with the dense, surrounding, jungle vegetation. I continued on north to Circe's home, which had been somewhat visible from my only ship. As I stridently advanced in my quest, my racing heart was turning-over many gloomy thoughts, and my encumbered mind mulled-over all possible escape scenarios."

"After I had sneakily tiptoed up to the unscrupulous sorceress's gateway, I just stood there and gave a lusty shout. The goddess heard my resonant voice, and at once exited her crystal palace, opened her glimmering portals, thoroughly evaluated my masculine visage, smiled, and invited me inside with a casual hand gesture. Naturally, I had misgivings, but trusting Hermes's intercession, I entered the charming female's opulent mansion, where the conniving witch sat my rear end upon a silver-studded chair, accompanied by a beautiful utilitarian stool to rest my weary feet."

"Now dear King Alcinous and Queen Arete, my captivating hostess mixed her normally effective potion into a golden cup and steadily-handed the preparation to my right hand for me to drink. I conjectured that her heart was bent on enacting mendacious mischief; that the hot-looking bitch wanted to rape me, and perhaps suck me off, and my biological side wished to make my fantasies convert into true reality. The horny hussy used her wand to touch my erect wand and uttered the following words."

"Off now, you human swine, to your assigned pigsty, and lie-down in the muck alongside all the rest of your slimy, stinking, oinking companions."

"The arrogant-but-surprised whore loudly screamed when I methodically drew the sharp sword that had been situated on my thigh, and I charged at her exposed pubic zone, as if the weapon was intent on either murder or unnatural, perverted penetration. Circe's throat emitted a second piercing expletive. The shrieking strumpet ducked to the tile floor, and her sweaty hands were reaching for my strong knees. Through her multiple tears, the viperous destroyer of men spoke to me in a queer sort of pig-Greek, which I shall now endeavor to interpret."

"What sort of superior man, who is immune to my magic, are you? What kind of womb are you from? Human or animal? Where is your native land? Are your' parents mortal, or are they' gods? I'm amazed you drank this drug and then were not bewitched or enchanted. No other shipwrecked sailor who's ever sampled my mixture has ever been able to resist its effect, once the secret compound has passed the barrier of his teeth. Inside that handsome chest of yours, a titanic spirit successfully thwarts against my spell. I assume that you must be fabled Odysseus; that resourceful hero who the reigning gods are both discussing and punishing. The Killer of Argus, Hermes of the Golden Wand, always predicted that the champion Odysseus, arriving in his swift black ship, would stop here on his classic odyssey back from Troy. So, Odysseus; put that nasty sword back in its sheath; put your big boy tunic on, and let the two of us go up into my bed and wildly roll around in the straw. After we've made passionate love, then that is when we can learn to trust each other."

"Once Circe had indicated that proposal, I sagaciously answered her entreaty. "Bitch Circe; how can you ask me to be kind to you? In your own home, I've learned that you've changed half my crew into pigs, and you intend to keep me here because you know that I would never leave your miserable, controlling demeanor without them. You're plotting pernicious mischief as you charmingly-but-erroneously speak in amorous tones, inviting me to go up to your bedroom, into your bed, so when I have no clothes, you can do me harm, and destroy my precious salami with your dagger-like teeth. But I will not agree to screw you with my apparatus and my nuts, unless, slut Circe, you will morally swear a solemn oath that you'll make no more plans to injure my dangling dingle and my testicles with some novel, devious trick."

"When I had stressed those specific, fabricated comments, the irascible witch made the suggested oath at once, promising that she'd not injure my pecker, nor mangle my alternately bouncing, dangling balls. Once the reputed harlot had sworn and finished with the pledge, I escorted Circe to her splendid bed and watched her exotically and erotically remove her sexy, sheer, bedtime apparel in what constituted a magnificent striptease."

"Meanwhile, four women attendants serving Circe's needs were busy gossiping about my incidental arrival inside the female magician's crystal palace. Truthfully, despite my oath of fidelity to Queen Penelope, I would have much-preferred to screw any of the four fat and ugly hussies than to have wild, unbridled sex with a distrustful, voluptuous witch."

"After giving me a bath and a full body massage, Circe's delicate hands rubbed me all over with rich oil, and then the whoring schemer fitted me in a fine cloak and tunic, and led me to a handsome silver chair, actually embossed with expensive silver. An obese maid brought-in a lovely golden jug, and poured-out water into an expensive emerald basin, so that I could thoroughly wash, and the accommodating servant set a polished table at my side. Then, the distinguished faggot steward brought-in stale bread and set the loaf before me, probably thinking that I was a vagabond loafer, and not, in the flesh, the famous wanderer Odysseus of Ithaca."

"But in my troubled heart, I had no appetite for either sex or food. So, I just sat there being contemplative and immobile, thinking of other more essential things besides mundane sex and available edibles. But my keen perception was soon sensing something quite ominous, but also very obscure."

"When Circe noticed my apparent lethargy, not reaching for the delicious food, or covetously scrutinizing her thick, brown muffin, the obsessed control freak came-up close and softly whispered in my ear."

"Odysseus, why are you just sitting here, like a deaf and dumb mute, wearing out your heart, and keeping your wonderful sperm juices all to yourself. You've never touched your food or drink? Do you think this is another devious trick? Don't be afraid, brave man. I've already made a solemn promise that I won't injure you. Don't you trust my' genuine words."

"Circe, I want you to listen to this incredulous bullshit I'm about to disclose. What King or Captain with any self-respect would start to gluttonously eat and drink before he had released his shipmates and could reunite with his crew face to face? If you're being sincere in wanting to have the poop pumped out of you on yonder mattress, then I'm demanding that you set my comrades free, so that my own eyes can see my trusty seamen before you receive your special semen. But in essence, Circe; your heart and your mind are so radically depraved that you would probably savor all of my twenty-two incarcerated, grunting hog-men pork the living daylights out of your sexually deprived love tunnel!"

"When I had spoken that hard-hitting remark, Circe angrily rushed through the wide hall with her supernatural wand clutched in her right hand, and the lady tiger, that I was taming, violently opened-up the pigpen's doors. The witch vociferously scolded the herd, and then using a whip from the wall, the lady dictator drove the whole herd out."

"Then, dear King Alcinous; my transformed mariners now looked like full-grown, nine-year-old pigs, oinking and snorting their guts out of their foul mouths. Circe paced through the putrid-smelling group, actively, smearing upon their disgusting backs a uniquely different potion that instantly changed my men back to their normal human appearances, with all of my acquaintances looking much younger, taller, stronger and more handsome than ever before."

"Odysseus!" one called-out, recognizing my illustrious presence. "Why have you caused your crew additional grief and sorrow on this never-ending, fucked-up odyssey? You're a horrible and terrible disgrace to Ithaca, and to all of Greece."

"Circe herself was moved to pity at the soldier's vile testimony, realizing what agony my heart had been suffering, along with the myriad perils, death and devastation that my return from Troy had destructively generated. Standing close to me, the lovely goddess uttered and intimated her sympathy."

"Resourceful Odysseus, son of Laertes and child of Zeus; go now to the seashore to your swift ship, drag it up on land, and stash your goods and all the things you need inside the caves. Then, come back to my crystal palace again, and bring your loyal companions in your second squad with you."

"Because my crewmen now hated my total being, Circe's illogical words easily persuaded my proud heart to comply. I left the premises, and my mind was in a nebulous quandary as I walked in a mental fog back to the anchored Bireme. I found *my* trusty comrades idly standing together, all lamenting sadly and shedding an abundance of genuine tears."

"I immediately sensed that their brains had been tampered with by the unethical witch, and that my sailors didn't need my guidance anymore, because the asshole idiots believed that they were now safely back in Ithaca, and were looking and waiting for impending merchant marine work."

"Meanwhile, Circe had been acting kindly to the rest of my companions still being held hostage as human hogs, against their free will, inside her crystal home. The devious witch had her fat, ugly servants provide the other squad members with soothing, warm baths, rubbed their scrotum sacs with rich olive oil, and had dressed their now-attractive asses in warm cloaks and tunics. All of the converted former pig-men were now feeling jolly in happy spirits, eating crackers and drinking diluted pussy juice mixed with rye whiskey. When my transformed subordinates recognized me again, the selfish dolts completely ignored both my rank and my military presence."

"Resourceful and erudite Odysseus, son of Laertes, come now; enjoy my food, and indulge yourself and drink my special wine. Revive once more the sensational need you once felt for sex and female company. You're weary now, and you have no spirit or appetite for pleasure, which essentially, makes human life both tolerable and satisfying. Your entire fuckin' existence is focused on always brooding about your painful wanderings and the misery that your odyssey has engendered and caused. There's no bland joy or thrill that is residing inside your saddened heart; you have endured so much misery since leaving Troy; crazy 24/7 daily sex with me can magically erase your ever-burgeoning plethora of cruel emotional excruciation."

"My proud ego was affected and further damaged by the irresistible witch's implausible lexicon. I stayed there like a moron for one whole year, feasting on sweet wine, and partaking of huge stores of meat. But as the months and seasons evaporated into eternal time, eventually, the long spring days returned. A full year had passed when my former trusty comrades summoned me to a showdown conference."

"You god-driven, self-centered, non-Cretan cretin!" my old friend Eurassisgras admonished me and my ranking authority. "Now then; you weak-minded dunderhead. The time has come when you must think again about your native land, about your wife Penelope, and about your son, Telawoman, er, I mean Telemachus. If you're really some special jerk-off especially selected by the gods, who's fate is destined or worthy to be saved, you might be able to reach your lofty home and native soil once more. Now is the correct time to act accordionly, er, I meant, 'to act accordingly'."

"My conceited heart was drastically altered by Eurassisgras's irrational argument. So, all day long, until the sun disappeared on the western horizon, I sat there on an improvised picnic table, feasting on huge plates of meat and getting stone-cold drunk on sweet wine. When dusk faded and the pall of darkness settled-in, my pissed-off crewmen staying inside the crystal mansion, and no longer hogs, all lay down to sleep in the shadowy hall. I went to Circe, who was resting in her impressive bed; I clasped her knees, and then gently rubbed her massive, engorged, penis-sized clitoris. The sexually aroused sorceress listened attentively to my entire grief-laden request."

"Beautiful Circe; I plead that you fulfill the promises you had made a year ago to send me home. My spirit's keen to leave your protection, as are the hearts of my envious companions, who now aspire to eliminate my ass, colon and epididymis from this totally insane planet. Oh, strange lady warden; please release me and my destiny at once from your bureaucratic, local government protection program. I humbly seek your blessing for me to depart from your isolated island."

"Crying bona fide tears, the bitch/witch answered in a melancholy tone of voice, saying. "Resourceful and wet-fingered Odysseus, son of Laertes and Zeus's inane, insane child, if it's against your obstinate will, yes; you born with a gigantic stubbed head; you should not now remain in my crystal palace frustrating my sexual needs. But first, I've cleverly manipulated your complicated fate. You must complete another trip and journey-down deep inside the bowels of Mother Earth, and venture to the bleak kingdom of Hades and Persephone. In that terribly gloomy realm, you are hereby appointed to interact with the shade of blind Teiresias, the deceased Theban prophet. His mind is unimpaired, even though his body has disintegrated into dust decadent decades ago. Even though he's fuckin' dead as a dildo, dreaded Hades, who is the brother of Zeus and Poseidon, has granted the deceased prophet the power to understand your plight, and perhaps absolve your chronic curse, and afford your spirit a viable solution, or perhaps an appropriate remedy. All of the other fucked-up souls trapped down there in that unimaginable hellhole simply flit about, mere shadows and hazy two-dimensional apparitions."

"As Circe finished her brief summary, my desire to live and continue on my arduous odyssey was breaking like a fragile eggshell. I sat weeping upon her bed, for my heart no longer wished to survive, or even glimpse the light of day. But when I'd had enough of shedding tears and rolling around in mental distress, scratching my abominable hemorrhoids and also my crotch-itch, I politely answered her sense of compassion and requested for her to administer benign mercy."

"Circe; who'll be the guide on such a perilous underground trip? No black ship has ever sailed across the River Styx to subterranean Hades. What impossible task are you suggesting?"

"Resourceful Odysseus, son of Laertes and Zeus's illegitimate child who somehow popped out of your father's asshole; do not concern yourself with a competent pilot to adroitly navigate your one remaining ship. Raise the mast, spread-out your peaceful white sail, and just take your seat. And I now oracle that the breath of North Wind Boreas will propel you on your unknown misadventure. But once your Bireme has crossed the flowing Ocean, drag it ashore at Persephone's weeping willow groves; that is, upon the level beach where tall popular poplars grow. The dismal willows shed their fruit, right beside deep swirling Oceanus. Then, dear Odysseus, you must venture directly to disconsolate and dispassionate Hades' murky, sinister throne-chamber, where easy-to-spell Periphlegethon, along with grammatically-correct Cocytus, together form a precarious cascade of grand rapids, which streams and branches-off the dreaded River Styx. Act bolder and you'll locate a boulder precisely where those two foaming rivers have their confluence. Go there, heroic and singular human specimen, and honor my explicit instructions. Dig a deep hole at that place, approximately two-feet-square. Pour libations to the revered dead contributors to Greek Civilization around your shallow pit."

"That's more shit you want me to do than that which overflows a colossal cesspool!" I futilely objected. "Why the hell can't I just set sail for Ithaca?"

"Circe ignored my oral opposition and proceeded to give me more illogical directions. "Then, Odysseus; pray your swollen balls off in earnest to all the hapless, good-hearted Greeks who've died in the past, with a vow that, when you reach Ithaca, you'll solemnly sacrifice a barren heifer, a pregnant cow, and a really fat woman to Zeus and Poseidon. That uncanny promise will grant you a brief conference with the specter of Teiresias."

"When early Dawn appeared, glowing upon her eastern golden throne, Circe dressed me in a splendid cloak and tunic, and as part of her weird farewell ceremony, clothed her body in a long white robe. On her bald head she placed a transparent veil. Next, I dashed through her entire, hundred-room crystal palace, rousing, but not arousing, my pissed-off, rebellious companions. With words of reassurance, I addressed them all as strong warriors and not as dumb-ass pigs."

"No more sleeping now; by that, I mean no sweet slumbering and jerking-off while blissfully imagining hot sex in your fantasy white dreams. Let's go and re-embark on *our* more-than-challenging odyssey back to Ithaca. Lovely Circe has told me exactly what to do along the sacred way. Amazingly, King Alcinous; my remaining crewmembers did not protest and wholeheartedly agreed to comply with my nonsensical request."

Chapter 14
"ODYSSEUS JOURNEYS TO HADES"

"Once we had reached our previously damaged Bireme down on the beach, we strenuously dragged the vessel out into the gleaming sea, attached and hoisted-up the sail to the mast in the center of our black ship; led onboard the adequate supply of sheep, and of apples to prevent scurvy, and then embarked ourselves subject to Fate's volatile mercy. All day long, the sail stayed full of a favorable wind. We sped like a smaller version of Hermes across the wine-dark sea, until the sun went-down in the west, and soon the sky grew dark and spookily dreary."

"Yes, King Alcinous and Queen Arete; we gambled on our gambol. Our once-reliable ship then reached the banks of the deep stream Oceanus, a region, according to legend, that always had been wrapped in mist and cloud. We sailed into that fog rather easily, and upon completing our arrival, dragged our ship upon the shore of Oceanus, until we reached on foot the place Circe had graphically described and designated."

"Feeling frightened, Eurassisgras begged and urged me: "Dear Odysseus; please eminent Captain! Let's get the fog out of here!" The non-amusing asshole grieved and pleaded, obviously referring to the intense eerie mist that had spookily enveloped our patrol."

"Perimedes, Eurylochus, Periodontis and Eurassisgras firmly held the necks of the expendable sheep designated to be our sacrificial victims, while I unsheathed the sharp sword upon my thigh and dug the square hole Circe had commanded. I poured-out libations to give honor to all the dead, first with milk and honey, second with wine, and a third with water and semen. Around the sacred pit, I barely sprinkled gluten-free barley meal, oats and imported rice."

"Then, to pay homage to Hades and Persephone, and also to show reverence to the helpless, non-talking heads of the dearly departed, I offered many impromptu prayers, with attached promises that I'd humbly soon sacrifice, and in the future, permanently demonstrate good religious faith, once I returned safely back to Ithaca. And finally, throwing into the overall god-worshipping equation, a cheap, about-to-die, barren heifer would be offered upon an altar of volcanic rock in the center of the city, along with a fat woman. Citing an abundance of prayers and contrite pledges, I, a mere suppliant, called upon the families of the dead to recognize my patriotic allegiance to all Greeks, both living and deceased."

"Next, I held-out the chosen sheep above the hole, slit their throats one by one, and let their dark blood flow into the shallow hollow I had just excavated. Then, out of Erebus came swarming-up shades of the dead: brides; young unmarried men; old farts worn-out from arduous toil; young, tender two-dimensional girls with hairy bushes, and flat-imaged male teenagers with hearts still absorbing new grief. Their sorrowful existence also featured the ghosts of many warriors that had been wounded by bronze spears, who had died in battle at Troy, still wearing their blood-stained two-dimensional armor after being hammered and brutalized. Crowds of them came thronging in from all sides, scaring the living shit out of me, and also out of petrified Eurassisgras."

"Pale fear seized my heart out of hearing scary other-world cries that were emerging out of the pitiless pit. In my great confusion, I called my comrades, ordering them to flay and burn the dead sheep still lying there, and instructed them to pray to the gods like there would be no tomorrow for us mariners, and to especially beg for Pallas Athene's protection from mighty King Hades and pallid-faced Queen Persephone, sitting together in dismal darkness upon their ominous ebony thrones."

"In seconds, King Alcinous; to my expanding apprehension, there suddenly appeared the awesome ghost of my dead mother, Anticleia, Autolycus's deformed child. I had left her still alive when I had enthusiastically departed Ithaca and set-out for Troy in quest of selfish glory and earthly fame. Once I caught sight of her flat ghost swirling about my awed presence, I relentlessly wept and cried like a hungry infant, and I felt pity and remorse in all four chambers of my reprehensible heart. Nonetheless, in spite of my mounting emotional sorrow, I could not allow her nebulous, no-longer-alive specter, get too near the sacred slain sheep blood, until I had interviewed and questioned blind Teiresias, or perhaps first located his maternal ancestor, infamous Mother Teiresias."

"Now King Alcinous, the shade of the prophet Teiresias of Thebes eventually appeared, holding a golden staff that apparently represented his renowned wisdom and sagacity. The eminent savant immediately recognized my identity and began speaking some indiscernible, intellectual gibberish."

"Adventurous and fatuous Odysseus, Laertes' son, and Zeus's bastard child; what now do you seek, you very unlucky man? Why leave the sunlight, come to this horribly joyless place, and see the dead just for your own preposterous folly? Move from the sacred pit you have established, and put-away your lethal sword, so that I may drink the dark sheep blood and speak the truth, as I fathom it, to satisfy your' naïve, dumb-ass inquiries."

"When Teiresias had enunciated that profound rhetoric, I fearfully drew back and stubbornly thrust my studded sword inside its sheath. Once the blameless prophet had swallowed-up the dark blood, the acclaimed shade said these rather pathetic, prophetic words."

"Glorious Odysseus, you ask about your honey-sweet return to Ithaca, if and when it might occur. But an omnipotent and jealous god, who has many grievances and complaints against you, will make your journey absolutely bitter. My gifted vision, which I've somehow retained after death, informs me that as soon as you've escaped the dark blue sea and have reached the sinister island of Thrinacia, you'll find grazing in the resplendent pastures the sacred cattle and rich flocks of Helios Hyperion, who hears and watches over everything in Heaven, and everything occurring on Earth, which includes your plenteous and notorious bullshit activities."

"Now, Odysseus, if you wisely leave the cattle unharmed and keep your mind concentrated on your return home, you may reach Ithaca, though you'll encounter more perplexing, fucked-up difficulties. But if you dare even touch the sacred bovines, then I foresee widespread destruction for your crew, for you, and for your already-damaged Bireme. And even if you yourself miraculously escape, you'll arrive home again later than expected, and grieving your' ass off in someone else's ship; that is, after losing all of your crewmen at sea. And if I may add to your ongoing quandary, there'll be massive trouble waiting for you at home; insolent and reprehensible suitors, worthy of castration, will be parasitically eating-up your livelihood, and wooing your godlike wife by giving courtship gifts with money that had been pilfered from you. But if and when you return from your skein of tragedies, you'll surely take sweet revenge for all their prolific violence and their numerous immoral violations."

"And Mother; what should I be doing in Ithaca in regard to my properties, wife and son?"

"My mother's specter remained silent, so the prophet's shade again spoke. "Once you have killed the contemptible suitors, Odysseus, Teiresias's apparition informed; yes, those human worms egregiously dwelling inside your unkempt palace, then I suggest that you cunningly find a well-made oar and go and seek-out a people who know little of the sea, and who don't put salt on any food they eat, and who have no special knowledge of ships painted red, or who know any pertinent shit about well-made oars that serve those ships as ocean-gliding wings. Now great Odysseus, I'll tell you a sure sign you won't forget. When some wayward stranger inadvertently encounters you carrying a fractured oar and asks if you've got a shovel used for winnowing, then immediately fix that broken oar and offer a rich sacrifice to Lord Poseidon with a fattened ram, a bull, a whore, and a neurotic boar that breeds with many sows. Then quickly leave that fucked-up scene and frenetically race home, and in your back weed-infested garden, make sacred offerings to the immortal gods, who hold wide heaven and have jurisdiction over the entire known world. Your death, my senses perceive, will ultimately ascend out of the sea when you are feeble and bent-over at a ripe old age, but with your grateful people prospering around you. In all those futuristic events to come, I'm telling you the inflexible truth."

"The profit's mysterious shade finished speaking. Then, I replied in turn: "Teiresias; no doubt the gods themselves have spun the threads of this future horse-shit, clown show. But come, tell me now, and speak more essential truth. I can see over yonder the shade of my dead mother, sitting near the stench-odor blood saying nothing familiar like 'Fuck you Odysseus', just as she used to yell. I've noticed that her ghost does not dare confront the face of her own son, or even make an effort to speak to me. Tell me, my lord, how she may understand just who I am."

"I'll tell you exactly what the Hades is happening, Odysseus. It's all quite elementary to comprehend. Whichever shadow of the dead you let approach the blood will speak to you and tell the truth, but those you keep away and try to protect from Hades' tremendous wrath, will once again withdraw."

"After articulating those explanatory words, the shade of Lord Teiresias returned to the dark gates of Hades, having made his dramatic prophecy known. I stayed there next to the sacred pit, motionless and undaunted, until my mother's specter flitted around, instantly stopped, and greedily drank the dark sacrificial blood. Then, marvelously, she realized and knew me from our shared past. Full of sorrow, her ghoulish throat spoke: "My disobedient son; how have you come to this black, forsaken, subterranean world while still being alive? For living men, it's both impossible and sinful to discover these arcane things you're presently witnessing! Your occult experience will involve huge rivers, fearful streams, and frightening spirits and goblins. Stand between us, first and foremost, and pray to Oceanus, which no man can cross on foot, unless of course a low I.Q. idiot such as yourself has a death wish to drown. Please Odysseus; pray to Oceanus that you need a sturdy ship to complete your' infamous, fucked-up odyssey. Have you only now voyaged to this condemned territory from Troy? Have you still not reached depleted Ithaca, or seen your wife suffering humiliation and hardship within your own house?"

"Mother, I had to journey and arrive here to Hades', meet and interact with the shade of Teiresias of Thebes, and hear his infallible prophecy. I have not yet approached nor come near Achaea's shores, or disembarked into our ass-backwards native land. I've been aimlessly wandering around this hazardous part of the world in constant misery, ever since I left Ithaca with noble Agamemnon, bound for Troy, to fight against the all-too-fertile small-dicked Trojans. But now, Mother; tell me this unalterable truth! What grievous form of death took you away? Was your' demise a lengthy illness? Did archer Artemis attack and kill you with her sharp arrows? Did you die during a masturbation climax?"

"Obnoxious and incorrigible son; your grandfather had died of extreme heartbreak when you failed to return home after so many years of being absent. Even when you were a difficult toddler, you tried running away from the family palace at every given opportunity. And Odysseus, I gladly kicked the proverbial pottery bowl soon after your grandfather had died from ordinary old age symptoms."

"Mother, before you flit away and vanish, please tell me of my wife, Queen Penelope. What are her thoughts and plans? Is she still there with our son, Telemachus, faithfully keeping watch on everything? Or has my spouse been married to the finest of Achaeans pursuing her ivory-white hand?"

"Odysseus; you can rest assured that loyal Penelope has been both impatiently and patiently waiting for you to return to Ithaca, and is desiring to receive your loving embrace."

"Well, King Alcinous and Queen Arete, in my immortal soul, I thought about how much I yearned to once again hold my mother's shade, for in the past, she had owned many lamps. My spirit urged me to clasp her in my arms, and three times I moved towards her vague image, but on each approach, she slipped-away, like an elusive shadow, or like a hazy summer dream. Then, I mustered the necessary wherewithal to call-out in a disgruntled tone of voice: "Mother, why do you not linger longer with me? I'd like to hold your frail hands, so that even here in bleak Hades, we might throw our loving arms around each other and share our icy lamentation. Or are you a spying phantom, dispatched by royal Queen Persephone, sent to harass my presence and make me groan and grieve still more?"

"My foolish child-man; of all Greek warriors being most unfortunate, no, dreaded Persephone, daughter of Zeus, is not presently deceiving you, nor is the Queen of Death planning to put your breathless corpse on permanent cemetery lay-away. For you see, my son, once mortals die, this phenomenon flashing before your eyes is what's actually ordained for their restive spirits. The ethereal sinews of past heroes no longer hold flesh and bone together. The mighty power of a blazing fire destroys and cremates both temporal flesh and bones; that is, once our spirit flies from its earthly shell, our white bones gradually disintegrate over time. And before that process happens, the everlasting soul slips away like a vapor into time and space, and, like a cloudy dream, the soul flutters around in furious concentric circles, eventually ending-up swirling-around in this horrid, repugnant hellhole known as Hades."

"Just as my mother's haunting ghost mystically disappeared, a ghoulish, frightful incident occurred. My flustered eyes believed they were witnessing the specters of deceased Eurshiddenme and Eurballsourout swirling-around, and then arcanely vanishing into the surrounding gloom."

Chapter 15

"ODYSSEUS CONTINUES ADDRESSING THE PHAEACIANS"

Odysseus paused momentarily to clear his raspy throat, and soon resumed describing to the alert and attentive King Alcinous, Queen Arete and their silent, spellbound Phaeacian counselors how he had witnessed in Hades a large number of famous women's shades from olden times, including flat nude specters of strippers, lap-dancers, porno stars and prominent bordello prostitutes. King Alcinous asked his political allies how the incompetent politicians were evaluating Odysseus's stunning testimony.

"Phaeacians, how does this man seem to you in terms of beauty, stature, and honesty? Do you believe that this storyteller possesses a fair, well-balanced mind? Indeed, he is my honored guest, though each of you at this meeting shares in this presumed honor, too. So, don't be quick to send this garrulous fellow away from Phaeacia, and conversely, don't hold back your gifts to one who is in such great need."

Then, old coot warrior Echeneus stood and addressed the others in attendance, both old and young.

"Friends; what our wise Queen, er, I mean King has just stated, as we'd expect, is not wide of the mark. I hereby make a motion that the final decision concerning this odd fellow who claims to be the famed Odysseus rests with Alcinous. As for this Greek Odysseus, here, I'm inclined to tell the itinerant asshole to go to Hades, but by his own words, our prevaricating guest has already been there!"

Once the hoary codger Echeneus finished his opinionated remarks, King Alcinous spoke-out: "I maintain that my wife, Queen Arete, indeed should have the final word in this important matter. But though our guest is longing to return, let him agree to stay in Phaeacia overnight until tomorrow. By then, I'll have collected all our gifts and donations to finance his glorious trip back to Ithaca, wherever the hell that obscure island is located on the flat Earth. Now let our oddball guest resume his story."

"Noble Lord Alcinous; of all the most renowned residents on this island, if you asked me, Odysseus of Ithaca, to stay for one whole year, to arrange my escort and give me splendid gifts, then I would still amiably agree. It's far better to get back to one's own dear native land with more wealth in hand, which I intend and promise to fully repay in the future. I'll win more respect from my subjects and predicates, the city residents, most of whom will be lazy, indolent parasites depending on my generous goodwill to supply the general population with adequate welfare and ample food stamps."

"Odysseus, when we look at you, we do not perceive that you're in any way a lying fraud," King Alcinous stated. "You speak so well, and you have such a noble heart inside your community chest, just like a few carnival barkers who have recently ripped me off, and then the criminal scoundrels fled town in a hurry. You've so far told your story with a minstrel's skill, the painful agonies of the Greek Argives, along with your own singular obstacles and dilemmas, as well. Come then, tell me more of your stranger-than-myth accounting, and speak the honest-to-Zeus truth."

"What else do you want to hear from me?" Odysseus asked Alcinous. "I have a resilient will, and a stubborn disposition, but not a malleable soul."

"Did you see any of your deceased comrades in Hades; those godlike men who went with you to Troy and met their deaths there? This night before us will be lengthy, astonishingly so. It's not yet time to sleep with our favorite fabricated sex dolls; so, Odysseus, tell us more of your marvelous sequence of implausible events."

"Lord Alcinous; once Queen Persephone dispersed those female shadows here and there, wildly swirling-around before my amazed recognition, then the grieving shade of King Agamemnon of Mycenae, son of Atreus, appeared. The frightening ghost knew me at once, and after drinking the sacred dark sheep blood, the leader of the Greek forces against Troy wept aloud, shedding many tears, and stretched-out his cold misty hands to reach my warm grasp. But the dead brother of King Menelaus no longer had any inner power or strength, not like the force his supple limbs had possessed before, when the bad-ass son-of-a-bitch would beat the shit out of me before each ensuing battle. Pity filled my heart at then feeling his overall weakness and demise."

"Then, I called-out to the murdered leader of the Greek forces against Troy: "Lord Agamemnon, son of Atreus, king of Mycenae; what fatal net of grievous death has destroyed you? Did Poseidon stir the winds into a furious storm, and you died from a tremendous blowjob? Or, were you killed by savage enemies on foreign land, while you were confiscating their cattle herds, or purloining their rich flocks of sheep? Or were you fighting to seize their town and carry-off their wives who didn't care who or what screwed them, as long as the kinky whores got screwed up their wet, splashy love tunnels?"

"Ingenious Odysseus, Laertes's son, and Zeus's mentally unstable child; Poseidon did not kill me in my ships by rousing turbulent winds into a vicious storm. Nor was I slain by inspired enemy pyromaniacs performing scorched earth tactics upon the land. No, Odysseus. Scumbag Aegisthus, lover of my unfaithful, adulterous wife Clytemnestra, sister of Helen, contrived my assassination while I was away from Greece ten-years at Troy," Agamemnon's ghost somberly grieved. "That despicable ballbuster Aegisthus was amply assisted by my accursed spouse. The evil pair plotted and succeeded in murdering my ass. Clytemnestra hurled a fish net over me while I was splish-splashing, taking a bath, and then she and Aegisthus repeatedly stabbed me as if I was a common sacrificial tuna fish!"

"That's appalling, dear Agamemnon! Such an ignoble death for such a noble King! Surely, over the years, wide-thundering Zeus has shown a lethal hatred towards the family of Atreus, and also against myself, thanks to the conniving of some evil women behaving worse than Pandora had done with her box. Many Greek champions have died because of Helen, causing the Trojan War fiasco by foolishly eloping with Prince Paris to Troy, and then Clytemnestra arranging an assassination trap for you, while you, Agamemnon, were gallantly fighting alongside me over in Asia Minor."

"Now King Alcinous, poor Agamemnon didn't have a ghost of a chance from escaping his wife's conspiracy against him. I believe that Aegisthus was inspired to reenact the myth of Ares screwing Aphrodite, Hephaestus's wife, while the ugly blacksmith god was away hammering another sex-starved goddess!"

"Did you have any conversation with the spirit of that heel Achilles, who is also dead?"

"Yes, King Alcinous. Achilles, along with his close friend, Ajax, the detergent huckster, were killed at Troy. Ajax was also flitting around in that shadowy entrance to Hades, hysterically behaving as another haunting, uncleansed specter."

"What did Achilles say?" Alcinous wanted to know. "I hope that *that* heel wasn't pulling your leg!"

"Upon being solicited by my quivering voice, the famed hero Achilles addressed me in a creepy, screeching soprano tone:

"Adventurous Odysseus, Laertes's son and Zeus's obdurate child, what a bold and daring dick-head you were and are! What exploit will your vagabond heart ever dream-up to top this imaginative expedition you've undertaken down to doom-and-gloom Hades? How can you dare venture-down-here into this morbid Kingdom of the Dead, the dwelling place for the mindless shades of worn-out warrior assholes? Even the minstrel Orpheus scooted out of here like a bat out of Hades after finding the shade of his beloved sweetheart, Eurydice! Do you realize how mortified I feel being down here with mediocre dumb-shits who accomplished basically nothing of significance in their human existence? What a depressing psychological letdown it is for me, having to share this utterly bleak environment with idle, craven, brain-dead dumb-shits for all fuckin' eternity! Do you now fully understand my great frustration Odysseus, after, while I was still living, achieving such great fame and fortune throughout all of Greece?"

"Mighty Achilles, son of Peleus;" I respectfully replied to the awesome apparition. "I came here to Hades because I had to confer with Teiresias of Thebes, and hear his prophecy of my future return to Ithaca. I've not yet reached Achaean land, where I need to screw my wife Penelope, kill two-dozen suitors, and get laid some more. Ever since my fleet had left Troy, I'm in constant trouble with the mercurial-minded Powers-that-Be. But as for you, Achilles, there's no big or little-dicked man in former days who was more blessed with military success than you, and none will come in the future. Before now, while you were still alive, we Achaeans honored you as we did the gods. And now, the jealous gods have arranged your death, but because of your strong desire, you should rule down here with power among those less-ambitious cowards whirling around you, who have also died. So, Achilles, why the lugubrious expression appearing upon your pallid countenance? You have no cause to grieve, just because you are now stone-cold dead."

"King Alcinous; I then noticed that Hades had given Achilles a very humiliating punishment. The formerly virulent warrior was now stark naked, and the humiliated flat ghost's emaciated body featured a small, hollow weenie hanging between its legs."

"Don't try to comfort me about my unexpected, early death, glorious Odysseus," spoke Achilles' shade. "I'd rather live working as a common wage-laborer in Ithaca than preside-over all the lazy wasted dead-heads here in Hades, who incidentally, were just as lazy and wasted in their earlier earthly lives. Yes, Odysseus; everyone down-here is on the same fucked-up level and privilege, and we have all surrendered our precious free will in order to become lousy, lackluster, dull-minded slaves of apathetic King

Hades and Queen Persephone. Free will is positively everything, Odysseus. Down-here in this wretched Greek hell, there is none at all!"

"With those disconsolate words, King Alcinous, the shade of swift Achilles moved-off and filtered like a vapor into distant meadows filled with faded daffodils. The other macabre shadows stood around me, sobbing in sorrow, all asking an annoying multitude of questions about the ones they knew and loved. The only soul who stood apart from the rest was the shade of Ajax, the detergent entrepreneur, still full of heightened anger for my meritorious victory, when I'd beaten the shit out of his intestines during a minor quarrel that had developed on the shores of Troy beside our ships. In that epic competition between Ajax and me, mutually struggling for dead Achilles's weapons and breastplate, after a lethal arrow had pierced the hero's exposed tendon, which was *his* only vulnerable, unprotected body part, Ajax and I became bitter foes. The Trojan Prince Paris, who Achilles tried to plaster, shot the life-ending arrow, and it was Paris who stole-away King Menelaus's wife Helen from Sparta, and that abduction started the entire fucked-up Trojan War. Menelaus's brother, King Agamemnon of Mycenae, soon organized the major Greek expedition of one thousand ships against Priam, King of Troy, who had approved of his son, playboy Paris, stealing-off with whoring Helen, Menelaus's wife."

"Ajax, worthy son of Telamon, can't you forget our past altercation at the shores of Troy. Even when you're now dead, your vitriolic anger at me over those destructive weapons remains dominant inside your' envious spirit? The gods turned Achilles's armor into a curse against the Argives, and when we regrettably lost you, too, it was worse than visiting a popular brothel only to find gay homosexuals giving bad head to all the dissatisfied patrons. Now that you've been killed, I want you to know that Achaeans mourn your death unceasingly, just as they do that of Achilles, and of Agamemnon. No one is to blame for this ongoing tragedy but Zeus, who in his terrifying rage against the army of our Danaan spearmen regiment, implemented his arbitrary, almighty whims; that's precisely what brought on *your* untimely death. Come over here, my detergent guru, so that you can hear me say that your soul is supposed to be cleansed instead of your unwarranted duration here in Hades being disinfected by fire. Stop being so futilely antagonistic towards me!"

"Grudge-happy Ajax's ghost did not reply, but left, moving away towards Erebus, to join the other rotating shadows chaotically revolving-away in the far distance. For all his colossal rage, the formidable combatant would have talked more verbal garbage to me, or me to him, but at that brief moment, I wished to see and consult more shades of those revered war colleagues who also had died at Troy."

"And King Alcinous, after that session with Ajax, I saw Tityus, son of the glorious Earth, eternally punished for disposing of Leto. Tityus, who when living, looked like a giant female breast, was lying prone upon the ground in Hades, with his suddenly magnified body covering around nine acres or more in width. Two voracious vultures sat there, one on either side of his abdomen, ripping-out his liver and relentlessly biting his one huge nipple; the buzzards' sharp beaks were jabbing deep inside his guts and chest, for his paralyzed hands could not protect his vulnerable body."

"Then, King Alcinous; my astute pupils spotted Tantalus, suffering in perpetual agony. I cautiously advanced through a shadowy cave and entered the spooky area of eternal atonement where the pathetic, grieving ghosts of dead individuals were posthumously punished for violating the capricious gods' supreme laws. Even Sisyphus, who labored for all eternity, pushing a huge rock up a curved hill, only to have it roll down the incline so that the process would have to be repeated over and over again, stopped to greet my' intrusion. Sisyphus was so inspired by my company that the punished victim immediately organized his own underground, ungrateful dead band called 'The Rolling Stones', and instantly began mimicking the musician Orpheus's fine example. Even the crackling dancing flames, that flourished in leaping fences of fire in that atonement section of Hades, soon heated-up the whole damned area."

"Next, I advanced further into the darkened caverns of Hades and again encroached-upon Tantalus, who had been eternally punished by having to stand chained inside a pool that was filled chest-high with delicious water. An abundance of luscious fruits on tree limbs dangled above the hungry and thirsty dead man's head. When Tantalus was 'tantalized' to drink, every minute or so, the manacled figure would bend-over, and the cool water would rapidly drain out of the tank. When frustrated, chained and hungry Tantalus would reach for a ripe peach, or for a savory overhead apple, the desired fruit would either disappear, or be blown-away by a sudden wind gust. The penalized fellow was so enraptured and entranced by my appearance that he momentarily ceased performing his eternal sentence, and Tantalus's rejuvenated spirit fondly recalled, and briefly shared, how wonderful it was once like, just to breathe and be alive."

"And then, King Alcinous, I noticed my mighty idol Hercules's gloomy shade, or at least his flat image. Around the former discus champion, ghouls of the other melancholy dead were making eerie noises, sounding much like an irritated covey of large birds in distress, erratically fluttering their two-dimensional wings in a quite-terrifying manner. And like dark night, the strongest of Greeks was glaring all around him, almost dazed, turning his bothered head back and forth in rapid repetition. The still-muscular specimen, who when alive easily killed, with his bare hands, numerous bears, wild boars, and lions, and indeed, was always-triumphant in his various battles, fights and murders; along with him defeating a catalogue of very daunting evil adversaries. Hercules's saddened eyes alertly noticed my entry into his designated area of atonement, and the disconsolate, eternally sentenced fellow immediately recognized my three-dimensional identity."

"Odysseus, you resourceful warrior, son of Laertes and a disobedient foe of Almighty Zeus; are you now bearing an unhappy fate below the sunlight, as I, too, once did? What the hell are you' doing down here on the wrong side of the grass? I was a son of Zeus, and yet, I had to bear so many troubles, and had been forced by Olympus to perform those twelve demanding labors for a weak, craven king vastly inferior to me, but still, given the authority to keep assigning me the harshest tasks to complete for *his* satisfaction. On one occasion, the feckless royal son-of-a-bitch sent me here to bring away Hades' personal hound back to the surface. There was no other challenge the cowardly bastard could dream-up that would be more difficult for me than *that* superhuman enterprise. But I carried the ferocious three-headed, snarling dog Cerberus off, and bravely brought the fierce canine up from Hades."

"With those incredible words, recollecting one of his most famous exploits, Hercules's specter returned to its preoccupation of constantly searching left and right, which was representative of King Hades' cruel sense of amusement. I sadly stayed at that morbid place a while longer, but then I feared that spiteful Queen Persephone might assign a horrific monster, perhaps grotesque Medusa the Gorgon, to face me by surprise, and instantaneously turn my ass into an inanimate stone statue for all eternity."

"And then, dear Phaeacians; shivering from overwhelming fear, I hastily initiated my recollected path back up to the magnificent sunshine, the purpose of my memorized ascent from Hades being to be reunited with my cherished ship and with my unhappy crew, who habitually blamed me for all of their myriad emotional maladies. My disenchanted sailors reluctantly loosened-off the mooring cables at the Bireme's stern, and my dejected mariners angrily took their seats along each rowing bench. A rising swell gently carried our vessel away, moving along Ocean's swift-moving stream.

The sailors vigorously rowed at first, but then a fair wind blew, and assisted our sea passage onward toward our next unknown, perilous adventure."

Chapter 16

"THE SIRENS, SCYLLA & CHARYBDIS, AND THE CATTLE"

"That second night, our battered ship sentimentally sailed-on along the gentle waves, away from Oceanus's tugging stream, across the great wide sea, and in several more days, we reached Aeaea, the island being the presumed home and dancing grounds of Dawn, and the actual bailiwick of the wily witch Circe. Our Bireme sailed into the placid harbor, and soon we hauled our ship up the inclined beach, and then ambled along the serene shoreline. There, waiting for the emergence of bright Dawn, we surrendered to fatigue and fell asleep under a full silvery moon."

"Circe was well-aware of our return from Lord Hades' obscure subterranean realm. Dressed in her finery, the alluring, lonesome bitch quickly came to us with her mechanical-like servants, who were obediently carrying bread, plenty of meat, and flasks of bright red wine. Then, the devious sorceress stood in our midst and immediately criticized our reappearance on her fucked-up island."

"You reckless ninnies; you ludicrous jerk-offs must have toxic worms for brains; you death-wish retards have been down to Hades while still alive, to meet and defy death twice, when other mortals die just once. But come, enjoy this special food and drink this tasty wine. Take all day if you idiots so desire. Then, as soon as Dawn fully arrives, without her boyfriend, Tony, you'll sail-on to your next destination. I'll show you your course, Odysseus, and inform you each sign to look for, although there will be no billboards to view on the oceans. I augur that you'll not suffer any great pain if you adhere to discretion, and not dare to challenge the gods' dictatorial authority."

"Listen, Circe. First of all, close your beautiful legs. Your deep pink hole smells like cheap vinegar. Secondly, even though my crew and I distrust you, horny whore, our proud hearts and peckers agree with the language you've just regurgitated."

"And so, patient King Alcinous, Queen Arete, and all of you other sore-assed, petite Phaeacians sitting there hearing my extended story; all that day, until the sun retired from the sky in the west, we stuffed our stomachs while relaxing on that really weird island, eating rich supplies of delicious meat and drinking-down sweet wine mixed with pig's entrails, until darkness arrived. We slept beside our ship's stern cables, which that night seemed all-too-lenient. But that scheming strumpet Circe, who had the hots for any man's dingle-dangle, large or small, took me by the hand and led me away some distance from my dozing crew. Through her power of suggestion, the kinky doll persuaded me to sit in muck, while she stretched-out beside me upon the muddy, damp ground. I told her every detail of our trip ever since I had left Troy, specifically describing all of the sensational adventures and episodes from start to finish. I never saw anyone yawn as often as Circe did, and I noticed in the moonlight that her dry mouth was almost as wide, but not nearly as wet, as her alluring pink, deep-hole vagina. Then, saddened Circe spoke."

"All these things have thus come to an end, Odysseus, but unlike our imaginary sex life, at least your lengthy skein of troubles has had a definite beginning. But you must listen now to what I say. My gift of prophecy has me comprehending that a god himself will soon be reminding you of something I cannot reveal out of fear of being punished myself. First of all, you'll encounter the Sirens, mermaid chicks of the sea. Like me, the naked, big-breasted beauties seduce all men who come across their powerful beckoning, and no man who unwittingly sails past and hears the Sirens' call ever returns. But unlike my hairy snatch, the Sirens' scaley crotches smell like rotten tuna flesh. Now Odysseus, beware of the Sirens' clear-toned singing, which will captivate your heart and make your manhood erect. They'll be restlessly sitting upon a jetty, near a meadow, surrounded by an immense pile of heaped, rotting, human bones encased in shriveled skin, which stinks even worse than the mermaids' smelly crotches do. Any besides, Odysseus. How the hell do you have sex with mermaids, who are half fish? Believe me. I assure you, Odysseus; the Sirens beaver slits don't taste like chickens of the sea!"

"What will happen next?" I curiously asked Circe. "Now I fully fathom that these Sirens' song should always represent a warning signal, both now, and in the future!"

"Dear Odysseus; I advise that your dumb-fuck crew row-on past the lethal choir with having some sweet wax stuffed inside their ears, so that none of your' mariners can listen, be distracted, and crash your vessel straight into the jutting jetty. But if you're keen on hearing their hypnotic melody, make your crew tie you to the mast, if you enjoy being tantalized like Tantalus down in Hades. When your rebellious sailors have rowed-on past the beckoning Sirens, think about your wife Penelope, because your fragile marriage is also on the rocks. I cannot tell you which alternative to follow on your arduous route; for you yourself will have to trust your instincts to get back to Ithaca, wherever the hell that dump of a city-island happens to be located. You'll be on your own, Odysseus. I can only tell you about the Sirens' danger as your Bireme approaches their jetty!"

"Now King Alcinous, I humbly beg your indulgence. When I was down in morose Hades, the shade of the dead prophet Teiresias informed something important about me passing past a narrow passage having towering rock cliffs on either side. But remarkably, Circe knew about *that* circumstance, too!"

"Odysseus, I do not wish to share the gods' secrets as I like sharing my pussy. All that I can reveal to you are the names Scylla and Charybdis! One will be on the left, and the other on the right of the towering, and sometimes clashing-together cliffs, which will squeeze your vessel flat like the enormous vice belonging to the underground volcano blacksmith, fifty-foot-tall Hephaestus, possessor of the red, two-inch-long penis."

"Circe, the prophet I had consulted down in Hades also mentioned a place called Thrinacia. Do you know anything pertinent about it?"

"Since you have asked me, dear Odysseus, and the source of the inquiry has not originated from my mind or mouth, I can share some vital knowledge with you. Thrinacia, is a secluded, sacred land where Helios Hyperion, the sun god, keeps his quivering cattle to graze safely away from the danger of human arrows kept in quivers. His rich flocks, consisting of seven herds of golden cattle, and just as many lovely flocks of golden sheep, with fifty in each group, are revered by Helios, who believes that silence is golden; so, the sun god never mentions the secret grazing location to anyone! In short, don't dare to even graze the grazing sheep!"

"Will my mariners and I be executed if we trespass on this place Thrinacia, which you've so accurately described?"

"Not exactly, dear Odysseus. The golden cattle and sheep bear no young and never die. Their immortal herders are also divine. Now, if you leave these golden animals unharmed and exclusively focus on your long journey home, I think you may fortunately get back to Ithaca, although you'll meet other misfortunes along the irregular route. But please remember: if you harm the sacred cattle in any way in regard to these cows and sheep grazing, then like Eurassisgras, your ass will be grass! If you dare violate the vindictive sun god's stipulations, then Odysseus, I foresee destruction and ruin for your ship and your crew. Even if you yourself escape the devastating dilemma, a fucked-up debacle that you will have irresponsibly caused, I predict with certainty that you'll get back to Ithaca in great distress, and all alone, after all your shipmates have been killed by factors I cannot now reveal."

"When rosy Dawn finally fully appeared on her golden throne, frustrated Circe left my company to go up-island and search for her lost, magical vibrating dildo. So later, I returned back to the ship, where I urged my grumbling comrades to get on board and loosen-off the ropes, not disclosing to them that our mission was destined to be on the ropes, too. The brass-knuckleheads quickly clambered inside the ship, sat-down in proper order at each assigned rowing bench, and struck the gray sea surface with their splintery oars, as a favorable fair wind blew, just like more-than-decent fellatio, behind our damaged, dark-prow vessel."

"Several hours thereafter, the cooperating wind abruptly died-down. Everything was calm, without a hint of gusting. Some interfering sea god had stilled the waves, and our nautical passage was no longer a breeze. My comrades, whose dull minds were in the doldrums, stood-up, furled the sail, stowed the material inside the hollow ship's small storage hull, and then sat at their oars, churning the smooth water white with their polished blades carved out of fine pine. Wielding my sharp sword, I methodically sliced a large round chunk of thick wax into smaller bits, and then kneaded the pieces into functional shapes with my strong fingertips. My worried mind carefully considered the whole puzzling situation: my fucked-up sailors have so much grit and grime in their ears that the numbskulls might not really need this wax, but better safe than sorry! I theorized and assessed."

"Once I had sufficiently plugged my comrades' ears with the aforementioned thick wax, the fools, pretending to be rehearsing a mutiny, tied my hands and feet onto and against the ship's central pole, so that I stood upright, hard against the sturdy mast, and would not be able to masturbate. The fools next lashed the rope ends to the mast as well, but then returned to their separate work stations, and the rowers sat and struck the gray sea with their dependable oars. But when we were about as far away as a man often discernibly shouts 'Fuck you!', moving forward quickly, our swift Bireme did not slip past the singing Sirens sitting on the jetty. Once we navigated in close without me as the captain barking commands, the very fascinating mermaid bitches began orchestrating their clear-toned cry."

"Odysseus, you' famous, fucked-up, intriguing asshole; yes, great glory of the Achaeans; come over here and wonder at our splendid harmony. Let your sleek ship pause for a while, so that you can hear the marvelous songs we shall sing, like a beauty salon quartet. No man has ever rowed inside his black ship past here without attending his ears to absorb the beauty of our glorious songs; yes, our sweet-voiced melodies, like a Bohemian rhapsody, sung from our own chaffed lips. Our melodic music brings sailors unmatched joy, and mariners depart from here becoming wiser, instant smart alecks, just like you, Odysseus; you dumb-fuck wise-ass. We angelic Sirens, who in the future will be honored by police departments and fire houses, fully understand all the misfortunes your brave men had endured at Troy; yes, hardships faced by Trojans and Achaeans alike, who in truth, did not like each other's body odor. Now Odysseus, order your fucked-up crew to row closer to us, or you'll really make us pissed-off to the point where our entire chorus might be changed by the gods into gay male mermaids, simply because we could not effectively execute Poseidon's vengeful game plan! Thank Zeus that we Sirens are all female altos. We don't' have to have our balls castrated because we already alto-gether sound like high frequency, rap crap, effeminate, eunuch choir boys! We don't need that castration shit!"

"Now King Alcinous, the hypnotizing voices that reached me were so fine and transcendent that my ears could not resist listening any longer to the rhythmic cadence. I shouted at my crew to set me free from my mast tethering, sending the preoccupied rowers vividly clear signals with my eyebrows, which their dedicated activity thankfully ignored. Then, after the crew made a west turn on the eastern ocean, Perimedes and Eurylochus arose, bound me tighter with additional rope, and then being pissed-off, lashed me across my eyelashes. When the highly focused rowers had paddled my boat well beyond the Sirens' sound range, one of the mermaids was still singing solo, so low that I could barely hear her exquisite voice."

"Feeling safe and secure, my elite Phaeacian audience, my loyal sailors quickly removed the wax I had stuffed into each man's ears, and the two main crewmembers obliged by loosening the mast ropes that had wonderfully salvaged my men and me. But once we'd left the island's jetty trap far behind, I viewed giant waves rising, and smoke billowing into the sky not far ahead."

"Then, King Alcinous, my auditory perception discerned a crashing roar. My crew became terrified, fearing a crash of the nearby Titans. I paced through the ship, cheering-up the totally intimidated wimps, standing beside each one as I moved along, and speaking resolute phrases of reassurance."

"Friends, up to this point, we have not been strangers to all kinds of fucked-up misfortune. Surely, the bad omens we're presently hearing and seeing are nothing worse than when the one-eyed Cyclops kept us as trapped prisoners inside his expansive cavern. But even there, thanks to my superb excellence, keen intelligence, and coy planning, we escaped being eaten alive. Seeing no one in my audience being a trifle interested, I felt compelled to continue my superficial prattling."

"I think that someday we'll be remembering these prodigious dangers, too, and relate the tales to our great-grandkids, and emphasize to them how fucked-up mortal life is under the callous dominion of the insane Olympian gods. But come now, ancient mariners; all of us should follow what I say, even though everyone aboard knows that I'm a model asshole not fit to emulate. Stay by your oars, keep striking them against the surging sea, and we'll all sing redundant choruses of 'Row, row, row our boat!' Great Zeus, possibly being distracted by the furry entrance to Hera's entrancing snatcheroo, may somehow allow us all to survive."

"I deliberately did not mention the name Scylla, for I suspected that *that* creature was a monstrous threat for which I could devise no remedy. So, we kept moving-on, up the narrow strait, groaning as we worried about participating in a one-boat demolition derby. On one side of the narrow channel lay Scylla; on the other side, deep below the waves was divine Charybdis, who according to scholars who diligently studied mythology, was a mammoth maelstrom who swallowed-up massive amounts of salt water from the seething and bubbling sea, and then gargled both nearby ships and mariners, and next swallowed the victimized sailors along with the imbibed salt water, and finally, spit their twisted bodies at Scylla, who was standing upon the opposite high rock cliffs."

"When Charybdis began sucking the turbulent salt water-down to the sea bottom, everything in the surrounding environment looked totally hazy and confused; and soon, a dreadful roar arose around the perilous clashing rocks, and in the depths of the maniacal whirlpool, the dark and sandy bottom at the sea's floor was plainly visible. Pale fear gripped my comrades, who all had already shit their tunics at least three times. And when we saw the havoc that Charybdis had been causing, we were afraid we'd be destroyed, mingled with salt water, and then spit-out and propelled onto Scylla's towering crags while involuntarily participating in a real legendary cliff-hanger."

"Captain!" dumb-ass Eurcockisnum loudly shouted in my direction while referring to Charybdis. "I've finally found something that sucks more than you do!"

"During the disgusting encounter, Scylla had snatched-away six of my hysterical companions, right from the recently-swabbed deck; the plucked/fucked mariners being among the strongest and the bravest men I had, including Eurcockisnum, a callow virgin who always wished to be sucked and eaten by a female, but certainly not by the viperous thirty-foot-tall Scylla."

"I instinctively turned to watch as Scylla flipped the screaming sailors high over her head, quickly breaking three warriors' bodies in half with her dagger-like teeth as the awesome monster violently snapped her head back and forth in rapid succession. The doomed victims cried-out and screamed, calling my accursed name. My keen ears heard my ship's fourth mate Eurcockisnum shrieking: "This is not how I fuckin' wanted to be eaten'!""

"Then, King Alcinous, in the entrance to her massive cave, Scylla finished devouring her human quarry, licking her lips as her prey kept on screaming, stretching-out their useless arms in my direction."

"Of all the gruesome and catastrophic experiences that my eyes had witnessed in my hazardous journeying over the turbulent seas, the sight of Scylla gobbling-up my crewmen was without a doubt the most piteous, fuckin' nauseous, distressful adversity I've ever observed. But in the final analysis, it was much safer to drift closer to Scylla and lose a half-dozen sailors than to risk approaching the whirlpool Charybdis, and jeopardizing what was left of my nautical expedition from Troy."

"Once our pummeled vessel had made it past those crashing rocks and escaped the insane vicinity, fleeing from both Scylla and Charybdis, in two days of smooth sailing we reached the lovely island of the sun god, home to those fine herds of broad-faced cattle and plentiful, rich, golden-furred flocks, all belonging to Helios Hyperion, the greedy god of daily sunshine. I recalled the ultra-scary prophecy of the sightless Teiresias of Thebes down in Hades, and the collaborating prediction of Circe regarding the need to not abuse the obsessive sun god's golden cattle herds, or fuck-around with his coveted flocks of golden sheep."

"Shipmates; let all of you now swear this solemn *oath* dictated and offered by this big oaf, your incomparable Captain. If by chance we discover a herd of golden cattle, or a large flock of golden sheep, not one of you potential hoodlums will be so audaciously overcome with foolishness that you will avariciously slaughter a holy cow, or a sacred sheep. Instead, you'll be content to sit upon your scrawny asses and voraciously consume the sufficient food supplies that the witch/bitch Circe had so generously provided us."

"Once I'd emphasized those strict words of condemnation, I compelled the dumb-dicks to swear to Poseidon and Zeus that the sacred animals would not be tampered with, as I had just announced and commanded. When the thick-skulled muttonheads had made their impious promising, I ordered that we navigate our ship inside a nearby shallow harbor, situated by a spring having sweet, fresh water. My hungry companions disembarked and merrily prepared a welcome dinner."

"But later that evening, King Alcinous, when three-quarters of the night had passed, and the zodiac constellations had shifted their predictable positions, cloud-gatherer Zeus, with nothing better to do, stirred-up an extremely hostile wind, accompanied by an amazing storm, and torrential rain poured-down from the dark clouds upon both land and sea alike, and then as if foreshadowing a major calamity, ominous nightfall arrived and rapidly descended."

"Once rose-fingered Dawn arrived the following morning, as was our standard habit, we dragged-up our ship and then secured it inside a deep cave, which was a place that local nymphs used as a fine lap-dancing assembly hall, and also as a group sex therapy location."

"But then the obdurate South Wind kept blowing for one whole month, which seemed like Mother Nature was suffering her four-week period. No other wind had sprung-up, except those few times when the East or South Wind occasionally blew mild squalls. Now, while the partying crewmen still enjoyed their sweet red wine and soft bread, the undisciplined jerks obeyed certain orders and did not touch the sacred cattle or sheep. The temporary gentlemen were keenly focused on basically staying alive. But once the food and drink we had stored inside our ship was gone, the crap-brained cretins had to roam the island, scouring around for game, fish, and birds to swallow-down for supper. The inventive boneheads made bent hooks with which to fish, as sudden starvation gnawed-away inside their growling stomachs."

"At that point, I ventured inland, and then up-island, to the plateau's highest summit, to pray to the gods, hoping that one of the 'don't give a shit' tyrants would show me a viable way back to Ithaca. One time, I had moved across the island, far from my companions. I washed my hands in a protected spot, a shelter from the wind, and said my solemn prayers to all the eccentric gods who resided atop Mount Olympus, who mercifully poured sweet sleep across my weary eyelids."

"Meanwhile, doltish Eurylochus began lecturing truly bad advice to his hard-headed, low-mentality companions."

"Shipmates; although you're suffering diarrhea and distress, hear me out. For us wretched human beings, all forms of demise are hateful, including shitting ourselves to death because of dehydration. But to die from lack of food, to meet one's fate in such a hostile manner, *that* is the worst sort of death of all. So come; let's drive away the best of Helios's golden herds, and then we'll sacrifice several of the animals to the immortal gods, who hold dominion over wide Heaven and Earth. And if we ever get home to Mother Ithaca, we'll construct for Helios Hyperion a resplendent temple, and inside the impressive marble edifice we'll include many expensive gifts of thanksgiving, although we presently have no such national holiday. If spiteful Helios becomes enraged about his straight-horned cattle being killed for food, and desires to wreck our warship, and the other equally-powerful gods agree, I'd rather lose my life once and for all by choking on a wave, than starving to death on this miserable, abandoned wasteland."

"Eurylochus spoke very dangerous rhetoric, but his fellow comrades, valuing biological needs over rational thought, agreed with the jabberwocky-type polemics the knuckleheaded dunce had stated. The imbeciles quickly and eagerly rounded-up the finest beasts from Helios's herd, and also from the sun god's golden corral, which was situated close-by. The crazed fanatics stole sleek, broad-faced rams with curved horns, the animals being found grazing near our dark-ship's-prow. My lame-brained sailors stood around the selected rams and cows, their throats all praying to the gods for approval."

"Once the obsessed mob had falsely prayed to Olympus, the sinners cut the creatures' throats, flayed their flesh, and severed-out portions of the thighs. These slices the violators then hid in double layers of fat, and laid old raw meat on top to conceal their egregious misdeed. All of this evil action had transpired as I soundly slept inside a cove, lazily dreaming and fantasizing about my two favorite Greek tailors, Euripides and Eumenides."

"The noodle-brained sailors had no wine to pour-down upon the flaming sacrifice, so the lunkheads used some salt water for libations, and being asinine ignoramuses, the heretics roasted all the ram and cow entrails inside the blazing fire. Once the thighs were completely broiled, and the phony gourmets had a taste of delectable inner organs, the aberrant fools skewered the various portions upon burning spits."

"Now, dear Phaeacians; I meandered from the higher elevation and ambled-down by the shore to the vicinity of our swift ship. As I drew closer, the sweet smell of hot fat floated around and wafted into my sensitive nostrils. I immediately felt obligated to groan and apologize to the offended immortals, particularly Lord Poseidon and Lord Zeus."

"Father Zeus, Lord Poseidon, and revered members of your sacred family. You've forced this perilous travesty upon me in the form of that cruel sleep I just had, and your grand design was to bring about my impending doom. For my goonish companions who remained behind have planned and initiated something terribly disastrous."

"A messenger, presumably fleet-footed, sandal-winged Hermes, quickly came to Helios Hyperion, with the distraught herald bringing the regrettable news that a military contingent from Ithaca, leaving Troy, had brutally killed the fit-to-be-tied sun god's sacred cattle and holy sheep."

"Without delay, King Alcinous and Queen Arete; Father Zeus heard Helios's plea and contemplated taking his notorious vengeance-out on those pagan-behaving crewmen, whom the erratic Olympian King regarded as all being indolent, renegade companions of mischievous, diabolical Odysseus, Laertes's disobedient son."

"If those punk sailors don't pay me proper restitution for those marvelous beasts that the Greek nutcases have indiscriminately butchered, then I'll go down to Hades and aggravate your macabre brother by shining brilliant sunshine among the dead," Helios commented to Zeus.

"Friend Hyperion; I think you should keep on shining sunlight for us immortals, and also for mortal beings polluting and contaminating fertile Earth. With a dazzling thunderbolt, I myself will quickly strike at that swift ship of theirs and, in the middle of the wine-dark sea, smash the Bireme into tiny toothpicks. But first, I will take my anger out against one of the more flagrant violators."

"Zeus peered-down to Earth and witnessed horny Eurdicisin screwing, up the ass, one of Helios's sacred golden sheep. The king of gods raised his right hand and sent a wicked lightning bolt straight up Eurdicisin's anus hole, instantly killing both shocked Eurdicisin and the recipient sheep, in what amounted to a rather electrifying climax."

"Now King Alcinous; I later learned of all this bizarre excitement from the fair Nymph Calypso, who informed me in a vivid dream that she herself had heard the report directly from the lips of Hermes the Messenger."

"For six monotonous days, those delinquent comrades I had idiotically trusted, feasted there, eating the golden cattle that the dumb-fucks had rounded-up, indeed the finest beasts in Helios's herd. But when Zeus, son of Cronos, brought to us the seventh blustery day, the fierce stormy winds had died-down to a mere bland breeze. We climbed-aboard our warship at once, put-up the mast, hoisted the white sail, and promptly left the wholly dysfunctional island behind."

"Zeus was not satisfied with simply electrifying Eurdicisin up the ass with the powerful lightning blast, so the king god, with the assistance of his demented brother, Poseidon, produced a severe tempest that snapped the mast of my once-stellar vessel. The heavy pole landed squarely on my helmsman's skull, shattering the sailor's bones into tiny white fragments."

"On the tenth night thereafter, I was again guided to Ogygia by the influence of the gods; yes, we landed upon the fucked-up island which fair-haired Calypso called home. Still hot for my hurting body, the horny nymph welcomed and treated me with delicate care. But why should I redundantly tell you Phaeacians *that* same story again, now from which I had originally started? If you recall, King Alcinous and Queen Arete, it was only yesterday, in your palatial home, that I had told both of you the strange interaction I had experienced with the captivating nymph, Calypso. And quite frankly, it's an irritating disservice, I think, to re-tell a fantastic story that's been clearly narrated once before."

Chapter 17

"ODYSSEUS LEAVES PHAEACIA"

Odysseus paused to gauge the total impact that his narrative had had upon his seemingly mesmerized audience. All Phaeacians present sat in silence, motionless, and evidently spellbound inside the vast shadowy hall.

"So, you see, kind Phaeacians. I've tried to describe my crazy adventures to you noble residents in true chronological order, but one thing is certain. I've sadly lost all my sailors, and all twelve of my fifty-man Biremes. I've arrived to your admirable land alone, after my self-made raft had been demolished by Poseidon's cruel wrath, presumably caused by me blinding his inhuman son, the all-too-primitive Cyclops, Polyphemus."

"Odysseus; since you're visiting my meeting hall, with its brass floors and high-pitched roof, I think you won't leave here and go back to your Ithaca disappointed, although you've truly suffered much bad luck along the way. Clothing for you, our distinguished guest, is packed already, and stored in a polished chest inlaid with gold, as well as all the other gifts brought here by designated Phaeacian government counselors."

King Alcinous dispatched a staccato voiced herald to conduct his counselors to the dock where the fast Phaeacian ship had been moored. Once the farewell party had walked-onboard to inspect the sleek vessel, the dockworkers immediately carried the food and drink items, and stowed the abundant supplies inside the ship's hull. The assembled "departure entourage" spread a rug and a linen sheet upon the deck at the stern, so that Odysseus could relax and enjoy a peaceful sleep during his imminent sea passage.

The fatigued-from-speaking Trojan War hero ambled aboard, and lay down in silence. Each rower then sat in proper order at his assigned oarlock. The conscientious port laborers loosened the cable from the perforated stone. Once the muscular rowers leaned-back and stirred the water with their oars, a calming sleep fell upon Odysseus's eyelids, undisturbed and very soothing.

Not even reeling hawks zooming in flight, or the swiftest of all flying species, could match the beautiful vessel's speed, as the rugged sea conqueror raced ahead, slicing through the splashing ocean waves, bearing on board a special passenger whose mind was like a god's distinguished cerebrum. The main passenger's heart, in earlier days, had undergone much pain and duress, as the renowned warrior, known for his strength and guile, had maneuvered through conflictive wars and had suffered much hardship upon the formidable sea waves. Now, Odysseus slept in peace, forgetting all his troubles, and dreaming of how his return to Ithaca should be coordinated and executed.

The Phaeacian ship, named "Piece of Ass", was usually utilized as a floating whorehouse, but this current voyage was its first legitimate charter. The one-eyed navigator, had once visited Ithaca, and had a rough idea where the remote island was located, somewhere far from historic Lesbos, the very popular lesbian resort and spa destination.

When the most splendid of the morning stars appeared, which always comes to herald light from early Dawn, the fast sea-faring "Piece of Ass" was nearing Ithaca like a speeding piece of hanging antelope shit. Those athletic rowers' arms had so much strength that half the boat, which was moving quickly, was driven-up on shore and immediately created a burrow six-foot-deep upon the sandy beach. Once the crew had clambered from that well-built merchant ship onto dry land, first the mariners carried-off Odysseus, lifting him out of the hallowed hollowed hull on that isolated section of the ghetto island Known as Ithaca.

Odysseus was still wrapped-up in the linen sheet and splendid blanket, looking much like an ancient Greco frankfurter. The mariners next placed snoozing Odysseus down upon the shore, which was loaded with sandfleas and other bothersome, biting insects, but the hero was still fast asleep.

The sailors then brought ashore the fabulous gifts which the Phaeacian noblemen had given their illustrious guest; all thanks to the goodwill of powerful Athena, who had stimulated their donations, and who had subconsciously promised the junior stevedores good individual and group sex for the remainder of their mortal lives.

The workmen placed the extravagant golden chests containing silver and porcelain gifts, expensive jewelry, and versatile adult sex toys against the trunk of a decaying olive tree, and quickly, neatly stacked the rare metal containers in a conspicuous pile, situated some distance from a path, in case some staggering drunk or mendicant came-by and stumbled-upon the magnificent goods, before Odysseus could wake-up from his extended slumber. Then, the motivated Phaeacians climbed aboard their sleek vessel and set-off for home, ready to indulge in obtaining eager-beaver sex from the whores that Athena had cleverly suggested to their subconscious libidos.

In the interim, livid Poseidon complained to Brother Zeus about what the naïve, humanitarian Phaeacians were doing to assist Odysseus, and sympathetic Zeus immediately granted permission to his equally vengeful sibling to "severely punish the fucked-up do-gooders". So, Poseidon, using an accurate mask facsimile of Medusa the Gorgon, turned the Phaeacian ship and crew to stone, just as the "Piece of Ass" identification logo then remarkably read in etched stone, "Piece of Shit".

Meanwhile, brave Odysseus, asleep in his own land, finally woke-up. But the napper did not recognize just exactly where he was. And so, all things seemed unfamiliar to the returning king; the long straight paths; the majestic harbor with safe anchorage; the sheer-faced stony cliffs, and the deciduous trees in rich full bloom. So, feeling spry and energized, the returning king jumped-up and looked-out at his barren native land. Odysseus groaned aloud and struck his thighs with both his palms, and then cried out in sorrow:

"Where the hell am I now? Whose strange country have I come to this time? Are the inhabitants violent, unjust, and cruel? Do the natives of this dump welcome lost strangers? Do their minds respect the fucked-up Olympian gods? And all this treasure here; where do I take the extravagant gifts without getting robbed? What the fuck do I have to do to safeguard these priceless valuables?"

Then, overwhelmed with a severe longing for his native land, the new arrival weakly wandered upon the shore dunes beside the crashing surf. But then his Olympus patron, Pallas Athene, floated-in on a low cloud, and soon the talented goddess shape-shifted into the form of a handsome young man.

Odysseus, happy to catch sight of what he thought was another human, came-up and spoke to him/her.

"My friend; since you're the first one I've encountered here on this thorny, desolate beach, tell me the honest truth; where the hell are all the sun bathers? What country is this land? Are you also marooned on this island, even though your skin color is not lavender? Is this nightmare place some sunny island, or is this merely a small cape jutting from the mainland out to sea?"

Athena, goddess with the gleaming eyes, replied: "Disoriented Stranger, far from either China or Japan; you must be a full-fledged, wacky fool, or else you've come here from somewhere far away like Hades or the Moon. If you must ask about this land's identity, its name is not unknown. Many men have heard of it, either gay, straight or transgender. Ithaca is well-known, even to paupers in Sparta, in Mycenae, and also in Troy; all three cities being a long way from this accursed Achaean land."

Lord Odysseus instantly felt great joy, being happy to learn of his ancestral land firmly beneath his feet. Bright-eyed Athena smiled and stroked him with her hand. Then, the versatile deity changed herself into a lovely, sexy, tall woman, because the caring Daughter of Zeus was very adept at creating and projecting splendid and adorable visions.

"Odysseus, of all Greek warriors, you're the best at making plans and giving persuasive speeches, and among all gods, I'm well-known for my gentle subtlety, and my divine wisdom. Still, you failed to recognize in your midst Athena, daughter of Zeus, who's always at your side, whether the hell you can see me or not. Whether your diminutive pea-brain realizes it or not, I'm looking-out for you in every novel crisis. Yes, noble hero; it was I who had compelled all those feckless Phaeacians to love your worthy ass. Now, I've come to weave a looming scheme with you, and help you hide those luxurious goods you've stupidly placed behind that decaying olive tree."

"What is to happen to me upon my weary entrance into my own palace? Will my wife Penelope and my son Telemachus even recognize me?"

"I'll generally tell you what unchangeable Fate has in store for you, oh great adventurer. You'll find harsh troubles abounding within your now-dilapidated palace. Be patient, impulsive Odysseus; for you must endure all challenges to achieve desired success. Be vigilant. Don't tell anyone, man, woman or neuter, that you've just returned from wandering aimlessly around the known world. Instead, against your garrulous nature, keep silent as night. Bear the many pains as if you're giving birth to sextuplets. When grown men act like savages in your house, do nothing. By nothing, I mean 'no thing'. Now, brave Odysseus; let's not wait another second, but put away these treasures you've obtained from the idealistic, very gullible Phaeacians. We'll hide the precious gifts in some dark recess of yonder sacred cave, where the goods will stay safely stored inside. And then, let's think about how all these things may turn-out for the best. Like turnips, one never knows what will turn up!"

"After Athena and I hid the magnificent gifts inside the nearby cave, we sat-down by the sacred olive tree's gnarled trunk to seriously think of ways to eliminate the insolent suitors who had been courting and harassing Penelope."

"Listen-up, intrepid Odysseus. Think how your mighty hands may catch those unethical charlatans, who for three-years now, have been lording-over and cavorting inside your palace, shamelessly wooing your godlike wife, and offering Penelope their cheap marriage gifts. Most honestly, Odysseus; your faithful spouse longs for your return and your caress."

"Patron Goddess; if you had not told me all this contemporary insanity, I would've gladly shared the fate of Agamemnon, Achilles, and Ajax, and suffer and repeat endless redundancy down in Hades. Come, and weave a viable plan so I can pay those parasitic suitor bastards back for their brazen, evil greed. Stand in person by my side, beautiful Athena, and fill me with indomitable courage, as you had done when we loosened the bright diadem of Troy. Many think I am brave, but in my faltering soul, I feel both wimpy and craven."

"You can be certain I will stand by you, and I won't forget your myriad sacrifices when the real trouble starts. I predict that the blood of many suitors, who have consumed your livelihood, will be splattered, and their brains scattered, all over your palace's tawdry hall. But come now, Odysseus; I shall magically transform your appearance, so that no one on Ithaca, not even Penelope, will recognize your identity. You must first go to see the swineherd, who tends your scrawny, underfed pigs. He's well-disposed to you and loves your son, and also advocates for wise Penelope. If you have some pertinent questions, ask the loyal swineherd for guidance, for he has had some experience working with disruptive juveniles as a quack child psychologist. In the meantime, I'll speed-off to Sparta, and there, Odysseus, I'll summon back your dear son, Telemachus, who has gone to spacious Laconia, to the home of laconic Menelaus, to hear news if you are still alive, or if you are dead."

The benign goddess touched Odysseus's staff with her staff as a mild token of indirect affection. The Daughter of Zeus then mystically wrinkled the smooth skin on Odysseus's supple limbs, and transformed the dark hair upon the king's head and made it totally gray. The cunning goddess covered his arms and legs with an old man's dark-spotted skin, and next dimmed his handsome blue eyes. Odysseus next was amazed to find himself dressed in a beggar's ragged cloak, and a dirty tunic, both garments tattered, disheveled, and stained with stinking soot and stench-laden smoke.

When the two ancient schemers had finished reviewing their unique plans, Pallas Athene vanished, heading to Lacedaemon to locate and bring back Odysseus's nomadic son to Ithaca.

The returning king, disguised as a worthless tramp, left the secluded harbor, taking the rough path into the woods, and soon pacing across the rolling hills, ambled to the place where Athena had told the wanderer he would meet the uneducated-but-sagacious swineherd, who was, of all the servants that Lord Odysseus had, the one who faithfully took the greatest care of his master's hogs and pigs.

The returning warrior found the hoary gent squatting-down and taking a lengthy crap into a deep rabbit hole. But with the appearance of Odysseus, the swineherd's constipation ended when the silent intruder scared the shit out of him.

All of a sudden, the swineherds ferocious dogs observed Odysseus, and the canines howled and darted toward him, barking furiously. The returning King of Ithaca was alert enough to drop his staff and sit to show the attacking animals that he was of a friendly disposition. But the loyal swineherd hobbled-up as fast as his feeble legs could muster, hurrying and rushing forward, vociferously shouting a series of unpleasant expletives at his vicious dogs, and scattering the irritated canines by hurling a hail of stones in their' direction.

"Old Man; those dogs would've ripped you apart in no time, and then, like any lying vagrant-pedestrian, you would've heaped the blame on me. Well, I've got other troubles from the gods, for as I stay here on my master's estate, raising fat pigs for other sinful men to eat, I'm full of sorrow, for my noble master, who has been away for twenty-years, and I fully regret that countless miseries haunt and contaminate his family; all caused by a gaggle of fucked-up suitors. But come Stranger; enter into my ramshackle hut, and I shall provide you with adequate food and drink, because I pity your plight as an indigent seeking vital nourishment."

"Thank you, kind swineherd; your generosity is quite exemplary! May the gods reward you!"

"When you have had enough to eat and drink and your heart's content is satisfied, you can tell me where you come from, and what hardships and obstacles you've endured."

With those sympathetic words, the loyal swineherd entered the hut, waved Odysseus inside, and invited his new-found guest to sit and eat five-day-old leftovers. Odysseus was glad to receive that meager hospitality, so the master of the estate politely addressed the swineherd.

"Kind Swineherd; may Zeus give you whatever wishes you desire; I appreciate that your magnanimous heart has welcomed me into your troubled life."

"It would be wrong, Stranger, for me to disrespect a less fortunate guest," swineherd Eumaeus answered. "Even if one worse-off than you arrived, for every guest and beggar comes from Zeus, rich or poor, under the protection of the Olympian's Suppliant Law. Now where did you come from?" Eumaeus asked. "And please don't tell me from your mother's vagina!"

"I'm a traveler from Crete, but I got lost on my journey back home. I didn't have enough coins to pay my entire fare, so the captain ordered that I be dispensed with at the next island stop, which is this weird place, Ithaca, I believe," Odysseus lied.

"Well, if you're from Crete as you say, you must know all about Minos!" Eumaeus asked.

"What the hell is wrong with your nose?" Odysseus answered. "Do you have three nostrils?"

"Well now, mild-mannered, dirtbag Stranger. I'd like to know everything about the famous Minotaur."

"Most tours in Crete last much longer than an hour," the itinerant Beggar cleverly replied.

"Okay, anonymous Visitor," Eumaeus declared. "Please tell me about the advanced civilization on Crete."

"The Cretans are a very smart people. The Cretans definitely are not cretins!" Odysseus coyly and confidently stated.

As those two mental cases were sillily conversing, the younger estate herdsmen came-up, bringing home the property's twenty-two remaining hogs. The sows were shut-up and contained inside their customary pens, and the emaciated pigs gave-out weak squeals, as the animals were herded inside for sleep time.

"Bring a boar in here, the best there is, so I can butcher it for this peaceful Stranger, who has arrived from another country," Eumaeus ordered his young associate.

"Thanks again for your courteous hospitality," the shrewdly disguised beggar indicated to his sympathetic host. "You are most accommodating!"

"We too will get some benefit from pigging-out," the head swineherd joked. "We can't afford lamb chops, but pork chops are definitely on the menu. But Stranger; my mundane existence is quite boring, watching these slimy, stench-laden hogs porking each other all day long; that is, when I'm not actively slaughtering the squealing bastards. I've even learned and mastered their simple piggy language. One oink means 'Let's eat'; two quick oinks mean 'Let's sleep'; three fast oinks mean 'Get out of my damned way'; four consecutive oinks mean 'I gotta' take a shit', and five rapid-in-succession oinks succinctly mean 'Let's fuck'!"

Once Eumaeus uttered that informative declaration, the elderly swineherd used his sharp bronze axe to chop wood for kindling, while his protege led-into the hut a large tusked boar, five years old, and stood the snorter by the humble hearth. The kind-hearted pig-keeper solemnly prayed to the zany gods that his master Odysseus would return and reclaim his rightful, entitled estate.

The junior hog attendant proceeded to raise his arm, and holding a huge oak club, struck the boar's head, and life instantly left the beast. The subordinate herdsmen skillfully slit the dead creature's throat, singed its bristles, and, working quickly with both hands, deftly carved-up the carcass.

"Eumaeus, may father Zeus treat you as well as you are treating me with this abundant boar's flesh, and if I may add, the very finest cut of meat, even though I'm just an impoverished beggar sitting inside your modest hut."

"Eat plenty, god-guided Stranger, and enjoy the only kind of food I have to offer. A deity capriciously gives some favors and holds others back, as his or her fickle heart prompts, for the inimitable Olympians can do all oddball things."

According to tradition, Eumaeus prayed again and offered to the eternal gods the first and best pieces he had cut. The pig-master poured gleaming wine as a libation, handed another cup to Odysseus, fearless sacker of cities, and then sat-down to eat his portion.

Twilight soon converted to night, bringing stormy winds and inhospitable rain, with no moon visible in the black sky. Showing compassion for his frail guest, Eumaeus covered the sleeping Odysseus with his only blanket, as heavy rains penetrated the leaky, thatched roof, saturating both humans inside the dilapidated hut. The sleeping king appreciated the wonderful kindness of his old faithful servant, and Odysseus, realizing that he had knowledge of one dedicated ally on his side, was quite tempted to reveal his true identity to loyal Eumaeus, whose troubled mind only ever thought about his oinking hogs and his missing master.

Chapter 18
"TELEMACHUS RETURNS TO ITHACA"

In less than a blink of an eye, Pallas Athene zoomed-down to Sparta and visited Telemachus, telling the lethargic dreamer to return home and communicate with the swineherd Eumaeus. Meanwhile, back in Ithaca, Odysseus and Eumaeus continued to thoroughly discuss the treacherous situation prevailing inside the Ithacan royal palace.

After receiving his final full-body massage from seventeen spa attendants, Telemachus departed Sparta for equally-depressing Pylos, and next reluctantly set sail for his raunchy homeland. A week later, the assigned lesbian and transgender crew spotted the Ithacan coast and tossed the son of Odysseus into the raging surf, making the callow punk swim to shore after the adolescent refused to have wild sex with a homosexual male gorilla that had been stowed on board.

The feckless teen finally got his bearings straight, even though he was nowhere near fictional Alaska, and the soaking-wet trekker soon miraculously reached the farmyard and the herds of oinking pigs, among whom the loyal swineherd still lay asleep, always-contemplating nice gentle thoughts about his assumed-dead master and owner.

At dawn, Odysseus and the loyal pig custodian, Eumaeus, without any formal arson education, lit a fire inside the dingy hut and prepared their smelly breakfast of hog entrails and raunchy piggy-sausage.

As Telemachus approached the ramshackle hut, the yelping dogs stopped barking and fawned after recognizing the familiar human. Perceptive Lord Odysseus peered-out the only window, noticed what the vicious dogs weren't doing, and quickly relayed that irrelevant information to the half-asleep swineherd.

"Eumaeus, I believe that some friend of yours is either encroaching or approaching your hut. Your ferocious dogs aren't barking and are acting peculiar and friendly."

Soon, Telemachus was standing inside the unlocked entry portal, still dazed from being tossed into the surf and landing upon a surprised sand-shark, that had been eating a large crab. Recognizing the drenched kid's face, the amazed swineherd jumped-up to enthusiastically greet his current master, before addressing the seventy-five-pound weakling.

"You've come back to this sour land, Telemachus, you sweet light. I thought I'd never see your ass around here anymore. You know, I did study to be a proctologist when I myself was an ambitious youth. But now, once you had sped-off to Pylos in that ship paid for by the parasite suitors, and with your own money, I thought you had run-away from home, seeking a better life as a reckless recluse. Come in here now, dear boy, so that my heart can feel the joy of seeing you inside my humble pigsty, now that you've returned from experiencing your' experiment as an isolated, crabby itinerant playboy."

Immediately, hearing Eumaeus say his son's name, Odysseus stood and offered Telemachus his rickety stool.

"Stay put, Stranger. We'll find a stool somewhere, perhaps inside Eumaeus's potty outhouse. I'm surprised that the swineherd has taken you in. Usually, Eumaeus doesn't give a crap about a stool."

Odysseus went back and sat down again, thinking about his next bowel movement. Then, after a brief silence, Eumaeus heaped a pile of green brushwood upon the dirt floor, and spread a fleece on top where Odysseus's sore-assed son sat-down to soothe his burgeoning hemorrhoids. "Telemachus, let the three of us break our fast and have breakfast together. Then, you can review for my guest and me your dumb-fuck travels to Pylos and to distant Sparta."

Being filled with nostalgia and sentimentality, Telemachus felt compelled to speak the truth amongst the chorus of three growling stomachs. "Old friend, Eumaeus; you must go quickly and report to wise Penelope that I've returned," the wimpy adolescent related. "I felt most wanted and welcome in Pylos, where everyone there had piles and nasty hemorrhoids, just like myself. I'll stay here inside your hut, until you've told the news to my mother that I've returned with accomplishing absolutely nothing at all. No other Achaean must learn about my being back here in Ithaca, for I think that I'm too young to be violently castrated and beheaded. I suspect that the evil suitors are hatching a tailor-made, dangerous plot against me, and I fear being brutally executed for the first time. After you've informed my mother of the news that I'm safely back, then rush here to this shanty right away. Don't go roaming around the fields looking for senile Grandpop Laertes. Instead, tell my mother to send her maid, the housekeeper whose name I can't remember, but she should send the bitch quickly, and in secret. The housekeeper can report the news to the old man, not to my Old Man, but to forgetful Pop-pop Laertes, who erroneously thinks that Mother Penelope has become a nun working as the head priestess inside the downtown Metropolitan Holy Olympian Apostate Temple."

After Eumaeus scurried-out of the pathetic shack to report to Penelope that Telemachus had returned, Pallas Athene appeared upon the scene, only visible to Odysseus and the barking dogs, but not to Telemachus, who was itching to scratch his pimpled rear end.

"Son of Laertes, adventurous Odysseus, sprung from Zeus," Athena prefaced her declaration. "Now is the time to speak and address your only son, who after being evicted from your palace, will have no street address in which to call home. Make yourself known to the potential juvenile delinquent, and don't conceal the vital facts, so that together, you two awkward simpletons, along with Eumaeus, can plan the suitors' lethal fate. Then together, trek to your infamous city, and enter your palace with a pure heart, so stay-away from all the local bordellos and brothels until your vital revenge mission has fully transpired. I won't be absent from you for very long, Odysseus; for I'm an avid, vicarious battle witness, and I'm eager to view your upcoming fight against the leeching suitors."

After the enchanting goddess enunciated those cryptic words, Athena touched Odysseus with her golden wand, and immediately, an unblemished cloak appeared around his now-youthful body, which was much taller, and had been marvelously restored to a much younger age. The hero's skin grew dark once more; his countenance filled-out, and the beard covering his chin turned black-as-pitch again. Once the miracle-worker had initiated those dramatic changes, even before the days of plastic surgery, Athena vanished in a puff, and Odysseus stepped-back into the hut, thinking about what wild and crazy sex with a goddess would be like. His dear son was amazed at the sensational transformation of the former feeble mendicant. The timid lad turned his eyes away, afraid that his father was a god, ready to beat the shit and piss out of him.

"Stranger; now you look quite different than you did before. You're wearing different clothes, and the *pig*mentation of your skin has changed. Your new skin changes the complexion of everything! In this phenomenon I'm seeing, I'm noticing what actually happens when someone rubs the disgusting skin of filthy hogs all day long? I suspect that you're one of the fickle gods who rule over wide heaven. If so, be gracious, so that I can give you pleasing offerings, and well-crafted gifts, as soon as my irresponsible father returns home to reclaim his ass-backwards, bankrupt kingdom."

Long-suffering, regal-looking Lord Odysseus then answered young, still-shocked Telemachus. "Don't insult my intelligence, Foolish Fellow.

I'm not one of the fucked-up gods arriving here to break your' tiny stones. Why do you compare me to immortals? But indeed, and truthfully, Telemachus; I am your itinerant father, on whose account you are grieving and are suffering such tremendous distress, having to bear ambitious fools' committing acts of insolence, while still not being old enough to be a skilled mariner or warrior; I believe that you're now awkwardly navigating through the wimpy phase of your pre-adult life."

Telemachus reflexively embraced his noble father, whom the idiot still thought was a prankster Olympian god deliberately frustrating his emotions with a lousy impersonation of the Ithacan King. Both father and son lamented, and cried like irritated babies bawling for more breast milk. That's exactly how those two groaning grown assholes let tears of sorrow fall from underneath their melancholy eyes. And at that precise moment, light from the brilliant sun almost-disappeared, as the reunited pair incessantly wept. Telemachus soon found a greasy rag to clear his wet face, and then asked his rejuvenated father about *his* hanky-panky activities while being AWOL from Ithaca for two decadent decades.

"Father, in what kind of advanced ship did drunken sailors carry you here to Ithaca? Where did the stupid-shit fools say they were from? For I don't think you made it back here on foot, wading your way through the wine-dark Mediterranean."

"All right, my sperm-less child. I shall tell you the uncouth truth. Phaeacians, those famous sailors of yore that bards and retards often sing about, brought me safely back home. The bored idiots have nothing better to do than to escort lost castaways to their native lands and take them all over creation, as is *their* quixotic habit and reputation. But now, it's time to tell me the approximate number of leeching suitors there are, so that I may know exactly how many obnoxious fuck-heads are hanging-out like dirty laundry inside my palace, and what the human vermin are truly like. Then, once my noble heart has thought-over all possible and impossible contingencies, I'll make-up my disheveled mind, whether we two dreamers are powerful enough to take them on alone, without assistance, or whether we should seek-out and employ the fighting services of other stout-hearted, mercenary, Ithacan warriors."

"Father, I've often heard about your great renown, you being a mighty warrior in search of your destiny. Your hands are strong, and I'm sure that your plans will be intelligent enough for any low-level moron to fathom. But what you've now contemplating is far too big a task to initiate. I'm astonished that you believe that you and me alone could fight against at least two-dozen arrogant-and-powerful bellicose fucks, who prey upon your dwindling estate, all having fixations of marrying Mother Penelope, and then humping and pumping the poop out of your wife on your own hard mattress, or atop your tin palace roof, or on top of your pet camel, er, I meant to say, on top of your favorite dromedary!"

"All right, I'll tell you straight-up, Telemachus. Pay attention now, and listen with all three of your ears. Do you believe that Athena, along with Father Zeus, and possibly also legendary Mother Goose, will be enough support for the two of us inspired fools to combat the crazy suitors, or should I think about who else might help us? Perhaps if we prudently pray hard enough, we can obtain the aid of Hephaestus, the deformed blacksmith god, to hammer some volcanic lava up the freeloaders' colons and semi-colons!"

"Father, those Olympian allies you've mention are quite excellent. They sit high in the clouds, ruling others, immortal gods, demigods and men," Telemachus naively agreed. "We'd better include the easily-slighted, chariot-riding sun god, too, so that we don't have to apologize to Apollo for leaving Helios Hyperion out of our capricious strategy alliance."

"Yes, pathetic dumb-shit!" Odysseus agreeably boomed. "Only empathetic Athena cares a scintilla about what the hell happens to me. All of the other gods have amnesia about constructively helping us defeat this ravenous, diabolical horde of licentious vultures. But for now, Telemachus; when Dawn arrives with her hairless crack, go to the palace, join company with those haughty suitors, and cordially mingle with the demented scoundrels. The swineherd Eumaeus will accompany me to the city later on. I'll be disguised like a pretentious beggar, old and wretched with arthritis all over my body, except in my incomparable fadorkenbender. If the obnoxious dregs are abusive towards me, let that dear heart within your chest endure the cursing and derision of the nasty dirtballs, while I'm being badly mistreated and scorned, even if the diabolical scumbags drag me by my testicles all throughout the house, attempting to hold my feet and scrotum sac to the fire, and then meanly throwing my ass out the door, and then begin hurling sharp objects and weapons in my direction."

"How will I know when all the exciting drama and the trauma will commence?" Telemachus asked. "I want to get directly involved and not become a useless part of the Mr. Olympus protection program!"

"Keep looking forward with anticipation, vernal Telemachus, and hold yourself in check, until the appropriate time is ripe. When wise Athena plants the exact 'go signal' inside my mind, I'll give you the nod to participate in the melee by bobbing my head up and down like a neurotic mental patient. Once you see that symbolic gyration, remove all of the weapons of war ornamented upon the external hall walls, and stow the spears, bows and arrows in a safe place, perhaps in the lofty upstairs storage room, modeled after the one I had once seen in Attica."

"Any other directions, father?"

"Be sure to leave behind a pair of swords, two spears, and two ox-hide shields for the two of us to grab when we make a wild rush at the surprised, partying bastards; I'm confident that our colleague, Pallas Athene, will keep the son-of-a-bitches' minds preoccupied with visions of perverted and gay pornographic images. I'll tell you something else of a meritorious nature; if you are my son, truly of our family blood, let no one in Ithaca hear that Odysseus is back home."

"Can't I even tell grandfather? He won't remember anything I say, anyway!"

"Don't even let Laertes know, even if *my* senile old man has amnesia and has developed six brain tumors. And keep our secret away from the swineherd Eumaeus, and the remaining vigilant slaves, or even Queen Penelope herself must not know of my reappearance and planned insurgency. The goddess Athena, my son, had just told me in a vision that King Menelaus has sent a ship with additional gifts for me to the house of Clytius, the brother of Clitoris, for safe-keeping until our vengeance has been fully enacted and consummated!"

Meanwhile, back at the palace, Antinous, the chief suitor, was addressing his inebriated and apathetic colleagues. "My friends; to tell you tiny-pricks the blessed truth, in his great fantasy, Telemachus has carried-out his preposterous trip, and remarkably, the silly dumb-shit prince has had great success. We never thought he would complete his fruitless mission, but against all odds, the lucky oddball has been successful. So, fellow rogues; let's do something terrible and gruesome to him."

No sooner had vile Antinous uttered his devious plot that ambiguous Amphinomus, turning in his seat beside a dirty broken window, observed an alien ship anchored in the deep harbor. Mariners were bringing down the sail, while others were holding their oars. With a hardy laugh, Amphinomus lustily addressed his nefarious comrades, thinking that the foreign ship was carrying Telemachus and his ample supply of gifts from Pylos and Sparta.

"Well, this is certainly the worst news ever since all-too-curious Pandora opened her box, not the one between her legs, mind you, but the one sent by Zeus to distract humanity, since the god was afraid that mortal intelligence could eventually rival and conquer the Olympians, just as the foul Olympians had risen-up, rebelled against, and defeated their ancestor Titans," Antinous lectured. "And as we all know, all of the evils contained inside Pandora's chest, not the one under her neck, but the one that was a gift from deceitful Zeus, curses flew-out of the container to plague and bewilder mankind forever. This time, the devious gods have made sure that Telemachus has been kept safe from our plot to kill him, being entertained first in Pylos, and later by King Menelaus in Sparta. Our attempt at ambushing that little squirt Telemundo, er, I mean Telemachus, is much more resilient than I had originally imagined that annoying punk to be!"

"So, once that pesky pest Telemachus is satisfactorily eliminated, we can all fairly compete at wooing and courting Queen Penelope," snidely Amphinomus, wicked brother of Iamanignoramus maintained.

'Ludicrous Fool!' Antinous selfishly conjectured. 'Penelope will consent to marrying me, because I have the most wealth, and at three-inches in length, I own the biggest erect penis amongst all of us!'

Chapter 19

"ODYSSEUS AS A BEGGAR"

As soon as rose-fingered early Dawn appeared upon the eastern horizon, Telemachus, dear son of godlike Odysseus, tied dirty sandals upon his feet and ankles, grabbed a powerful spear that was well-suited for the scum-ball suitors' chests, and soon gathered enough courage to articulate a firm message to Eumaeus, the pig-herder.

"Old brain-dead friend; I'm now leaving for the city, so that I can see and possibly commiserate with my saddened mother. I don't believe that the Queen's dreadful grieving, along with her sorrowed sobbing, will cease tears from cascading down-her cheeks until Penelope, not through commonplace hearsay, but through actual and true interaction, gets to communicate with me face-to-face. So, I'm telling you, Eumaeus; although I'm not a medical doctor, I prescribe that you do this particular event in the exact order which I'm now commanding. Take this vagrant Stranger now dozing in *my* bed into the city. Once there, the Vagabond can beg for food and charity from any well-bred person who'll offer him moldy bread and cups of stagnant water. I can't take on the weight of everyone, not when I have these myriad sorrows inhabiting my heart. As for the stranger-than-fiction Stranger, if he's especially upset at this plan, things will turn-out worse for him."

Odysseus, who was eavesdropping on the oddball monologue, rose from the hut's only bed and stated to the swine-keeper. "Friend; I myself am not all that hot-to-trot to be held back here in suburban Ithaca. For a beggar, it's better to ask mealy-mouthed people for a meal inside the city instead of asking for bullshit from the cows and steers in yonder grazing fields, that ironically, the pastures themselves never graze. Whoever's willing to give me alms from their palms should voluntarily contribute to the sustenance of my general welfare. I still possess a zest for living, despite my ragged, disheveled appearance."

"Oh, marvelous Beggar," Eumaeus commended. "You seem to possess artificial intelligence coming directly to you from the clouds! May Almighty Zeus be praised for the mental telepathy your brain is receiving from Olympus's supreme transmissions!"

Telemachus walked-away, moving at a rapid pace, and making sure the hut's squeaky door didn't hit his skinny ass on the way out. The lad's only thought was his strong desire to sow seeds of trouble for the covetous suitors, while Penelope was preoccupied upstairs, sewing and unsewing her huge tapestry.

When the sole son of Odysseus entered the deteriorating palace, Telemachus stepped through the main hall, tightly gripping his sharp spear which he had never used. Two swift-but-ferocious dogs accompanied him into the edifice, to be commanded to attack pond-scum villains if necessary. The arrogant suitors thronged around the newly-arrived youth, making phony, courteous conversation to awkwardly conceal their deep, vitriolic hatred dwelling within their minds and inside their dark souls.

Telemachus' marvelous mother had abandoned her upstairs sewing pursuit and sat across from her son, by the doorpost of the hall, leaning from her seat to spin fine threads of delicate fabric and to tell family yarns. The pair reached-out with their hands to partake of the meager crumbs and scraps prepared and set before them. When the twosome had satisfied their stomachs with rancid-tasting food and drink, the first to speak was the son.

"Mother, since this poor-diet meal, which consisted mostly of meat morsels and tasteless vegetables, I say that this low-budget dinner could only be described as being totally fruitless!"

"Telemachus, get serious for a moment! Once I've gone upstairs to my quarters, I'll lie in bed, which has become for me a place of despair, always damp with tears, ever since Odysseus sailed-off to Troy with Atreus's vengeful sons Agamemnon and Menelaus. Yet you don't now dare to tell me clearly of your father's twenty-years' absence, before the haughty suitors come back here and again shame my home and your father's legacy; in short, you've provided no substantial word of what the hell you have recently learned fucking-around down south in Pylos and in Sparta."

"All right then, Mother. I'll tell you the meaningless truth as I know it. First, my entourage and I had sailed to Pylos and reached Nestor, shepherd of his flock. The older elder welcomed us into his home with hospitality and kindness, like a genuine father-substitute would do; that's how Lord Nestor looked after providing for my stomach, but-not-after-my-great sexual needs. But as for brave Odysseus, alive or dead, Nestor had nothing worthwhile to offer that his defective ears had heard from any visiting horse's ass living on Earth. The old coot sent me off, providing me with a primitive chariot with wobbly wheels, to visit that famous spearman Menelaus, son of Atreus. In Sparta, I met Argive Helen, for whom countless Achaeans had desperately struggled hard to liberate from Prince Paris's sexy charm. Menelaus, skilled at yelling war shouts, at once questioned me, asking: Why had I come to Sparta? Was I looking to lose my virginity to the million whores humping and pumping their diseased genitals all over the city, even in the public streets? I'm telling you the honest-to-Zeus truth, Mother, describing every minute detail as I recollect them."

"Did Menelaus give you any new information concerning my husband?" the Queen wondered and asked. "That's why the hell you traveled there in the first place!"

"That travesty over in Ithaca that you're inquiring about is disgraceful and sinful!" Menelaus impulsively replied to me and my earnest plea. "The good-for-nothing two-dozen predators wasting your inheritance inside your' father's house all now-desire to lie-down in the bed of a courageous warrior and pork his faithful wife, when they themselves are cowardly jerk-offs. I predict that intrepid Odysseus will soon arrive and bring those avaricious shit-heads to their disastrous end."

"That can't be all you learned!" Queen Penelope exclaimed. "You could learn more going to a teachers' college!"

"That's exactly what great spearman Menelaus said, Mother, and in plain Greek, that's about all she wrote."

Meanwhile, indomitable Odysseus and the loyal swineherd were hastening to leave the stenchy pig-fields behind and start walking toward the city, striding past veteran battle-weary warriors in trances, and passing by the historic Ithacan National Shrine, the Sacred Country Cunt-tree. Eumaeus amiably offered Odysseus his smelly staff that he himself often used to shove-up the asses of uncooperative hogs, instantly sending the giant pigs down to swine hell as newly snorting hog-goblins.

Then, the clumsy pair approached the city center, while barking dogs and apathetic herdsmen remained two miles behind to guard the farmyard, and to spend their time pissing and shitting into rabbit, snake, chipmunk and rat holes.

The faithful swineherd casually led his anonymous master deeper into the inner city, himself also appearing much like a beggar; yes, another old-and-wretched vagrant, with his filthy body covered by shabby, threadbare rags. But as the dirty duo made their way along the cobblestone path, finally leaving the odor-laden outskirts, the twosome reached a well-made spring, with a steady flow, where townsfolk drew their daily water with pails, and not crayons.

At that crossroads, Melanthius, son of doleful Dolius, approached, driving a herd of unshaven goats, all sporting exaggerated goatees beneath thin chins; the finest ones in all the flocks, designated to serve as delicious dinner for the demanding palace suitors. When Melanthius started yelling shameful insults at his goats and at his servant underlings, Odysseus became enraged at such abuse being vocalized in public.

"Now, Eumaeus; here we have a truly filthy man vehemently cursing at another filthy scoundrel. As always, a god matches like personality with like character. Buzzards of a feather, generally always flock together! The wretched, self-important goatherder!" Odysseus the Beggar explained to Eumaeus, the don't-give-a-shit pig-master.

"Where are you off to with this disgusting beggar asshole, a tedious bore who'll most-certainly interrupt our palace feast?" Melanthius screamed at Eumaeus. "Beggars can't be choosey, but *you* certainly can!" the suitor's favored servant criticized.

Melanthius, the unethical goatherd buffoon, soon entered the decaying palace, and at once sat among the never-satisfied suitors, directly opposite Eurymachus, who was fond of the nasty dumb-shit more so than the other garrulous grubbers were.

Meanwhile, Odysseus and the wifty swineherd paused as the two came closer to the former gleaming fortress. Around them rang the music of the hollow lyre, for minstrel Phemius was about to sing another gay tune. But then a hunting dog, Argus, Odysseus's favorite, raised its head and pricked-up its ears. But before the master could enjoy being reunited with the gray-hound, the King of Ithaca's heart sadly regretted leaving the comforts of his dog and palace to venture-off to distant Troy on his twenty-year odyssey.

Odysseus looked away and brushed aside a tear he wished to hide from the swine-herder's scrutiny. "Eumaeus, it's strange that this seemingly familiar dog is lying prone here, resting in the dung without his costumed canvas dungarees that I've heard Queen Penelope had sewn for him," the master observed and commented. "Indeed, according to scuttlebutt all around the Mediterranean, the once-formidable boar-hunter had a handsome body twenty years ago. I'm not sure right now if his speed once matched his awesome looks, or if Argus is presently like those table-mooching canines that weak men perpetually pet, the extremely-spoiled pooches that their masters raise and keep for show and tell."

"Yes, clever Stranger. This muscular dog belongs to a courageous man who probably has died somewhere far away. If the gray-hound had the form and acted as he did when Odysseus had left him, and voyaged to Troy, you'd quickly see his speed and strength, and then you'd be amazed at the animal's incomparable dexterity. No wild animal that Argus had vigorously chased into the forest ever escaped his pursuit in the deep, thick woods, for that tenacious gray dog could track a scent; especially nasty ones emanating from between a horny woman's legs. But poor Argus is in a bad way now. His master's more-than-likely dead in some foreign land, and careless older women don't look after him because the elderly hags no longer enjoy having their dried-up pussies smelled. For when self-centered masters can no longer exercise their assumed power, observant slaves no longer demonstrate any desire to do their work properly."

Eumaeus carefully led the Stranger deeper inside the formerly stately mansion, walking straight into the main hall to join the ignoble, always-protesting, confiscators. But once he'd seen and recognized the odor originating from his master's crotch, after twenty years of separation, Argus's legs collapsed, and his remaining dog spirit was suddenly gripped by the fatal clutches of ever-stalking Death.

Ignoring the demise of Argus, Telemachus was the first to notice Eumaeus making the palace scene. The alert Prince, in essence, a royal pain in the ass, quickly summoned the pig-herder by nodding his head like a neurotic parrot. Eumaeus cautiously looked-around, and then picked-up a stool, placed it where a servant usually would sit, and proceeded to carve massive cuts of meat to serve the unruly, rowdy, vitriolic, fucked-up suitors.

Odysseus, looking like an old, miserable, impotent beggar, had entered unnoticed into the huge chamber directly behind Eumaeus. The returning King, with his curved back bent-over, was leaning upon his staff, with his totally covered body dressed in putrid-smelling rags. The pathetic-looking beggar sat upon the ash-wood threshold situated inside the termite-infested doorway, and the lit fireplace embers burned his sensitive ass, and nearly set his entire attire ablaze. Then, like a Greek theater actor, Melanthius, the cynical goatherder, called-out to the gathering, and imperatively yelled derogatory remarks at the newcomer to the daily feasts.

"Listen to me, those of you courting the glorious queen, about this impudent Stranger who has just entered. I've seen him before, and I've also noticed that the lowly swineherd was the one who had brought him here. I don't know the intruder's identity, or the family he might claim to have come from, but I have *bad vibrations* about this stinking trespasser, and the feeling I'm receiving doesn't exactly send me to any fucked-up, idyllic blossom world, either."

Then, Antinous turned on Eumaeus, to reprimand, embarrass, and scold the pig-keeper, and also mock and ridicule *his* apparent association with his peculiar Stranger-Beggar-acquaintance.

"You really are a nuisance scum-wagon. Yes, Eumaeus; you who cares for wallowing pigs without demonstrating any cultural esteem for your' sophisticated superiors. Why are you' so intent on bringing this scruffy fellow here into the center of town without giving the dirty piece of shit a decent ten-hour bath? As far as drifters and vagrants go, do we not already have too many of these dependent freeloaders indiscreetly panhandling around this city and inside this palace; yes, worthless bloodsuckers who cavort with impunity around the local straight, the gay, and the tri-gender communities; obviously being troublesome, greedy tramps who recklessly disrupt our elite banquets, simply to ask for our benign mercy?"

"Antinous," Eumaeus audaciously addressed the detestable head glutton. "You may be an aristocrat of sorts, but what you've just articulated, insulting this humble guest to the House of Odysseus, is indeed not a commendable and honorable speech. You are sinfully abusive, and a poison to my master's slaves, more so than any of the other detestable suitors in your company; and your harsh tongue and stinging language are especially offensive to me. But honestly, I don't give a flying fart; not while suffering Queen Penelope lives here in this once noble mansion, reigning with brave Telemachus."

Noticing Odysseus moving around the vast room begging for food, Antinous spoke-out against "lowlife from outside entering the great hall".

"What insane god sent this filthy dirt-bag into our midst to interrupt our festive feast? You're basically an insolent and shameless beggar, with no respect for educated, august noblemen. You confidently and presumptively approach each of us without conscience, one by one, and we generously give you scraps and tiny edibles, with no holding back, for we prestigious fellows religiously obey the laws of the gods without exhibiting sinful deviation."

"Well now, repugnant and pugnacious Antinous," Odysseus the Beggar defiantly challenged. "It seems as if that phony, conniving mind of yours does not match your ugly looks. You'd refuse to give even a grain of salt from your own house to a disciple of yours, and now you sit in someone else's home and do not even offer me a half-cup of diluted wine. And yet, there's plenty of sour vino in that jug sitting right in front of you."

The chief suitor glared at the stubborn mendicant and, with a wide scowl upon his countenance, gave his derisive response.

"I no longer think you'll leave this hall unharmed, decrepit Stranger; now that you've begun babbling lowlife insults in my direction. I believe that you're begging for elimination besides asking for charity!"

After perturbed Antinous screamed those derisive words, the incensed blowhard grabbed a stool and threw the heavy piece of furniture, which in seconds impacted Odysseus at the base of his right shoulder. But the brazen recipient of the toss stood firm, like a rock, and the Beggar did not stagger or buckle one iota, while Antinous became somewhat befuddled and astounded.

At the time of the ensuing argument, Queen Penelope was conversing with her chief servant women, while later, Lord Odysseus sat quietly and munched on paltry scraps and petty morsels. But then, Odysseus's dignified wife slowly stood and calmly called-out to the steadfast swineherd.

"Good Eumaeus," Penelope affably beckoned. "Go and ask the extraordinary Stranger you've brought here to come meet me, so that I can greet him warmly, and ask if he perhaps has heard any news about my brave Odysseus; or perhaps our guest might have somehow caught sight of my husband with his own aged eyes. For indeed; our unexpected, withered visitor looks like a weary man who's spent a very long time wandering all over the scientifically-proven Flat Earth."

"Honored Stranger," Eumaeus calmly said. "Wise Penelope is summoning you and your alien ideas to have a parley. For her heart, in spite of bearing much anxiety, is urging her to inquire about her husband's travails since Troy."

"Eumaeus," Beggar Odysseus sternly answered. "I'll tell the honest-to-Athena truth, along with all the significant details, and reveal the facts to discreet Penelope, daughter of Icarius, and I'll accurately describe everything pertinent rather quickly. Frankly, Eumaeus; I happen to know King Odysseus fairly well. Please tell Queen Penelope, for all her restless eagerness, to patiently wait until the predictable sun goes down in the west. Let the Queen ask me at that time about her husband's itinerant drudgery; and about the day of his wonderful return, and about everything else that the intrepid adventurer has both endured and survived. But right now, let me sit close by the warm fire, for the clothes that I'm wearing are rather thin and pitiful, and my garb stinks-to-High-Olympus, like a putrid gallon of skunk piss, and as you well-know from your own offered hospitality, and from your dreadful occupational experience, I directly came to your hut first for help, smelling and reeking like a lousy, dirty, rabid rat. In the sense of existing parallel odors, Pig-master Eumaeus, you and I are indeed kindred brothers."

Chapter 20
"EURYCLEIA RECOGNIZES ODYSSEUS"

Irus, a frequent beggar to the palace, came inside and started abusing Beggar Odysseus, whom the wise-ass regular suspected had been representing new competition for food and charity. The pair fought, and Odysseus easily knocked-out Irus, hitting the bully double-crosser with a flurry of left hooks that beat the brown feces and the yellow urine out of the aggravating son-of-a-bitch. Penelope, very impressed with the Beggar's pugilistic ability, encouraged the parsimonious suitors to bring presents for her, and the want-to-get-laid, in-heat idiots did so with dispatch. Meanwhile, Beggar Odysseus admonished the female servants, criticizing them for being too sympathetic to, and too friendly with, the belligerent suitors. Eurymachus decided to ridicule Odysseus in return, and in imitation of Antinous, threw a stool at the disguised King, but missed his target and hit the wine steward, knocking the servant unconscious. Being amused, the inebriated gluttons continued feasting, and then the contented moochers departed thereafter to their separate residences.

The wimpy Prince and the camouflaged King quickly and surreptitiously removed the weapons on display from the empty hall and stealthily concealed them in a remote storage room.

Telemachus, becoming fidgety, paced through the main hall, moved below the flaming wall torches, out into the room where he used to rest when sweet Sleep trespassed into his troubled mind. Lord Odysseus also stayed, lingering and pensively contemplating how to kill the contemptible culprits; of course, with Pallas Athene's guidance and inspiration.

After unraveling her daily tapestry enterprise upstairs, wise Penelope emerged out of her quarters, looking like a combination of huntress Artemis and golden Aphrodite. Beside the fire where the Queen used to sit, an alert servant placed an elaborate chair for her, inlaid with ivory and silver. Penelope sat, and then spoke to Eurynome, her often-preferred housekeeper.

"Fetch a comfortable chair over here with a thick golden fleece, so that the visiting Stranger can sit and share sincere conservation, er, I mean 'sincere conversation' with me. Although I know nothing about police work, I want to thoroughly interrogate the Beggar."

Obedient Eurynome quickly brought-in a polished chair, placed the object by her Queen, and as instructed, threw a clean sheep fleece over it. Lord Odysseus, who had endured so much hardship, sat-down next to his grieving wife, who found special interest in conversing with lowlife guests.

"Stranger; you appear to be a cultural moron! Who are you among men? What is your' nationality? From what city, town, land, or village do you originate? And where the hell are your negligent parents who have not adequately provided for your prosperous development?"

"Noble lady; wife of gallant Odysseus; all right, I'll tell you everything, even though it's impossible for anyone who is mortal to know everything. I've been wandering all over flat Earth, traveling through many towns of men, and suffering great distress. Still, there's a place in the middle of the wine-dark sea called Crete, where I had been born, son of Deucalion and his wife Decalian, who liked to draw logos and glue the artistic renditions onto babies' asses for identification. I am a grandson of Minos, and please don't ask me if I was born out of one of his nostrils. In regard to your absent husband, I had seen Odysseus in Crete, where the fickle wind's whims had forced his warships to land, as his twelve Biremes were sailing for Troy. So, I invited your spouse into my house, and I entertained him well with a warm welcome."

As Odysseus spoke and fibbed, the disguised tramp made his many falsehoods sound just like truth without consequences. But he held his pupils steady between his eyelids, and the prevaricating King adroitly kept-up his verbal deceit and deftly concealed his tears. But then, when Penelope had had her fill of shedding tears and sobbing her laments, the curious Queen austerely spoke to the shrewd visitor once more.

"Now, marvelous Stranger. I think I'd really like to test you out, to see if you did, in fact, entertain my husband in Crete, along with his fine companions as you've just claimed. So, describe the style of clothing Odysseus was wearing then, and the kind of man he was. And also, tell me all about his principal comrades who had loyally accompanied him."

"My Fair Lady; it's difficult for an aged beggar such as myself to recall exactly what I had observed twenty long years ago, but I'll do a mental deep-dive and delve-down into my hazy memory. In contempt of the gods, Lord Odysseus wore a double woolen, purple cloak. The brooch on it was made of gold, and it had a pair of clasps along with a fine engraving on the front. The first clasp featured an angry dog, and the second one a dappled fawn. Everyone standing and observing him at the dock was astonished at viewing those magnificent gold animal representations; the dog held-down the fawn, as the canine throttled the weaker animal, and the fawn was apparently struggling with its feet, trying to flee the predator's powerful grasp. I noticed the transparent tunic on your husband's body glistening like a dried-out onion skin. I mean, what is the purpose of clothing? Why would a man wear a see-through tunic and show his pubic area in public?"

As Odysseus spoke his wily rhetoric, Penelope sobbed and wept more, because the Queen had recognized signs of truth in what the unique beggar had just revealed.

"Stranger-than mythology, Stranger; though I had pitied you upon first impression, you'll now find from me genuine welcome and respect. I was the one who had dressed my husband in those exact clothes you've just so eloquently described. I brought them from the room, smoothed them out, and pinned on the shining brooch to be an ornament, a unique conversation piece."

"Wife of famous and infamous Odysseus, don't mar your lovely skin or waste your heart by weeping for your careless husband," the Beggar insisted. "Dry your tears, and listen to my factual words that will sound like absolute fiction. I've already heard gossip and discussions around Ithaca about Odysseus's recent return. He's close by, hanging-out in the wealthy land of Thesprotians, still barely alive in the Thespian and Lesbian Colony, and in quest of additional exploration and adventure."

"Oh, Stranger with the smelly clothes; I wish what you've just divulged is true. But my injured heart has a sense of what will certainly materialize in reality. Odysseus won't be coming home again, and you'll not find an escort out of this decaying palace, because there are no leaders of Odysseus's prowess and pure character in this enemy-occupied fortress. Despite these tremendous adversities, I'll command my servant women, to wash your stinky feet, that emit a foul odor even worse that my husband's had emitted two decades ago."

"Honored wife of great Odysseus, it's now time for me to be completely honest, and not facetious. I've hated cloaks and shining coverlets since I first left the snow-draped mountains of Crete, when I departed on my long-oared ship a full week after your husband's sandal scandal you have failed to mention. So, I'll resolve to lie-down, as I have done before through hundreds of sleepless nights. And having my feet washed brings me no afternoon delight, nor sky meteors in flight, into my heart, because in truth, I love the odor of grimy toes and heels. No woman serving in this house will ever touch my feet, unless there is an old one, who reveres true devotion, and who has suffered in her heart as many emotional pains as I have hurtfully endured in my many frustrating travels."

"Are you explicitly saying that you don't wish to have your smelly feet washed with stagnant water?"

"I'd not resent it if the old bag touched my feet, because in the end, everything comes-out in the wash," replied Odysseus, imaginatively inventing a novel cliché.

"Dear Stranger; no visitor from far-off lands who has come into my house has ever been as wise at spewing magnificent profundity as you have by inventing crazy and fantastic idiomatic expressions. Now, I have in my service a wrinkled old hag who possesses an understanding heart. She had often provided my helpless husband her fine care, ever since the day his mother gave birth to him. Although she's presently quite weak and feeble, she'll wash and clean your feet and rub sandpaper cloth between your' grimy toes. So come now; stand up, wise Eurycleia. Bathe this man's walking arrangements the same as if he's your former master."

The old woman clasped her hands and then spoke with certainty to the warrior having the gross athlete's feet condition.

"And I'm willing, For Queen Penelope's sake, to bathe and wipe your stinky feet as if they were your smelly asshole."

The old servant used a bright bowl to commence with her washing assignment, but then realized that she needed water to continue her task. Eurycleia slowly poured-in plenty of cold liquid, and soon added warmer water to rub-off the inch-thick crud and excess dead skin. Odysseus then turned and sat some distance from the hearth, and quickly turned around towards the central darkness. The disguised beggar was afraid that the old hussy would notice a prominent scar shown upon his left ankle, and also a red birthmark upon his right heel, and then the Beggar's actual identity would be readily discovered.

When Eurycleia (a former Ithacan national spelling bee champion) began her specialized cleansing, the hoary, foot-cleaning specialist immediately recognized the inimitable scar, a wound that Odysseus had suffered at Mt. Parnassus, years before Troy, that had been obtained from the razor-sharp, white tusks of a ferocious, wild, hungry boar.

After recognizing the scar along with the associated red birthmark, the scrubwoman dropped the heavy foot, worrying that she had rubbed the beggar the wrong way.

"Either this is a remarkable coincidence, or it's positively genuine truth. Queen Penelope; I've seen ugly clodhoppers similar to those belonging to this old goat, and I can attest that this ancient codger is indeed your husband Odysseus. Nobody has body odor to this horrendous extreme than your husband does. The stench is enough to exterminate every fly, mosquito, ant, cockroach and spider in the entire palace."

While Penelope was preoccupied swatting disturbing flies and mosquitoes landing upon her legs and crotch, Odysseus's arms quickly reached-out for Eurycleia's throat.

"Stay silent, old bitch, so that no one roaming the hall finds-out what you have just identified. For I'll tell you something, and it will soon happen. For the time being, shut the fuck up, and don't utter either a vowel or a consonant."

Frightened to death and aware of Odysseus's notorious temper, Eurycleia frantically left the room and sprinted like an athletic teenager down the adjacent hallway. After swatting a bevy of flies and mosquitoes, Penelope again addressed the stench-laden Beggar.

"Stranger, my body requires sleep and masturbation. So now, I'll ascend the rickety steps up to my chambers and lie on the bed, where I sometimes think and mumble to myself the truth."

Chapter 21
"THE BOW CONTEST"

When twilight in the form of Dawn arrived inside Odysseus's former fine home, the women servants were already up kindling the fire. Then, the male attendants who fearfully served the loathsome Achaean lords arrived inside to perform their duties. Behind them came the swineherd, leading the three chosen corpulent hogs, the best oinkers of all he currently had in his pens. The hog guardian turned the squealers loose to feed inside the butchering room, and while multi-tasking, the versatile fellow exchanged assuring lingo with Beggar Odysseus.

"Stranger; these fucked-up, voracious Achaeans have no regard or deference for your plight. The vain assholes are mocking and insulting you the same way that the privileged scum-wagons had meanly done yesterday."

"Well, Eumaeus. I hope the gods pay back the injuries that the egocentric, fucked-up leeches so recklessly have planned in another's home; yes, and the disgusting pond scum are obviously showing no evident sense of guilt, shame, or remorse for their transgressions."

A few seconds later, Melanthius, the antagonistic goatherder, came-up close to the pair of conferees. The coy, ill-tempered fellow was leading the very finest she-goats in his flocks, designated to be the major part of the suitors' feast.

"Stranger; are you still bothering us here, inside this confiscated house, begging food and copper coins from the kind Achaeans?" Melanthius prefaced his nasty derogation. "Why don't you get the fuck-out while you still have an ass from which to shit? I think it's obvious that you and I will not say goodbye until after we've had a taste of one another's fists. The way you contemptuously beg is not ethically correct. Achaeans, particularly well-mannered suitors, are valid authorities on practicing proper etiquette at feasts, you know."

Shrewd Odysseus recognized Melanthius's bravado as being sheer braggadocio, and the Ithacan King remained reticent and said nothing in return, shaking his oversized head in disgust.

Then, a third more civil servant Phuloshitus, an outstanding man when he wasn't standing inside the palace, brought-in a sterile heifer for the suitors' banquet. Phuloshitus tied-up the noisy beast with care, approached Odysseus, and spoke to the laconic Beggar.

"Greetings, honored Stranger. Though you're facing many troubles now, may you find pleasant happiness in future days. When I recall Odysseus and think of his illustrious presence in this once-magnificent house, I start to perspire, even though my wife tells me, 'Don't sweat the small stuff'. My eyes fill-up with abundant tears. For wandering Odysseus, I think, if still alive, would be dressed in tawdry rags just like yours, roaming around this flat Earth, and admiring the sunlight while drinking plenty of moonshine."

"Herdsman; you don't appear to be a fellow who's bad in character, or one who lacks common intelligence, for I can plainly sense that your sympathetic heart is functioning well-above the moron level of meditation," the cleverly disguised King replied. "And so, I'll swear a mighty oath to you. I predict that your mentor Odysseus will soon come home. With your own eyes, you'll see the evil suitors slaughtered like oinking pigs and squealing goats, if that's your secret wish."

"Ah, philosophical Stranger," Phuloshitus acknowledged and muttered. "How I wish Cronus's erratic son might bring about what you've just told me. Then, with Zeus's awesome assistance, you would find-out how strong I truly am, and what my hands can do during Odysseus's battle, should my master ever triumphantly return to retake Ithaca."

Eumaeus also prayed a similar plea in a low tone to all the Greek gods, the pig-keeper's theme hoping for Odysseus to return to his own home and reclaim his righteous jurisdiction over the island.

The ball-busting degenerates continued to feast and verbally abuse Odysseus, still-masquerading as a common, dependent panhandler. Bright-eyed Athena then placed inside the heart of Penelope, the creative idea that Telemachus' mother should set-up inside Odysseus's main hall the lord's incomparable bow, along with a series of a dozen gray iron axes for the suitors to engage in a friendly competition for the Queen's hand in marriage; but in reality, the unique bow was a secret prelude to the vile fiends' impending deaths.

Graceful Penelope stepped cautiously and furtively into the storage chamber and collected Odysseus's bow and his favorite axes. Once the lovely lady returned to the great hall and reached the suitors, the elegant and eloquent Queen stood beside the door-post of the deteriorating chamber, and a bright thin veil covered her still-beautiful face. On either side stood loyal women attendants, wishing that they would soon die and speed directly down to dismal Hades, and lead more normal existences as flitting spirits.

"Listen to me, emboldened, sex-driven suitors, who've been ravaging this home with your incessant need for food and drink. Now, my husband's been away so long that I could never recognize him if he were present standing or sitting next to me in this great room. The only story you fools could offer-up as an excuse to acquire the wealth of my husband's estate is that you all desire to marry me and take me as your wife. So, since I want to marry only one of you, come now, suitors; and since I seem to be the prize you falsely seek, I'll place this great bow right here; the favored weapon that once belonged to brave Odysseus. Whichever one of you clumsy goons who can grip this incomparable bow and string it with the greatest ease, then shoot an arrow straight as a dart through the dozen carved openings inside the positioned twelve axes, all of them lined-up in a row, one after the other, I'll promise to go with him to the altar and then to the bed where I'll make the lucky winner the Principal at my Beaver Academy."

When Penelope declared her vowed intention, the Queen told Eumaeus, the swineherd, to set the twelve iron axes for the suitors' imminent contest. But to the suitors' alarm and surprise, Telemachus spoke-out with new-found royal authority.

"Well now, Zeus, son of Cronus; your power of suggestion must have made me foolish and frivolous. My dear Mother; although quite sensible in her offer, says she'll shack-up with one of you professional jerk-offs. But now, it's prime time for you amateur archers to axe-tually get started!"

As Telemachus uttered that ludicrous nonsense, the impulsive lad quickly threw-off the purple cloak covering his back, and then impetuously jumped-up and removed the sharp sword hanging and dangling from his wimpy shoulders.

Fortunately, the greenhorn fool didn't have to carefully set-up the axes in a straight line, which had already been deftly accomplished by Eumaeus and Phuloshitus, the pig-master's occasional animal-tending confederate.

Amazement gripped the suitors' souls as the cruel critics looked at Telemachus and watched how the youth had directed Eumaeus and Phuloshitus to properly align the axes, though before then, the neophyte archer had never even seen those particular weapons.

Then Antinous, who had graduated Magna Come Loud from the Ithacan Orgasm Institute, nervously addressed the assembled rabble. "All you courageous suitors; get-up in order of strength now, two lines from left to right, in order of height, beginning from the place where the steward pours and spills the wine."

Antinous spoke, and what he had proposed, the rest of his ilk found agreeable. The first suitor to stand was Leiodes, who often bragged about having three-and-a-half large testicles, along with an enlarged clitoris bulb situated at the top of his hairy asshole.

Leiodes, was the first contestant who picked-up Odysseus's bow and the accompanying arrow. After moving to the threshold and standing there, the famed archer tried pulling and bending the bow, but unbelievably, the strongest among the suitors could not string the weapon. Much to his embarrassment and chagrin, the nutcase's powerful hands and arms soon grew weary, before the contestant could ever succeed in hooking-up the string, which was a rather simple process that Leiodes had performed thousands of times before with ordinary bows.

"My friends and colleagues in practicing mass palace mooching; despite my unrivaled hunting reputation, I'm not the man capable of stringing this trick bow. So now, let someone else take hold of it who perhaps has the savvy to figure-out the damned, confounded device. As for me, this fuckin' bow is a puzzling conundrum! And I'm not being arrow-gant when I humbly state those wimpy words of surrender."

Chief suitor Antinous felt obligated to denounce the champion archer's concession. "Leiodes; what wretched, sorry words filter from your' fat lips! As I listened, your craven remarks made me extremely angry. Your royal mother did not produce a feckless coward who lacks sufficient strength to draw an ordinary bow and shoot a regular arrow. But I'm convinced that some other motivated man among these noble suitors will succeed in his endeavor. Come now, Melanthius, you uncouth goatherder," Antinous prodded. "Light a fire in the hall and next set a large chair in front of it; and after doing those simple procedures, spread a fleece all across. Then, if your raisin-sized brain can remember, I want you, lard-ass, to fetch a hefty piece of fat so that these young competitors here can warm the bow and rub heavy grease onto it, making the bow more flexible. That precautionary measure should easily eliminate any particular margarine for error!"

Feeling threatened by the disreputable bully, Melanthius soon lit a tireless fire. Then, the volatile-tempered goat-herder carried a large chair next to the hearth, draped a fleece upon it, moved and set the seat-down beside the roaring flames, and then a minute later, from inside the kitchen, fetched a large piece of fat to respect and butter-up Antinous.

So, then the young servants in attendance followed directions and warmed the bow and tested it, but even the strongest among the palace security guards could not string the hunting mechanism. Antinous and Eurymachus, the lead suitors, still remained as scheduled participants slated to test their bow-stringing ability.

Melanthius, the moody goat-herder, and Eumaeus, the benign keeper of the swineherd, both aged servants to Beggar Odysseus, soon left the palace to monotonously shovel pig and goat manure onto a crap-corroded donkey cart, the animal dung to be later used for crop fertilizer.

So, harried Lord Odysseus moved and slinked away to also silently leave the palace unnoticed. The costumed King walked through the weed-infested backyard, and swiftly followed *their'* irregular path. When the pig and goat custodians had passed beyond the rear courtyard, and then sauntered past the classic-designed gates, Odysseus called to the preoccupied laborers, and uttered certain reassuring words.

"You there, yonder goat-herder and swine-keeper. Shall I tell you something, or should I keep my secret all to myself? My Athena-stimulated spirit tells me I should not speak goat or pig-shit; not horse-shit; not dog-shit, but instead, important bullshit to you two paragons of virtue. Now then; if Lord Odysseus were to come back suddenly, brought by a god from somewhere like the moon, perhaps as a fucked-up, disoriented space alien, would you two degenerates be the sort of loyal underlings who would volunteer to defend his legitimate return? Would you support the exploitive suitors, or would you actively fight with, and for, noble King Odysseus?"

"Oh, by virtue of Father Goose, er, I mean Father Zeus," Melanthius the goatherder yelled-back. "May that virtuous King return, and may his actions be led by some fickle, mercurial-minded god. Then, if that impossibility ever happens, you would know the kind of strength I have, and how my hands can easily demonstrate my strangling power. Instead of choking goats, I'll just transfer my knowledge to strangling a suitor or two."

And then, Eumaeus, too, made the same sort of commentary to all the apathetic gods, wishing that wise and insightful Odysseus would return to his own home and "royally kick ass".

Once the Beggar King had clearly realized how resolute the dual animal attenders were in their cited testimonies, the King spoke to the common dregs again, in an authoritarian voice.

"Well, kind servants; here I am in person, after suffering much hardship and distress for two decades. I've managed to finally return to Ithaca in the twentieth year to righteously reclaim my own wife and property. Of those who had worked for me, I recognize that you're the only two males who want me back as the main decision-maker. Among the rest, I've heard no one praying that my return would bring harmony, and also melody, to my seized palace. I'll tell you both how this is going to go-down, and I'll speak the truth, if, on my puny behalf, some empathetic god will assist me in overcoming and vanquishing those illegitimate scoundrels."

"What's in it for me?" the very interested goat-keeper and pig-herder simultaneously hollered to the astonished Beggar, whom the pair believed was being facetious in making his extraordinary, unorthodox statements.

"And furthermore, I promise that if our ultimate battle is victorious, both of you lackluster dimwits will be amply rewarded with expensive gifts, elite homes, and either wall-to-wall heterosexual or homosexual activity for the remainder of your happy life' tenures."

"Count me in!" both Melanthius and Eumaeus screamed in unison. "Count me in!" the dumb-dick assholes reiterated.

Odysseus pulled aside his rags, exposing the great scar that verified his true identity. Once the two animal-herders had recognized the identification mark and noted every unique detail, the bisexuals both threw their arms around the wise Odysseus, and the wimpy snowflakes burst into tears. Melanthius and Eumaeus kissed their master's head, shoulders, left nipple, scrotum sac, and finally, both nutjobs kissed his kisser.

"Okay; stop these dumb-ass laments immediately, you stupid-shit faggots," Odysseus chastised the two all-too-affectionate idiots. "Let's have no more crying, or homo' kissing. Someone might come-out from the hall, see us, and tell people in the house that we're three active members of the anti-conservative LBGTQRMSV community. Let's go into my palace, one by one, at one-minute intervals. I'll go first. And let's make this our sign for us to initiate action. Eumaeus, as you carry that massive bow of mine around the hall, put it first into my hands, and tell the women servants that they must lock and bar the hall doors from the outside to keep all of our prospective victims trapped inside."

Odysseus paced back into the hall and nonchalantly sat-down upon the stool where he had been sitting before. The two animal keepers, godlike Odysseus's servants, went in after him, farting and crapping their dirty tunics out of amplified anticipation and general excrement excitement.

Eurymachus already had the challenging bow in hand, warming the sturdy weapon here and there in light and heat from the blazing fire. But even doing that, the frustrated fuck-head could not competently string the bow after several failing tries.

"It's too bad. I'm disappointed for myself and for all of you," humiliated Eurymachus apologized. "I'm not that unhappy about losing the marriage with Penelope, although I'm upset about losing these nightly feasts and our merry camaraderie. There are many more convivial Achaean women with serious abdominal maladies to pump the poop and intestinal gas out of, some here in sea-girt Ithaca itself, and other harlots screwing-around in various neighboring towns and villages. But if we distinguished noblemen are so weak compared to godlike Odysseus, so puny that we can't even string his favorite bow, then our failure is a disgraceful embarrassment which future generations will learn about from their history lessons in years to come."

Antinous, desiring to delay his turn at stringing the bow, then felt compelled to offer his evaluation of recent events. "Eurymachus, that's not going to happen, as you yourself well-know," the chief suitor maintained. "At this moment, in the country, there's a special feast day, sacred to the gods, but I can't recall which one. So, who would bend the irrelevant bow? It really doesn't matter. Set the trick item aside without mentioning any more gossip about it. Come now; let the steward begin pouring fresh wine in our size D cups, so we can make libations and get plastered like Paris had done over in Troy. In honor of the anonymous religious feast day, let's put the curved bow-down, and in the morning, we'll test the weapon again when one of us remaining rivals will abruptly end this moronic contest."

Antinous finished his self-serving recommendations, and once the compliant stewards had poured the libations, and the already-intoxicated suitors had drunk wine to their hearts and stomachs' content, Odysseus, a very crafty and scheming fellow, thought it was time to gain the attention of the pursuers of Penelope's hand.

"Suitors of the most splendid Queen," Odysseus began his response to Antinous. "Listen to me, so that I can assess what the heart beating inside my chest is prompting me to state and do. It's a request, a plea, especially to you Eurymachus, and to you Antinous, since what the Chief Suitor had just suggested was most appropriate. I do believe for the moment that you should postpone this business involving the bow contest until another date and time. Give me the polished bow, Eumaeus, so in this hall I can test these hands of mine and determine if my supple limbs still possess the strength and the dexterity I used to have, or if my wandering, and my lack of nutrition have quite destroyed my muscular potency."

Hearing the intense bravado originating from the already-despised Beggar, the freeloading drones instantly became extremely agitated, but in their black hearts, the human parasites were fearing that a lowly beggar might capably string the polished bow.

"You wretched, warp-headed Stranger," Antinous rebuked the bold Beggar. "Your mind lacks any sense of decent respect for Ithacan culture and advanced Greek civilization. You possess no academic education, and have little rudimentary knowledge of laws, religion, ethics, morality and traditions, whatsoever. Aren't you content to feed your grimy face and share a feast with us, such eminent men, and to have the privilege of listening to the sagacious word exchanges that we philosophically speak to one another?"

"Antinous," Penelope vehemently chimed-in. "It's neither good nor proper to deny guests of Telemachus a chance to democratically participate in discussions and debates, no matter who it is who comes as a welcomed guest to this house. And if, trusting in his strength and power, the ragged Stranger in our midst manages to successfully string Odysseus's great bow, do you believe that this Beggar will take me home and make me his valued wife? I'm sure he himself bears no such hope inside that tanned chest of his. So, none of you prospective husbands should grimace and criticize this flesh and blood Beggar at our daily dinner hour. It is your nasty derision, along with your harsh brow-beating that dishonors this house, and not this unfortunate Beggar's rather insane comments."

"Among Achaeans, especially those present too weak and afraid to go to Troy, *no man* has a right stronger than my own to offer this bow to anyone I wish, or withhold," Telemachus asserted and contributed. "Among these same assembled crooks and hoodlums, no one will deny my will by force, if I wish to give the bow to this feeble, frail Stranger as an outright gift, it is my explicit privilege to do so, for in terms of character, none of you swine are as straight-as-an-arrow. But Mother; you should go to your own rooms and keep busy with your proper duties, weaving the complex tapestry upon the loom and spindle. The bow-stringing will be a matter for the men to decide, especially me, since power in this house is justly mine," Telemachus chauvinistically indicated.

Penelope, astonished at witnessing her formerly wimpy son's stellar oration, went-back up to her rooms, taking to heart the prudent words recently uttered.

The worthy swineherd, as instructed, had picked-up the curved bow and was carrying it in the direction of the disguised King. Eumaeus came to the chair of shrewd Odysseus and placed the device into the Beggar's worthy hands. Then, the often-forgetful pig-herder summoned the nurse, Eurycleia, and said to her, "Wise servant; listen carefully. Telemachus is telling you to lock the closely-fitted doorway to this dining hall. If any valet hears groans and death screams coming from inside this room, or detects any noise emanating from the throats of scared men within these walls, he or she is to remain busy with work responsibilities, and is to ignore any shouts or shrieks, or yells of 'What the fuck'!'"

Without any hesitation, Eurycleia rapidly departed the huge room, and the anxious nurse frantically raced to bolt all the doors to that enormous hall. And the old woman's female colleagues, without ever even whispering a word, slipped-out of the large chamber and soon obediently also locked the courtyard gates.

Odysseus already was holding the awesome bow, turning it this way and that, and testing it in different ways to see if, while its lord had been away, still had the same feel and flexibility. The shrewd archer, getting used to the string-resistance of the shooting device, in five seconds easily strung the difficult bow. Then, the champion marksman picked-up the arrow lying by itself upon the nearby table, and set it against the bow, right upon the bridge. Next, he pulled the notched arrow and the bowstring back, and still casually sitting inside his chair, and with the sure aim of Cupid, let the old arrow fly. Amazingly, the projectile sped through every single hole near the top of all twelve axe heads. The projectile, weighted-down with bronze, emerged unscathed, exiting out of the last opening.

"Telemachus," the Stranger-turned-archer summoned his amazed son's attention. "I have not disgraced you. I did not miss my aim, or work too long to string my cherished bow. Now it's time to get a dinner ready for these lecherous Achaeans, while there's still some daylight, we'll entertain ourselves with your minstrel singing diriges, and playing the various lyre lyrics."

Telemachus, recognizing his father's repetitious head-nodding signal, cinched his sword belt tight, closed his fist around a bronze spear, and moved-in close beside his father.

Chapter 22

"THE KILLING OF THE SUITORS"

Ingenious Odysseus stripped-off his tattered rags, grabbed-up the nearby bow and accompanying quiver full of arrows, and sprang-up from his chair. The returning King then loudly shouted at the suddenly alarmed suitors.

"This contest to determine who is best bow-stringer is now over. But there's another target in which to aim; one that *no man* has ever struck. I'll soon find-out if my past ability can hit the mark. May Apollo grant that I receive the desired glory I seek."

As Odysseus spoke his astonishing words, which were both cryptic and obscure to the appalled moochers, the returning King aimed an arrow straight at Antinous, who was just about to raise-up to his lips a fine double-handled goblet. Among those feasting, who would have ever thought that a lowly Beggar would or could also be a formidable assassin? Odysseus had taken steady aim, and his lethal arrow hit Antinous right in the neck, with its honed point passing directly through the victim's tender throat. Thick spurts of blood came flowing quickly from the targeted creep's nose and mouth. When the other suitors had observed Antinous falling to the slate floor, the frightened rogues raised an uproar and profusely shouted and cursed expletives at the keen-eyed Beggar.

"Vile Stranger; you'll pay for luckily shooting an arrow at that innocent nobleman. You'll pay heavily for your malicious violation. It's certain you'll be killed, and now vultures are going to feast upon your evil flesh and blood," Eurymachus shouted above the rest.

The drunken freeloaders did not realize that Odysseus had deftly killed Antinous on purpose. In their folly, the fools did not imagine that they, the onerous villains, were now tightly enmeshed in destruction's unfailing net. Shrewd Odysseus scowled at his bitter enemies, and sternly communicated his vengeful intent.

"You mangy dogs; because you had fallaciously speculated that I was never coming back to Ithaca from Troy, you've been wildly ravaging my house, incessantly raping innocent women, bullying my son, and, in devious ways, evilly wooing my faithful wife, while I was still alive defending Greece's honor. You exhibit no fear of gods who hold reign over wide heaven, or of any mortal who might take his revenge in days to come. And now venomous assholes, a cleverly planned fatal snare has caught you all."

As Odysseus articulated his great animosity, pale fear seized his adversaries' hearts and minds. Each craven egomaniac looked-around to see how he might flee the imminent administration of complete destruction. Only loquacious Eurymachus mustered sufficient gumption to answer.

"If, in fact, it is true that you are the invincible Odysseus of Ithaca, arriving back home again, you're absolutely right in what you say about the actions of us Achaeans' demonstrating reckless conduct inside your home. Our many foolish behaviors in the fields and in your' palace have been reprehensible. But the instigator who had been responsible for all that mayhem is repulsive Antinous, who has just been killed. Now that the misfit is dead, and deservedly so, his warped mind taken out of commission, you should spare the rest of us because the snake's head has already been severed. Later on, we'll contribute adequate compensation to pay for what food and drink we've abundantly consumed over the years, and I hereby promise that you'll be reimbursed annually with large amounts of oxen, with bronze objects, and with gold and silver coins."

"Eurymachus; I believe that you're trying to save your own ass from death while attempting to place the entire blame for your enumerable felonies on dead Antinous. Even if you offered me all the goods you' retards have inherited from your own fathers, everything which you now own, and offered that total sum to me as retribution, I would decline out of pure principle; for from my point of view, none of you dumb-fucks deserve to be safe from slaughter. Now you miscreants have a distinct choice: you can either fight me here in my palace face to face, or you can run away. But I think that there's not one of you slimy bastards who will luckily escape being utterly destroyed, since all of the palace doors have been locked tight; so therefore, your simple choice is either to fight, or to fight!"

"Friends, this unsavory bum claiming to be Odysseus won't dare box all of us with those all-conquering hands of his," Eurymachus yelled to his suitor associates. "Instead, now he's got the polished bow and quiver, and the lunatic bastard will just keep on shooting arrows and insults at us, until the crazed fanatic has killed us all. So, colleagues; let's think now about how we should fight this unethical renegade. Pull out your swords, and set-up turned tables to block his wicked arrows, and then let's charge the son-of-a-bitch, going directly at the pestilence all together in an unstoppable assault."

Showing what the gifted orator considered a good example of resistance, Eurymachus pulled-out his double-edged bronze sword, and then recklessly charged forward, rushing at Odysseus with a blood-curdling shout. As the attacking fool did so, Lord Odysseus shot a sharp arrow, piercing the hostile bloodsucker directly in the lower chest, and penetrating right through his spine. Eurymachus's sword slipped-down from his bloody hand onto the slate floor. The fatally wounded braggart bent-over, writhing upon a blood-laden table, and soon collapsed into death's throes. The antagonist's forehead kept hammering upon the now-crimson floor, and with his heart writhing in agony, and with both of the knave's feet futilely kicking at the nearby chair's legs, making it shake and shimmy twice, the vile suitor's heavy breathing quickly expired. Soon, a hazy veil fell over both of Eurymachus's non-blinking eyes.

Another possessed, nutjob, marital candidate Amphinomus, brother of snake-like Amphibius, charged straight at glorious Odysseus, the attacker wielding his raised sword, but Telemachus aimed and threw a bronze-tipped spear, hitting the aggressor from behind in his behind, although the youth had as his target the blade landing between the assaulter's shoulder-blades. With a loud crash, Amphinomus fell forward upon a turned table, his dazed forehead then striking hard against the slate floor. Telemachus quickly sped across the supper chamber to his arrow-shooting father, whose reliable quiver never quivered.

"Father; now I'll bring you a shield, two spears, a helmet made of bronze; one that fits your exposed temples. I'll also hand weapons to the petrified swineherd and to the paranoid goat-keeper, both of them now lying on the floor, pretending to be dead! It's better if we fully arm ourselves, just in case we lose a wrist or an elbow."

"Hurry son! Get those battle weapons to me fast, while I still can shoot arrows to protect my humorous funny bone and my shoulders," Odysseus yelled. "If I am disarmed, I'll have no appendages left to hold and swing my sword!"

Telemachus obeyed the explicit orders and hurried to the house's storeroom area. From a cabinet, the harried youth removed four shields, eight spears, and four helmets with horsehair plumes, and clumsily rushed across the chamber and tripped over a table, thus inadvertently supplying the suitors with additional weapons and battle equipment with his clumsy fall.

"It would be easier for chickens to fly the coop, than to have you cooped-up trash-mongers escape your imminent doom!" the abused Prince awkwardly stood and illogically hollered.

The two apprehensive servants arose from playing possum and grabbed available dropped spears and helmets, audaciously joining the bloody imbroglio. But skilled Odysseus needed no new weapons or armor, using the bow and arrows he already had to kill his scared-shitless adversaries, one by one. As the suitors' bodies began piling-up, the remaining combatants finally realized that they, the illicit scoundrels, were soon to also be in a heap of trouble.

But once Odysseus shot and used his last arrow from his quiver, the incensed King could not again shoot his *bow* towards any other prospective marital *beau* in pursuit of Penelope's hand. So, the creative archer then propped his hunting weapon against the dim room's massive doorpost, and let the weapon lean beside the mammoth entrance.

Suddenly, ageless Agelaus yelled-out, calling to all his frantic colleagues scurrying around, but before the old geezer could finish his death sentence, or even his death phrase, Odysseus picked-up the loudmouth curmudgeon, and despite the fact that the King had no undertaker training, the husband of Queen Penelope easily lifted and tossed Agelaus's wrinkled ass above the hearth, and flung the elderly coot directly into the raging fire, in what amounted to an instant ancient cremation."

"That elimination of Agelaus felt better than making a killing in the city livestock market," Odysseus screamed across the room to Telemachus' ears. "The old asshole's hopes and dreams have all gone up in smoke!"

Goatherder Melanthius, demonstrating his true traitor nature, picked-up several shields, spears, and bronze helmets that had been accidentally dropped upon the floor by Telemachus, and the deceitful turncoat began distributing the items to various suitors that were still scurrying around the vast room, still searching for a means of escaping Odysseus's intense wrath.

"Telemachus, it seems that one of the women residing in this house has stirred-up a nasty fight against us, or perhaps the suspect goat-herder Melanthius is a stupid-ass transgender who has somehow impressively grown concave tits and a quite useless, very dry cunt."

"Father, I'm an inexperienced cub cadet, and I bear the entire blame for inadvertently arming the enemy! But now I intend to mow them all down!"

Melanthius, the dastardly goatherd, jealously shouted a coarse insult at his master. "Guileful Odysseus; you indeed are a devious ass-wiper! You've penned-up the suitors like I daily pen-up my goats!"

"Fuck you, Melanthius! If you had eight brawny suitors standing behind you, you'd still be asinine! I'm not a cowardly scapegoat standing here to suffer from your false allegiance! You're on your way to goat heaven, that's for damned sure!" Odysseus shouted as the proud king flung a sharp-tipped bronze spear at the two-faced scumbag, whose skull immediately shattered in half.

Since Odysseus's bow and his swift arrows had brought-down and executed the principal suitors, the remaining rabble of insurgents were all in a panic-stricken, hysterical mode, being picked-off one by one.

Led by spiteful Amphimedon, brother of Trachodon, who generally looked-like a gigantic prehistoric lizard, the terrified suitors that were still standing kept on throwing spears, tables, lamps and porno' paintings at their good-guy opponents with frantic haste, but benign Athena appeared upon the battle scene, and the biased goddess made their in-flight projectiles amazingly veer in opposite directions, killing their comrades instead of impacting valiant Odysseus, Telemachus and Eumaeus. But dastardly Amphimedon, flailing-away with a lengthy knife, got lucky and managed to cut Telemachus' left hand with a glancing blow across the wrist. However, the minor injury proved to be a badge of honor to the inspired youth.

Being stimulated at receiving his first battle wound, Telemachus managed to hit the bronze metallurgist Leocritus, striking the brass-balled, tin-headed combatant squarely in the groin. Leocritus lurched forward, his entire face and forehead quickly smashing against the slate floor, coincidentally earning valorous Telemachus the lad's future title, "Expert Ballbreaker Son of Odysseus!"

And then the minstrel Phemius, who had been compelled to sing against his will while standing before the suitors, attempted to evade his own disastrous fate. The gay entertainer set-down his hollow lyre, left the musical instrument upon the slate floor, awkwardly placing it between the mixing bowl and the silver-studded chair. The scared musician rushed-forward and quickly knelt-down to clasp Odysseus's knee, and then addressed the monarch with a desperate plea.

"I implore you, King Odysseus; show me respect and pity. Show me mercy! I was forced to sing for the abominable suitors, but I will gladly praise you in my songs!"

"Hold-on, Father. Don't allow your sword to injure this innocent minstrel. We should save Medon the Herald, too, who faithfully delivers news all over your square square. Please spare those two cowardly gay guys from your tempestuous rampage!"

Medon the Herald, was also pouting and acting like a crying baby, cowering beneath a high-chair, but then the fool jumped-up and pleaded to young Telemachus.

"Here I am, my friend! Tell your father to restrain himself, in case, as he exults in his great strength, he accidentally, in his fury, strikes my' shoulder blades with hist sharp bronze blade. If I fortunately live through this crisis, I promise that I'll stop sleeping and having unnatural sex with Phemius the Minstrel. I now realize that both mine and his assholes are exits and not entrances. And I also pledge to forget all this homosexual gay stuff, too. I promise to marry a plump, ugly female who is a fine cook, and I also promise to go straight, thrusting my diminutive dingle right into the sex-starved whore's wet, pink love tunnel!"

"Don't worry, Medon!" Telemachus exclaimed. "My Father will spare your life, even though he despises all of your bullshit lyrics and your perverted homo' life style! But I believe you'll luckily be making the right choice. Never make a pretty woman your wife! Instead, marry an ugly whore who can cook!"

Satisfied that all of the suitors had been killed, Odysseus, Telemachus and Eumaeus dragged all twenty-four enemy combatants, and Melanthius too, out of the great hall, sliced-off their testicles and limp peckers from their abdomens, and left the severed reproductive organs in a small, putrid mound for the hungry hounds to eat and savor. The rest of the suitors' bodies were then heaped into a putrid pile. Thus was the demise of Antinous and his wicked confederates, along with the emancipation of Penelope; all wonderfully accomplished by the incomparable and persistent Odysseus, who had salvaged his land from utter destruction.

"Now Telemachus, I believe that the famished canines can have a temporary food source from their everyday dog-eat-dog existence! The eager hounds can now relish the suitors' severed wieners without consuming their buns!"

"But Father, where did you ever get the idea to dress like a beggar and isolate the two-dozen suitors into a closed hall, and then systematically execute the bastards one by one."

"Well, Telemachus," Odysseus objectively explained. "When I had visited the fantastic palace at Knossos, and conferred with King Minos, and also with my fellow hero Theseus, slayer of the frightful Minotaur, the dual geniuses gave me some very excellent abstract and con-Crete military strategies to seriously consider!"

Chapter 23

"ODYSSEUS AND PENELOPE"

Old wart-faced Eurycleia climbed-the steep steps to an upstairs room, laughing to herself, so the old dame could merrily tell her Mistress Penelope that Odysseus was again triumphantly present in the house. The exuberant nurse stood beside her lady's head, happily bent-down and spoke into her ear.

"Wake-up now, Penelope, my dear child, so you yourself can see with your own eyes what you've been wanting and desiring each and every day. Odysseus has arrived home. Better late than never, but he's back and has been kicking ass downstairs. And he's just killed those screwball-haughty suitors who have maligned and upset this home, used-up his possessions, and also his financial resources, and victimized his only son."

After twenty-years of mounting disappointment, Penelope held her emotions in check and did not immediately rejoice. The Queen, who had been deep asleep, tossing and turning while dreaming about wild fighting in Troy in regard to the loud noises occurring downstairs, hastily jumped-up out of bed, hugged the old woman, and soon an abundance of' tears fell from her eyelids and cascaded down her cheeks.

"Come now, fanciful Eurycleia, my dear nurse. Tell me the truth and cease with all of this fictional mythology nonsense you profess. If Odysseus is truly here, back in lackluster Ithaca as you've maintained, then how could he ever contend with and defeat those shameless suitors? He was alone, and in this house, and those scurrilous harebrains were always causing havoc when together in a large two-dozen group."

"I didn't overtly see any actual violence or massive massacre occurring," the nurse admitted. "I only heard the haunting groans of grown men being methodically killed. I slinked myself downstairs and took a brief glimpse of the aftermath. My disbelieving eyes found King Odysseus standing victoriously with the bodies of numerous dead crackpots laying upon the slate floor; yes, lying all around him. The carcasses of the heinous assholes were heaped-up together, which indeed was a heart-warming sight for my' eyes to witness. And your valorous husband was standing there, covered with blood and gore, just like a successful lion after a great hunting pursuit. Come along with me, my Queen, so that you too can be reunited and build content within your heart. You've been through so much misfortune, and now the joyful occasion you've both been anticipating for so long has finally arrived. He's come by himself; home without any observable entourage; home to his own hearth, ready to be warmly welcomed by Telemachus and you. After enduring countless trials and tribulations, and gaining his sweet revenge upon all the insufferable suitors, our King has finally liberated his home; and Odysseus must feel wonderfully vindicated in eliminating the two-dozen leeching crazies, while freeing his property and family from their horrific exploitation. I can't wait to hear your husband's proclamation of emancipation!"

"But quixotic Eurycleia. This fantasy story you're telling me can't possibly be true. It totally defies reality! I prefer to believe that one of the immortal gods has killed the sinister suitors out of sheer unhinged rage, reacting to the dirt-bags' heartless pride and shameless deeds. The impostors have met disaster through their foolishness, and their fate had been enacted by Zeus's imperial decree. But in some place far-away, I still fear that Odysseus has given-up his journey to Achaea, and that he himself is lost forever from my sincere embrace. It is exceedingly hard to fathom the complex plans of the eternal gods, even though, my aide, you're truly wiser than most straight and homo sapiens. But let's go to my son, so that I can praise Zeus, and witness the vile crackpots all dead, and closely view the special man whom you claim had killed the odious purveyors of repugnant evil."

"But Mistress; I've heard from fairly dependable palace-intrigue gossipers that the suitors' bodies are now stacked-outside in the courtyard with their tiny dingles and testicles sliced-off! Your hungry hounds are now feasting off their piled wieners and buns!"

Penelope rose and soon left her upper room, descended the rickety steps; slowly crossed the stone threshold; entered into the virtually empty hall, and gently sat-down near the blazing fire-crematory, positioning herself opposite shabbily-clothed Odysseus the Beggar.

The fatigued King was just sitting stationary, resting by a tall marble column, symbolizing the monarch being a definite pillar of the community. And while staring at the bloody slate floor, the exhausted king was waiting disconsolately to find-out if his elegant wife would speak to him. But Penelope quietly sat-down and stayed silent for a long time, trying to manage the mounting wonder and apprehension residing inside her charitable heart. Sometimes, the Queen's eyes peered straight at the grimy visitor, fully gazing at his heavily-bearded face, but at other times, Penelope turned her head in the opposite direction, disbelieving the silent, shabbily-clothed Beggar's claimed identity.

Telemachus then spoke-up, addressing a stinging rebuke directly at his mother.

"Saddened Woman; you're a cruel and conceited female displaying an unfeeling, dispassionate marital heart," Penelope's son criticized. "Why turn aside from my father in this unnatural and peculiar way? Why not sit over there, close to him, and ask relevant and irrelevant questions? No other woman's heart would be so hard as to make her so distant from a husband who has miraculously come home to his native land in the twentieth year, after surviving so many harsh ordeals. That heart of yours is sometimes harder than the stone columns that support the palace roof."

"My impetuous, idealistic child; inside my head and inside my chest, my mind and heart are quite astounded. I feel alienated from reality, and cannot speak with confidence, or ask applicable questions, or even look this mute Beggar in the eye. If indeed it's true that our visitor is Odysseus, and he is home again, surely the two of us have more certain ways to know each other that both of us stubbornly giving each other the silent treatment. But we do have uncanny signs which only the two of us can understand; a sort of mental telepathy, and other observing people are not able to recognize the established pattern."

As the abashed Queen spoke her mind, Lord Odysseus, who for two decades had borne so much travail, smiled and immediately addressed his son's perceptive inquiry.

"Telemachus; let your mother thoroughly test me in this all-too-familiar, bloody hall. Soon, the Queen will possess more certain knowledge of my personality and character. Right now, I'm filthy, but twenty years ago, I was filthy rich, with disgusting expensive clothing worn upon my body. Your mother has always preferred the finest and most costly attire, and I believe that she presently rejects me because I look grossly pathetic, and appear as a derelict pauper in her blurred eyes; all because of superficial external appearances. Why she repels me and will not admit so is because of her greed for materialism, and in that monetary aspect, your materialistic mother is much like the dead suitors. Even when your mother was a hot-to-trot teenager, she was without a doubt a material girl, living in a material world. But as you are obviously convinced, Telemachus. I am your authentic father and patriarch, Odysseus, King of Ithaca. Thank Zeus that I've been guided by good-hearted Pallas Athene on my arduous ten-year odyssey, despite my infatuation with me wearing the color purple!"

Once Odysseus had articulated those pertinent remarks, Eurynome, the veteran tri-sexual housekeeper, gave the great-hearted king a comprehensive bath; thoroughly rubbed him all over with rich oil; administered to the Ithacan monarch a full King-sized body massage, and finally placed a purple tunic upon his body, along with a resplendent purple cloak. In an invisible state, Athena interceded, and poured magnificent handsomeness upon her favorite hero, providing Odysseus with an abundance of blond hair; a much taller stature, and much more robust arm and leg muscles.

"Strange Lady, to you, those simpletons who live in marble temples atop Mount Olympus have given to you more than to any other wife, a two-valve half-heart. No other woman would harden herself and keep her distance, if her husband, in the twentieth year, came back to his spouse in his own native land, after going through so much agony with so little ecstasy to remember. So, come now, Nurse; you old ill-tempered hag; spread-out a bed and blankets meant solely for me, so that I can lie-down by myself and dream about my incredible wanderings, and not about this cold-crotched bitch sitting across from my aching ass. The cold heart beating inside her frigid breast must most-definitely be made of futuristic iron, even in this obsolete Bronze Age."

Wise Penelope then answered her perturbed husband: "Strange Man," Penelope retorted. "I'm not making too much of my lack of passion at this moment, or ignoring your somewhat familiar voice. Nor is it the case that you've offended me in any way, sounding much like the petulant jerk-off I had once known, whose identity I cannot presently recall. I understand the sort of narcissistic hardhead Odysseus was when he had left Ithaca in his long-oared ship. So come, Eurycleia; set-up for this guest outside my well-constructed bedroom, that strong bed my husband had carefully made for himself in anticipation of marriage. Put that sturdy bed out-there in the corridor, and throw some random blankets upon it, consisting of itchy fleeces and unclean cloaks taken from the palace cloak room."

"Small City Woman," perturbed Odysseus rankled. "Those sharp words you have just uttered are each one a painful dagger. Who has ordered my bed shifted to somewhere else, other than it staying inside the master bedroom? That task would be difficult, even for someone truly skilled, unless an ambitious god like fucked-up Hephaestus came-down from Olympus in person to strenuously perform that complicated maneuver. Quite frankly, Woman; your sarcastic, negative attitude sounds like penis envy to me!"

Hearing no oral response, Odysseus stubbornly continued his melancholy oratory. "But among men, there is no such adept asshole living, no matter how much energy the mortal fellow possesses, who would find it easy labor to shift that bed into the nearby hallway. In fact, if I were a carpenter, and you were my lady, I still wouldn't do that difficult bullshit at your command. For built into the alluded-to, well-constructed bedstead is a great symbol, which I had made myself, with no one else's assistance. A long-leaved olive tree was growing in the yard. It was in full bloom and flourishing, and the fluffy thing reminded me of my pretty girlfriend's hairy bush when I was a mere carpenter's apprentice, and she was a young lady studying to be a beautician at the now-defunct Ithacan Trades and Cosmetology School."

"Tell me more, anonymous Beggar," Penelope demanded.

"In woodshop class, I had built my palace bedroom around that fluffy olive tree, until I had finished the project with well-set stones. I had constructed a fine roof upon the growth, and added closely-fitted jointed doors, one leading to the adjacent cloak room. After that enterprise had been completed, I cut-back the excess foliage, all-the-while imagining that I was getting turned-on by meticulously trimming Lady Penelope's bush gardens. I carefully carved-off the tree's trunk, upward from the root, trimming it skillfully and honing it true with bronze sides, so that my enormous endeavor followed a straight line. Once I'd made the bedpost, with an auger, I bored-out the entire structure. Then, I cut-out my bed, until I was done my project, and my colossal effort received an A-Plus grade from the woodshop teacher. And that's the romantic symbol I now describe for you. Now Lady; I honestly don't know if that bed of mine is still in place and usable, or if some other man has cut that wonderful olive tree down at its base, and set the tree-mendous bed up in a different spot."

Haggard Lady Penelope felt a weakness in her knees, and her heart grew softer than her aroused clitoris button. For her hard-to-persuade mind finally recognized that the Strange Beggar-turned-King-Charming's stirring words were truer-than-fact. The Queen's blue eyes filled with tears; her cataracts almost as large as the Nile's; the Queen rose from her chair, and rushed across the room to the male whom Athena had now wonderfully and magically transformed into a handsome, strong, virile young warrior. Penelope instinctively threw her arms around Odysseus's neck, kissed his head, and suddenly, her crotch lips became wetter than those around her mouth.

"Don't be angry or sad, dear Odysseus; not with me and my characteristic cold nature upon our original contact. In every other matter to date, you've been the cleverest of men I've ever known. The fickle gods have brought us a plethora of sorrows that weren't exactly pleasant bestowments. The jealous deities atop Mt. Olympus were not willing to decide that we two should stay merrily married, and to happily enjoy the recollection of our shared youth, and now we have reached together with dignity the threshold of old age. It is not the time to rage at me, resenting what misery I've caused you upon your return to this decaying palace, first dedicated to Pallas Athene."

"I feel likewise, my dear wife and Queen!"

"There are many avaricious men such as deceased Antinous, who dream-up terribly wicked schemes. Argive Helen of Sparta, reputed to be a child of Zeus, would never have had sex with a man who came from somewhere foreign, if she had known Achaea's warrior sons would ally and bring her back to her native Greek land, after temporarily experimenting with being Helen of Troy. But now Odysseus, you have accurately described that clear symbol meticulously carved into *our* bed's headboard, which no one else of elite status has ever seen, other than the two of us romantic lovebirds. Odysseus, you once took my virginity; now you can take my twenty-year frigidity!"

While the reunited couple kept reminiscing shared memories with each other, Eurynome prepared the bed with soft coverlets, with the master bedroom being illuminated, the light originating from flaming torches. Once the servants had hurriedly arranged the soft bed sheets, the chief servant, Eurynome, led the couple on their way to their mattress, with a flaming torch gripped in her right hand. Once the servant had solemnly escorted the King and Queen, horny Eurynome went-away nearby to eavesdrop on the expected humping and pumping that the nosy whore anticipated were about to be heard. Odysseus and Penelope approached with joy the place where their bed still stood from earlier days.

After Odysseus and Penelope had enjoyed making love together for the first time in over two decadent decades, the pair entertained themselves by telling family stories, and also by playing games of 'Pin the Asshole on the Asshole'. and then the more popular afterglow sport of 'Spin the Dildo'. The rejuvenated Queen talked of all she had to bear in her own home, dealing with that destructive group of greedy parasites, who, because of her royal title, kept butchering so many cattle and fat sheep, and shamelessly draining so many large jars of vintage wine. Odysseus, told his attentive wife of all the troubles he had brought and wrought upon men, and of all the grief the famed wanderer had stubbornly caused for himself; the many troubles occurring because of the itinerant's stubborn defiance of vengeful Lord Poseidon.

"Let's have some good, old-fashioned *Bed*lam," the zany King suggested as Odysseus used his favorite word for 'crazy sex'.

"Oh, Odysseus; now I know for sure that you are indeed my long-lost husband! A tiger never changes its stripes; a leopard never changes its spots, and true to your past disgusting habit, you never change your smelly undergarments!"

Penelope was extremely happy listening and reviewing the many fond memories from the nostalgic past, and Sleep did not zoom-down and close her eyes until her spouse's complete story had been thoroughly told, and when her sex appetite had also been fully satisfied.

Then, Pallas Athene, radiant goddess with the extraordinary glittering eyes, came-up with something rather special. When Zeus's daughter thought that Odysseus and his wife had strengthened their hearts with pleasure and with sleep, the prankster-goddess stirred-up Dawn, enthroned in gold, to rouse unaroused Odysseus from his soft bed.

"Now that we've come back to the bed we love, you should seriously tend to our remaining wealth inside this once-opulent palace," the King lectured the Queen. "As for the flocks that those haughty-naughty suitors had stolen and consumed, I'll seize many area beasts as acquired plunder on my own pursuit; and Achaeans will gladly pay more taxes to merrily finance our numerous bad habits. Now, obedient Wife. I'm going to wander outside the city to check my forest lands, and there I'll see my noble father, Laertes, who, on my accursed behalf, has suffered so much worry and grief. So, dear Wife; since I know how wonderfully intelligent you are, I'm asking you to closely follow my sage advice. Once sunrise comes, the story will be out in the city about the suitors being viciously slaughtered inside our home. So, you should go now to your upstairs room with your female attendants and stay there. Do not visit or question anyone. As you can plainly fathom as I head for the hills, my attitude towards life has not made any significant adjustment in over twenty years."

"Wow, Father!" Telemachus exclaimed as the jolly pair left the palace to explore and hunt wild boar inside the forest. "Like father; like son! But Pop. I can't wait for you to tell me all about your fantastic adventure with the extremely dangerous Cyclops!"

"Well, my dear son," Odysseus explained. "The Cyclops was indeed a ferocious monster, and besides, the awesome brute also was a very dangerous enemy. So naturally, to protect my delicate ass, I had to always keep an eye out for the formidable bastard!"

Chapter 24
"ZEUS AND ATHENA END THE FIGHTING"

Once Odysseus and his son had left the city, the pair soon reached his father's once fertile, well-managed farm, which Laertes had won by his own efforts, after many earlier years of unsuccessful dice gambling. Laertes's crumbling estate was still there, with numerous sheds surrounding the formerly stately mansion, where the old codger's servants, having no other means of subsistence, still worked diligently to carry-out the old coot's austere wishes.

An ancient Sicilian woman, imported from Syracuse, lived inside the codger's house; looking after the about-to-die asshole; carelessly caring for aged Laertes, and baking large brick-oven tomato and cheese pizzas for the constipated old fart to swallow-down every single day.

"You hungry men should now go into the poorly-built home and quickly kill the finest pig they have, so that we can eat and greedily pig-out," Odysseus commanded several of his father's lethargic slaves. "Now Telemachus; I'll follow the snoring sounds and try to locate the field where my Old Man is napping. I'll awaken the neurotic nutcase, who was already-sleeping twenty-three hours a day twenty-years ago when I had embarked with my twelve ships to Troy."

"Why the hell have we come here to this horrible dump?" Telemachus wanted to know. "I thought you desired to bond with me by taking me hunting and hiking in the forest?"

"I want to see if my blind father still recognizes me," Odysseus answered. "I'm assuming that your grandfather Laertes is now totally blind, because when I had departed for Troy, the then almost-blind idiot thought that I was a kinky female prostitute standing at his door to whom he owed money."

Odysseus roamed the vast, run-down estate with Telemachus and eventually located Laertes, assiduously digging his own grave in a not-so-well-tended vineyard. The old man's Old Man was garbed in a disgusting, shabby, patched-up tunic, with laced-up, ox-hide shin pads upon his lower legs, stitched to protect his bony knees and ankles from abrasive scratches and painful insect bites.

On his aged, wrinkled hands, daft Laertes wore gloves to protect both his palms and fingers from needles and thistles that grew all over the entire farmland. On his head the senile fellow wore a tattered goatskin cap. In those tawdry clothes, Laertes was dealing with failing health, with esteem-less self-confidence, and with an obvious lack of wealth.

As Odysseus gazed and sniffed at his decrepit and miserable-looking father, the sorrowed King could feel sharp pains shooting-up his nostrils. The Ithacan King jumped over, embraced Laertes, and kissed the grunting fogey's farting asshole twenty times, once for every single year the famed warrior had been away.

"Father; I'm here, back home in the twentieth year, sauntering around on my own native island. Stop your grieving, and producing all these tearful sighs. I'll tell you everything, although my' lips have to move at triple speed, since I don't think that neither you nor I will live for all twenty years of my exciting oration. I've killed the parasitic suitors who had been traducing my palace, and I've avenged their malignant evil, along with their heartless insolence."

"If what you're now relating is true, self-proclaimed Odysseus," Laertes remarked, "this estate is still my damned land; and Telemachus, you are not down on junior's farm."

"But Father; I am indeed your son Odysseus returning home from Troy! Don't your ears recognize my voice?"

"Well, if you are indeed my lame-brained son and have come back to salvage your property, then show me some clear evidence of your identity," Laertes demanded. "I wish to see something tangible so that I can be quite certain of who the fuck you are, and who the fuck I'm talking to."

"First, let your eyes inspect this scar that an insane wild boar had inflicted upon me with its sharp white tusks when I had visited Mt. Parnassus to commiserate with the family of Autolycus, Queen Penelope's father. My real purpose in visiting the asses in Parnassus was to obtain the dowry gifts that the stubborn bastards had previously promised me."

As Odysseus spoke and complained, his skinflint father's fond heart fluttered with an irregular rhythm, and the old fart's feeble knees buckled. Unaware of his father's short aortic valve spasm, Odysseus proudly showed Laertes his foot-long limp fadorkenbender, and the hoary curmudgeon was finally totally convinced that Odysseus was truly his boner-fide offspring.

Being overwhelmed by excessive emotion, Laertes threw his frail arms around the son he so loved, and the aged coot's lungs struggled hard to breathe. Lord Odysseus, who had endured so much hardship and duress during his ten-year odyssey, held Laertes upright, hoping that he didn't have to administer CPR to a faltering geezer having a really bad case of halitosis.

After Laertes revived from his brief seizure episode, and the half-assed nutcase's spirit and will to live were miraculously restored inside his scrawny chest, Odysseus's father addressed his companions.

"Father Zeus, it appears that your gods are still interfering with human affairs from atop high Olympus," Laertes enigmatically hollered-up to the sky. "If it's really true that those intrusive suitors have paid the ultimate price for their deplorable arrogance, I am exceedingly grateful to you and your majestic family, for Odysseus will be staying inside his palace and not bothering the hell out of me here on my country farm. But now my alert heart contains a dreadful fear that all the vengeful men of Ithaca will soon rush here like barbarians onto my worthless estate and then rebel against the three of us. And they'll send-out messengers for reinforcements to every town in Cephallenia, wherever the hell that dumb-shit place is!"

"Take courage, Father, and do not allow these ass-backward ideas weigh-down your all-too-weak heart. Let's go into your three-seat outhouse, the one close by the fruit orchard, so that you, Telemachus and I can take triple dumps and review the past twenty-years in a delightful, aroma-filled atmosphere."

Meanwhile, several of Laertes's more conscientious servants had finished working the fields, pastures, and orchards, and dinner was being prepared. After leaving the three-seater outhouse without moving their clogged-up bowels, Odysseus, Laertes and Telemachus sat-down at the supper table, parking their rear ends upon wooden chairs that sounded like flimsy objects that were about to collapse. As the three diners were reaching for table-food, old Dolius appeared, carrying a large greasy tomato pie with anchovies, pepperoni and sausage. The bitchy Sicilian hag, thinking that she had recognized King Odysseus, dropped the hot pizza upon Laertes's head, and soon ran over to kiss Telemachus, whom the woman's poor vision had mistaken for his father, King Odysseus.

"My friend and most excellent King," Dolius began with thick cataracts evident in her eyes as her active lips were still kissing and caressing Telemachus' astonished face. "You're finally back here in Ithaca with us coinless paupers. I've longed for your wonderful return, but my eyes never thought I'd either see your head, or your ass again! Gods themselves must have been leading you at every step of your challenging journey. Joyful greetings, my Lord! May the gods grant you continued success and many years of enjoying prolific, volcanic-type ejaculations!"

While that annoying bullshit was going on at Laertes's kitchen table, rumors, gossip and scuttlebutt abounded and sped swiftly throughout the entire island, spreading distorted, false news about the suitors' appalling deaths.

Relatives of Antinous heard about the great palace massacre and sprinted all over the city in all directions, gathering with mournful sighs before Odysseus's run-down mansion. Each demonstrator vehemently protested, shouting a chorus of expletives outside the king's neglected mansion. The agitated mourners then found and carried the corpses of the deceased suitors off the ruinous property, vociferously cursing Odysseus for committing his grave revenge, and eventually tossing their dead relatives onto awaiting donkey carts. Antinous and his lifeless companions were soon to be put on permanent lay-away inside the local, weed-infested cemetery.

Up on Mt. Olympus's dazzling summit, adorable Pallas Athene, perceiving a massive insurrection developing against Odysseus, Penelope and Telemachus, respectfully approached Almighty Zeus, sitting in purple attire upon his majestic throne. And the apprehensive virgin goddess earnestly pleaded that all future violence performed against her earthly champion should be prevented from occurring.

"Father of us all, and son of Titan Cronus," Athena prefaced. "Answer and grant me my fondest wish. In regard to wandering Odysseus, who has suffered unbearable calamities for two decades now, issued mostly by your vindictive brother Poseidon, can you please inform me exactly what fate you are concealing inside that erratic mind of yours? Will you now foster further savage wars and fearful battles among the Greeks and their neighboring mortals?"

"My favorite child, why are you asking this petty human nonsense of me?" Zeus annoyingly replied. "Why do all these meaningless, unimportant questions about one dumb-ass, insignificant human down on Earth concern you so much? Were you not the one who put this last plan in motion all by yourself, so that your hero Odysseus could take-out his revenge against those avaricious Ithacan suitors, after he got back from Troy? Do as you wish, Daughter. But to appease you, I'll devise an appropriate solution that I think might be right. Since your Lord Odysseus has now accomplished his sweet revenge upon his bitter enemies, I decree to let the remaining Achaeans living in Ithaca swear a binding oath that your' hero shall remain their king for life, and let us make them all forget the way their brothers and their sons had been killed, and the population should learn to love one other as the dumb-fucks had done before the start of that petty Trojan War. And let there be wealth and peace to satisfy all the puny assholes living now, and also in the future, in deplorable Ithaca."

Being allotted the appropriate divine authority to act, Athena anxiously swooped-down from lofty Mount Olympus to implement erratic-minded Zeus's favorable command.

Meanwhile, back at the dysfunctional suburban ranch, after Telemachus and the returned King had satisfied their appetites for pizza, and while Laertes was blasting quantities of methane gas out of his dual exhaust assholes from suffering massive intestinal *fart*itude, Lord Odysseus, who had borne so much adversity, was the first to speak.

"Father," the wandering hero commenced. "I haven't said a word all-meal-long because I remembered that you had taught me from when I was a toddler to never speak with my mouth full. But now, someone should go outside, pretending that he is a weather vane, looking around the vicinity in all directions, and seeing if the livid relatives of the killed suitors are getting close to our vicinity."

Telemachus rose from his seat and paced to the termite-infested doorway, and his vision detected a loud crowd of armed men rapidly advancing toward Laertes's decaying domicile.

"Father, our enraged enemy from the city is here and closing-in already! Let's gather all available weapons! We'd better hurry, as if we both had the runs!"

The inspired twosome moved quickly to Laertes's storeroom, and Odysseus put-on tarnished, bronze armor. Laertes, although he had sparse gray hair upon his head, but no semen inside his withered testicles, donned his thin tin breastplate, and was then artificially ready to join the imminent battle.

Odysseus led the two nitwits out of the humble dwelling, but then Athena, with the shape and voice of Mentor, appeared before the three idiots, and soon stood by totally senile Laertes, instructing the old coot in a forceful tone: "Child of Arcesius, by far the dearest of those old farts I cherish; pray to Father Zeus and to me, Pallas Athene. Then, without delay, brandish that long spear that you're holding, and when you have the chance, hurl the weapon at Antinous's cousin Eupeithes's scrotum."

Pallas Athena spoke those dramatic words, and then breathed into Laerte's limp fadorkenbender enormous power, making the old codger have his first significant erection in twenty-years. Laertes offered a short prayer to great Zeus, and another to the god's benign Daughter, and then, the old fuck slowly lifted-up his long-narrow spear. The uncoordinated old geezer awkwardly threw the ancient projectile at flabbergasted Eupeithes, piercing the aggressor's vulnerable scrotum sac, and permanently incapacitating and busting the belligerent asshole's balls.

Next, before Antinous's insolent cousin could collapse to the wet turf, Telemachus also tossed his sharp spear that hit Eupeithes upon the attacker's bronze helmet, finishing-off and decapitating the uncouth loudmouth for good.

"My Son!" Odysseus proudly shouted. "You're learning and discovering correct combat methods quickly! You've just demonstrated the best way to get a head in this world!"

Odysseus and his splendid son together boldly charged at the opposing combatants standing in the front line, attacking them with their remaining swords and double-edged spears. The King and his livid son would have killed all of the crazed aggressors; but then, Pallas Athene intervened in the conflict, and cried-out in a bellowing, loud-soprano voice:

"Men of Ithaca; you must stop this disastrous, low I.Q. warfare at once, so that you mortal fools can quickly go your separate ways without spilling any more blood, and without pissing and shitting your tunics from experiencing overpowering lightning attacks from my father Zeus, reigning atop Mt. Olympus."

Athena, in skilled imitation of Almighty Zeus, spoke thunderously. And instantly, a pale fear gripped the combatants' minds and throats. The avenging assaulters were so terrified at the booming sound of the goddess's earsplitting voice that the intimidated retards dropped their weapons to the damp ground and dizzily spun around like toy tops. The terrified mob hustled like prostitutes soliciting quickies, frenetically scurrying back in the direction of the inner city.

Then, much-enduring Lord Odysseus's larynx emitted a most-distinct, blood-curdling shriek. Startled because his voice-box had been operating independent of his addled brain, King Odysseus soon gathered his normally confident composure. But at that particular moment, unpredictable Almighty Zeus shot-down from Mt. Olympus a flaming thunderbolt that struck between the sandaled feet of bright-eyed Athena, who in the process, had suffered a mild hotfoot.

"Intrepid Odysseus," the goddess addressed her most-admired hero, as Pallas Athene wobbled while holding her slightly-scorched right foot with both hands. "You have certainly encountered much sorrow during your wild odd sea odyssey. Please now, Laertes's son. I insist that you stop this senseless feuding and fighting, for unlike non-compassionate Poseidon, my father, Great Zeus, who sees far and wide, grows disenchanted with your misbehavior, and will decide to give you two nutcases shocking lethal hotfoots instead of just one."

When the famed Ithacan King had heard Athena's electrifying words, Odysseus, fearing the nuts and bolts of his predicament with his testicles possibly being scorched by hot lightning bolts, the returned ruler then respectfully obeyed his patron goddess's command, and the Greek champion suddenly found a small amount of peace developing inside his vengeful heart.

And then, Pallas Athene, beloved daughter of aegis-bearing Zeus, both in shape and form, appeared as a judicious instigator in the image of famed sage Mentor. The talented shape-shifter compelled both Odysseus and Telemachus to swear dual solemn oaths professing community tranquility, with their pledge of allegiance specifically designed to put a cessation to all hostility against the hostile, pugnacious relatives of deceased Antinous, and equally dead Eurylochus.

"As my future heir, Telemachus," Odysseus explained and emphasized on the mile-long trek back to Ithaca City. "I've learned from my lengthy twenty-year ordeal that eternal life would be unbearably monotonous and boring, and I now fathom that it's the challenges and problems in human existence that make our lives interesting. If you don't like challenges and problems, then you won't enjoy living!"

"Father; philosophically speaking, do you have any other relevant advice for me to consider?"

"First and foremost, Telemachus; never kiss ass, but always kick ass! Someday, dear son; you will proudly become a royal pain-in-the-ass, just like your stubborn Mother and your' obstinate father have always been, and just as we will continue to be until the bitter end!"

About the Author

Jay Dubya is author John Wiessner's pen name and also his initials (J.W.) John is a retired New Jersey public school English teacher and he had taught the subject for thirty-four years. John lives in southern New Jersey with wife Joanne and the couple has three grown sons. John is the creator of sixty-eight books.

Jay Dubya has written adult satires *Fractured Frazzled Folk Fables and Fairy Farces* and *FFFF and FF, Part II. Black Leather and Blue Denim, A '50s Novel* and its sequel, *The Great Teen Fruit War, A 1960' Novel* and *Frat' Brats, A '60s Novel* are adult-oriented literary endeavors constituting a trilogy.

Pieces of Eight, Pieces of Eight, Part II, Pieces of Eight Part III and *Pieces of Eight, Part IV* are' short story/novella collections featuring science fiction, paranormal and humorous plots and themes. *Nine New Novellas* is the companion book to *Nine New Novellas, Part II, Nine New Novellas, Part III* and *Nine New Novellas, Part IV*. And *So Ya' Wanna' Be A Teacher* is a satirical autobiography describing the author's thirty-four-year educational career in American public schools.

Ron Coyote, Man of La Mangia is adult humor and the work is an imaginative satire/parody on Miguel Cervantes' Don Quixote, published in 1605. *Mauled Maimed Mangled Mutilated Mythology* is a work that satires twenty-one famous ancient tales. *The Wholly Book of Genesis* and *The Wholly Book of Exodus* are also adult satirical *humor. Thirteen Sick Tasteless Classics, Thirteen Sick Tasteless Classics, Part II, Thirteen Sick Tasteless Classics, Part III* and *Thirteen Sick Tasteless Classics, Part IV* are adult satirical rewrites of famous short fiction.

John has also authored a trilogy of young adult fantasy novels, *Enchanta, Pot of Gold* and *Space Bugs, Earth Invasion. The Eighteen Story Gingerbread House* is a new collection of eighteen diverse and creative children's stories.

Jay Dubya likes '50s rock and roll music and he also enjoys pop' songs by the Beach Boys, Fleetwood Mac, the Eagles, the Rolling Stones, ELO, John Mellencamp and by John Fogerty.

Author Biography

Born in Hammonton, NJ in 1942, John Wiessner had attended St. Joseph School up to and including Grade 5. After his family moved from Hammonton to Levittown, Pa in 1954, John attended St. Mark School in Bristol, Pa. for Grade 6, St. Michael the Archangel School in Levittown for Grades 7 and 8 and then Immaculate Conception School, Levittown, Pa. for Grade 9. Bishop Egan High School, Levittown Pa was John's educational base for Grades 10 and 11, and later in 1960, the aspiring author graduated from Edgewood Regional High, Tansboro, NJ. John then next attended Glassboro State College, where the future author was an announcer for the school's baseball games and also read the nightly news and sports over WGLS, GSC's radio station.

John Wiessner had been primarily an English teacher in the Hammonton Public School System for 34 years, specializing in the instruction of middle school language arts. Mr. Wiessner was quite active in the Hammonton Education Association, serving in the capacities of Vice-President, building representative and finally, teachers' head negotiator for 7 years. During his lengthy teaching career, John had been nominated into "Who's Who Among American Teachers" three times. He also was quite active giving professional workshops at schools around South Jersey on the subjects of creative writing and the use of movie videos to motivate students to organize their classroom theme compositions.

John Wiessner was very active in community service, being a past President of the Hammonton Lions Club, where he also functioned for many years as the club's Tail-Twister, Vice-President and also Liontamer. John had been named Hammonton Lion of the Year in 1979, and in 2009, the community helper earned the prestigious Melvin Jones Fellow Award, which is the highest honor that a Lion can receive from Lions International.

John also was a successful businessman, starting with being a Philadelphia Bulletin newspaper delivery boy for two years in the late 1950s in Levittown, Pennsylvania. After his family moved back to New Jersey in 1959, John worked at his grandparents and his parents' farm markets, Square Deal Farm (now Ron's Gardens in Hammonton) and Pete's Farm Market in Elm, respectively. He later managed his wife's parents' farm market, White Horse Farms in Elm for three summers.

Also, in a business capacity, for 16 summers starting in 1966, John Wiessner had co-owned Dealers Choice Amusement Arcade on the Ocean

City, Maryland boardwalk and also co-owned the New Horizon Tee-Shirt Store for eight summers (1973-'81) on the Rehoboth Beach, Delaware boardwalk. In addition, "Jay Dubya" was a co-owner of Wheel and Deal Amusement Arcade, Missouri Avenue and Boardwalk, Atlantic City. And then, for 18 summers beginning in 1986, John had been the Field Manager in charge of crew-leaders for Atlantic Blueberry Company (the world's largest cultivated blueberry farm), both the Weymouth and Mays Landing Divisions.

After retiring from teaching in 1999, writing under the pen name Jay Dubya (his initials), John Wiessner became the author of 68 books in the genre Action/Adventure Novels, Sci-Fi/Paranormal Story Collections, Adult Satire, Young Adult Fantasy Novels and Non-Fiction Books. His books exist in hardcover, in paperback and in popular Kindle and Nook e-book formats.

In January of 2022, John Wiessner (Jay Dubya) had been nominated into Marquis Who's Who in America, and in April of that same year, the author had been selected as one of nine distinguished Who's Who in America members honored with Lifetime Achievement Awards, all nine sharing an article of recognition appearing in the Wall Street Journal.

Google: Jay Dubya books
Google: Walmart.com, Jay Dubya